Destiny's Path

ANNA JACOBS

Destiny's Path

**HODDER &
STOUGHTON**

First published in Great Britain in 2011 by Hodder & Stoughton
An Hachette UK company

I

Copyright © Anna Jacobs 2011

The right of Anna Jacobs to be identified as the Author of the
Work has been asserted by her in accordance with the Copyright,
Designs and Patents Act 1988.

A CIP catalogue record for this title is available from the British Library

Hardback ISBN 978 0 340 95409 6
Trade Paperback ISBN 978 1 444 70831 8

Typeset in Plantin Light by Palimpsest Book Production Ltd,
Falkirk, Stirlingshire

Printed in Great Britain by
Clays Ltd, St Ives plc

Hodder & Stoughton policy is to use papers that are natural,
renewable and recyclable products and made from wood grown in
sustainable forests. The logging and manufacturing processes are expected to
conform to the environmental regulations of the country of origin.

Hodder & Stoughton Ltd
338 Euston Road
London NW1 3BH

www.hodder.co.uk

To Ros Merefield, dearest of friends, with lots of love

Acknowledgements

Thanks again to the wonderful library system of Australia and to the State Records office of Western Australia for their help in research.

And thanks to Eric Hare, for his generous help with the ship details.

I

Late February 1866

X anthe Blake stared out of the kitchen window at the parched Australian landscape. The grass outside the paddocks was beige because it was summer and hadn't rained for two months. Leathery dried leaves lay in drifts here and there, rotting more slowly than English leaves did. Since water was precious, she picked up the tin washing-up bowl and carried it outside, tipping it carefully along the nearest row of vegetables. A sudden longing for the green fields and soft air of Lancashire swept over her. She'd grown up there, had been forced to come to Australia and work as a maid nearly three years ago – and didn't intend to stay here for much longer.

'Penny for them.'

She realised she'd been standing there lost in thought and turned to see her employer standing in the doorway, giving her one of his serious, assessing looks. She had a great deal of respect for Conn Largan, who might have come here as a convict, but he'd been convicted on political charges, which didn't make him a criminal in her eyes. Anyway, his mother had assured them he'd been innocent and Mrs Largan wasn't a liar.

'My thoughts aren't worth a penny.' She tried for a light tone, but could see from the way he tilted his head to one side and studied her that he wouldn't be deflected. As an ex-lawyer he was a very shrewd man, but he was kind, too, and she was tempted to confide in him.

'You're an intelligent woman and your thoughts are usually well worth listening to, Xanthe,' he urged gently.

So she told him, because she was aching to talk to someone about her problem and this was one time when she couldn't confide in her twin. 'I'm trying to work out two things: first, where I should go from here and second, how to persuade Maia to let me go on my own and leave her here at Galway House where she's happy.'

He was silent for so long she nearly went back into the kitchen.

'It'd be better for Maia if you took her with you,' he said at last.

'How can you even think that? I want to travel, but she's a homebody – and besides, she's absolutely devoted to your mother.' Maia was devoted to her master too, though Xanthe was never quite sure whether Conn knew that her sister loved him. She was fairly sure his mother was aware of it, but open as she was about most things, Mrs Largan had never even hinted at it.

He began pacing up and down, avoiding looking directly at her. 'I can find other maids to do the housework and care for my mother, if you'll give me a little time.'

She was puzzled by that. Did he really want to get rid of them both? 'That's not easy in the Swan River Colony. There are ten men to every woman here and people with money are desperate for maids. You might not realise it, but Maia and I have had lots of other offers since we started working for you. Men come to see you about horses but they also come to me and Maia secretly, begging us to go and work for their wives.' One or two had wanted more from her, but she wasn't going to sell her body, however much they offered. No less than three of the younger men who lived nearby had proposed marriage to her, on the briefest acquaintance. She'd had no hesitation in refusing.

She wished sometimes she was ugly, then men wouldn't pester her in that way. Unlike the other young women she'd known, she'd never met one with whom she wanted to spend her whole life, so had decided there was something wrong with her. But since she and her sisters had inherited money from their uncle, she didn't need to marry to find a man to support her, wouldn't even need to work for a living as long as she didn't live extravagantly.

She was lucky, or she would be once some of her inheritance was sent to her in Australia. Until then, she was as short of money as she'd always been.

'I could send back to Ireland for a maid or two,' Conn said. 'Though I realise that would take nearly a year and you may not be willing to wait so long.'

'I can't go anywhere till our money comes through. When Pandora wrote to let us know she'd got back safely to England, she said it might take some time to sell the cottages my uncle left us, then find someone to bring the money to us here. She and Zachary want to buy the shop from us, so there'll be more money to come later from that, as well.'

He frowned again. 'It's not going to be easy to get money out here safely. And even when you get it, where would you keep it? The Post Office Savings Bank or the Perth Building Society? Neither has been open long enough to prove themselves safe. Other banks here haven't lasted long, either. I wonder now . . .' He turned away, staring into the distance, then said thoughtfully, 'A close friend of mine is thinking of coming out for a visit, possibly to settle here. I'd trust Ronan with my life. He could perhaps bring you some of the money at the same time. There's nothing like good golden sovereigns safe in your purse or strongbox.'

He paused to let her think about it, strolling to the fence to stare across the grassy paddock, the grass of which was kept more or less green by regular watering from the well.

Conn Largan was like that, Xanthe thought, watching him. He never tried to force a quick reply or impose his opinions on others. Had he always been so reasonable or had being transported done that to him? she wondered. Most men brought up with a privileged background like his were not nearly as courteous towards their servants – especially a servant who was thinking of giving notice.

'That might be a good idea,' she said at last. 'I shan't want all my money bringing here anyway because I'm definitely going back to England at some stage, and will probably stay there, so—'

There was a gasp behind her and she swung round to see her twin staring at her in dismay from the kitchen doorway. Seeing her sister was always like looking at a slightly altered image of herself in the mirror. Physically, they were almost identical, tall and with the same dark hair and eyes, but Maia was slightly plumper and softer looking. In character they weren't at all alike. Xanthe knew she was far more decisive, while Maia was too gentle for her own good.

Her twin rushed across to grab her arm. 'You can't mean that, Xanthe. I know you said last year that you weren't staying here for ever, but I thought you'd settled down. You've seemed happy enough.'

'I made up my mind to enjoy the experience of living in Australia until I could see my way clear to moving somewhere else. I haven't changed my mind at all. I just – didn't see the point of upsetting you.'

'When must we leave? Can we at least stay until I find a replacement to look after Mrs Largan? Oh, I shall miss her so much!'

Xanthe looked at her sadly. 'You don't want to leave at all, love. You know you don't.'

'I'll not be separated from you.'

'You hate travelling and I want to do quite a bit of that, though at least you're not seasick like poor Pandora was.' When her sister would have spoken, she held up one hand. 'No, let me finish, Maia. You prefer staying at home, being with people you know, while I like to meet new people. That was the best part of the voyage out here, talking to people, going to the classes on the ship, learning new things.'

She looked over her shoulder and saw to her relief that Conn had moved further away, leaving them to talk privately. Still, she lowered her voice. 'Besides, how can you leave? You love him, don't you?'

Maia's eyes filled with tears. 'You know I do. But it's hopeless. He's an educated gentleman and I'm just a mill girl, even if I do have a little money behind me now. He'd never look at someone like me in that way.'

'You're not *just* anything. Our father didn't only give the four of us fancy Greek names, he made sure we grew up with a love of books so that we could keep our minds fed as well as our bodies. You're the equal of anyone else in understanding.'

'As if other people care about that! What they think important is *knowing your place in society* and behaving accordingly.'

'When have we ever done what was expected of us? We're our father's daughters in more ways than one. If not, we'd be long married with a gaggle of children tugging at our skirts. Well, I shan't ever—' She saw her sister's expression change. 'Oh, I'm a fool to talk like that! There's nothing you'd have liked better than a gaggle of children, is there?'

Maia tried to smile. 'It wasn't to be. I'm twenty-seven and I've never met the right man, even though quite a few tried to court me when we lived in Lancashire. I'd not settle for anything less than a husband I could love. Look how happy Cassandra and Reece are. I want that sort of marriage or none. He's a fine brother-in-law, isn't he?'

'Yes, she's fortunate to have found him.' Xanthe gave her a hug and there they left it.

But she hadn't changed her mind. Once she got her money, she was leaving Australia – and on her own. Life here was too limited for her taste and sometimes she felt like screaming at the boring repetition of her daily routines. She didn't enjoy being the housekeeper, though she did her work as well as she could, out of sheer pride.

In Lancashire a few months later, Pandora Carr woke up feeling sick. She lay still and closed her eyes, willing it to go away, but it didn't.

'Are you all right?' Zachary asked.

'No. I'm feeling sick again.' She heard him suck in his breath and knew what he was hoping. 'I must be expecting a child,' she admitted.

'Oh, my darling girl! I'm so happy.'

She risked a slight movement to look at him. His plain bony

face was lit up with joy. He'd never be handsome but he was attractive to her and to others too because of the kindness of his nature. 'I'm not sure how I feel about it,' she admitted. 'It's too soon.'

He laughed softly. 'Children come when chance wills it. And anyway, didn't we say we wanted three or four?'

'Not yet, though. I've hardly settled into the routine of the shop. We've not even been back in England for a year. You and I have so many plans now that the war in America is over and the town's mills are coming to life again.' She and Zachary intended to buy her sisters' share of her uncle's shop, where he'd worked since he was twelve and which he loved.

'I know, love, but we'll manage just fine with a baby. I'll make sure my children never want.' He watched her anxiously. 'Can I help in any way? There must be something wrong if you're not bouncing out of bed.'

She smiled wanly. 'I've a sudden longing for a cup of tea, very sweet. Could you ask Dot to bring one up, please?'

He leaned forward to press a kiss on her forehead. 'I'll do it straight away.' He'd heard their maid get up a little while ago.

Half an hour later Pandora got up and although she felt a little dizzy at first, her body soon settled down again. She was even more grateful than usual for the wonderful indoor bathroom and smiled wryly as she remembered her days working as a maid in Australia, sleeping in a tent, fetching all the water from the well, using a trench for a privy at first. It had been hard, especially after her eldest sister Cassandra got married and left her on her own with their employers.

The thought of her three sisters brought tears to her eyes, as it often did. She'd been so desperately homesick in Australia, she'd been wasting away with unhappiness, but the others had loved it there and refused to come back to England with her.

She knew they'd always keep in touch by letter but that wasn't very satisfying and it still hurt to be so far away from them. Things would never be the same as when they'd lived together. Why, it took over six months to send a letter and get a reply.

She'd been expecting to hear from at least one of her sisters for the past few weeks.

Sighing, she finished getting dressed and went down to the kitchen to discuss the day's work with Dot – she still wasn't used to having a maid – then into the shop to see Zachary before it opened.

'Feeling better now?' he asked with a smile.

'Much better. What are you going to do today? How is the new tea blend you created?' She felt shut out of the shop, because only men served there and they didn't like her even making suggestions openly, so she had to do that through Zachary, for his sake.

'Blake's Best Tea is selling well. Your uncle always said I had a good sense of taste and smell, and I think I've achieved as good a blend as he did. Today I'm going to look at the shelving in the shop. I'm sure we can arrange things more efficiently. I want your help there. We can study it together then draw up plans. So have a think about it.'

She loved the way he tried to include her. 'Breakfast is ready now. You'd better hurry up or the shopmen will be here.'

Just as Blake's Emporium was opening, the postman arrived at the house door with a letter from Australia. Pandora beamed at the mere sight of it. How marvellous that a small thing like a letter could come so far in safety! She blinked away tears as she traced out Xanthe's handwriting on the envelope with her fingertips.

Closing the house door, she went to stand at the inner entrance to the shop, waving the envelope triumphantly at her husband. He grinned and waved back, knowing this letter would make her day.

Then she could wait no longer and hurried upstairs to the parlour to read it. A quick glance showed her that it was mostly in Xanthe's handwriting this time. There would be inserts from both Maia and Cassandra, though, there always were.

Only there weren't any inserts this time. It was a long letter in which Xanthe poured out her heart. And what she read both upset and delighted Pandora. It might mean she'd see her sister again.

And whatever Xanthe said, she didn't think Maia would let her twin go so far away.

2

Ronan Maguire waited till he was alone to open the letter from his friend Conn in Australia, reading it with great interest and locking it away carefully afterwards in his travelling writing desk. His mother wasn't above going through his things and as he could never stay angry with her, he found it easier to keep his private papers secure.

Down in the parlour he went to stand by the window, looking out over the rain-swept landscape at the big house at the far end of the drive. Ardgullan had been in the family for generations. It must be ten times as big as the dower house, where his mother had lived since she was widowed. His mother's house was set back in a small patch of woodland near the gates and he sometimes wondered if the ancestor who'd built it had deliberately placed it as far away as possible from the main family residence.

An even heavier downpour pounded against the window panes. Fine summer weather this was! He heard his mother come in behind him and said with a sigh, 'It's done nothing but rain lately.'

She linked her arm in his. 'This is Ireland. We're famous for our rain. Why don't you go for a ride anyway?'

'I'd come back drenched and cold. That's not my idea of enjoyment.'

'Going to Italy and Greece spoiled you. Though I do get fed up with the rain too. But the gardener says it'll be fine tomorrow. I haven't ridden since I was a girl and I don't miss it. So smelly, horses! I suggested your brother put in a croquet lawn at the big house. It's all the rage, croquet. It'd give us something pleasant to do.'

'Who would you play with? Our village is too small to provide you with any suitable partners.'

She shrugged. 'I could play with you when you're here.'

'As I'm not here half the time, it'd be a waste. Hubert wouldn't play. He's not a sociable animal, my brother. Anyway, I doubt he could afford it. Have you seen the condition of the estate cottages? The whole village is in a sorry state. I wonder he doesn't do something about that. It's much more important.'

'You're always going down to the village and talking to common people. You should spend more time with people of your own class.'

'I grew up with some of those men in the village and we played together as boys.'

She let go of his arm, moving away to fiddle with the ornaments on the mantelpiece. 'Well, you're not boys now. What you need, my dear, is to settle down with a wife and children. That would steady you.'

'Hubert isn't married and he's the eldest. Turn your matchmaking on to him.'

'I've got one or two young women in mind but he's as stubborn as you. He says he wants to get the estate in better order before he thinks of marrying.'

'Because of Father's gambling.'

'Yes.' She didn't comment on her late husband's weakness for cards; she never had. 'Well, at least my youngest son has married well and Patrick's given me grandchildren, too – though they're in England so I hardly ever see them.'

She'd been saying that sort of thing for years, introducing Ronan to a string of eligible young ladies, but he hadn't met a single one who wasn't a dead bore. Hubert hated social occasions and avoided them when he could, even though he was the landowner now. He avoided his own family too, preferring to sit on his own in the evenings. Ronan had never understood him and if they hadn't been brothers wouldn't have bothered with him at all.

His mother shook his arm to get his attention. 'You're not

listening. Do think about finding a wife. I'm sure it'd make you happier.' She flung herself down in a chair.

'I doubt it. And I'd need a house to put a family in, which I don't have.'

'You've the money to buy one. You had a very comfortable legacy from your great-aunt Mary. You could live nearby and make your poor old mother happy. You're thirty, Ronan darlin'. If you wait much longer, it'll be too late for you to father children.'

He didn't let himself smile, but he doubted he'd have trouble with that. He'd fathered one illegitimate child already and had seen it well provided for.

She began drumming her fingers on the arm of her chair. 'It's all that travelling that's unsettled you. Have you any idea how much I worry when you're off on one of your trips?'

'I've always been perfectly safe.'

'Then perhaps you could take me with you one day. I get very bored here sometimes when you're away.'

He'd hate to travel with her. She'd be fussing about every little thing. 'I think you like your comforts too much to travel, Mother.'

'It might be worth the discomfort. I get very lonely here when you're away.' She forced a smile. 'Maybe one day I'll surprise you all, and go off to see a bit of the world. London. Paris. Rome. You make them sound so interesting.'

The wind suddenly howled round the house and he thought longingly of warm, lazy days in Italy and Greece. But the less frequented parts of southern Europe weren't very safe at the moment so he didn't feel inclined to risk his life there till things settled down. There had been years of patchwork troubles, with the shifting of territories and minor kingdoms from Austria to Prussia to France. Who knew what would happen next? He'd no mind to run into danger.

'Well, I'd better go and write some letters.' He left her with her embroidery.

In his bedroom he unlocked the writing desk and took out the newest letter, rereading it carefully. He was very tempted to accept the invitation to visit Australia. Conn wasn't guilty of conspiring against Queen and country, but his cousin Michael had given convincing evidence against him. All Ronan had been able to do was sort out the finances so that when his friend arrived in Australia, there was money waiting for him.

How could justice go so awry? Conn had received no support from his damned father, either.

Someone rode up to the front door. Good. A caller. That would cheer his mother up. But a few minutes later she called up the stairs, her voice urgent. 'Ronan! Come quickly! They've just sent a message round from Shilmara. Poor Mr Largan has had a seizure and is like to die. We must call on Kathleen at once, to offer our sympathy and help.'

'Didn't I tell you I'd never cross that threshold again?'

'You'll respect our neighbour in his last hours, if you respect nothing else, Ronan Maguire, or you're no son of mine.'

When she spoke as sharply as that he usually did what she wanted. And in any case, it occurred to him suddenly that if he did go to Australia, Conn might like to know how things were at his old family home.

'I'll go and have the horses put to,' he called back.

When he came back into the house to tell her the carriage was ready, his mother met him, arms akimbo, cheeks flushed with anger. He looked at her in puzzlement. Fenella Maguire's temper was mercurial at the best of times, but this sudden change of mood baffled him. 'What's upsetting you now?'

'Your friend Conn seems to think you've agreed to go and visit him in that heathen place.'

'You've been reading my letters again.'

She tossed her head. 'And why should I not? You left the latest lying about. How was I to know it contained secrets? I'm your mother, aren't I? And anyway, I've a right to read what comes into my own house. I'll not have you going so far away! You're staying here in Ireland and that's my final word.'

Her prying made up Ronan's mind for him. He was going, but he wouldn't tell her that until he'd finalised his plans. No use trying to change her. She'd interfere in their lives and nag them for as long as she had breath in her body. She meant well, he'd grant her that, but he didn't want her pushing him into a marriage like his brother Patrick's, one where neither cared about the other, only about money and their position in county society. Ronan intended to follow his own destiny, wherever it led.

'Are you ready to leave, ma'am?'

Something in his voice and the formal way he called her 'ma'am' instead of 'Mother' must have warned her that he was seriously annoyed. She looked at him a little warily, hesitated and when he said nothing more about Conn's letter, put her hand on his arm and let him lead her out to the waiting carriage.

He could see Shilmara long before they got there, a sprawling, two-storey building on a rise overlooking a small lake. He'd not visited it since Conn sailed for Australia and wondered what they'd think of him coming here today. Well, who cared what they thought? He was here for Conn's sake, not because a scheming, lying old man lay on his deathbed.

A groom came running to open the carriage door, whispering, ''Tis grand to see you again, Mr Ronan. Have you heard from Mr Conn lately?'

'I heard only yesterday. He's doing well in Australia, breeding horses. You know how good he always was with animals.'

'And his mother?'

'She's in better health there in the warmer climate, though still not able to move about easily.'

'It's good to be hearing that. The poor lady used to suffer terrible bad from the rheumatism.'

A cough from inside the carriage reminded them of their obligations and Ronan went to help his mother get out.

'Do you have to chat to grooms like that?' she snapped as they climbed the stairs to the front door.

'I've known Bram since we were lads together. It's only natural he'd be asking after Conn and Mrs Largan.'

'That woman didn't know her duty to her husband. I can't even bear to speak her name.'

To his mind, when she fled to join her son in Australia, Mrs

Largan had been obeying a higher duty, serving the cause of truth and justice rather than staying out of duty with the husband who'd allowed them to jail his son on a trumped-up charge without making a single protest. Ronan thought less of his mother for her changed attitude towards a woman who had been her closest friend for years. 'We'll not be arguing about that again.'

She tossed her head and led the way through the front door, which had been opened by then. The Largans' housekeeper was waiting to show them in.

He slowed down to greet her by name as well, to his mother's annoyance.

'It's nice to see you again, Peggy. I hope your mother is better.'

She nodded but after a glance towards his mother said only, 'Mrs Kathleen is waiting for you in the parlour, Mrs Maguire.'

'Thank you.'

As they entered the room, Kathleen Largan moved forward from the window, where she must have been watching their arrival. 'Won't you sit down?' she asked her female visitor. She didn't attempt to greet Ronan, hadn't spoken to him since he helped her husband. As if he'd disown a good friend like Conn. He went to stand on the other side of the fire, one hand resting on the mantelpiece, and prepared to endure a boring visit.

His mother shot him a glance warning him to behave, then said in the cooing voice she used when out in society, 'We heard about Mr Largan and came to enquire. How is your poor dear father-in-law?'

'Holding his own, the doctor says. That's all we can hope for at the moment.'

'Was it a bad seizure?'

'Yes. One side of his body is completely paralysed and he's only half-conscious. I've sent for Kieran – in case.'

Well, Ronan thought, Conn's oldest brother would be a much nicer person to have as a neighbour. *He* wouldn't make his tenants' lives a misery as that wicked old man had done. James Largan had sat in the pocket of the English from the moment he'd inherited, even changing his religion to suit, furious when his wife and sons hadn't followed his example.

The two women chatted for perhaps five minutes. Kathleen didn't address a single remark to Ronan, which suited him just fine. She really was a strange woman, rigid in her ways and he knew Conn had only married her under strong pressure from his father.

As he listened, Ronan studied the room, thinking how shabby it was looking these days. Were the Largans also short of money, then?

When he and his mother took their leave, he was again ignored by his hostess. He wondered what she'd do without her father-in-law to look after her. He knew Kieran couldn't stand her and doubted he'd let her live at Shilmara after his father died.

The visit made Ronan wonder whether he'd ever be coming back here again himself. Perhaps he'd stay in Australia. Or if he did return to Ireland, he might buy himself a house somewhere else. Oh, who knew what the future held?

But the thought of buying a house depressed him. He hadn't unlimited money and would need to buy the sort of estate that brought in a regular income – and tend it carefully, too. So there would be no more travelling, except maybe to Dublin or London.

Did he want to settle down?

Did he know what he wanted?

Pandora paced up and down the parlour above the shop, staring through the window at the main street of Outham. Why, she thought rebelliously, were pregnant ladies supposed to hide away as if there was something indecent about their condition? Nothing was more natural than having a baby. And heaven forbid she should show herself in the shop now! Why the whole town might vanish in a clap of thunder if she did that!

Not that she considered herself a lady. She was neither fish nor fowl in that respect. She had worked in the mill when she was younger but now had money and property, so people didn't know how to treat her.

She saw their lawyer's clerk moving down the street and when he turned into the shop, she wondered what he wanted with Zachary. He'd better not avoid her if he was here on her business, because she wasn't going to let anyone exclude her from helping manage her own inheritance.

Mr Dawson didn't come out into the street and she wondered if Zachary had brought him out of the shop to have a private conversation in the hall that linked the two parts of the building. She went out to the head of the stairs, to see if she could hear them, annoyed that she had to resort to eavesdropping.

Sure enough, Zachary's voice floated up to her. 'I don't like to disturb my wife with this, in her condition, so perhaps I can come to Mr Featherworth's rooms in about an hour, when things will be less busy in the shop?'

Angry at this, she called down the stairs, 'You won't be disturbing me and if it concerns me or my sisters, I insist on being involved.'

There was a brief silence and she could imagine the two men exchanging glances, then Zachary called, 'I'll send Mr Dawson up, then, and I'll join you in a moment or two, my dear.'

She heard the sound of footsteps and Mr Dawson came round the turn in the stairs. She was quite prepared to say something sharp if he avoided looking at her and her baby-filled stomach, as some men did, but instead he gave her a beaming smile as he got to the top.

'No need to ask how you are, Mrs Carr. You're blooming.'

'Do come and sit down. How is your wife?'

He blushed. 'She too is – um – in a delicate condition.'

She looked at him in surprise. Both he and his wife were in their mid-forties and recently married, so no one had expected them to have a child. 'How wonderful for you!'

He smiled but there was anxiety in his eyes. 'She's rather old for a first child, I'm afraid.'

'Alice is in good health and was well-nourished during the Cotton Famine, so I think she stands as good a chance as any of a safe delivery.'

'Yes, you're right. I daresay I'm worrying for no reason. But since my sister died, Alice is all I have. If I lost her . . .'

She didn't try to reassure him, because as far as she could see, women risked dying every time they bore a child. She was relieved to hear Zachary run lightly up the stairs and turned to stare at him challengingly, answering his most frequent questions even before he asked them. 'No, I'm not tired and no, I shouldn't be resting.' She turned to Mr Dawson with a smile. 'My husband fusses too much over me. I find it more than a little trying because I'm in excellent health. I hope you're not driving your wife mad!'

Zachary gave her a wry, apologetic look and of course she couldn't help smiling back at him. Impossible to stay angry with him. She turned back to the lawyer. 'Well, Mr Dawson, please tell us why you're here.'

'You'll be glad to hear that I've sold two of the three cottages you inherited, and for the prices we expected.'

Pandora clapped her hands together. 'That's wonderful news! So we can send a decent amount of money to my sisters. Have you worked out how we do that?'

'Mr Featherworth has been looking into the matter, but it seems all the methods have their disadvantages. The main safeguard, we feel, is not to try to send the money all at once. If we send everything and the ship founders, as the *London* did in January in the Bay of Biscay, then the whole inheritance is lost. With the recent bank failures, we don't feel sure of the banks, either. And they seem to be opening and shutting banks rather frequently in Australia, as they are here. So . . . the best thing would perhaps be to send some of the money in the form of gold sovereigns in the care of a responsible person. But I don't know how to find someone one can trust absolutely.'

'I know someone,' she said, feeling smug at the surprise on their faces. 'I had a letter from my sisters in Australia recently. Xanthe is going to leave the Swan River Colony and come back to England as soon as she gets some of her money, though she hopes to do some sightseeing en route. She said a friend of her employer is probably going out to Australia to visit the Largans,

so Conn has written to him to ask if he'll take some money out
for them. He'd be very reliable, I'm sure. He's not a poor man.
And if he's a friend of Conn's we can definitely trust him. Until
she gets some money, Xanthe can't even afford her fare back,
you see.' She couldn't withhold a sigh. Her three sisters were all
so very far away!

'Who exactly is this person?'

'He's called Ronan Maguire and is from a landowning family
near Enniskillen. Xanthe's sent me his name and address so that
I can write to him.'

'Perhaps it would be better if your husband did that?' Mr
Dawson suggested.

She breathed deeply. 'I think I can manage to scratch a few
words down legibly.'

Zachary smiled. 'My wife has some very firm views on what
she wants to do – and it is her money, after all.'

'Legally, it's yours now, as her husband.'

'Then the law is wrong,' he said quietly. '*She* inherited it. Were
I to take it for my own use without her permission, it'd be no
better than stealing.'

Pandora looked at him, feeling emotion bring tears into her
eyes. Few men were so liberal in their views about their wives'
money. 'Thank you,' she said quietly.

The look he gave her said he perfectly understood how she
was feeling.

Strange that he was so liberal about this, yet would not countenance the idea of women serving in the shop. He insisted customers
would regard it as lowering the tone, which would perhaps make
them go elsewhere. She had to abide by that for the moment,
because he did understand about running the grocery emporium,
loved what he did, had been trained by her uncle, who'd made
such a success of what had been quite a small shop before.

When a letter arrived a few days later, Ronan's mother studied
the envelope with a frown, not tearing it open as she usually did.
He guessed it was for him and twitched it out of her hand.

'Now, who would be writing to you from England?' she demanded.

'I don't recognise the handwriting so I won't know till I've read it.'

She looked at him expectantly but he took it up to his bedroom, promising himself that this time he'd make sure his writing desk was locked.

Dear Mr Maguire,

My sister Xanthe Blake works for Conn Largan in Australia. She's written to say you're considering visiting her employer there, and Mr Largan thinks you might agree to carry some money out to the Swan River Colony for us.

Would you be so kind as to do this?

If you agree, perhaps you could visit us before you start your journey? My husband Zachary and I would be happy to give you a bed for the night and to pay any expenses you incur in making this detour.

Pandora Carr (Mrs)

He smiled. Conn had mentioned the four sisters, two of whom worked for him, saying how unusual they were and how well-read. This one certainly wrote a fine, educated hand. He'd have expected it to be the husband who contacted him, though.

He'd certainly take up her invitation. He'd never been to Lancashire before and dearly loved to visit a new place. Were the industrial towns really as bad as William Blake's poem suggested, with 'dark satanic mills' belching forth smoke?

Someone tapped on his bedroom door. 'Mr Ronan, Bram Deagan is here to see you, says it's urgent.'

'I'm coming.' Ronan carefully locked his writing desk and ran lightly down to the kitchen.

He found Bram sitting at the table with a cup of tea, looking utterly miserable. 'What's wrong?'

'She's dismissed me, sir, Mrs Kathleen has.'

'Whatever for?'

'Asking you about Mr Conn. She had a window open and overheard us.'

Ronan felt anger surge through him. That woman was as bad as old Mr Largan, harsh in her judgements, cruel to those who served her, but unlike her father-in-law she acted irrationally at times, so that you could never quite guess what she'd do or say next.

'I wondered, sir, if you'd have a word with her? She refuses to pay me my wages, even. They're surely owing to me? I've done the work, over two months of it, because it's not long to quarter day.'

'That's not fair.'

'My mother's packing my things, sir – and crying her heart out. Mrs Kathleen says she'll turn my parents out of their cottage if I'm not clear of the estate by nightfall and they're to be grateful they're allowed to stay. What am I to do without my money? I give most of my wages to the Mammy, so I've only a few shillings to my name.'

'You'd better come here. We'll find you a bed for the night, if only in the stables.'

'We'll do no such thing!' his mother exclaimed from behind him.

Ronan turned round. 'Mother, surely—'

'I'll speak to you in the parlour. And you!' She turned to Bram. 'Finish your cup of tea and wait outside. I'm sure Mr Maguire will give you a coin or two to help you on your way, but that's all he'll be doing.'

Ronan followed her into the parlour. 'Are you really refusing to give Bram shelter for the night?'

'Of course I am. It'd be disloyal to our neighbours to do otherwise.'

'I thought you kinder than that, Mother.'

She glared at him. 'Your first loyalty is to your own class and we've always been particularly close to the Largans.'

'My first loyalty is to truth and justice – the same as Mrs Largan's was.' He waited, willing her to speak, but she kept her lips firmly pressed together. 'If you'll not change your mind, I shall leave with him.'

She gaped at him for a moment. 'You can't mean it! You'd turn on your mother and neighbours for a *servant*?'

'I do mean it. I was leaving anyway, but this has only brought it forward. I'm definitely going to visit Australia.'

The colour drained from her face. 'You're going to *him*, aren't you, Conn Largan?'

'I am. And I'll not be coming back to live here, either, not after what you and Kathleen have done today.'

She drew herself up. 'Then may the Lord forgive you, Ronan, because I shall have trouble doing so.' She turned and left the room, head held high.

He stood there for a moment feeling desperately sad. His mother would regret these harsh words in a day or two, she always did after her temper flared up. But it'd be too late then. He'd be gone. Ah, he'd let a little time pass and then write to her. She'd come round.

He went to speak to Bram, now standing outside the back door. 'I'm sorry my mother won't let you stay here, but as I'm leaving today, you can travel with me. In fact, I have a proposition to put to you, a possible job.' He knew from Conn's letters that a man who was good with horses would be sure of finding a job in a new country like Australia – probably with Conn himself. And Bram was more intelligent than most. Emigrating might give him chances he'd not find if he stayed here in Ireland.

His friend looked at him sadly. 'I could hear you and your mother arguing from here. I'll not be coming between you and your family, Ronan lad – sir, I mean. If you can lend me a pound or maybe two, and write me a letter saying I'm a good worker, I'll manage somehow. And you can be sure I'll pay you back one day, I swear to that.'

'Don't do anything hasty. We'll talk further tonight. In the meantime, will you do me a favour? If I lend you a horse, will you take a message to John Docherty and bring back his answer?'

'Of course.'

'He's a good friend, is John, and will lend us a carriage to take us and our luggage to the railway station in Enniskillen. It's shocking how behind the rest of the world for rail travel Ireland is. Why, they've lines everywhere in England, and branch lines even to the smallest towns. Everyone uses that form of transport.'

'Are you going to England, then?'

'*We* are going to England, Bram. It's only our first stop, though.' He pulled out his watch and clicked his tongue in exasperation at how late in the afternoon it was. 'Look, I'll explain later. Will you trust me and come with me?'

Still the groom hesitated. 'Are you sure you want to do this, sir? You've upset your mother and now you'll be upsetting the Largans.'

'I am sure. Very sure. *That woman* treats her servants badly and I for one can't stomach it any longer. Why, she and old Mr Largan have even set my mother against Conn, a man we've all known and liked since boyhood. I can't be doing with the hypocrisy and the downright cruelty of it all, Bram lad. I was going to leave anyway, I promise you.'

If Kieran returned, he might give Bram his job back, because Bram was a good worker. But there again, he might not. Being several years older than Conn and Ronan, Kieran hadn't been one of their group of friends and had spent a lot of time away from the estate since he grew up. No, it wasn't worth risking.

He saw that his old playmate was wavering and added firmly, 'I'm leaving today whether you join me or not.'

'Then I'd be honoured to travel with you.'

3

Xanthe hummed as she cleared up the kitchen. It'd been months since Conn wrote to his friend who might be able to bring some money out to Australia for them. She needed to be patient but it was hard sometimes and she felt trapped here, even though she worked for such nice people.

Hearing a sound behind her, she spun round to see her mistress standing there, leaning on her walking stick.

'You should have rung for me, Mrs Largan. It's no trouble to come and see what you need.'

'I wanted to catch you on your own. Maia's cleaning my bedroom so perhaps you and I can have a quiet little chat? I'm worried about her, you see. Your decision to leave once your money comes through has made her so unhappy.'

Xanthe sighed. 'I know. But I can't help how we're both made. I always felt we'd go our own ways one day, and I've tried to prepare her for it, but she refuses to believe me.'

'Will you sit down and tell me about what you want to do? Or should I mind my own business?'

Xanthe helped her mistress to ease herself down into a chair then pulled up another for herself. 'It'd be good to talk to someone who isn't part of the problem, if you don't mind, ma'am. The trouble is, I've always wanted to see the world. And Maia – well, she doesn't want that.'

'Do you want to become a lady explorer like Louisa Anne Meredith? I've read her accounts of her travels in the Antipodes and always envied her.'

'You *envied* her?'

Susannah Largan smiled. 'Yes. I was very interested in botany when I was younger and more able to go out and about. Does that sort of travelling interest you?'

'No, not at all. I've no wish to go exploring wild places or living among savages.' She smiled. 'Growing up in the mill terraces with no gardens didn't give you much chance to grow fond of plants, let alone study them, and I was always more interested in books than flowers. No, I want to see the other countries I've read about, especially Greece. My father loved the Greek language and myths so much. I want to go there for him. And then . . .'

'Then what?'

'I don't know. See something of my own country, or yours, or Scotland. Visit Paris. I've read that a man called Thomas Cook is taking groups of people travelling to France and Germany. I could maybe go on some of his tours now that I have money.'

'And where would you live in between your journeys?'

'I could visit my sister Pandora or rent a little cottage some-where pretty once she and Zachary have paid us something for our shares in my uncle's emporium, because to be honest . . .' She looked round, listening, not wanting Maia to hear this. 'I don't see myself ever coming back to live in Australia.'

'That'll upset your sister. And what will happen to Maia if I die?' Mrs Largan asked. 'She'll be on her own then.'

Xanthe hesitated, unable to think of an easy answer to this.

'You must both realise that her love for my son can lead nowhere.'

That was obvious to both her and her sister. Maia wasn't stupid, after all. But Xanthe hadn't realised Mrs Largan was aware of Maia's feeling. Even this kindest of mistresses wouldn't tolerate a marriage between her son and a young woman from the labouring classes. 'I don't think she expects anything to come of her feelings, to be truthful, ma'am. She knows gentlemen like your son don't marry mill girls.'

'Expecting is one thing, dreaming is another. If I didn't need her so badly, I'd help her find another position, for her own sake.' Mrs Largan looked down sadly at her twisted hands. She wished they'd told their maids the truth about Conn being married from the start. It might have stopped Maia falling in love with Conn – or perhaps not. Who could deny love? 'Well, your other sister lives nearby. Maia could go to Cassandra if anything went wrong here. And in the meantime, if you do leave, I'll look after her as best I can. Will that set your mind at rest a little?'

'Yes. It will.' Was her mistress hiding something? Xanthe wondered. Why was she talking of dying? Had her health deteriorated? She watched as Mrs Largan got slowly and painfully to her feet and left the room. Clearly the conversation was over.

But it had done little to solve Xanthe's worries. She'd always been the strong one, protected her gentler sister, and she felt guilty about leaving. But she couldn't give up her whole life for Maia, much as she loved her.

Two weeks after he left his mother's house, Ronan got off the train in Outham and looked round with interest, smiling wryly to see that it was looking like rain here, too, with heavy grey clouds hanging low. His travels hadn't included a Lancashire mill town before and he was hoping to get a tour of one of the huge monoliths with their towering chimneys. He'd not like to live here, though, fenced in by rows of streets on either side and with even the sky barred by ribbons of black smoke from the mills.

He realised a lad had asked him something and forced his attention back, having difficulty understanding the accent. 'What? Oh yes, I would like a handcart for my luggage. I'm going to Blake's Emporium.'

'It's just down the main street in that direction, sir,' the lad said, not cheekily but as one equal to another, which was very different from the way poorer people in Ireland talked to the gentry.

The rest of Ronan's things were in Southampton, waiting to be loaded on the ship. Bram was in London waiting for him. He'd given Bram enough money to look round the famous capital city of England, which he would probably never have a chance to visit again, and his boyhood friend had been as excited about that as a child.

Ronan had written a brief note to his mother to tell her he was sailing to Australia, but hadn't received a reply. It didn't usually take her more than a few days to get over a disagreement and he couldn't think why she was staying so angry.

The lad stopped and gestured to the emporium, which had a handsome frontage with a big plate-glass window to the right of the entrance and a smaller one to the left. The name of the shop was written in big gold letters against a maroon background above the sparkling clean windows. A few tins and packages were arranged neatly in the narrow shop window and the whole of the inside seemed full of shelves containing groceries of all descriptions, some dry goods already weighed and set out in neat rows of packages of various colours. It had the air of a thriving business.

'House door or shop, mister?'

'I think it'll be the house door,' Ronan said, so the boy used the knocker and they waited patiently.

A young woman with a cheerful face and the white apron and cap of a maid answered it.

'I'm Ronan Maguire. Your master and mistress are expecting me.'

She beamed at him. 'Oh yes. Welcome to Outham, sir. If you'll please to come in and leave your luggage here in the hall, I'll get someone from the shop to carry it up to your bedroom in a few minutes.'

He paid the lad and followed her upstairs, where his hostess was waiting for him. She was glowingly beautiful, as some women are when expecting a child.

'Mr Maguire. How kind of you to come and see us!'

He took her hand and shook it. 'I'm always interested in visiting new places.'

She smiled. 'You sound like my older sister Xanthe. She's intending to use some of the money we've inherited to travel.'

'With her husband?'

'She's not married.'

He hoped he'd hidden his surprise but he couldn't help saying, 'It isn't usual for single ladies to travel on their own.'

'I doubt we're any of us "usual", Mr Maguire. Our father worked in the mill and yet was learning Greek, while my sisters and I usually have our heads in a book when we have time.' She sighed and glanced at an open book, lying beside her on the sofa. 'At the moment, I have all too much time on my hands.'

He could only assume that her sister didn't share her beauty, because it was normally dried-up spinsters who became globe trotters, a modern phrase he rather liked. He'd met a few such women on his travels and found them eccentric, bizarrely dressed and sometimes rather free in their behaviour.

Mr Carr didn't come in from the shop to join them until the evening meal, which was served at six o'clock and which everyone called 'tea'. After that he apologised for needing to go back to the shop, which didn't close until nine o'clock.

'Your husband works hard.'

'Yes, but he loves it. I do the accounts but women aren't welcome to serve in the better class of shop.'

She'd surprised him again. 'Would you want to?'

'Oh, yes. It'd be much more interesting than sitting here twiddling my thumbs.' She smiled. 'Most men wouldn't let their wives near the accounts, but I've always been good with figures.'

'Tell me about your sisters and how they wound up in Australia. Did you not want to go with them?'

So she explained about their aunt forcing them to go to Australia by kidnapping Cassandra and threatening to kill her. As their aunt had already killed her own husband, they'd been too afraid to refuse. 'But I could never settle in Australia and was so homesick I became ill. In the end I had to come back to England on my own, but I miss my sisters dreadfully.'

It was said simply and quietly, but he could sense the deep sadness behind the words.

'They're starting to reduce the travel time now that steamships are coming into their own, and once the Suez Canal is finished, it'll be even easier to get to and fro. If they prosper, and from what you've told me they sound very capable, I'd guess that one day they'll come to visit you here.'

Her face lit up. 'Do you really think so?'

'I do indeed.'

'Then you've given me a bright hope to comfort me.'

Fenella Maguire sat stabbing at a piece of needlework, bored with her own company and wishing she hadn't quarrelled with her son. Ronan would come back, though, she knew he would. Didn't they always make up their differences?

When she heard a carriage outside, she went to peep out of the window and saw Kathleen Largan get out, her black clothes fluttering in the breeze.

Fenella hurried to greet her in the hall. 'Are you all right? I thought you'd be resting after the funeral.'

'That was over a week ago.'

'What shall you do now?'

She shook her head, frowning. 'I don't know. Kieran has told me he doesn't want me staying at Shilmara. He's offered to buy me a house wherever I like, Dublin, Belfast or England even, but I'd be among strangers and I don't like that. I've always lived near here. I like living in the country. Why should I leave and go to live in a town, where I'd not be able to ride?'

Fenella wondered what to say to this. Kathleen wasn't an easy person to live with, so she didn't blame Kieran. James Largan should never have made his son marry her, because any children of the union might be like their mother, but everyone had supposed she'd brought a large dowry with her.

Kathleen hadn't had any children, which was perhaps a good thing, but Fenella felt sorry for the younger woman, she did indeed. She'd once promised James Largan that if he died she'd keep an eye on his daughter-in-law. Strange how kind he'd always been to Kathleen. The younger woman didn't have the knack of making friends, or even of getting on with people. Perhaps that was because of how her parents had treated her, keeping her always at home with a very strict governess. Children needed kindness and love, but Fenella doubted she'd ever had any.

Kathleen scowled down at her clasped hands. 'There's another thing I've been thinking about. Mr Largan's wife won't know he's dead so I thought I might go and tell her.'

'*Go to Australia?*'

'Why not? It was his dying wish that his wife come back where she belongs and Kieran refuses to go and tell his mother or even to write to say she must come back, and cousin Michael won't go, either. So . . . I thought maybe I could go. I'd do anything for Papa Largan. He was always so kind to me, kinder than anyone else ever has been. What do you think, Mrs Maguire?' She began to fiddle with the material of her skirt, pleating it then smoothing it out.

'You could just write to her.'

'I don't like writing letters.'

'I could write for you.'

'No. My mind's made up. I want to go and see her myself, persuade her to help me.'

'You know she's living with Conn. You said you never wanted to see your husband again.'

Kathleen's fingers stilled for a moment. 'I don't want to see him, but I must if I'm to see her. Since Mr Largan died, people have started treating me differently, as if . . . I'm a divorced woman or something terrible like that. It's all because of Conn being a convict. I hate being married to a traitor.'

'You are in a difficult position,' Fenella admitted. Only James Largan's influence had made sure that Kathleen was still accepted in the houses of the local gentry after her husband was transported.

'So I've decided to go to Australia, see Mrs Largan, tell her what her husband wanted and try to persuade her to come back and live with me. That'd be more respectable, don't you think? People would talk to me again if I was living with her.'

'What about your husband?'

'Conn can rot in hell for all I care!'

Fenella didn't know what to say to that. If Kathleen moved out of the district, she didn't think anything would make up for the fact that her husband was a convict who'd been transported to Australia. Socially, her young friend was ruined and would remain in a sort of limbo unless Conn died and she remarried. Even then, some people would refuse to socialise with her.

Fenella too would have looked askance on a convict's wife if she hadn't known the family and Kathleen all her life. She'd never been able to believe that Conn was a traitor. 'Australia. That's a long way to travel on your own.'

'That's why I came to see you. You told me your son wrote to tell you he's going to Australia and you're all on your own here now. You said last time I saw you that you were bored, so I thought perhaps you'd like to come with me, to make it all respectable.'

Fenella stared at her in shock, unable to speak or move for a few moments, then slowly the idea began to seem . . . possible . . . interesting even. She'd never travelled, never really wanted to until now, but she didn't enjoy being a widow, particularly now that all her children had left home. In fact, life had become rather tedious and without Ronan to cheer her up, she couldn't see it improving.

She sat and thought about it, vaguely aware of Kathleen staring at her, grateful that her companion didn't say anything to interrupt her thoughts.

Should she go? Dare she go?

The alternative was to stay here and die of boredom. She'd had more than enough of that.

She was only mildly surprised to hear her own voice, sounding to come from a long way away. 'Yes, I'll do it. I'll go to Australia with you. Why not? What have I got to keep me here at Ardgullan?'

Maia went to sit on the front veranda on her own. She felt too restless to sleep and since the night was mild with a full moon shining, she went to stroll round the gardens, which were only half-finished. They didn't have proper flower beds yet, but there were paths winding among the remaining trees and a few bushes had been planted, some of which were in flower. There was always something in flower in Australia.

She didn't try to stop the tears tonight. She tried not to weep at the thought of being separated from Xanthe, especially in front of her twin, but sometimes she just couldn't help it. They'd always been so close, she and Xanthe.

After a few minutes she ended up on the far side of the stables and went to lean on the rough fence, made from sapling trunks alternating in a zig-zag pattern, each one set on top of another. She didn't realise someone else was there until a man moved forward and she couldn't help crying out in shock.

'It's only me.'

She'd recognise Conn's voice anywhere. 'It's – um – a beautiful night, isn't it?'

'Too beautiful to be crying. What's wrong?'

She scrubbed at her eyes, not knowing what to say, but the tears wouldn't stop.

'Ah, Maia!' He pulled her into his arms and held her close. 'Are you fretting because your sister wants to leave?'

'I don't think I can bear it. We've never been parted before.' She sobbed against him, unable to hold back the tears that had built up over the past few months.

When her weeping eased, he fumbled in his pocket and pulled out a crumpled handkerchief. 'Here. It's more or less clean.'

She tried to take it from him but her hand was shaking so badly she dropped it and when he picked it up, he clasped her fingers around it with his big warm hands and then stilled. She heard him suck in his breath sharply and looked up at him. The moonlight was shining down on them both like a blessing.

For a moment neither of them moved, then he pulled her close to him and said simply, 'It won't go away, this feeling between us, will it?'

'No. Conn, I know I'm only a maid, but I lo—'

He pressed his fingers to her lips. 'Shh. Don't say it. I must tell you something. I should have done it before now, once I realised how you felt.' He turned her to stand with her back to him, wrapping his arms round her, so that she fitted comfortably against his body. 'Maia, I'm attracted to you, too, of course I am, but I'm already married.'

It was the last thing she'd expected to hear. 'Married!' she whispered, through lips that suddenly felt icy cold. 'But you have no wife here, and you've never mentioned one. Nor has your mother.'

'She's in Ireland still and I hate her, hope I never see her as long as I live. It wasn't a happy marriage – wasn't really a marriage at all – but my father and hers were eager for it; and my father was upsetting my mother, blaming her for my refusal to consider the marriage. Kathleen seemed pleasant enough while we were courting, eager to please. Best of all, she had a love of horses to match my own. I thought that might be enough to get by with and I'd never met anyone else I'd had a fancy for, so in the end I said yes.'

His laughter was low and yet harsh, seeming full of pain. 'It wasn't long before I found out how badly I'd been fooled. Kathleen refused point-blank to let me into her bed. What's more, she's a shrew, treats her servants and everyone she considers beneath her badly. When I asked her not to be so harsh she began to quarrel with me. I was always hobnobbing with servants, you see, giving away my money to any fool who told me lies, not behaving properly. I think her idea of good manners had been beaten into her by her parents and she seemed unable to change any of the "rules" they'd set in her mind.

'And then, when they arrested me, she immediately believed the worst. She didn't come to see me once in jail, sending a message that she wanted nothing to do with a traitor.'

'Oh, Conn! That's dreadful. How sad you must have been.'

'Yes. I should have had the marriage annulled. I had grounds for doing so. But once I was in prison I didn't have any chance to do that and since I've been here, I've not seen any reason to bother. It'd take years and what decent woman would want to marry a convict, anyway?'

'I would.' She heard him suck his breath in sharply and wondered if she'd been too forward.

'Oh, my dear, you're the last person I'd burden with a convict husband. You're young and unspoiled, and I pray you'll stay that way. You deserve so much more.'

'Not so young. I'm twenty-seven.'

'And I'm several years older.'

'What if I don't change my mind?'

'Then I'll have to send you away, so that you can recover from your madness. I love you too much to mar your life.'

There was silence and she didn't know what to say, how to persuade him that she'd never be able to forget him. Before she could think, he'd gone on speaking.

'My father was as bad as Kathleen. He didn't believe me when I told him I was innocent, I don't know why.'

'When did he die?'

'He isn't dead. Crippled as she is, my mother left him and ran away to join me here because—' he hesitated.

'Because she believed you were innocent,' Maia finished for him.

'Yes. She's a wonderful woman, with a keen sense of justice. She knew I'd been wrongly accused. But my cousin Michael provided so-called proof and I was convicted out of hand.'

There was silence but they didn't move apart, then he said quietly, 'So you see, I can do nothing about our love without ruining you. And I won't do that, my dear.'

She waited for a moment to be sure she meant it, because she knew what she said would damn her in most people's eyes and perhaps in his, but she loved him so much, she couldn't bear to think of leaving him, living without him. 'I'd be honoured to become your mistress, Conn.'

'*Honoured!*' He pushed her away, turning her to face him as he did so and giving her a little shake. 'Do you think I'd do that to a wonderful, decent girl like you? Maia, I love you far too much to ruin you. I'd have sent you away before now if my mother didn't need you so much.'

She smiled and lifted one hand to caress his cheek, something she'd longed to do for months. 'I'd not go, not now that I know you love me.'

'Then heaven help us both, because if it was hard to keep my distance before, it'll be a Herculean task now.'

'I don't want you to keep your distance, Conn.'

'I must. I couldn't live with myself if I ruined an innocent girl.'

He didn't push her away, though, so she allowed herself to nestle against him. Once he sighed softly and a little later dropped a kiss on her hair, as ephemeral as a butterfly landing there.

She could have stood there in his arms all night, but she heard Xanthe calling from the kitchen door. With a sigh, she pushed away from him.

He pulled her back to press another of those gentle kisses on her cheek, then turned away and walked back towards the stables.

Drawing a deep breath, Maia took a moment to calm down, then turned towards the house.

4

R onan and Bram boarded the steamship at Southampton on
    a stormy evening that had even that large vessel heaving up
and down at its moorings. It was an auxiliary vessel using both
steam and sail, but the masts were bare of canvas just now. The
two men were immediately separated, he to go to a cabin he'd
paid extra to keep to himself and Bram to go into the single
men's quarters in the steerage section below.

His cabin had been described by the agent as 'spacious' but
it seemed very cramped to him once his huge cabin trunk, which
opened out like a set of drawers, was in place. His previous journeys had meant a brief Channel crossing then travelling on by
train usually for all the longer stretches. For the first time it sank
in that he'd be spending more than two months in this restricted
space. He'd have to spend a lot of time out on deck, hated the
feel of this dark place with its tiny porthole window.

There would be some respite from the cramped conditions in
Egypt, where they had to leave this ship and travel overland from
Alexandria to Suez to board another vessel. He felt a moment's
temptation to run off the ship and give up this foolish idea, then
smiled at himself. Was he such a weakling that he couldn't stand
a journey which many thousands had taken before him?

It'd have been nice to have company, though, someone like
Conn in the cabin next door. Travelling would be a lonely business unless the other passengers were very congenial. Bram didn't
count because apparently cabin and steerage passengers lived
fairly separate lives.

Within the hour Ronan was feeling a faint nausea and when
the steward came to tell him that dinner would shortly be served

in the day cabin, he shuddered and waved one hand in dismissal. 'I don't feel like eating.'

The steward gave him an assessing look. 'Feeling sick, are you, sir? It'll soon pass, but I'll fetch you a bucket and fasten it beside the bed. Just in case. Ring if you need anything else, but I can't promise to attend to you immediately, I'm afraid, because it's always very busy just before we set sail and you're not the only passenger who isn't feeling well.'

The weather continued stormy and Ronan grew rapidly worse. He missed the moment of sailing and felt vaguely sorry not to be able to say farewell to England, but couldn't face the thought of staggering up to the deck and perhaps disgracing himself in front of other people.

He spent the next two days lying in his bunk suffering from debilitating seasickness, and if he could have turned round now, he would have done. The steward kept assuring him that for most people this was just a temporary phase which lasted until they 'got their sea legs'. It didn't feel temporary. He seemed to have been ill for a black eternity.

He ate nothing, but kept forcing cups of tea and boiled water down. He didn't need the steward to urge him to do that, because it stood to reason you needed liquid to keep your body functioning. You could go without food for a long time if you had to, but not without water.

On the second day at sea, the steward showed Bram into the cabin and left them together.

'They told me you were ill, Mr Ronan.'

'Damned seasickness. Are you all right?'

'Right as rain. I've got some very clean, pleasant neighbours below decks, which makes a big difference, and I'm nicely settled in. Now, shall I tidy the cabin a bit and perhaps you'd like me to read to you? There's talk of starting a ship's newspaper, did you hear that?'

'How can I hear anything lying here?'

Bram grinned at him. 'It'd make me grumpy, too, to be seasick – sir.'

Ronan was surprised into a smile. 'Yes. Sorry. You can tidy up, but don't bother to read to me. I can't concentrate. My head's muzzy and my mouth tastes like a dungheap.'

'Could I borrow a book, do you think, sir? I'll be careful with it.'

'Yes, of course.' He'd forgotten how well Bram had done at the village school, how the teacher there had urged the family to let the boy continue his education. But James Largan had been furious, saying education wasn't for the lower classes and only gave them ideas above their station. He'd insisted on the boy going to work as a stable lad and since the family all worked on the estate and knew he'd turn them all off if they upset him, Bram's parents hadn't dared refuse this job for their son.

Ronan and Conn had lent Bram books from time to time as they all grew up, doing this with great secrecy, however, for his sake. And Bram had bought others when he could, tattered volumes of anything at all from passing pedlars, just to feed his brain.

While he set the cabin to rights Bram chatted quietly, describing the steerage quarters with their rows of narrow bunks in small compartments of four, with long central tables between the compartments. The steward had kept things clean here, bringing water, emptying slop buckets, but hadn't had time to tidy up properly because several of the other cabin passengers were also suffering from seasickness.

Bram must have been born tidy, Ronan thought as he watched. His friend had been the same when working in the stables. Even the smallest piece of harness was always where it should be. Kathleen had lost a valuable employee for the Largans when she dismissed him. Her brother-in-law wouldn't be pleased about that.

The groom's gentle voice was so soothing that Ronan found himself drifting towards sleep, welcoming the brief respite from sickness.

When he woke, it was morning and he was surprised to have slept so long. He felt much better, only slightly queasy now.

He smiled, able now to believe the steward was right and his sickness was a temporary thing. He went across to stare out of the porthole and saw that the sun had come out and the sea was much calmer.

He thought he could face a cup of tea and a piece of dry toast. He'd not try anything else till that had stayed down.

But he was feeling hopeful again, and looking forward to seeing some exciting new places.

Fenella led the way on to the ship, shivering in a downpour of rain and feeling that twinge in her belly again, just a niggling pain that sometimes happened, so annoying. It always went away again, but it made her uncomfortable for a while.

Behind her Kathleen was grimly silent, her heavy features not flattered by long strands of hair that had blown out of the tight bun. The two of them were followed by Kathleen's maid Orla, whom they'd agreed to share while they were travelling.

The two ladies were also going to share a cabin, though how that would work out, Fenella had no idea. She was wondering if she'd been right to come, though she wasn't going to back out now, not after the way her son Hubert had carried on about this venture. Why shouldn't she travel a little? She wasn't that old! He wanted her to sit quietly in her parlour till she died, probably of boredom, and she wasn't going to do that.

It was strange that she'd had three sons so different in personality. Hubert was a quiet, reclusive man, who cared more about his acres and horses than he did about any human being, while Patrick, now living in England, was hunting mad and moved with a fast set, thanks to his wife's money. But Ronan, ah, her middle son was the darling of her heart, such fun to be with, and sometimes she couldn't help being glad he'd never married and kept coming back to live with her – though this couldn't go on, if she was to have grandchildren from him. Such splendid children they'd be if they were anything like him.

She felt a little apprehensive about what he'd say when he found out she was travelling to Australia on the same ship as him – and worse, travelling there with Kathleen, whom he couldn't stand. Ah, the two of them would settle down after they'd been on the ship for a while, and that'd end their quarrelling, surely it would? It wasn't good for neighbours to be on bad terms.

Kathleen was foolish to refuse to speak to him just because he'd helped poor Conn get his money through to Australia. And Ronan shouldn't blame her for abandoning Conn. Surely he of all people should realise Mr Largan had been telling her what to do. Fenella suspected Conn's cousin Michael was involved. He was a cunning devil, that one. She'd never liked him. Though what he'd hoped to gain from it, she couldn't work out.

It had occurred to her more than once that Kathleen might have had more chance of happiness if Conn had died, as convicts sometimes did, but no, he'd survived, gone to Australia and been released there. And she was glad, really. She didn't wish him ill, whatever he'd done. He'd been a nice enough lad, always polite, though he'd grown very solemn after his marriage, looking years older.

It had shocked everyone when his mother had run off and followed him to Australia, but why Ronan had to go chasing after him, too, Fenella didn't understand. She intended to make very sure her son came back to Ireland once the visit was over. She wasn't having him buying property and settling there, however cheap land was.

That was the main reason she'd come, though she hadn't told Kathleen that.

The ship was heaving up and down, even here by the dockside, and she staggered as she made her way across the deck. Oh dear! She hoped it wasn't going to be rough or that she'd be seasick. No, of course she wouldn't. She'd never been a sickly sort of person, not even when she was carrying her children.

She laughed and shook the rain off her cloak as she and Kathleen were shown into their cabin. 'What a wild day!'

'I'm afraid I'm going to have to ask you ladies to stay either in your cabin or the day cabin until the storm has passed,' the steward said. 'It's not safe for you to go up on deck.'

Kathleen didn't answer him, just glared round the cabin and said, 'Can they do no better than this for their passengers? I've never slept in such cramped quarters in my life.'

'Sure, we'll be all right here.' Fenella gave the steward a coin and winked at him as he left.

'We should ask them for a better cabin,' Kathleen said as the door closed on him.

'All the other cabins are booked by now. You know the shipping agent said this was the last one, which is why we're sharing. This was the only way for us to get to Australia, otherwise we'd have to wait weeks longer.'

Kathleen let out a sigh and plumped down on the bed. 'It's all Conn's fault.'

Fenella had learned not to argue with this statement. Kathleen blamed everything that went wrong on her husband and you couldn't persuade her otherwise. James Largan, on the other hand, was quoted as the fount of all wisdom, which Fenella thought rather strange, though she had to admit that he'd been kinder to Kathleen than to anyone else.

It was very obvious from the way she talked about her parents that the poor girl hadn't been loved as a child. Not surprising, therefore, that she would cling to anyone who was kind to her.

'I'm going to take my cloak off, then start arranging our things,' Fenella said briskly. 'Come on. Let's make ourselves at home.'

'Orla should do that. That's what she's paid for. Papa Largan always said one should never do servants' jobs for them. Besides, I can never make things neat.'

'Well, I'll help you. Orla has to stay in the steerage quarters till after we sail, because of the stormy weather. And anyway, I'd rather do it myself so that I know where everything is.'

But to her surprise Kathleen seemed completely at a loss as to how to arrange her things. 'I don't know what each drawer is for,' she said several times as Fenella chivvied her to set her garments and other possessions to rights for the journey.

In the end Kathleen flung herself down on the bed. 'How do I ring for Orla? I can't do this.'

'I told you. She can't come here till the storm has died down.'

'But she's my maid. She *has to* do this work.'

Fenella gave up and put everything away herself. Was Kathleen really as helpless as she seemed?

It wasn't until four days after the ship had left England that Ronan ventured on deck, turning his face up to the watery sunshine and hoping those clouds didn't mean more rain or – heaven forbid! – further stormy weather.

He walked along the part of the deck reserved for cabin passengers, saw Bram on the lower deck and waved. Unless he much mistook it, his friend was staring at something beyond him on the upper deck with a shocked expression.

Ronan turned round to see what was wrong and froze where he was, unable to believe what he was seeing.

Kathleen Largan!

After a moment's hesitation he marched up to her. 'What the hell are you doing on board this ship?'

She turned away as if he'd not spoken and he grabbed her arm.

'Take your hands off me!' She spat the words at him, well laced with her usual venom.

'I will when you answer my question.'

'It's no concern of yours where I go or what I do. And I haven't changed my mind about talking to someone who supports traitors.'

Just then someone came across to join them and he had a second, even greater shock. *'Mother!'*

'Hello, darling. I thought I'd join you on your visit to Australia.'

He was bereft of speech, could only gape at her like a landed fish. She gave him one of her sunny smiles, but her eyes were wary, and well they should be!

'I'm glad you two have started talking to one another, Ronan darlin'. It's so foolish for neighbours to keep quarrelling.'

'I've no intention of talking to your son, Mrs Maguire. What *he* says or does means nothing to me.' Kathleen turned and walked away.

'How could you bring her to Australia, Mother?'

'She's bringing me. This was all her idea.'

'Then you should have refused to come.'

She shrugged. 'That'd not have stopped her coming. She's got it into her head that she has to see Mrs Largan and tell her that poor James is dead, and you know what Kathleen's like. Once she's decided on something, she won't change her mind.

'Anyway, you aren't the only one who gets bored in the country or who longs for sunshine. Ah, come on now, darlin'. There's no use staying angry with me, because I can hardly turn back now, can I?' She gave him one of her twinkling smiles as she added, 'I never did learn to swim.'

He rolled his eyes at heaven for what it had thrown at him, then gave her a hug anyway. 'I'm not sure you're going to enjoy this journey.'

'Of course I will. I know it's going to be uncomfortable some-times, especially when the weather's rough, but at least I shall be with people. I shan't be sitting in that parlour on my own hoping someone will call, anyone, even Kathleen, who is not the most amusing companion in the world.'

His voice grew gentler. 'Is that what you do when I'm not at home?'

She smiled and gave a quick shrug. 'Sometimes. I've missed your father sorely, for all his faults.'

He put one arm round her shoulders and gave her another hug. 'Then we'll have to make the most of travelling together, shan't we?'

'Indeed we shall. I intend to enjoy myself. And Ronan, darlin', you'll do your best to get on with Kathleen, won't you? Just for me?'

'A saint couldn't get on with that woman for more than a few minutes. She's the one who's not speaking to me, you know. It takes two to hold a conversation.'

'I'll have a word with her. By the time we get to Australia, you two will be on good terms again, I'm sure. After all, she is your best friend's wife.'

He wished his mother wouldn't try to reconcile them. He didn't trust Kathleen. She was so chancy, you never knew what she'd do next.

What the hell was Conn going to say when she turned up at his house in Australia out of the blue? He only hoped his friend didn't blame it on him.

Something had changed between Conn and Maia, Xanthe was sure of it, but couldn't put her finger on what exactly it was. Her sister wasn't sleeping with him, she was fairly sure of that. She caught Mrs Largan watching them, too, with her forehead furrowed in thought.

In the end she could stand it no longer. 'What's happened between you and Conn?' she asked her sister as they lay in the bed they shared each night.

'Nothing. What should be going on?'

'Exactly that – nothing. But I can sense something and you won't persuade me otherwise.'

Maia rolled over to stare at her sister. 'What's between Conn and me is nothing to do with you or anyone else.'

'But surely you're not—'

'Sharing his bed?' Maia sighed. 'I wish I was.'

'He'll never marry you.'

'I know that. But I'd go to him anyway, if he'd take me. Only he won't.'

Xanthe gasped in shock. 'You can't mean that?'

'I do.'

'You offered yourself to him?'

'Yes.'

'That isn't love; it's insanity.'

'You've never really loved anyone, so you don't understand. And I'm not discussing this again. You're going off travelling, so grant me the right to do what I choose with my own life.'

Xanthe knew her decision to leave and her insistence on going alone had hurt her twin badly, but she couldn't bear to waste her life like this, not when she had the resources to do other things. There didn't seem to be any way out of this tangle. If Conn really loved Maia, he'd marry her and be damned to what people said. After all, he was a convict and that would place restrictions on who would associate with his wife, however well-born she was. And it wasn't as if they met many people here in the middle of nowhere.

Oh, why hadn't her home-loving sister met someone else? Anyone but a gentleman who clearly didn't think of her as a potential wife.

A few days before the ship reached Alexandria, Fenella woke in the night with a pain so great she couldn't help moaning. She tried to stifle the sound in the pillow but it got worse and worse, till she found herself screaming helplessly.

She could sense Kathleen trying to speak to her, but she couldn't listen let alone answer, couldn't think of anything but the pain that was surely tearing her belly apart.

Someone else came into the cabin and she heard Ronan's voice, felt him lift her and clung to him for a brief intermission when the pain had abated enough not to take away her senses.

'I love you, son,' she gasped.

'I love you too, Mother. We've sent for the doctor. He'll be here in a minute.'

It took the man five minutes to get there and Ronan realised in horror that he was drunk.

The doctor asked questions, palpated Fenella's abdomen then sat with bowed head next to her, seeming impervious to her screams and writhing.

'For heaven's sake, can you do nothing to help her?' Ronan asked.

The doctor looked at him sadly. 'No. There are doctors in America who advocate a laparotomy, cutting open the abdomen to remove the corrupted portion of the intestines. Hancock did this in 1848. And it worked.' He gave a bitter laugh. 'I enjoy reading about such advances. When I was younger I used to think I'd be like those doctors.'

'Can you not try the same thing, then?'

'No. This is a bold treatment, still controversial, and only to be assayed by surgeons of considerably more expertise than myself.'

'Maybe if you were sober you might make the attempt,' Ronan flung at him.

'Not even if I were stone cold sober would I attempt this. I do not have the skill and I do not have the equipment. All I can offer is to stupefy her with laudanum and let her die peacefully.'

'*Die?*' Ronan stared at him in horror. 'You'd let my mother die?'

'I can't prevent it. All I can prevent is the pain – well, most of it.'

When Ronan didn't speak, Kathleen moved forward from the far corner. 'Then do it, doctor. We can't let her suffer like this. My mother took laudanum when she was dying.'

Even with the drug, Fenella was clearly still in pain, but at least she wasn't screaming now.

Kathleen stayed with her, but it was the maid Orla who cared for his mother and kept her clean. All he could do, for decency's sake, because he knew his mother would hate him to see her naked body, was to turn away when she needed cleaning. The rest of the time he stayed, helpless to do anything but be with her.

Food was brought for them and his went away largely un-tasted, though Kathleen continued to eat with her usual hearty appetite.

It took Fenella two days to die, by which time Ronan was praying for her to be released from this travail and the doctor was grimly sober. Kathleen's face was mostly expressionless except when she was scowling.

When his mother eventually breathed her last, Ronan bowed his head and wept, not caring who saw him.

In the end they had to bring Bram to force him to leave the

cabin while Orla laid out the body and a sailor sewed it into a canvas shroud.

Ronan came back only to kiss his mother's cheek before they finished their sad task.

He looked across her body at Orla. 'I'm grateful to you for your help.'

'She was a kind lady.'

'If I can ever help you in any way . . . ?'

'Thank you, sir. Who knows what we'll need in Australia?'

Kathleen stood cold and tearless on the deck as the passengers all gathered to see Ronan's mother's body consigned to the deep the following morning. He was relieved that his mother was blessed by a clergyman, at least, a man travelling to the Swan River Colony. He couldn't help shedding a few tears as the solemn words were spoken and the canvas bag containing his mother's body was tipped into the water. He felt as guilty as if he'd killed his mother himself. She'd not have been on this ship but for him.

That evening he tried to get drunk and couldn't do it. He'd never been a drinker and alcohol made him sick well before it could blunt his senses.

The following day, his mother's possessions were delivered to his cabin by the steward.

He stared at them in horror. 'Why did you bring these?'

'On Mrs Largan's instructions, sir.'

Kathleen had to be the most insensitive woman in the world. He shook his head, not wanting to touch them, and almost told the man to toss them over the side of the ship. But then he realised they contained valuable items like her jewellery. 'Put them over there, then. I'll go through them later, then you can toss what I don't want over the side of the ship.'

The steward did as he'd asked and left. A few minutes later Bram came into the room without knocking.

Ronan scowled. 'What are you doing here?'

'That poor ould steward doesn't know what to do with you,' Bram said.

'My instructions to him were quite plain.'

'Only a rich man would even think of tossing all that stuff over the side of the ship.'

'I'm not rich.'

'You seem rich to people like me.'

Ronan shrugged. 'That's easy then. Once I've gone through them, *you* can have my mother's things, to keep or to throw away, whatever you choose.'

His childhood friend didn't move, just stared thoughtfully at him. 'Are you sure about that, Mr Ronan?'

His calm patience made Ronan feel ashamed and he looked down at the trunks then back at Bram pleadingly. 'Will you help me go through her things?'

'Of course I will.'

It felt like a violation to go through the trunks and bags, fumbling through underwear and corsets, stockings and gloves, fans and shawls.

Ronan found her jewel case and set it aside. There were a few other bits and pieces that he thought he should keep, including her Bible. It seemed to take them a long time.

Once the steward knocked on the door and put his head round to ask, 'Anything I can get you, sir? It's mealtime.'

'I'm not hungry.'

Bram intervened. 'How about a tray of sandwiches and cakes, and a pot of tea?'

'I'll bring it right away.'

'You can eat it,' Ronan told his friend. 'I'm not hungry.'

'Well, I am.'

When it arrived Bram ate some of the food and cajoled Ronan into eating a little too. He continued to open the boxes and trunks, rendered speechless at how many clothes Mrs Maguire, bless her soul, had considered necessary for this voyage. 'It doesn't seem right for me to be doing this,' he muttered at one stage.

'Nor me,' Ronan said, brushing the back of his hand across his eyes.

When they'd finished, he got out a bottle of cognac and poured them both a drink. 'Slàinte.'

'To your mother's memory,' Bram said quietly.

Ronan raised his glass and sipped, then sat down on the bed.
'What are you going to do with those things?'

'Sell them. They're worth quite a bit of money. Do you mind?'

'No.' And somehow, he felt his mother would not begrudge
them to Bram now. She'd always had a kind heart, even though
she didn't like Ronan being friends with people from the lower
classes. Her servants had thought the world of her.

It didn't escape his notice that Kathleen came nowhere near
him, let alone offering to help sort out his mother's possessions.
She didn't even send her maid.

After they'd finished, Bram stared at his new possessions and
couldn't help feeling a sense of elation. This represented more
money than he'd ever seen or hoped to see in his life before. For
the first time he began to wonder what opportunities he'd meet
with in his new life, what he could make of himself. He was in
an anomalous position with Ronan and it'd be the same with
Conn, neither friend nor merely a servant.

But on his own, could he do more?

What if he earned enough money to buy himself a smallholding,
or a shop, or found some other way of being independent? He'd
talked to people on the ship who said others had made a fortune
in Australia. Could he do it too?

He smacked one fist into the palm of his other hand. He could
try, couldn't he? What had he to lose? He'd left Ireland with only
a few clothes and the family's tattered Bible, which his mother
had insisted he take, as eldest son.

He closed his eyes for a moment, then took a deep breath. If
he ever had children, he didn't want them to be treated like a
possession of the estate owner, as he had been. He'd want them
to be educated and free to make what they chose of their lives.

He didn't need to make a fortune, which would be asking too
much of fate, just a decent living. He wasn't a stupid man but
he'd never run a business, wasn't even sure how to start.

But he could try, couldn't he? Some of his travelling companions had worked in shops. He'd talk to them more carefully. There were self-improvement classes on the ship. He'd attend more of them, however boring they were.

He could try, couldn't he?

The doctor came and stood beside Ronan at the rail the day after the burial. 'It's no use blaming yourself,' he said abruptly.

'But I am to blame. If I hadn't come to Australia, she might still be alive.'

There was silence, then the doctor said, 'I doubt it.'

'What do you mean?'

'With cramp colic like that, most people do die, wherever they are. If they recover, it's due to their own bodies not the doctor's efforts. As I said when I first examined her, some doctors are starting to cut the abdomen open, but unless your mother lived in a city where there were skilled surgeons experimenting in this treatment, she'd not have been likely to be operated on and would still have died. And even with the wonders of chloroform to block the pain of an operation, a large percentage of patients die from sepsis, an infection carried, some think, by the air.'

Ronan was silent as this information sank in.

His companion added softly, 'And at least she spent her final days enjoying your company instead of being alone. She was a lively woman, was she not? Everyone liked her.'

Ronan nodded, his throat too clogged with emotion to speak. He continued to stare blindly out across the ocean and when he glanced sideways, he was alone.

Further along the rail he saw Kathleen, also on her own. The other women were sitting in a group, chatting and doing embroidery or other handwork. After the first few days, she'd had little to do with them and he'd seen them whispering and staring at her. His mother had told him sadly when he asked, that she'd let slip that her husband was a convict and they'd immediately ostracised her.

Was Conn so determinedly shunned in Australia? How did a gregarious man like him cope with that?

Ronan pushed himself away from the rail and began a slow circuit of the deck, waving to Bram, who was in earnest conversation with an older man.

Life went on, however sad a blow it had dealt you.

5

Two days later they reached the port of Alexandria. Those days had passed in a blur for Ronan, who still couldn't accept that his mother had died in such a terrible way. Was it really only three weeks since they'd left England?

Some of the passengers were staying in the city for a few days, wanting to explore its ancient wonders, and chatted about that excitedly. He wasn't in the least interested in going sightseeing. He couldn't even settle to reading at the moment.

The small travelling bag containing his mother's jewellery and a few other trifles lay in a corner of his cabin, seeming to accuse him of being a bad son. In the end, he locked it in one of his trunks, but he couldn't bear to open it, just couldn't bear to see the things she'd loved and know she'd never touch the jewels and trinkets again.

Before they took the train, most of the passengers went to inspect the great earthworks where the French were constructing a canal to link the Mediterranean with Suez. Bram went with them and came back full of wonder about the huge numbers of men employed to dig the canal, not to mention the size of the earthworks, far larger than that needed for a railway.

Ronan couldn't rouse himself to do more than listen half-heartedly and nod occasionally.

The train was hot and vendors crowded at the carriage windows whenever they stopped. Covered in sweat, Ronan soon came to the conclusion that there was little pleasure to be had in climates this warm. He'd thought Greece in the springtime warm, but this was like living in an oven.

He began to wonder whether Australia would be as bad. He wanted to see it once, but if it was as searingly hot as this, he'd not stay for long. One of the other passengers laughed when he said this, reminding him that the seasons were in reverse and it'd be early spring there, not the hot season.

The captain and officers of the P&O Line had been mildly scornful of this canal, saying their company didn't consider it at all necessary because it had set up a perfectly adequate system for transporting passengers and mail, which included the railway Ronan had just travelled on. The canal was a folly and would probably silt up quite quickly.

After the uncomfortable train journey, Ronan decided that he disagreed with them. It'd have been far easier to stay on the ship and let it move him in comfort from one sea to the next.

At Suez they took a ship to Galle in Ceylon and during the two-week journey Ronan gradually began to recover from the worst of his grief, though the first time he laughed he felt horribly guilty all over again. But nothing he could do would bring his mother back, and she'd be the first to tell him to get on with his life, he knew.

He wasn't sure how long they'd have to stay in Galle because he'd already been warned that he might have to wait there for the mail ship to Western Australia. It seemed there wasn't nearly as much shipping traffic to such a small place, population-wise, as there was to India and the Far East. People joked about 'the ends of the earth'. He seemed to be heading there.

Each time he gathered more information from the crew or other passengers, Ronan reported his findings to Kathleen, who listened to what he had to say then inclined her head. She was still avoiding speaking directly to him if she possibly could, and she was still spending most of her time on her own, her expression stoic.

He wished he could travel ahead of her and warn Conn of her impending arrival, but he knew he couldn't leave a woman to find her own way in a strange land. Perhaps he could send Bram ahead, though he wasn't sure there would be any chance of that. From what other passengers said, travel in Western Australia was very primitive, with no railways to take passengers from one town to the next. And anyway, Bram would be as much a stranger to the place as he was, as likely to go astray.

Ronan found Galle and its people charming and wouldn't have objected to lingering there a while, but Kathleen turned up her nose at it.

'You aren't trying to find a way to get us to the Swan River Colony, Ronan Maguire. It's bad enough for me to be travelling with a man, but to linger here is absolutely wrong.'

'Do you think I can magically produce a ship?'

'There are ships in the harbour here. Why not hire one of them?'

'Because I'm not made of money, that's why. Nor are you.'

The next day Bram, who had the rare ability to talk to anyone and everyone, came back from a walk looking smug.

'I've found a ship we could take passage on, Ronan.'

'You have?'

'Yes. It's a smaller trading vessel, that's been blown off course and has sought shelter and minor repairs in Galle. It's going to the port of Fremantle, which is what we want, isn't it?

'No, it isn't. We have to go to Perth,' Kathleen said, nose in the air.

'Fremantle is the port for Perth, which is a few miles inland,' Ronan told her for the third time.

'But we were going to a port called Albany.'

'That's where the mail ships go. This ship isn't a mail ship. And anyway, Fremantle is nearer to Perth.'

'Should I ask them if they could carry us all?' Bram asked.

Ronan nodded. 'I'll come with you.' As they walked down the street he said through gritted teeth, 'The sooner we finish this journey and I get rid of *her* the better.'

'But you won't be getting rid of her, will you? You'll both be staying with Mr Conn.'

'If she stays there for long, I'll be moving on after a few days. I thought it strange that he married her. Now I've spent time with her, I can only think he went temporarily mad. Or that she's losing her mind.'

The captain of the trading vessel had two cabins and sometimes took passengers. Ronan inspected them and decided they'd do, since the journey would only take two weeks or so. He could share one cabin with Bram, and Kathleen would have to lower her standards to share with the maid. He didn't envy Orla that!

They were the only passengers. Bram watched the crew and the others in their party because there was little else to do on a trading vessel where no activities were provided for passengers. It didn't have the smooth service offered on the larger passenger ships, either, and the food was plain and often downright unappetising.

He didn't mind that. It filled his belly, which was what mattered.

As the days passed, Bram spent a lot of time with the captain, with whom he was soon on first-name terms. He was fascinated by the way Dougal made his living, and quite a good living too.

They discussed the merits of various trading goods and he began to wonder if fate wasn't showing him an opportunity.

'Do you – carry goods for other people?' he asked Dougal one day.

'I carry anything that will pay.'

'Small consignments, even?'

Dougal grinned. 'Thinking of going into trade?'

'Wondering.' For the first time he said it aloud. 'I want to do more than work as a groom for someone else.'

The discussions continued, each day teaching him something new. He was especially interested in finding out which items had sold well in the past in the Swan River Colony. Dougal was still paying off his ship, the first he'd ever owned, old but sound. He was expecting to pick up a cargo of sandalwood in Western Australia, as that fragrant wood sold well in the Orient and grew wild in the colony.

Towards the end of the voyage Dougal said casually, 'If you *are* thinking of setting up for yourself and you did happen to open a shop, I could sell my own stuff there and perhaps you'd take less commission than others do.'

'Perhaps I would.'

★　★　★

Kathleen coped with sharing a cabin by excluding her maid from it in the daytime. When she wasn't attending her mistress, poor Orla sat on deck under an awning for hours on end, staring at the horizon. Kathleen sat under another awning, ignoring her.

'She's not an easy mistress,' Ronan said one day as the two of them leaned on the rail.

By now, Orla was comfortable enough with him to speak the truth. 'She's a terrible woman. You don't know the half of it. If I can find another mistress, I'll be leaving her.' She clapped one hand to her mouth. 'You won't tell her I said that, will you, Mr Maguire?'

'Not me. I heard nothing. Anyway, I don't blame you. Why did you come here, then?'

'I wasn't given a choice. My family are tenants of the Largans. Mrs Kathleen said they'd be thrown out if I didn't.'

'What did Kieran Largan say?'

She looked at him in puzzlement. 'I never spoke to him.'

'I doubt he'd have supported that threat.'

Tears filled her eyes. 'You mean . . . I didn't need to leave my family?' The tears overflowed and she bent her head, trying to hide her weeping.

How dreadful! he thought. Kathleen takes no heed of other people's needs. She's like one of those automatons, doing what she's been taught, not going beyond that. He'd noticed before that she was at a loss in new situations and grew flustered and upset when she didn't know what to do.

As the pilot guided the ship from Rottnest Island towards Fremantle, Ronan said quietly, 'Not even three months, and yet this voyage seems to have been going on for ever.'

No one answered him. All four of them stared at the flat shore-line in dismay. It looked untamed and not at all attractive, low-lying with scrubby vegetation.

'Is this really the main port of the colony?' Ronan asked.

Dougal, who was leaving the pilot to his work, grinned. 'Not much to look at, is it? Albany is about the same size. That's where the mail ships call. It's a coaling station, mainly, even less trade going on from there.'

Bram nodded. 'Someone told me on board the other ship that there are only about thirty thousand people in the whole of Western Australia – and yet it's far bigger than England. He said there'd be even fewer if they hadn't brought in the convicts and they've been a godsend to the colony, making roads and bridges. Their crimes have certainly benefited the locals, eh?'

Kathleen breathed deeply and moved away from him, as if even to hear talk of convicts annoyed her.

'I heard that too,' Ronan said. 'A few people on the first steamer were returning to the Swan River Colony and I made it my business to talk to them.'

The ship came to a halt and with much yelling the anchor was dropped. The pilot returned to shore and a boat came for the passengers, who were invited to climb down into it by a rope mesh which formed a sort of ladder.

Orla clutched Bram's arm. 'I can't do it. I just can't climb down there. It makes me dizzy even to look at it.'

'You can do it, lass. Just remember how you used to climb trees when you were a child.'

'I never did any tree climbing. I was too busy looking after my little sisters and brothers.'

With a scornful sniff, Kathleen moved forward to let the sailors help her over the side. 'If you don't follow me, Orla, you can stay here and rot,' she said by way of encouragement.

Bram took the maid's arm. 'Come on, lass. Let's get it over with.'

She muttered a quick prayer, crossing herself.

Ronan stepped forward. 'I'll go down first and help you into the boat, Orla.'

'Thank you, sir.' With an audible gulp, she let the men guide her down the rope netting hanging over the side of the ship, desperately trying to keep her skirts from flying up in the light breeze.

Ronan steadied her and with a groan of relief she sank down

next to her mistress on one of the planks that served as seating in the boat.

Kathleen didn't even look at her, but sat stiffly upright studying Fremantle, which looked more like a village than a town, with buildings scattered here and there up a slope, not always set out in streets, but looking as if they'd been dropped higgledy-piggledy.

After being rowed to shore, they waited on the dock for their luggage, then Dougal came over to join them.

Knowing what he wanted, Ronan turned to his companions. 'Will you check that all your pieces of luggage are there?'

When they'd counted and nodded, he paid the final amount agreed on for safe delivery of themselves and their possessions to Fremantle, shook the captain's hand and turned to seek conveyance to a hotel, since it was now late afternoon.

Kathleen watched him discussing their needs with a lad who'd approached with a handcart. He nodded and smiled at the lad, who left the two men loading luggage on to the handcart and ran off to find more help. Ronan Maguire would smile at anyone, she thought sourly.

She was trying not to let her shock show, because she'd found out when she was smaller that it was dangerous to let your feelings show to people of your own class. Servants didn't matter and convicts certainly didn't matter. But sometimes her feelings escaped her, try as she would to hold them back, especially when she was angry.

If she'd known what it was like here, how small and uncivilised a place it was, she'd not have come, whatever she had to put up with back in Ireland as the wife of a convict. But she was here now, and without Mrs Maguire, so had to rely on Ronan, of all people, to help her. She hated him because he'd helped her husband when he'd been transported. If he hadn't, maybe Conn would have died and good riddance to him.

Well, just let her husband try to lay one finger on her! She'd keep her distance from him. Surely Mrs Largan must be tired now of living in such an uncivilised place? Surely she was missing Ireland? And surely if Kathleen was living with her, people would speak to her and invite her to their houses again, as they had when she was living with Mr Largan?

As she followed the procession of four handcarts up a sandy street, Kathleen passed buildings of all types, from cottages of unpainted wooden boards, to small brick houses. None of them was suitable for a lady to live in. And none of them could hold a candle to Shilmara.

Tears came into her eyes at the thought of her old home. She was no longer welcome there since James Largan's death, but she still dreamed about it. She'd loved the house on first sight, had been so happy to be away from her mother. She hadn't thought she'd have to leave it – or James, who had been so kind to her, so loving. No one had ever loved her as he did. She'd not been frightened of him, as she had of Conn.

She'd had to leave her horses too, though Kieran had promised to look after them and see they were properly exercised. She couldn't wait to get back and go riding again.

All it needed now, she thought angrily, was to find that Mrs Largan was also dead and this long, horrible journey in vain. If that was so, she didn't know what she'd do with herself. She wasn't going to live permanently with Conn, never that.

But where could she go back to? What could she do with her life when no one would even speak to her once they found out her husband was a convict?

She realised everyone had stopped moving, so paused to look at the building to which the lads had brought them. It was another colonial hovel, a rambling, two-storey structure made of wood, with a sagging veranda on each level.

'Is there nothing better than this?' she asked Ronan.

'Apparently not. It'll do for one night, surely?'

When they were shown to their rooms, she pointed out to the owner that the floor needed sweeping. He rolled his eyes but sent up a skinny maid with a broom, who proceeded to whisk it round, making little difference to the corners or the dust and light sprinkling of sand under the beds. Once again, she'd have to share the room with her maid.

'I'll unpack your nightclothes and a towel, shall I, Mrs Kathleen?' Orla asked quietly. 'They said they'd send up some hot water when we needed it.'

'Yes. All right.' Feeling exhausted and miserable, Kathleen sat down on the narrow bed for a moment, closing her eyes to shut everything out.

Conn had better agree to let his mother come back to England with her, or she'd be driven to desperation, and she never knew what she'd do when her temper took over. She'd been trained in self-control by a very strict governess and a strap wielded with all her mother's strength, but even so she sometimes couldn't help letting go of her temper and lashing out at the world.

She couldn't cry herself to sleep with a maid in the same room, wouldn't demean herself. But she ached to weep.

How long would this nightmare continue? she wondered. How long could she cope on her own? She'd never had to do that before. There had always been someone to tell her what to do.

There was only Conn left now to turn to. Oh, how she wished she'd never come!

In the morning Ronan and Bram went out to make enquiries about getting transport to where Conn lived. They found it was over a day's journey south of Perth so ended up hiring two men and two carts, which would take them first to the south bank of the River Swan, where they'd stay overnight at an inn the men knew, then on to Conn's homestead, as the men called it, a journey of three days in all, probably, 'barring accidents'.

'What sort of accidents?' Ronan asked.

'Could lose a wheel or break an axle but we don't do that as often nowadays because the roads have been improved. They aren't bad that way, what with the mail going down from Perth to Albany in the south. It's a made road, you see, that one, which means the convicts worked on clearing it properly, so it doesn't have to wind its way round obstacles like big trees.' He grinned. 'But it's still just a dirt track, when all's said and done.'

'Where shall we stay the second night?'

'We'll see if we can find a farm or else we'll have to sleep in the wagons.'

Ronan almost laughed to see the indignation on Kathleen's face, but managed to hold back his amusement, because he didn't want to upset her. She was difficult enough without that.

A moment or two later she pulled him aside. 'Can you make no better arrangements than these for my travel?'

He noticed she only said 'my'. It was as if she lived in a world of her own and couldn't see other people's needs or feelings. 'No, I can't make better arrangements. I did ask around in Fremantle and these men were highly recommended for their reliability.'

'They're impudent wretches!'

'The lower classes are different here, Kathleen. Haven't you noticed that? Freer, more independent.'

'They don't know their place and should be soundly whipped. As for the Swan River Colony, it's not what *I* would call civilised at all.'

'They'd not send convicts somewhere civilised, now would they?'

Her face tightened and she turned away.

A short time later he saw her slap Orla, taking out her temper on the poor maid. He didn't feel he could intervene, but the sight of the lass's reddened cheek made him feel angry and he could see that Bram felt the same way. He felt desperately sorry for poor Conn, who'd said in one of his letters that getting free of his wife was the biggest benefit of being transported.

What a shock her arrival was going to be for his friend!

What would Conn do with the woman? He'd found it hard enough to live with her before in a large house. From what he'd said in his letters, his Australian home was more like a farmhouse, so they'd not be able to live separate lives here.

★　　★　　★

Maia was talking to Mrs Largan on the veranda when she saw two carts turn off the track that passed their house. A woman was sitting bolt upright in the back of one, scowling at the world.

'Oh, dear God, it can't be! It is!' Mrs Largan clutched her chest. 'Go and warn Conn quickly. That's his wife. What in heaven's name is Kathleen doing here?'

Maia gaped at the cart. *Wife? Conn's wife was here?*

'Hurry!'

She ran into the house, calling for Xanthe and explaining breathlessly what Mrs Largan had said, then went rushing out to the fields to find Conn.

'Where's the master?' she asked the stable hand.

'Out riding.'

'Which direction?'

'He went to see the Grahams on the next farm. He should be coming back down the side track any time, I reckon, because he went a while ago.'

Without thinking, Maia set off running to find him.

To her relief she met Conn after a couple of hundred yards and stopped to try to regain her breath, as he reined in and slid down from the horse.

'What's the matter? My mother's all right, isn't she?'

'Yes. But she sent me – to warn you. Two wagons arrived – your wife is in one.'

'*My wife?* Are you sure?'

'I'm sure that's what your mother said. I've never met your wife. The woman in the cart looked . . . very angry.'

'That's the right word for Kathleen. She was always angry with the world. Nothing was ever right for her except her horses.'

He stood for a moment or two like one carved from stone, looking suddenly years older, then let out his breath slowly. 'Come on. I'll give you a ride back to the house behind me.' Without waiting for her answer, he remounted and leaned down. 'Put your foot on my stirrup. There.' He pulled Maia up and she managed to get one leg across the horse, heedless that she was showing her lower legs.

Conn clicked his tongue and the horse set off as soon as she was securely seated. 'I can't believe the woman would follow me out here. It's not as if she cares for me – never did.'

Maia put her arms round his waist, resting her head against his back and wishing the ride could last longer, but all too soon they arrived at the stables.

'Get down quickly.'

She slid off the horse, stumbling as her feet touched the ground.

'Sean! You're needed.' He was dismounting even as he called for his head groom, and when no one came running, he thrust the reins into her hands. 'Here. Hold him till Sean can take him off you.'

So she was left standing in the stable yard with the sun shining down as if it was mocking her and the horse moving restlessly to and fro. She kept wondering what was going on inside the house, worrying about Mrs Largan – and him.

He had never seemed so far out of her reach.

6

Xanthe reached the veranda before the wagons stopped outside the house. 'Maia's gone to find Conn,' she told her mistress in a low voice.

Mrs Largan nodded, looking relieved. 'Good. At least he'll have a little warning.'

'I didn't know—'

'That he was married? Didn't your sister tell you? He told her. I insisted he did.'

'No, she didn't say a word.' It explained a lot, though.

'His wife is a dreadful woman. She'll try to take over here and she— don't let her hit you.'

Xanthe gaped at this comment. '*Hit me?* Just let her try!'

'She hits out blindly if she's upset. She has a terrible temper.'

What sort of a woman was Conn's wife that such a warning was necessary?

Her mistress's face took on an expression of grim distaste as she watched the carts, a look Xanthe didn't remember seeing on her face before. Normally Mrs Largan was the gentlest of women, with time and a smile for everyone, whatever their faults.

'Remember, *I* give you your orders here, Xanthe, not her. Don't be afraid to check with me first about anything that doesn't seem reasonable. She can cause mischief, as well as messing up domestic arrangements on a whim. We don't have enough staff here to run round after her. My husband used to find her silly behaviour amusing; I never did.'

'I'll remember that. Don't worry. I'm not afraid to stand up for myself.'

'Tell your sister too.' Mrs Largan eased herself to her feet, leaning on her walking stick as she studied the newcomers. 'The gentleman with her is Ronan Maguire, a good friend of Conn's, the other man is Bram Deagan, who used to work in the stables at Shilmara, and the maid looks like – it must be little Orla. My goodness, how she's grown! I can't think what's brought them all here, but I wish with all my heart they hadn't come. Wherever Kathleen goes there's sure to be trouble.'

It was the second time she'd said that, Xanthe thought, studying Conn's wife carefully. She was a stocky woman dressed in clothes which didn't flatter her at all and had a rather plain, masculine-looking face.

The two women on the cart sat waiting while Ronan jumped lightly down and strode towards the veranda.

Xanthe saw Conn's wife look after him indignantly, one hand stretched out to be helped down, but he made no effort to help her. The man called Bram hesitated, then turned to assist her.

As Ronan Maguire came closer, Xanthe forgot the rest of them. He wasn't handsome but he was an attractive fellow with his brown hair gleaming in the sun, which lit it to almost auburn. His face looked as if it was made for smiling, though at the moment his expression was as grim as Mrs Largan's and he seemed full of suppressed anger.

Ronan? Why did the name sound familiar? Then she realised it was the man who was to bring their money from England and her heart leaped in anticipation. If she had her money, she could start making plans for travelling.

He took Conn's mother's hand, clasping it in his for a moment. 'Mrs Largan. I'm delighted to see you again. I hope you'll forgive us for turning up without warning.' He bent his head to say more quietly, 'And sorry I am to have brought *her*. I didn't know she was on board till after the ship had sailed, or I swear I'd have had her kidnapped and locked away till it left Southampton. We both know she'll upset everyone. She always does.' He kept his hostess's hand clasped in his as he looked questioningly towards her companion.

'This is our housekeeper, Xanthe.'

He smiled at her, and Xanthe felt a tingle run through her. She'd heard of dazzling smiles before but never seen one. Heard how people could be attracted to one another on sight, but had never expected it to happen to her. As she was fumbling for words, something unusual for her, he spoke again.

'You must be Pandora's sister. There's a strong family resemblance. Doesn't Maia live here too?'

'Yes. She's my personal maid,' Mrs Largan said. When neither of them spoke, she looked at them in surprise. They didn't even seem aware of her. Instead, they were staring at one another with a look of – well, she could only call it recognition, as if they knew each other, which they didn't. Her heart sank. That could only mean one thing. Wasn't it bad enough that her son had fallen in love with Maia? Now Ronan had taken one look at Xanthe and forgotten the rest of the world. What was there about these Blake sisters that attracted men so quickly? Thank goodness they weren't immoral and didn't encourage men's attentions.

Xanthe looked at Ronan eagerly. 'You've seen Pandora?' At his nod, she asked, 'How is she? We all miss her so and—'

A harsh voice interrupted them. 'I'd not have thought a maid's gossiping took precedence over greeting a guest.'

Mrs Largan drew herself up and stared coldly as her daughter-in-law walked towards them. 'Or that a guest would take it upon herself to speak so rudely to her hostess.'

'If this is Conn's house, then it's I who will be mistress here from now on. I'm still his wife.'

'A wife who abandoned him in his hour of need.'

'Papa Largan said he was a traitor and we should all cut him out of our lives.'

Mrs Largan let out a sound that was so anguished Xanthe wanted to put an arm round her for comfort.

'I can't believe a father could treat his son so badly.'

'He said Conn deserved it.'

Xanthe watched the newcomer's hands clench into fists. What a way to start a visit, by being rude to an older woman who was not only her hostess but her mother-in-law! And what a gargoyle of a face she had! The woman could never have been pretty, even when she was younger, but now lines of discontent were scored across her forehead and down her cheeks. She must be years older than Conn, surely?

No wonder he'd found gentle Maia attractive.

But her sister could hardly stay here, because if ever trouble was brewing it was now.

Conn heard Kathleen's remarks as he was walking quietly through the house and his step faltered for a moment. He felt almost physically sick at the thought of seeing her again, but he wasn't going to let her insult his mother – or anyone else. 'You're not mistress here, Kathleen, and never will be,' he said as he stepped out on to the veranda.

She spun round to stare at her husband, her mouth pinched as if she'd just tasted something sour and spots of red flying across her cheeks. 'You've not changed, Conn Largan. You still have no sense of what's right. I'd expected them to have taught you a few manners in prison. Your father said they would.'

She waited but no one spoke. It was as if they were all frozen, not knowing what to do next.

She moved forward. 'Well, since you've not seen fit to invite me to sit down, I'll take a seat anyway. The roads in this benighted place leave a lot to be desired. And I'd not mind a cup of tea. Surely that housekeeper of yours can provide some?'

Conn took his wife's arm before she could sit down. 'I think you and I have some talking to do first. On our own.'

She tried to pull away from him, but he held on tightly because he wanted to get her away from his mother as quickly as possible. As he forced her to walk with him into the house, he remembered other times when she'd fought him and won by using her nails and feet. She had refused point-blank to let him into her bed when he visited her room on their wedding night. The only thing he'd really wanted from her had been children, so he'd tried to persuade her – not force, persuade – but she'd still gouged deep marks down his cheeks and screamed for help at the top of her voice.

After that, if he so much as entered the bedroom that had always been his before she'd begin to scream and throw things at him.

She'd quickly revealed her true nature in other ways, the utter disregard for other people's wishes or needs, the viciousness when someone offended her. Soon he'd been glad the marriage was unconsummated and had spoken to his father about getting it annulled on those grounds. But his father had refused to countenance the idea, saying the family would lose too much if they had to pay back the dowry. Conn wasn't the heir so it didn't matter if they never had children. He could always find a village girl to satisfy his needs.

But Conn couldn't face a life with Kathleen and made enquiries about arranging an annulment. That caused the greatest row ever with his father, after which he left the family home – without taking his wife. Clearly Kathleen's parents must have paid James Largan a hell of a lot of money to marry her off to his son. Money was his father's god, always had been.

Conn stopped walking as he realised suddenly it was only a few weeks after that final row that he'd been arrested and imprisoned. He'd never connected the two things before but now he had to wonder. No, it couldn't be. Surely a man wouldn't do that to his own son?

But someone had planted false evidence. He didn't think his cousin Michael was clever enough to do that. And Kathleen had continued to live at Shilmara with his father.

As he frog-marched his wife into the house, Conn realised he was much stronger than her nowadays – and mentally stronger, too. He'd been far too easy-going before.

But was he strong enough to get rid of her? He had to be. He wasn't going to live with her again or impose the misery of her presence on his mother. As well live with the devil. In fact, he'd rather live with the devil.

They met Maia coming along the hall and Kathleen stopped

to stare at her in surprise. 'Didn't we just leave you outside on the veranda, girl?'

'That was my twin, ma'am. I'm Mrs Largan's personal maid, Maia; Xanthe's the housekeeper.' Maia's voice was cool, her expression giving nothing away.

'I've never seen a matching pair of maids before. Are you convicts too?'

'No, ma'am. We're free settlers.'

'Excuse us, please, Maia. My wife and I need to talk.' Taking Kathleen's arm again, Conn forced her to move into the room he called his library, sparsely furnished as it was with books at the moment.

He let go of her wrist and shut the door. 'What the hell do you mean by coming to Australia?'

'I had nowhere else to go and you're still my husband, after all, so you have a duty to support me.'

'My father gave you a home. Why have you left it?'

'Your father's dead and your brother threw me out of the house.'

'Father's dead? How? When? Have you told Mother?'

She rubbed her wrist. 'Not yet. You didn't give me the chance.'

'That still doesn't explain why you're here. I'm sure Kieran offered you somewhere else to live, even if he didn't want you at Shilmara, and arranged an allowance too.'

Her lips curled in that scornful way he remembered so well. 'A six-room hovel in Dublin! I'm not lowering myself to that, whatever *you* may have done. You need a bigger house than this.'

'No, I don't. And never mind that. Why did you really come here, Kathleen? You must have some reason and I'm sure it wasn't me.'

'I thought to ask your mother to come back and live in Ireland with me, but I can see she won't make old bones. She'd probably die on the voyage like Ronan's mother did, then I'd be back where I started, having to live on my own. No one would come to call and—'

He stared at her aghast. 'Ronan's mother died on the voyage?'

'I just told you that. It made things very difficult for me. None of the other ladies would speak to me when they found out I was a convict's wife.' She looked round. 'This place could be made into a gentleman's house if you built a new wing and doubled its size. And you'll have to hire more servants while I'm here.'

She'd grown even more selfish over the years, he realised. No, it was more than selfish. He'd soon realised that there was something wrong with her mind which affected the way she thought. She could only see how things concerned herself, had no thought for others. 'I don't have the money to make the house bigger, besides which we don't need the space. And it's nearly impossible to find servants here, so even managing a place this size is difficult.'

'You can't possibly run a house with two maids.'

'We can and do, with a little help from a local woman who scrubs floors and helps with the washing. But I'll tell you now, Kathleen, *you* won't be staying here for long, so that won't matter.' Not an hour longer than necessary, he promised himself, even if he had to drag her away tied hand and foot. He resisted the temptation to say that, trying to retain some semblance of civility between them.

'I've nowhere else to go and once the men have taken away the carts, no means of travelling. And I don't have much money left, either. I don't know how I'll get my next quarter's allowance from here.' She rubbed her wrist where his finger marks were still visible. 'Is that an example of your new convict manners?'

'I'll pay your fare back to Ireland and give you something to manage on till my brother can provide you with a house. You'll have to go back to Shilmara – or to your parents' house – yes, that'd be best. Your parents will help you.'

'I've nothing to go back to. My parents are both dead, too. My brother has their house and he's worse than *your* brother, won't even let me visit them since you were arrested. You *ruined* my life!'

'I was innocent. How did I do anything?'

'Your father said you were guilty. He looked after me. Now you must look after me.'

Conn didn't bother to argue the point or say that being transported had affected him a lot more than it had her. 'Look, if Kieran offered you a house of your own before, I'm sure he'll still find one for you. He won't see you homeless. And surely your parents left you *some* money?'

She shrugged. 'Yes. But what use is money if I only get a little bit of it every quarter? That soon gets used up. And besides, without your father beside me, no one will even talk to me.'

'You'll make new friends if you live in Dublin. No, don't start arguing. We can discuss the practicalities of your going back later, but go back you will. There was never a question of my mother returning, as you'd have found out if you'd written. Her health is better here, but still not good, so—'

She raised her voice to a near scream. 'I won't go back on my own. I won't! And you can't make me!'

'Then I'll find you somewhere to live in Perth.'

'Without a husband – even one as bad as you – to give me some shadow of respectability? No, thank you! Besides, what would I do in a city? It'd be as bad as Dublin. You can't ride horses properly there.' She fell silent for a moment or two, frowning in thought.

He watched her, trying to work out what to do.

'If your mother can't come back with me I'll have to stay here. Ronan says you breed horses so at least I'll be able to ride. And I'll have the protection of your presence. I'm *not* living anywhere on my own.' Another pause, then she added more quietly, 'Anyway, I can't do it. I'm not good at managing a house.'

Unfortunately he agreed. Even in the short time they'd been together he'd seen how useless she was at handling money. He abandoned the argument for a moment to ask, 'How did my father die? And when? I thought only the good died young. He was barely sixty.'

'He died of a seizure. It was very sudden. His face turned red and he fell down.'

She didn't sound in the least upset about that, and yet she'd been living with his father for over two years. 'I must go and tell my mother. Stay here.'

'I've no intention of sitting here, thirsty and in need of a wash. Does that so-called housekeeper of yours do any work round the place, or is she just here to warm your bed?'

'Don't be ridiculous. I've not taken anyone to bed since I was thrown in prison, let alone one of my own servants. I'll send Xanthe to you. You have my assurance that she's the housekeeper and that's all! She'll show you to a bedroom where you can wash and she'll bring you some refreshments.'

'Xanthe? Fine name that is for a maid! No wonder these people get above themselves. You should call her by a maid's name. Susan would be better. It sounds close to Xanthe so I shall call her that.'

'I doubt she'll answer to it, since it's not her real name. A word of warning. You'll get no subservience here, Kathleen, and I don't want it. Your requests for service should be made politely and through my mother, who is and will remain the mistress of Galway House.'

'I'm your *wife*! Now that I'm here, the servants must answer to me.'

How many times did he have to say it to her? 'You've never been a wife to me. Never. Marrying you was my penance for every wrong I've ever done, and for every sin I may ever commit in the future.' He watched her, but her expression didn't change. Did she even understand how he was insulting her? He doubted it. Her comprehension was very limited.

'Send that maid to me, then.'

He went to find Xanthe. 'My wife wishes to wash and needs some refreshments. Perhaps you could show her to the spare bedroom and attend to it?'

'Of course, *sir*.' She smiled mischievously as she called him that, had clearly realised that with Kathleen around they could not relax or seem too friendly.

'And remember, Xanthe, my mother is still mistress here and . . . if my wife doesn't use your real name, don't answer her.'

'I've met that before. They called me Susan at the soup kitchen in Lancashire. I suppose because it's similar in sound.'

'They had no right to do that – and nor does she.'

'Might is right. Only money gives you freedom.'

'And sometimes, not even then.'

It seemed to him that her look was full of sympathy. She didn't yet understand quite how bad Kathleen could be, but a few days would enlighten her.

Oh, hell, what was he going to do?

Conn walked slowly back through the house to the front veranda, where he found Ronan sitting beside his mother, his arm round her shoulders as she wept. His friend must have told her the news.

Conn went to her other side and knelt beside her. 'I didn't expect you to weep for my father.'

'I'm not. I'm weeping for sheer relief that I no longer have to fear him coming here to drag me back to live with him. It'd shock a priest, but you both know what a harsh man he was and I was always afraid of him, always.' She mopped her eyes. 'I'm forgetting my duties. Could you find Maia and ask her to help her sister sort out bedrooms for our guests?'

'You'll be all right?'

'I'll stay with her,' Ronan said.

It was then that Conn remembered what Kathleen had told him. 'I'm sorry about your mother.' He saw a bleak look come into his friend's eyes.

'Yes.' Ronan looked at Mrs Largan. 'My mother died on the ship coming here. There was nothing the doctor could do to help her.'

She stared at him. 'You've just lost your mother?'

'It's over a month ago now.'

'Oh, Ronan, I'm so sorry. I know what a loving mother she was.'

He gave a wry smile. 'In her own way. I'm getting used to it now. Actually, Kathleen was quite helpful at the time. In her own way. At least she stayed with my mother. I was surprised by that.'

'She was always good with sick horses. And she's had it drummed into her what you should do in every situation.' Mrs Largan sighed. 'Beaten into her, from what she told me. She's not had an easy life.'

'*Beaten into her?*'

'Yes. Her parents were very strict and her mother whipped her regularly.'

'Poor thing. I didn't realise.'

'That still doesn't excuse the way she behaves!' Conn said. 'I'll not have you feeling sorry for her, Mother, and letting her upset the household.'

'She'll upset it anyway. Where is she now?'

'In the only spare bedroom that's furnished. She can use it while she's here, because it's at the far end of the house from you and me.' He looked at his friend. 'We'll have to move some furniture around and I'll ask your help in putting the beds together for the other rooms. We never did get round to finishing them. Well, there was no reason. Not many people are likely to want to come and visit a convict.'

His mother patted his hand as if understanding his pain. 'Shh now. We'll get through this.'

He couldn't think how.

Maia went through into the kitchen, where her sister was putting some refreshments on a tray.

'*She* has decided to eat in the dining room, not her bedroom,' Xanthe said with a grimace in that direction. 'I'm not dusting it for her. I've enough to do with all the guests.'

'Shall I go and set the table?'

'Certainly not. I'll take in a tray. But you could start getting some refreshments ready for the others. I'm hoping Orla will help us too, once her mistress is eating.' She turned towards the outer door and saw the groom who'd come with Ronan standing on the veranda. 'Come in, do. I'm Xanthe. This is my sister Maia.

We're all at sixes and sevens, but we'll find you something to eat presently.'

'I'm Bram. I'm not needed in the stables, so can I help you at all here?'

'You can. If you'll watch the kettle and fill the big teapot when it boils, it'll be a help. I've put the tealeaves in already. Thank you.' She turned back to Maia. 'Conn made a point of saying we were to refer any orders that weren't reasonable to his mother, who will remain in charge.' She bent closer to whisper, 'Be careful not to give yourself away!'

When Xanthe carried the tray into the dining room, she found Kathleen sitting at the head of the table. She set down the tray in front of her, not commenting on that. 'Please ring when you need this cleared away, ma'am.' She turned to leave.

'I'm not eating off a tray. I want this table setting properly. I can't believe Mrs Largan accepts such shoddy service.'

'I don't have time to set tables. There are other guests needing food.' Xanthe turned to leave the room.

Behind her, Kathleen yelled, 'Come back! Come back this minute!'

Xanthe carried on walking, wincing at the shrillness of the other woman's voice.

She stopped dead in shock when she heard the sound of smashing crockery.

When he heard the noise, Conn set off running. It had started.

With a quick word of excuse to his hostess, Ronan followed him, passing Xanthe, who was staring open-mouthed into the dining room. Both men stopped in the doorway.

Kathleen was sitting at the head of the dusty dining table.

'I *will not* accept such shoddy service.' She thumped the table to emphasise her words. 'How *dare* that servant speak to *me* like that? She must be dismissed instantly. Instantly, I tell you.'

Conn stared at the tray, which was lying upside down on the floor on top of a welter of food and smashed crockery, then looked back at his wife's furious face.

'You will get rid of her! Dismiss her at once,' she repeated.

He said nothing because silence was as good a weapon as any with her. Kathleen glared at him, but when he didn't move, she began to fight for control over her emotions, something he'd seen her do before. He didn't think he'd ever seen her struggle for so long, though, nor could he remember her acting quite so outrageously.

'Wait for us in the kitchen, please, Xanthe. I'll deal with this.' Conn turned back to his wife, horrified to see how much crockery she'd broken. The mess was so far from the table that she must have hurled it. This was the act of a child in a tantrum or . . . he looked at her flushed face and wild, staring eyes and couldn't help thinking *a madwoman*.

'I'll pick that mess up,' Ronan said quietly, 'and I'll stay here in case you need help.'

Conn realised then that his friend was thinking the same thing.

Halting footsteps made them both turn round.

He forced a smile. 'No need to worry, Mother. Kathleen just had an – accident.'

'I won't be served by sluts and when I reprimanded her, *she* threw the tray on the floor. I'm a lady born and bred, the wife of a man who was born a gentleman, at least, and I *will not* be treated like this. That lazy creature must go.'

Surely she didn't think he'd believe this lie? Conn was utterly certain that Xanthe had not thrown a tray of food on to the floor, not because she hadn't had time to run out of the room before he got there, but because it wasn't in her nature. Kathleen had changed for the worse in the years since he'd seen her. No wonder his brother Kieran didn't want her staying on at Shilmara. No wonder her own brother didn't want her living with him and his family. The wonder was that they'd not locked her away before now. They must be delighted that she'd come to Australia.

'Perhaps we'd better send for Orla to help you to your room.'

'Why?' Kathleen's gaze was wide. 'I don't need her help just now, Conn. What I want is some food, served properly by those whose job it is.'

Ronan began to pick up the broken crockery and food. As he passed Conn, he whispered, 'Don't send for the maid. She beats poor Orla.'

Kathleen stood up, shoving her chair back so hard it fell over. 'What are you whispering about?'

Conn's mother moved forward. 'Why don't you come and sit with me on the front veranda, Kathleen. We often eat out there.'

'You've lowered your standards.'

'It's a different country. Different standards apply here.'

'That's not what the women on the ship said. I used to listen to them talking. They didn't bother to lower their voices. They said the gentry had to *maintain* their standards here. That's what I'm doing.'

'Some try to do that and they live miserable lives because it's impossible. There aren't enough servants here.'

The younger woman blinked her eyes furiously. 'I wish I'd never come.'

'It would have been better to write first. Anyway, you're here now, so come and sit down with me, Kathleen. We'll both have a piece of cake and a cup of tea.'

His wife stood there for so long Conn was about to intervene, but gradually the wild look faded from her eyes and she moved forward.

'You're moving very stiffly,' she told her hostess, 'worse than before.'

'My joints are less painful than they used to be in Ireland, however.'

'Stay with them,' Conn whispered to Ronan. 'I don't want to leave her alone with my mother.'

Ronan gave him a pitying look and nodded.

When they'd gone, Conn went to speak to the maids, his heart heavy with fear about what his wife would do next. In the kitchen he asked for tea and cake for his mother and wife on the veranda. While he waited for Xanthe to get it ready, he studied Orla, who was looking subdued and had a red mark across one cheek. He went across to study it. 'Did my wife hit you?'

The maid shrugged. 'She does sometimes. It's not so bad, sir.'

'I'm not having it.'

She looked at him, her eyes dull and hopeless. 'How will you stop her, sir?'

Silence, then. 'Why do you stay with her?'

'The old master said he'd throw my family out if I tried to leave.'

'Did Kieran say the same thing?'

She looked puzzled. 'I don't know. It's not for me to ask the new master about such things. He did say he was pleased she had me.'

It wouldn't occur to Kieran to worry about whether Orla was happy. He usually left the servants to his wife. Conn turned to the two maids. 'I'm sorry my wife is behaving – strangely. I think you two had better not be alone with her from now on. She's very strong and can be quite violent. Orla, you must call for help if she hurts you again. Whoever's nearest will come to make sure you're all right.'

'Better not, sir. She'll get even angrier. It's just a slap or two.'

Before he could argue with her, Xanthe pushed a tray forward. 'Here you are.'

'I'll take it.' Maia picked up the heavy wooden tray.

Conn followed her along the passageway, waiting out of sight while she took it to his mother. Kathleen was sitting staring out across the gardens, looking spent and weary now, as she often did after a tantrum.

He watched his mother pour some tea and keep up a gentle flow of conversation.

Kathleen responded briefly to her questions, ate two pieces of cake, then said, 'I'm tired. I think I'll go and lie down for a while.'

'Do you remember the way to your bedroom?'

'Yes.'

Conn slipped into a nearby room and waited till his wife had walked past, then went to sit with his mother. 'She behaved better for you.'

'She always did. Her mother used to whip her, you know, to teach her self-control. I speak to her gently.'

'She didn't show much self-control today, did she? I've never seen her behaving so badly.'

'That poor girl should have led a quiet life in the country with the horses she loves. Instead her parents filled her head with foolish ideas that people should wait on her hand and foot.'

He looked over his shoulder and whispered, 'Is she insane, do you think?'

'I don't know. Her aunt was very similar, you know. Strange as a girl, getting worse as she got older. They'd have had to lock her up but she drowned herself when she was twenty-two.'

'I never heard that.'

'Her family threatened trouble to anyone who spoke of it. Poorer people were too afraid for their livelihoods to do so. Most people of our class were too considerate to gossip about it.'

'And yet my father insisted I marry Kathleen.'

'For the money. I argued with him, but he threatened to disinherit you and throw us both out if I didn't keep quiet.'

'He threatened the same to me. He said he'd make you pay.' He'd never told her that before, not in so many words.

'I argued with him but he wouldn't change his mind. You weren't the heir so it didn't matter to him what your children were like. I'm sorry, Conn darling. I wasn't very good at standing up to him. He always found a way to hurt you if you defied him.'

'And yet you risked running away from him?'

'Oh, I planned it all very carefully, believe me. I'd not have left if I hadn't been utterly certain I could escape. I can never thank Sean enough for the help he gave me.' She got to her feet with painful slowness. 'I think I'll go and lie down too. I'm a bit tired today. We don't need to talk about this again, do we? It's over and done with.'

She was looking so pale and moving so slowly, he knew she was having one of her bad days, though she never complained. Even when she arrived in Australia unexpectedly, she'd not said much about his father. It was her idea of loyalty.

He rubbed his forehead, which was aching. He couldn't seem to think straight. The only thing he was certain of was that he wasn't going to let Kathleen stay here and make his mother's life a misery.

7

Xanthe went to check the unused bedrooms in the east wing. Only the one now occupied by Mrs Kathleen had been fitted out properly, though not lavishly. The others didn't even have the beds set up. She decided Orla should have the room next to her mistress, and she'd have to ask if Bram was to stay in the house or the stables. The trouble was that Sean had the only proper room out there and the other lads who helped came in daily and took it in turns to sleep in a corner of the hay store in case they were needed at night.

She could only hope they had enough bedding for everyone. Conn has been more interested in building accommodation for his horses than in improving the house, and since they never had guests and Mrs Largan wasn't able to do much, no one had bothered with the rest of the inside rooms.

She walked across to the French window of the first spare room and opened it to let some fresh air in. The bed frame was still in its various parts, leaning against the wall, and there was a proper mattress nearby. Thank goodness! At least their gentleman visitor could sleep in comfort.

She went into the other two rooms and they were in even worse condition, with bed frames but no mattresses. She'd have to get some ticking filled with hay, a poor substitute, but the best she could manage at short notice. She'd better start a list for next time someone went to Perth.

She tried to move one of the bed frames and found it heavy. No, she definitely couldn't manage this on her own. She'd have to get Conn and Ronan to do it. He must know where the tools were to fit the bed frame together.

Ronan looked up as Xanthe came out on to the front veranda again, thinking what a striking young woman she was. She seemed to have more spirit than her equally lovely twin and though she'd said nothing, her eyes had flashed with anger at Kathleen's rudeness. 'I've got a letter for you and your sister from Pandora and Zachary, as well as the things she sent you.'

'You mean the mo—' She stopped as he shook his head, putting one finger to his lips. Clearly he wanted to keep the money a secret. She'd guess it was something to do with Mrs Kathleen. 'We'll have to talk about that later, Mr Maguire, I'm afraid. At the moment I'm trying to get the rest of the bedrooms ready and I need some help. I gave Mrs Kathleen the only one that had the bed properly set up.'

Conn's voice came from behind her. 'Is she quieter now?'

'I've heard nothing since she went to her room. Could you help me move the heavy furniture around in the other bedrooms, Conn – sir, I mean. And the bed frames need setting up. We never did get round to sorting out this wing of the house.'

'I'll help too.'

Ronan smiled at her and she felt a hum of energy go through her. He had a lovely smile that made his eyes crinkle at the corners.

'Thank you.' She walked briskly back to the first bedroom, with Ronan beside her. When she glanced back, she saw that Conn had stopped to speak to Maia. She clicked her tongue in exasperation. Her sister gave her feelings away every time she looked at him. She saw Ronan watching them as well and said hastily, to distract him, 'This is the guest wing, Mr Maguire – though we've never had any guests. The family sleep in the other wing, and so do Maia and I.'

'I'll be the one to keep a watch on the dragon, then, in case she wanders at night.'

'Will she do that, do you think?'

'She sleep walks occasionally, did it a couple of times on the ship. She panicked when someone woke her and hit out at them.'

'I see.' Xanthe glanced at him and immediately looked away again, wondering why he was staring at her so strangely.

'Don't put up with any ill-treatment from Kathleen. She slaps her poor maid regularly.'

'If she slaps me or my sister, I'll slap her right back.' She hesitated, then added, 'I know it's not my place to comment, but as my sister and I have to deal with her . . . Well, I hope you'll forgive me for saying that she seems rather . . . strange.'

'She is and always has been. Very strange. She made Conn's life hell, even though they didn't live together for long, but she's been a lot worse since she's had to leave Shilmara. I think, in her own way, she loved it. And for some reason no one can figure out, she got on very well with old Mr Largan. I think he found her amusing. He was like that – malicious.'

'I see.' She stopped at the door of the first bedroom. 'You'll want to be at this end of the corridor, I think.'

'I'll fit in wherever it suits. I've slept in far worse conditions when I was travelling.'

'Have you done much travelling?'

'I've been to France, Italy and Greece.'

'I'd love to hear about it when you have time. I'm going to travel now that I can afford it.' She saw his surprise. 'Why do you look at me like that?'

'Women don't usually want to go travelling.'

'Well, I do. I'd go mad staying at home and doing housework.'

'That's what you do here.'

She shrugged. 'I have to earn a living, but I don't *enjoy* it.'

'You're an unusual woman.'

She smiled. 'So they tell me. Blame our father. He was an unusual man and brought us up to think for ourselves. That's probably why we've been slow to marry.'

'What sort of a husband do you want?'

'None. I don't intend to marry or have children.' She decided she'd said enough about herself and was glad when Conn came into the room just then. Ronan Maguire's bright blue eyes seemed to see too deeply into her soul, made her feel uncomfortably exposed.

She didn't normally talk about herself to anyone except Maia. Why had she confided in this stranger, told him about her dreams? Why had he asked? He was a gentleman and she was only a servant.

Ronan watched Xanthe walk across to some pieces of bed frame and bend to pick up the little sacking bag of nuts and bolts needed to hold the heavy pieces of wood together. He couldn't take his eyes off her, she was so unlike any other servant he'd ever met. She wasn't at all subservient, though she was polite and helpful. She was beautiful but didn't seem conscious of her looks in the way other beautiful women he'd met had been. And though she'd been born to the lower classes, she had enough money to be independent – though he suspected she'd have been of an independent turn of mind even without the money.

How did you treat a woman like that? Especially when attraction and desire had flared up within him the minute he'd set eyes on her.

Conn joined them just then and under Xanthe's direction the two men moved furniture and bolted together the bed frames for Ronan, Bram and Orla, sharing out the bits and pieces of furniture that were left from Ronan's room between the two servants and putting a couple of broken pieces into a smaller room whose window was boarded up.

'I'll get them mended one day,' Conn said. He waved one hand towards the window. 'Glass isn't easy to come by here in the country. I don't know how that got broken. I've ordered some from Perth but it's not arrived yet. It'll take even longer, I think, to order replacements for the crockery Kathleen broke today.'

Ronan smiled. 'It must be difficult pioneering.'

'This isn't pioneering. Another man cleared the forest and built the house, and I'm grateful to him. He was the true pioneer. I'm just finishing off what he started.'

'Did he die?'

'No, his wife did and after that he moved back to Ireland. I bought the place from him at a very reasonable price. There are about a hundred acres, more than I need to raise my horses, and there's a good well that never runs dry. Half of the land is still virgin forest and it can stay that way.'

'Your animals look to be in good condition.'

'I was fortunate enough to have a bumper hay harvest this year, and I've gradually been buying sturdy animals. We don't breed for looks here, but for work capacity.' He turned to Xanthe who had come up to join them.

'I can't make up the other two beds till we've made straw mattresses for them,' she said.

'I'll get Sean to do that and perhaps Bram will help him. You and Maia have enough to do. Is the girl able to come and help you?'

'Sean's sent one of the stable lads to ask.'

'Thank you for sorting everything out with your usual efficiency.'

She smiled. 'It's not hard to count how many people need bedrooms, is it? Now, if you'll let me know when the ticking is stuffed with hay, Maia and I will make up the other beds.'

Before she could turn to go, a voice interrupted from the doorway. 'Does your maid always order you around?'

Conn turned to see his wife standing in the doorway, looking neater physically, but clearly still spoiling for a fight. 'I pay Xanthe to organise the household and she does it well.'

'That's a matter of opinion.'

As she glared at her husband, Ronan noticed there were tears in her eyes. He didn't blame Conn for speaking to her so curtly. She was impossible to live with and had tried Ronan's patience to the limits on their journey down here from Fremantle. He'd never been able to understand why she seemed to go out of her way to antagonise people.

Conn must have noticed the incipient tears too because he

moved forward and said more gently, 'Perhaps you'd like to see the stables and my horses, Kathleen? You'll be wanting to stretch your legs if you've been sitting in that cart for three days.'

Her face brightened. 'Yes. I would like that. How many horses do you have?'

To Ronan's relief, the two of them left. He stared after them, pity in his heart for his friend.

'Excuse me, sir, but could I get past? I need to clear up Mrs Largan's bedroom now.' With a nod, Maia walked away and he was left with only Xanthe, who was still staring after her master and his wife, brow furrowed.

He watched her, admiring the blue-black sheen of her hair and her trim figure.

Maia came back to join them. 'Mrs Largan is having a lie down. Poor lady, she doesn't deserve this.' She didn't need to explain what she meant.

Even her voice was gentler than her twin's, he mused. 'You two are very different.' Then he realised this might sound rude. 'Sorry. I feel I know you after spending a couple of days with your sister Pandora. I'll hand over the money this evening if there's somewhere we can be private. I need to explain a few things to you.'

'We'll go out on the back veranda,' Xanthe said. 'The family sit at the front and we servants at the back.' Her eyes were dancing with amusement at this, as if she found it ridiculous.

'I'll get Conn to keep an eye on *her* while we have our chat.' He grimaced. 'I don't trust the woman an inch and haven't told her about any of your business.' His grimace turned to a smile. 'Though I'd love to see her face when she finds out you and your sister have inherited money and are quite independent.'

'I don't think anyone can be totally independent,' Xanthe said thoughtfully. 'I mean, we can't grow all our own food, or make all the fabric needed for clothes and household furnishings. There are all sorts of things which rely on other people's efforts.'

'No man is an island, eh?'

'No. He has a telling turn of phrase, but I don't like Donne's poetry as much as others'. It doesn't have the beauty of Keats. But he does sometimes make me think about life, and he's right about no man being an island, no woman either.'

He looked at her in surprise at a maid discussing Donne's poetry and offering philosophical views about life. Yet for all her free manners, he was quite sure Xanthe and her sister were decent young women. He could always tell.

'Well, we'd better get back to work,' Xanthe said. 'I haven't time for poetry at the moment.'

'Yes, of course. Um – I need to use the necessary, if you'll tell me where it is.'

Without the slightest sign of embarrassment Xanthe pointed out a shack with two doors across the stable yard. 'Right hand side is for men.'

When the twins were on their own, Maia said quietly, 'Isn't Mrs Kathleen dreadful? Poor Conn.'

'Poor Conn indeed,' Xanthe agreed.

And poor Maia too, she thought with a sigh. Why did her sister have to fall in love with a married man?

Conn and Kathleen walked out to the stables in silence. 'I've set up as a horse breeder, as you know.'

'A poor occupation for a lawyer. Can you not practise the law here now that you've been released?'

'I don't want to. The law that brought me here – an innocent man – is not worth serving. I want no hand in putting other innocent men behind bars.'

'Are you still claiming to be innocent?' She sounded surprised.

'I *am* innocent.'

'But they had proof of your guilt. Michael and your father both explained it to me.'

'I'm quite sure Michael was the one who set a trap for me, and that Father knew about it.'

She stopped walking to stare at him, open-mouthed. 'I don't believe you. That's a terrible thing to say of your father without a scrap of proof. He was very upset about what you'd done.'

'Was he? He must be a better actor than I realised. All the so-called proof was faked by someone. Who else could it have been? Michael and my father told lies in court, on oath. I thought it was because they believed it, but now that I've had a lot of time to think about it . . . well, I'm sure they did it on purpose.'

He was glad he hadn't suspected back then that it was his own family or it might have sent him mad with the pain of such a betrayal from those who should be closest to him. Now, he'd learned to endure so much that such knowledge seemed like only one more problem to add to his basket of troubles. Basket? Cart load, more like, now.

They started walking again.

'Why did you never come and visit me in prison?' he asked. 'I could have explained my side to you.'

'Your father said I shouldn't go to such a dreadful, dirty place. He promised he'd look after me when you couldn't. And he did, right until he died. He was *kind* to me, let me ride all his horses, took me to visit his friends. I was happy at Shilmara.'

Her tone rang with pain and Conn was surprised to find that he felt sorry for her. He changed the subject, though. He didn't want to hear any praise of his father. He stopped at the paddock where two or three yearlings were kept, horses he was proud of breeding.

'We need strong horses here. That's more important than whether they're beautiful or not. Look at those! Great animals, they are.'

She stood by the rails, studying them. 'They look well fed and exercised. Good glossy coats. But I prefer beautiful horses.'

'The roads are rough here and many of the riders use a horse to death.'

'I'd have the riders whipped for that. I like the looks of the chestnut stallion over there.'

'Yes, he's fathered two good foals already. I'm trying to find another mare or two for him.' He waited for her to look her fill, then asked gently, 'Why did you come here, Kathleen? Tell me the truth, now.'

'I told you: to ask your mother to come back and live with me.'

'I can't understand why you thought that would help.'

She looked at him in surprise. 'I was received socially when I lived with your father, but once he died, except for Ronan's mother, people didn't even speak to me after church – so I thought if your mother came to live with me, I'd have some chance of a decent life again.'

'My mother isn't fit to travel back to Ireland. You must have seen how hard she finds it to move now. Maia has to do nearly everything for her.'

There was a long silence and he didn't interrupt it.

'Yes, I can see that,' she said at last. 'So I'll have to stay here too. But I'm still not sharing your bed.'

Why did she hate the idea of him touching her so much? He wasn't vain, but he knew women found him attractive. 'Don't worry. You'll not be invited into my bed.'

'No. You've got your eyes on your mother's maid, haven't you? She's a slut, so she should satisfy your needs.'

'How did you—?' He broke off, realising he'd betrayed himself. 'I've not touched Maia in that way, and I won't. She's a decent young woman.'

She looked at him thoughtfully. 'I believe you. You always were too soft with servants. But you want to bed her, don't you? And you will one day. You men are all dirty-minded like that. No better than stallions when a mare's in heat. Your father explained it to me. *He* was different.'

'If you feel that way about men, I think you should go into a nunnery. You'll be quite safe from men there.'

'You'd like that, wouldn't you? Locking me away. That's what my brother wanted to do. I'd go mad locked up behind stone walls.'

She reached out to stroke the nose of a young mare and the animal let her, though normally it shied away from strangers.

'You can't stay here, Kathleen,' he said, but without the heat of his earlier remarks. 'We'd make each other unhappy.'

'I don't have anywhere else to go. And I'm unhappy already.'

'You can stay till I find you somewhere else to live, but

remember, this is my mother's house, not yours. She gives the orders here and I'll not have you ill-treating my servants.'

Anger flashed in her eyes but she didn't say anything, just pressed her lips together.

'We'd better rejoin the others.'

'I'll stay with the horses till it's dinner time.'

'I'll send someone to fetch you when the food is ready.' He looked up as someone moved out of the stables.

She followed his gaze. 'That's Sean. I remember him from Shilmara. He helped your mother escape. Your father was very angry. You shouldn't keep such a villain working for you.'

'I was glad to have him, glad he'd helped my mother. He's very good with horses.'

'That's all you care about, your mother and your horses.' She turned away and began to walk along the edge of the field towards the next enclosure where some yearlings were grazing.

He hesitated for a moment or two, not liking to give her free rein to wander around, but unable to think what else to do with her. At least out here she wasn't being rude to his mother and servants, and he trusted her with animals.

He turned to Sean. 'Don't let her order you around.'

Sean shrugged. 'She'll try. But she'll not hurt the horses, that's the main thing, and being here gets her out of your mother's way.'

Conn smiled briefly as he walked back to the house. Sean always knew what was going on, even though he spent most of his time in the stables.

After hesitating for a moment, he went to find Ronan. How terrible that his mother had died on the journey here. No wonder Ronan looked so sad at times.

8

An hour's drive away from Galway House, the eldest of the four Blake sisters, Cassandra, sat beside the bed of her old friend, Kevin Lynch.

She wiped his brow and smoothed back his sparse white locks. 'Can I get you a drink?'

'No, lass. I'm beyond . . . thirst . . . now.' He paused a moment to catch his breath. 'I'll not be . . . troubling you . . . much longer.'

She didn't try to deny that. He'd lived longer than anyone had expected him to and they'd all been happy together. 'We shall miss you, Kevin. You've taught us so much about farming in Australia. I don't know how we'd have coped without you.'

He smiled. 'You've been like . . . the children I never had.'

Reece came into the room as Kevin said this and went to sit on the other side of the bed. He raised one eyebrow at his wife and she gave a little shake of her head. He took Kevin's wasted hand gently in his.

'Need to tell you.' The old man fought for breath. 'I've left everything . . . to you, lad.'

'I thought this farm would go to your nephew,' Reece said.

'He never wrote back. Doesn't deserve it.'

'That's very kind of you,' Cassandra said.

A small child began crying in the next room and Kevin smiled at her. 'Go and tend to . . . little Sofia.'

When she'd gone Kevin said, 'Conn has the will. Drawn up properly . . . and witnessed.'

Reece bowed his head, thinking that fate was being very kind to him and his wife. They'd come to Australia with almost nothing and now they'd have a farm of their own, small but promising.

When he looked up again, Kevin was asleep, breathing shallowly and slowly.

He sat on for a few minutes, still holding the old man's hand, thinking what a difference it'd make to him and his family to own this farm, then something about the silence made him look more carefully at the figure on the bed. Kevin had simply stopped breathing. His expression was tranquil. It had been an easy passing.

Reece closed the staring eyes, murmuring, 'Thank you. And not just for leaving us the land, but for everything you've given us.' Then he raised his voice. 'Cassandra?'

She came to the door, the child in her arms.

'He's gone. So peacefully I didn't notice it at first.'

'I'm glad it was easy for him. Eh, but I'll miss him.' She went to pat Kevin's cheek with her free hand, then became practical and set her little daughter down while she covered his face with the sheet. 'We'll bury him tomorrow, shall we?'

He nodded.

'You'd better go and tell the Southerhams. They may want to attend, out of respect for a good neighbour, even if he was once a convict.'

Reece grimaced. 'I don't enjoy going there. The farm is in a worse mess every time I visit them. Leo does his best, poor lad, but except where animals are concerned, he doesn't think to do something unless they tell him – and half the time Livia has her head in a book or Francis is sitting with his beloved horses, so they don't guide him as they should. It's a good thing they're not relying on the farm to bring in money, because it never will as long as they're in charge. That's gentry for you!'

'Not all gentry are as impractical as them. Conn's doing very well for himself.' She looked round in a kind of wonderment. 'It's kind of Kevin to leave everything to us, isn't it? Imagine owning our own home! That'll make a big difference, won't it?'

He gave her a quick hug, as he often did. 'We'd have bought a place once your money came through from England, but this way I'm bringing something substantial to our marriage as well and that makes me feel good. I did wonder if Kevin might leave us something, from remarks he's made lately. He never said it outright, though.' Then he shook his head. 'It seems wrong to be rejoicing when he's just died.'

'Life goes on and he'd want us to be happy. We didn't care for him for gain, after all.'

'I suppose you're right.'

'Go on! Let the Southerhams know. We won't be able to get a priest here to bury him, but we can certainly hold our own cere-mony and say the prayers. He's already picked out the spot where he wants to lie. It's beautiful there at the top of our little hill.'

Reece gave her another hug and dropped a light kiss on Sofia's nose as the child came to cling to her mother's skirts. 'I'll do that and afterwards I'll ride over to Conn's and see if they want to come to the burial. I'll ask him what we need to do about the will while I'm at it. There's plenty of time to get there and back before dark and I don't think it'll rain for a while yet. I'll dig the grave first thing in the morning.'

'I'll lay him out.'

'Do you want me to help you with that?'

'No. I did it for my father and I'm happy to perform this last service for Kevin.'

'You're a wonderful woman and I'm lucky to marry you.' He patted her stomach, which was just starting to swell. 'If this one is a daughter, I hope she's just like you.'

She chuckled. 'She couldn't be much more like me than Sofia is.'

His face softened into a smile. 'Eh, she's a little minx, that one.' They both turned to smile at the child, who had dragged out a box of wooden blocks Kevin had made for her and was building a tower.

A short time later Cassandra saw Reece go striding off along the path through the bush that linked the two properties. She had so much to be thankful for, but most of all the fact that although Sofia wasn't his child, her husband loved her as if she was. He always said she'd been sent to replace the child he'd lost when his first wife died in childbirth.

Cassandra turned to attend to Kevin, the last thing she could do for him. Keeping one eye on her daughter she brought water to wash the body and dressed him in clean clothes for his final journey.

Reece saw Leo digging in the Southerhams' vegetable garden and waved to him. The two of them were lucky to have him, but he was lucky to have found a home with them, as well. His step-father had sent him to Australia to get rid of him because he was slow-witted. He had a gift for looking after animals, though, which gave him the means to earn a living anywhere. He kept the stables in perfect order for the Southerhams without needing telling what to do, but wasn't nearly as much use at the other farm jobs.

Reece shook his head at the sight of the ramshackle collection of sheds that he'd helped Francis build when he was working for him. Francis had begrudged the money to buy milled timber, so they'd used fallen trees and whatever they could find, just as Reece would be doing now that he had his own farm. The outbuildings might not look pretty, but they were waterproof and spacious enough for several horses, which was the main thing Francis cared about.

As he'd expected, Reece found his former employer sitting near his favourite horse on a sawn-off piece of tree trunk which he often used as a stool. He was shocked at how much Francis had gone downhill, even in the few days since they'd last met, and sighed at the thought of another death. They had no other near neighbours in this lonely place.

Livia had been nursing her husband devotedly for the past two years, but nature had decreed this was the way Francis Southerham should die. Even coming to a warm climate hadn't helped him, though it had probably prolonged his life. Livia had once said she'd leave Westview Farm and start a school in Perth once her husband died. He couldn't imagine her doing that, though. She wasn't practical enough.

He hesitated, but it had to be said. 'I came to tell you Kevin's just died.'

Francis winced and Reece added hastily, 'It was so peaceful that it was a minute or two before I realised he'd gone.'

'I'll probably die in agony with a coughing fit tearing my lungs apart.'

Reece sighed. Francis had been tossing remarks like that at him lately and it was hard to know how to answer them.

'Did Kevin tell you he's left you everything? Livia and I witnessed his will soon after we arrived. You fell on your feet there.'

'He did mention it, but only at the very end. I didn't realise he'd made the will so long ago. Why, he hardly knew me then! Conn has the will, apparently.' He turned round as footsteps came towards them. 'Good morning, Livia.' He explained why he was there and saw her eyes flicker towards her husband.

'I'll come to the burial, but I think it's a bit far for Francis to walk.'

'And at the same time a bit too close to home.' Her husband laughed bitterly at his own joke.

She didn't answer, just took his hand and he clung to hers tightly.

'We thought to bury Kevin tomorrow morning about ten, if that's all right with you?' Reece said. 'We'll have to perform the burial service ourselves. The travelling clergyman won't be making his monthly visit to this district for another two weeks, and even then he won't have time to ride out here to bless the grave. I'm going to ride across to Galway House now to let Conn and the twins know what's happened.'

'Give them our regards. I'll walk with you to the path. I'll be back in a minute, Francis.'

As they walked, she said, 'Don't take offence at how he speaks to you. He's getting worse rapidly and that's upsetting him. Leo had to help him walk to the stables today.'

'It'd upset me too, if I was dying, so I'm not likely to take offence.' Reece stopped to clasp her hand. 'Don't forget that we're nearby if you need us. Any time, day or night. Just send Leo across.'

'I know. Thank you.'

He turned just before he was out of sight to see her standing staring into the distance. She was a strong woman mentally, but it was hard to watch someone you loved die and how she found the strength to stay serene and supportive, he couldn't imagine.

If anything happened to his wife, Reece didn't know what he'd do. He'd lost his first wife, but hadn't loved her nearly as much, poor lass. Marrying Cassandra was the best thing he'd ever done. They were partners in every way, sharing hopes, plans and the sheer hard work necessary to make a success in this new country. As for little Sofia, she had his heart held tight in her rosy little hands and she felt to be his daughter in every way that mattered.

Reece went home and saddled the horse, which now belonged to him, he supposed. Like Conn, Kevin had had an eye for a sound horse, and though she was rather ugly, Delilah was equally at home between the shafts or carrying a riding saddle. He patted her affectionately. He'd barely been able to ride or drive a cart when he came to Australia, but now he was confident about using either mode of transport. Today riding would be quicker.

Cassandra sent her love to her sisters, then went back to sorting out a clean nightshirt to bury Kevin in. Her child played at her feet, too young to be aware of what was happening, just knowing instinctively that she was safe.

It took Reece only an hour to ride to Galway House. He was surprised to see a stranger sitting on the veranda all alone. She was sour-faced but clearly a lady by her clothing, so he doffed his hat to her politely as he passed on his way round to the stables.

Conn was leaning on the fence having an earnest conversation with another stranger. They turned at the sound of the horse's hooves and Conn murmured something to his companion then led him forward towards Reece.

The two friends shook hands then Conn introduced Ronan. 'He's brought your wife's inheritance from Pandora. They've sold two of the cottages.'

Reece shook hands with the newcomer. 'I'm glad to meet you.' He turned back to Conn. 'I've come with sad news, I'm afraid.'

'Kevin or Francis?'

'Kevin. He died peacefully this morning. We're burying him tomorrow morning and wondered if you'd like to join us?'

'I would normally, but I don't care to leave my mother on her own at the moment.' He hesitated then explained about his wife's unexpected arrival and the fact that Kathleen was rather difficult to deal with.

Reece tried to hide his surprise at this news, but wasn't sure he'd succeeded. No one had known that Conn was married. The poor fellow tended to keep himself to himself, having been snubbed many times because of being an ex-convict, but they all knew how Maia felt about him and it seemed unfair that he'd let her go on thinking he was free to love her. He became aware that Conn had said something. 'Sorry. My mind wandered for a moment. What did you say?'

'Xanthe and Maia may like to come to the burial,' Conn repeated. 'I can spare Sean to drive them across.'

'Or I could do it,' Ronan offered. 'I'd like to see as much of the countryside as I can while I'm here.'

'Aren't you tired after your journey here?'

'Not particularly. And I gather it's only an hour or so away.'

'Well, I'd certainly trust my horse to you, but you'll probably have to sleep on the cart tonight and the weather doesn't look very promising. There's only a small house, you see. Kevin built it himself, as people do here.'

'I've slept rough before and it's not exactly cold, is it?'

'No. Even in winter we rarely get frosts and never any snow, just a great deal of rain. Let's go and tell Maia and Xanthe, and ask if they want to go. And I suppose I'd better introduce you to my wife, Reece, or she'll take offence.'

'Look out, here she comes,' Ronan muttered.

Conn turned and said coolly, 'Ah, Kathleen, there you are. We were just coming to find you to introduce a neighbouring landowner, Reece Gregory. He's married to Xanthe and Maia's oldest sister.'

She gave Reece a curt nod. 'Are you another ex-convict? My husband says normal people don't visit him.'

He stared at her in surprise at this gratuitous rudeness.

'Kathleen, there was no need for that,' Conn said, with a certain weariness in his tone. 'Mr Gregory isn't a convict.'

'But he's a servant's husband. Why did you introduce him to me? Have your standards slipped so far? Fine friends you've made here.' She turned and walked off.

Conn closed his eyes for a moment and the other two men exchanged pitying glances.

'Kathleen has always been – difficult,' Conn said after a moment or two, 'but she seems to have got worse since I last saw her.' He took a deep breath. 'Let's go and join my mother. We'll ask the girls if they'd like to spend the night with you and Cassandra. It's better if they're out of the house at the moment, at least until I can find somewhere else for Kathleen to live.'

Maia's eyes filled with tears when she heard Kevin was dead. 'I'm so sorry. He was a lovely man. I don't think I should leave your mother, though, Conn. I know he'd understand that.'

'I'm sure she'll cope without you for a day or two. Kathleen's maid can help her if necessary.'

But Maia shook her head. 'Your mother never mentions it, but she's having one of her more painful times at the moment and I know exactly how to help her.' She looked at her sister. 'You go, Xanthe. One of us ought to. Give Cassandra my dearest love. You can sort out the things we got from England while you're there.'

Conn looked at Maia, his eyes softening involuntarily. 'I'm continually grateful for your care of my mother. Now, if you'll go and pack your things, Xanthe, I'll tell Sean to harness the small cart.'

Xanthe clicked her tongue in exasperation as she went to her room. Even the tone of his voice showed how much he cared for her sister. The pair of them seemed unable to hide their feelings.

Kathleen wasn't too stupid to have noticed – and any wife would feel angry about that, whether she loved her husband or not.

With Xanthe sitting beside him, Ronan drove the light cart slowly for the first mile or two, following Reece on horseback and getting used to the rough conditions. This meant he didn't like to take his eyes off the road for more than a few seconds. But the gelding Conn had harnessed to the cart was a fine animal, seeming happy to be out and about, so gradually he relaxed.

After a while she said, 'Tell me what's happening in the world. We're so late getting the news here. Is Lancashire recovering from the lack of cotton? Are the mills all running again? We were so glad when the war in America ended last year, though sorry to hear of poor Mr Lincoln being assassinated. I'd like to see America one day but it's a long way to go on your own, so I probably won't ever get there.'

He spoke for a while and she listened with great interest, asking questions and making intelligent comments.

They travelled for a few minutes in silence, then she asked suddenly, 'Tell me about your voyage out here. Pandora didn't tell us about hers in great detail because she was seasick and then she suffered badly from the heat, poor dear. Did you take time to visit Alexandria and Suez en route? What were they like? And did you see the new ship canal they're building? I've heard it's a marvellous thing and will make the journey to Australia and the Far East much easier.'

'You're a strange young woman,' he said before he could stop himself.

'I know. But now that I have some money I can stop pretending to be meek.' Not that she did go that far, really, but she certainly had to keep quiet when she'd rather have spoken out.

He threw back his head and laughed.

'What's so amusing?'

'Any maid less meek than you I've yet to meet, Xanthe Blake, so I doubt the money will make that much difference.'

'I do my job, and do it well.' Her voice was defensive.

'Yes, I can see that. But I shouldn't think you've ever been *meek*. Even the way you hold yourself is different from other women – you stare the world straight in the face.' His eyes were admiring.

'I'm polite, at least. Anyway, never mind that, tell me why you didn't stop to see places on the way here. I thought you enjoyed travelling.'

'After my mother died, I was too upset to go sightseeing. I was very fond of her.'

'Oh, no! I'm so sorry. I wasn't thinking. I didn't mean to stir up your sadness.'

He sighed. 'The thought that she's dead continues to make me feel sad, but that's not your fault. She was a lively woman and a good mother. I shall miss her greatly, and not just because I lived with her when I was in Ireland. Life goes on, however, and one grows more used to a loss, I suppose.'

'You never get completely used to it. I still miss my father greatly and think of things to tell him, even though it's years since he died.'

She laid her hand on his arm in a sympathetic gesture and he caught his breath at the picture she presented, cheeks glowing with health, eyes alight with intelligence and compassion. Did she realise how lovely she was? *She* never seemed conscious of it, but she'd be a temptation to the men she encountered if she went travelling on her own and that might put her in danger.

She certainly tempted him. Being so close to her stirred his senses. Already he wanted her and he was starting to like her too, not an emotion he usually associated with the women he bedded.

He was glad when she pointed and changed the subject. 'The Southerhams' farm is up that track to the left. They've called it Westview, for obvious reasons. Kevin's farm is this way, to the right – no, it's Reece and Cassandra's now, isn't it? He didn't give it a name. We just say Lynch's Farm. I wonder if they'll change that. Oh, it's good to be here again. I'm dying to see Cassandra and little Sofia.'

She jumped off the cart as soon as she saw her sister at the door of the farm and ran across to hug her, then pick up her niece and swing her round and round.

He watched, bemused. The fourth Blake sister was also beautiful. Pandora was the most classically perfect, Maia had a gentleness that dimmed her beauty a little until you looked more closely, Cassandra looked like the goddess of fecundity, her belly just filling with a child, and Xanthe . . . ah, she had a mind as bright and sparkling as her smile, such a dangerously attractive combination.

He reined in the horse and got down from the cart. Reece had dismounted by now and after a quick wave to his wife, he turned to his guest. 'Do you need any help to unharness the gelding?'

Ronan grinned. 'I'm not such a fine gentleman that I can't deal with my own horses.'

'I've plenty of room and feed for yours. Conn would never forgive me if I didn't look after it. He treats his animals more like children than horses.'

'Perhaps to make up for the fact that he has no children, nor is he likely to.'

'His wife is . . .' Reece hesitated, not knowing how to describe her.

'A vile creature, full of spite and nastiness,' Ronan finished for him. 'I don't know what poor Conn is going to do with her now. She was mad to follow him to Australia.'

'I pity him. My own wife is a wonderful woman.'

'They're an amazing group of sisters.'

The two men finished tending the horses, then washed their hands and went to join the women.

Cassandra greeted them with an offer of a cup of tea, which she went to make in the kitchen, a separate building at the rear of the small house.

Xanthe looked up. 'That sky's growing darker. I was hoping the threat of rain would pass but it's winter, so we can expect wetter weather now.'

'I always thought Australia was a hot, sunny country,' Ronan said. 'I haven't found it so.'

'Western Australia is very hot in the summer – too hot sometimes – but this is winter.'

Sure enough, as they were finishing their evening meal, it began
to rain and water was soon pounding on the roof and bouncing
up from the parched earth, making even the veranda uninhabit-
able as the wind drove the slashing spears of rain against the
front of the house.

'You'll have to sleep inside the house tonight, Mr Maguire,'
Cassandra said with a frown, 'though where we're going to put
you with Kevin's body lying in his bedroom, I don't know. You
could sleep on the floor there.'

He shuddered. 'I'd rather not keep a corpse company.'

'No, I'd not like that myself.'

'Mr Maguire can sleep in the living room with me,' Xanthe
offered.

Ronan nearly choked on his mouthful of food.

She pulled a cheeky face at him. 'I don't mean in the same
bed, Mr Maguire, but at the other side of the room.' She placed
one hand on her chest and pretended to be terrified. 'I'll sleep
near Reece and Cassandra's door, in case I have to scream for
help during the night.'

Everyone else laughed; he couldn't. The picture she'd raised
in his mind had shocked him for a moment. He was surprised
how relaxed they were about an unrelated man and woman
sharing sleeping quarters. He looked doubtfully at his host
and hostess.

'When people are travelling, they're welcome to stay in most
houses they pass, but have to take what's available. There are so
few settlements of any size outside Perth, you see, and therefore
few inns. We're not immoral, just practical. You can't sleep in the
cart or on the veranda in a downpour like this, nor can we fit
Xanthe in our bedroom, now that Sofia is sleeping there, but of
course we'll leave our door open for propriety's sake. Not that I
think you'd cause us any trouble.'

'No, no! Of course I wouldn't.' He tried not to smile at the
thought of how his mother or sister would have reacted to this

situation. Neither of them would have ever considered sleeping with the bedroom door open and a stranger a few feet away.

He wasn't going to cause anyone trouble, of course he wasn't, but the presence of the beautiful Miss Xanthe Blake so close by would cause him trouble and make it extremely difficult for him to get to sleep.

At Galway House Maia fetched Conn to carry his mother to the sitting room for the evening. He knew she mustn't be feeling well, because she rarely asked him to carry her. Outside it was threatening to rain and the sky had grown dark early, but a fire had been lit and a couple of oil lamps, so the room was cosy.

Kathleen was still pacing up and down the front veranda, muttering to herself, so he left her to it and sat down to chat to his mother.

After a while he heard Kathleen come inside but she didn't join them and he looked at his mother doubtfully.

'You'd better check what she's doing.'

He got up and went out quietly, following the harsh sound of his wife's voice to the kitchen and standing quietly outside the door to see what she was up to now.

'What are you doing, Mary?'

'My name's Maia and unless you use it, I'm not answering you.'

Conn tensed as Kathleen took a step forward and half-raised one hand as if to slap the maid.

Maia picked up the ladle. 'Don't you dare lay a finger on me!'

'How can I call a servant Maia? It's not a suitable name for a person of your class.'

'If you don't use my real name, how will I know it's me you're speaking to? Your requests for service will probably go unanswered.'

Conn smiled and watched Maia go on with her cooking. But he could see that she was keeping an eye on the woman still standing by the kitchen table. He too wondered if Kathleen was going to attack the maid and he tensed, ready to go to Maia's aid if needed.

'I'll ask again, then. What are you doing, *Maia*?'

'Cooking a hearty broth for our evening meal.'

'What's for the main course?'

'That's it, broth. With Xanthe away at Kevin's burial, there's no one to do any fancy cooking, and no time for it, either.'

'I can't believe my husband would only offer broth to his guests! That's poor people's food.'

'Broth and bread, with apple pie for dessert is plenty to fill a stomach – any stomach, rich or poor. There are fruit trees here and we bottle our own apples, though we've nearly used up last year's supply now.'

Kathleen stayed where she was, silent, but from what Conn could see of her face, she was puzzled, frowning as if she didn't understand the situation. He saw Maia stealing a couple of glances at her, as if trying to guess how she was feeling.

'Why don't you sit down for a moment or two, Mrs Kathleen? You must be tired with all that travelling.'

His wife stood quite still for a moment or two longer, then took a seat. 'It is tiring.'

Her voice had changed and she sounded calmer, the way she did when she was with horses. 'Why are you doing that?'

'I'm making the pastry.'

'I've never seen pastry made before.'

Had his wife never sneaked into the kitchen when she was little? he wondered. He could remember Cook letting him roll pastry and make his own little pies, his brother too.

Once he'd made sure his wife had calmed down, Conn slipped back to join his mother, feeling more sure that Maia could stand up for herself in all but the most extreme circumstances. And if she needed help, he'd hear.

Kathleen watched carefully for a moment or two as Maia filled the pastry shell with apples and moistened the edges with beaten egg. 'I've never seen anyone making apple pies before.'

'Haven't you? I used to watch my sister cooking when I was a child. My mother died when I was quite young.'

'I was never allowed in the kitchens.'

'What a pity!'

After another silence, Kathleen said suddenly, 'Conn's living like a peasant! He surely has enough money to live in better style than this.' She gestured round the room.

'I don't know anything about his money.'

Kathleen got up, paced up and down for a while, then came back to watch Maia decorate the apple pie crust with pieces of pastry cut out as leaves. 'What does pastry feel like when it's not cooked?'

Maia passed her a piece. 'Try it. You could make some leaves for the other pies, if you like.'

Kathleen felt the pastry, squeezed it, then spread it out and picked up a small knife. But her leaves were clumsy.

Maia could see her getting frustrated, so said quickly, 'It takes years of practice to do it right, but I thought you'd like to try.'

'Yes. It was interesting.' She pushed the bits aside, got up and began pacing to and fro again, then stopped to ask, 'What do people here do in the evenings?'

Maia was surprised that Conn's wife was bothering to talk to a servant when she'd been so scornful about them. If she wasn't able to see that her companion was a grown woman, she'd feel as if she was talking to a child, and an unhappy one at that. 'My sister and I work long hours, but we enjoy reading in our free time, especially in winter, when it rains a lot. Mr Largan usually sits with his mother. Sometimes they chat, or he reads to her – he has a lot of books if you want to borrow one – other times they sing. They both have lovely voices. I don't understand the words of the Irish songs, though.'

'I don't like reading. It makes my eyes hurt. Do neighbours not call to visit Mrs Largan?'

'They're as busy as we are and most go to bed early. Besides, although Mr Largan was jailed for political activity, people still treat him like a criminal.'

'He *is* a criminal. His father said so. But I'm not a convict and people don't talk to me, either. It isn't fair. Where do people of our class meet one another?'

'Once a month there's a church service in a local barn. I don't know whether you'll consider the people there your class, though, because they're mostly farmers.'

'Are there any other convicts?'

'Your husband received a conditional pardon when he arrived here, so he's not a convict. They call people like him emancipists. And no, there aren't any others like him near here, not now. The man whose burial Xanthe and Ronan are attending was an emancipist.'

There was no answer so Maia peeped sideways. She saw Kathleen smear away a tear. Against her will, she was beginning to feel sorry for Conn's wife, who seemed so limited in her thoughts and so angry at the world. What had made her like that?

She heard footsteps come along the corridor and Conn joined them in the kitchen.

'I've been watching your mother's maid make apple pies,' Kathleen announced. 'I've nothing else to do.'

'Would you like to sit with me and my mother now, Kathleen? I was going to read to her.'

'Yes. All right.'

Maia carefully avoided looking at him as they left. That had been one of the strangest conversations she'd ever held. She remembered a young woman who'd lived a few streets away in Outham, who'd been very similar to Mrs Kathleen, set in her ways, always certain these ways were right and aggressive about sticking to them. Was it possible Conn's wife was the same?

But what sort of life had Mrs Kathleen had? If she had to hazard a guess, she'd say the poor woman had never been loved. No child deserved to grow up without love.

But why in heaven's name had Conn married a woman like that? He was comfortably off and pleasant looking, could have chosen anyone.

She wished he wasn't married, wished she could still allow herself to dream about him. Oh, she was a fool! He was married and she must learn to turn her thoughts elsewhere.

Only, how did you stop yourself dreaming of what could have been when you loved someone so much?

The room was dark, except for the glow of the embers in the iron stove. Ronan was finding it as hard as he'd expected to get to sleep, with Xanthe sleeping only a couple of yards away. Or was she sleeping? Her breathing hadn't slowed down.

As if she could sense that he was thinking about her, she suddenly said in a low voice, 'Are you awake too?'

'Yes. It's not easy to get to sleep in strange surroundings.'

'Especially on a hard floor. Never mind, you'll be lying in a soft bed again tomorrow night.'

'But you won't be nearby.'

He heard a soft gasp as if what he'd said had surprised her. 'I'm sorry. I shouldn't have said that. But you're a beautiful young woman and that does affect men who come near you.'

'It's so annoying. They stare at me but they don't see me, not really.'

He knew what she meant. 'I'm beginning to see you, I think.'

'You still stare.'

He chuckled. 'I'll try not to from now on.'

'Where are you going after you leave here?'

'I don't know. I have to go back to Ireland to tell my brothers about Mother and deal with her affairs. I don't know anything about her will, but I suppose she's left everything to me and my brothers. After that, well, I don't know what I'll do. I used to live with her; now I'll probably find somewhere of my own.'

'Did your mother live with your oldest brother?'

'No. She lived in the dower house in the grounds of Ardgullan. When Father died, she thought Hubert would get married within a year or two, so insisted on moving into her own house. But he hasn't married.'

'You'll have to clear her things out of the house then, which is such a sad task. Or is there a woman relative who will do that for you?'

'No one but me and my brothers. I'd not ask Patrick's wife to do that. She looks down her nose at everything Irish. I can't understand how she ever came to marry him.'

She didn't say anything else and he heard her breathing slow down and deepen, so knew she was asleep. He wasn't as fortunate. Their conversation had been perfectly innocuous and yet he'd enjoyed the intimacy of chatting in the darkened room. The trouble was, his body was now reminding him it was a long time since he'd had a woman.

But he wanted *her*, Xanthe, not just any woman.

And couldn't have her. A gentleman did not seduce a decent young lass like her.

9

In the morning Reece got up early, slipped on some old working clothes he'd left ready and crept out past the huddles of blankets where Ronan and Xanthe were still sleeping.

As he walked up the hill to dig Kevin's grave, he enjoyed the morning chorus of bird calls and watched a flock of galahs chattering to one another raucously in the treetops, their pale grey plumage and pink crests making them stand out against the dull green of the gum trees. These cockatoos were his favourite among the parrot-like birds. He'd thought they actually were parrots when he first came here and had been corrected by Kevin, who had spent a lot of time enjoying the wildlife when he lacked human companionship.

The previous day's rain had passed and the sky was growing brighter by the minute. Reece sank his spade into the ground, hoping he'd not encounter any rocky outcrops, and began to pile the earth beside the grave

He was working so hard he didn't hear Ronan approach and jumped in shock as a voice said, 'Let me help you.'

He leaned on his spade for a moment or two, taking a breather. 'Thanks for the offer, but you'll get muddy and you've no other clothes with you. I seem to have fallen lucky here and the recent rain has softened the ground.'

'Do you have a coffin? I noticed the body was still lying on the bed.'

'I have some planks and I'm hoping to cobble them together into a box after I've finished this.'

'If you'll tell me where they are, I'll make a start. I'm quite handy with wood, used to hang around the village carpenter when I was a lad.'

Reece pointed down the hill. 'There's a pile of sawn timber stacked behind the stables. My tools are inside the stables, hanging on the wall above the workbench. I've not even sorted out the planks. Use any pieces you think might be suitable.'

Ronan was greeted by Xanthe as he passed the kitchen at the rear of the house.

'Do you want a cup of tea?' she called.

'I'd love one. I'm very thirsty.'

'I'll make it in a half-pint enamel mug, if you don't object to that. Everyone gets thirstier here than back home, and the mugs hold far more than a cup.'

'I'll be round the back of the stables, sorting out wood. I'm going to help Reece make a coffin.'

Her smile faded. 'What a sad task! Is there anything I can do to help?'

He couldn't resist saying, 'Keep me company for a while, perhaps.' He cocked one eyebrow at her and waited for an answer.

She gave him a long, level look, as if considering this, then nodded. 'All right. I'll just make the tea and take a cup to Cassandra, then I'll come and drink mine with you.'

He felt as if he'd passed some sort of test with her during their recent conversations. Maybe he had. But he didn't know what he'd done right – or what he was going to do next, right or wrong.

The coffin was a rough, splintery affair, because Reece said ruefully that the only glass paper they had was too precious and hard to obtain. No use smoothing a surface which would only lie and rot in the earth. But the coffin was at least made of good solid pieces of wood, with rope handles nailed on the sides. A blanket covering it lent an air of decency to the proceedings. Ronan was pleased with his work, given the circumstances.

Livia, the closest neighbour, arrived just before ten, having walked across from Westview Farm accompanied by a young man

called Leo, who in spite of being slow-witted was clearly on good
terms with everyone and of a cheerful disposition. Ronan didn't
think he would have been so well accepted back in Ireland.

That made six people and one small child to say farewell to
Kevin Lynch, all of whom spoke of him very fondly.

Reece and Leo carried the coffin up the hill and didn't seem
to find it too heavy. Reece was a strong man and Leo was a
young giant.

Xanthe moved closer to whisper, 'Leo may be slow thinking,
but he's marvellous with animals and he saved Cassandra's life
when she was having her baby. We're all very fond of him and
if there's anything seriously wrong with an animal we fetch him
to tend to it. Some of the neighbours do too, now they're used
to him.'

Ronan didn't comment but he hoped he wouldn't need Leo's
doctoring while he was here. He'd been fortunate so far in his
life, had been very healthy and hadn't even broken a limb as a
child, even though he'd been a devil for climbing trees or getting
up on roofs. He turned to study the neighbour, a charming lady
with a sad expression. He had to wonder what someone like her
was doing here on a farm.

She smiled at him. 'I brought my prayer book, which contains
the burial service, but it's not the Catholic one, I'm afraid.'

'I'm sure Kevin wouldn't mind,' Reece said. 'It's the same god,
after all.'

They took it in turns to read from her prayer book and the
most fluent readers were the two sisters, which surprised Ronan.
Xanthe in particular read with great feeling and listening to her
was extremely moving.

Afterwards they all sat and chatted quietly for a while on the
veranda, remembering Kevin fondly and telling tales of him.

'This is like an Irish wake,' Ronan commented.

Cassandra smiled. 'Kevin told us about them and said this was
how he'd like to be farewelled.'

Once Livia and Leo had left, Ronan took off his money belt
and produced the shiny gold sovereigns he'd brought from

England. 'There's a note from the lawyer handling your affairs in England, a Mr Featherworth. I'd appreciate it if you'd count the money and sign the statement he gave me to verify that it all arrived here safely.'

'As if we'd doubt you!' Xanthe exclaimed, then blushed slightly as her sister stared at her in surprise.

'You should doubt every stranger,' Ronan said. 'Those who trick people can be very plausible.'

'Not if they're long-time friends of Conn. He doesn't give his trust easily.'

'No, perhaps not.'

'Why didn't you want to talk openly about the money when we were at Galway House?' Xanthe asked.

'Because of Kathleen.'

'You think she'd steal it?'

'You can never tell what she'd do. Hurl it in a river, hide it somewhere where we'd never find it. Having been brought up to be scornful of servants and people like them, she'd probably be outraged about you even having an inheritance like this. The less we can upset her, the easier it will be for Conn.'

'She treats servants like idiots,' Xanthe said. '*You* don't do that, though, and nor does Conn. He even asked us to use his Christian name, which is unusual in an employer, even here in Australia. He said he'd learned in prison that one person was not superior to another simply because of birth, and he'd been treated kindly by people others would spit on.'

'I think he lost all his pride when he was in prison, poor fellow. But I'd like to follow his example and ask you all to call me Ronan.' He looked round but it was Xanthe's nod that he was after and as usual, she thought for a moment before agreeing.

Cassandra counted the money, then divided it into three piles, putting those meant for her sisters into two little drawstring bags that clinked satisfactorily.

Xanthe put hers and Maia's into a pair of old-fashioned hanging pockets that Mrs Largan had given her. They tied round the waist and hung underneath her skirt. They felt more secure than the

smaller modern pocket let into the side seam of her skirt, though
she had to lift her skirts to get at them. She could feel the coins
through the skirt and two petticoats, which were all she wore
here. Even ladies didn't usually wear crinolines in the country.

'I must ask Pandora to keep the rest of my money in the safe
at the shop till I go back and decide what to do with it,' she said
thoughtfully. 'Zachary told me when he was here that my uncle
didn't trust banks and had bought a safe from a man in Sheffield
called Thomas Milner. It's old-fashioned now but very strong
and it's even supposed to be fireproof. Imagine that!'

Ronan was surprised. 'Don't you want to put the money in a
bank?'

'So many banks have failed in the past few years that I don't
want to risk that.'

'Safes don't pay interest on your money, though.'

'I know. It's a dilemma. I've never had enough money to worry
about before. What do you do with yours?'

'I own various houses here and there, and my agent collects
the rents. Most of my wealth lies in them. I keep my money
reserves in two banks for safety, and I also have cash on hand
in a secure place. I ought to buy myself an estate, but I've never
yet wanted to settle down. And when I wasn't travelling, my
mother was always happy for me to stay with her, or I could have
stayed with Hubert, so it wasn't urgent. I'm very fond of the
place where I grew up. There's nowhere like Ardgullan. Though
it won't be the same without my mother.'

His expression was so sad when he said that, Cassandra looked
at the sky to give him time to recover. 'It must be nearly one
o'clock. We'd better get you some food before you leave.'

When the two sisters were alone in the kitchen, she said
abruptly, 'Don't let your heart settle on a gentleman like that.'

'Why do you say that?'

'I've seen the way you two look at one another. But however
attractive he finds you, he won't marry you. He'll marry one of
his own kind.'

'I don't intend to get married, as I keep telling you.'

Cassandra smiled. 'Neither Pandora nor I were looking for a husband, but when you meet the right person, you change your mind about marriage very quickly.'

Xanthe tossed her head. 'Well, I shan't.'

'Just don't – let him be too free with you.'

'You didn't need to say that.'

'I did! I know how loving someone changes people.'

'I'm *not* in love with him or anyone else, either.' Xanthe changed the subject firmly and her sister followed her lead, thank goodness. For some reason she didn't understand, she didn't want to talk about Ronan to anyone. She agreed with everything Cassandra had said about him, though, and at twenty-seven she was past being foolish about a good-looking man. Even one with a smile like his.

After their meal, Ronan harnessed the horse and Xanthe said farewell to her sister and family. It felt strangely intimate to sit together on the wooden bench of the cart as they set off alone on the drive back – almost as if they were good friends who had known one another for years.

Neither of them spoke for a while, but she was very conscious of his strong body beside hers, and saw him glancing towards her every now and then. In the end she decided it'd be more comfortable to break the silence. 'You're very quiet. Are you tired? If not, perhaps you could tell me about Ireland? I hope to visit it one day.'

'I'd rather talk about you.'

She looked at him sideways. 'Why should a gentleman like you want to talk about me?'

He hesitated then matched her frankness. 'I'm very attracted to you, you must realise that, and I think you feel that same tug of attraction.'

She stared down at her hands then looked back at him, not shirking his gaze. 'I feel it, yes, but I'm not going to do anything about it. I know where that sort of attraction can lead. I don't plan to marry and even if I did, a gentleman like you wouldn't marry a mill girl like me.'

'You like to speak the truth boldly, don't you?' She was right. People like him didn't marry mill girls – unfortunately.

'Yes. It's better to face up to things.'

His eyes lingered on her face and he smiled ruefully. 'I can face up to things too and I'm definitely not going to do anything to hurt you, but that doesn't stop me wanting to know more about you.'

'Oh. Well, there's not much to know.'

He chuckled. 'A mill girl called by an unusual name because her father was learning Greek, one who is better read than most men I know, who is not only beautiful but extremely intelligent – I think there's quite a lot to know. Now what have I said to make you blush?'

'I'm not used to lavish compliments. I wish you wouldn't talk like that.'

'I meant every word.'

'Well, I still don't like it. I wish my looks didn't – please people. It'd make life so much easier. I feel embarrassed when people comment on them. And as I've not known many educated people, I can't compare myself to them. I only know I love reading and that I want to see something of the world. Is that so unusual?'

'For someone like you, yes. Oh, look!'

A kangaroo suddenly leaped across the road ahead of them, followed by two others, one with a joey peering out of its pouch. As he reined in the horse to watch them, some whitetailed black cockatoos flew out of the trees, shrieking. No melodious singing from them. They sounded as if they were quarrelling and hurling insults at one another.

'I'm in Australia,' he said in tones of wonderment once the birds had flown away. 'I really am and—' He half-turned to her and what he'd been going to say vanished from his mind. She was smiling at him indulgently and her beautiful lips were only a few inches away. Before he could stop himself, he leaned sideways and kissed her quickly, moving back almost immediately.

She clapped one hand to her mouth. 'I wish you hadn't done that.'

'Was it so bad?'

'No. It felt very – sweet. I wish it hadn't.'

He drew her towards him, surprised when she allowed him to kiss her again. And it was more than sweet, it was . . . the perfect kiss. He wanted very much to kiss her again, but when it ended he smoothed her hair back from her forehead and forced himself to move away. The sun had burnished it to blue-black and he'd been dying to touch it to see if it was as soft as it looked.

After giving him one of her grave looks, she too moved back a little and put out one hand to stop him when he gave in to temptation and tried to pull her close again. 'No. Please don't. I couldn't resist that one kiss, just to see . . . but that's all it was. One kiss. We have to be sensible.'

He leaned against the backrest. 'Sometimes I don't feel like being sensible.'

'I have to be. It's the women who carry the fruit of wrong-doing and it can ruin their whole lives.' She frowned. 'I must say, I've never seen why women are so easily tempted before, but I think I can understand it better now.'

Not a woman's usual reaction to a kiss, but her serious deliberation about its effect on her enchanted him. He almost wished she'd said something stupid. If she'd mouthed inanities, it'd be much easier to forget how delightful her lips felt against his, how right it had seemed to hold her close!

He told the horse to walk on and it was a few minutes before either of them spoke. He kept his eyes on the road this time and tried to keep his thoughts on it, too. The ground had dried very quickly after the rain of the previous day, because the soil was quite sandy, but he could see from the deep, sun-baked ruts to one side of the track that even these rough roads got waterlogged in winter.

'How soon do you intend to leave Australia?' he asked when she made no effort to break the silence.

'I wish I could leave straight away and get it over with, because even the thought of me going is upsetting Maia so much.' She sighed and added, 'And me. We've never been apart before and twins are closer than other sisters, but the life I want wouldn't suit her at all – and I'm not prepared to lead a dull life, even for her.'

'Why can't you leave now?'

'Because servants are hard to find here and I wouldn't feel right leaving Conn and Mrs Largan in the lurch. And because there aren't a lot of ships sailing to and from Western Australia.'

'I don't like the thought of you travelling back to England on your own.'

She smiled. 'I'd not be on my own. There would be a ship full of people and this time I'd be a cabin passenger. How exciting to travel in such luxury!'

He thought of his cramped cabin and couldn't help grimacing. 'I'd not consider it luxury.'

'It is compared to conditions in the steerage section. I ought to be quite safe as a cabin passenger, don't you think?'

His voice came out more harshly than he'd intended. 'Someone as beautiful as you will never be safe travelling.'

Her smile faded. 'Even if I dress plainly and behave modestly?'

'Even so. Beautiful women tempt unscrupulous men and if you don't understand that, let me tell you that the urges men feel are very strong and sometimes overrule their common sense, even when they're trying to behave decently. And there are some men who have no scruples, who take what they please if the opportunity arises, by force if necessary.'

'I'm not completely ignorant, you know. Women of your class may be very sheltered from life, but we weren't. And my father warned us when we grew older, told us how men feel. I know it isn't going to be easy, but I'm *not* going to give up my dreams. There must be a way to do what I want. Perhaps I'll have to hire a travelling companion, an older woman. Do you think that might help?'

'A little. If you hired a strong man to protect you as well, it'd be even better.' He couldn't think of anything he'd like more than to be her guide and protector. It'd be a joy to take her travelling and show her other lands. But if he did, who would protect her from him?

No, he'd better keep his distance. This attraction couldn't be allowed to lead anywhere because the last thing he wanted to do was hurt her.

'Well, I've got plenty of time to work something out.'

Her chin was jutting out and her expression was quietly determined.

No, he thought, you'll not easily be deflected once you set your mind on something.

'It's on the left here!' she called, jerking him out of his thoughts. 'You nearly missed the turn.'

When they arrived at Galway House, Ronan was swept away by their host and Xanthe went back to work. Their lives were separate here, even though Conn treated his staff kindly.

It was just as well.

Conn took Kathleen out riding, pointing out the things to look out for in the Australian bush. She was at her best on horseback, not only a good rider, but also careful about her horse, and she listened carefully to his instructions.

But as soon as they came back into the house she reverted to her demanding and unpleasant ways, speaking so rudely to Maia that he saw tears well in the latter's eyes. He didn't dare step in to protect her or it'd have made matters worse.

It was a relief when Ronan and Xanthe came back in the late afternoon and there was someone else to share the burden of talking to Kathleen, who had no resources for entertaining herself.

In the late evening after the ladies had gone to bed, Conn and Ronan went out to stroll round the gardens.

'What are you going to do with her?' Ronan asked.

'I'm damned if I know.'

'Do you want me to go back to Fremantle and make enquiries about when ships are sailing?'

'I'd have to drug her to make her leave, I think.'

'Have you asked your mother's advice?'

'No. She's not well at the moment and I don't want Kathleen snapping at her. It's for me to sort this out.' He hesitated, then said, 'I think I'll go up to Perth first and take advice about annulling the marriage.'

Ronan gave him a quick look, opened his mouth then snapped it shut again to hold in his surprise.

'I never bedded her,' Conn said. 'I thought it my duty to try, because that was the main purpose of the marriage for me, but she fought me like a tigress and I soon gave up trying. I'm glad of that now.'

'It'll take a while to get an annulment.'

'Yes. But surely I can arrange it? And if she'd go back to Ireland while I did so, we'd all be a lot happier.'

'Why don't you go to Perth to see the Bishop soon? If you like, I'll stay here and keep an eye on things.'

Conn looked at him quickly. 'I think I'd better talk to Kathleen first. She might not agree to do this amicably.'

He took the opportunity to speak to her the following day while they were out riding, trying to explain in simple terms what he wanted to do.

Kathleen frowned at him. 'I don't see the need.'

'I don't think we're happy together, and I want a proper family one day – children, a loving wife.'

'I don't see why. Your brother can have children to inherit the land. Having children hurts women. Your father told me that before we were married.'

Conn stared at her. Had his father tried to stop him having children – on top of everything else? He could well believe it. His father had liked to control every facet of his family's life, and had not been pleased when Conn became a lawyer and went to live away from Shilmara.

They rode on in silence, then Kathleen asked suddenly, 'If we weren't married, what would I do – afterwards?'

'You'd make a life for yourself somewhere, a happier life I'm sure, because you'd not be a convict's wife any longer, so people would talk to you again.'

'But who would look after me?'

'Your brother would help you, I'm sure.'

'He hates me. And I hate him. He wanted to lock me away. I heard him saying that to my father once.'

'He wouldn't see you in difficulty and as long as you don't buy a house near him, I'm sure he would help you. How about finding somewhere in Dublin?'

'I'm not going to live in a town.' She looked suddenly as if she wanted to cry as she said, 'I want to go back and live at Shilmara. I was happy there after you left. Your father was kind to me.'

Conn tried to stay patient. 'You know you can't do that. Shilmara belongs to my brother Kieran now. You have no choice but to make a new life for yourself.'

She rode on for a few yards, then reined in her horse. 'If I'm your wife, *you* have to look after me so I don't want to end our marriage.'

'You'll have enough money to look after yourself.'

'I can't.'

'Of course you can.'

Her scowl grew more fierce. 'I *can't!*'

'Why are you so sure of that?'

She hesitated and he waited patiently, but he didn't expect what she said.

'Because I can't read or write.'

'Of course you can. I've seen notes you've written!'

'Orla writes them for me. I tell her it hurts my eyes to write, that's what my mother said I should do. Orla reads the letters to me as well.'

'She's never even hinted at that.'

Kathleen's expression became smug. 'When she became my maid, your father said he'd have her family thrown out of their cottage if she told anyone. And I said it too.'

'Did your other maid do that for you?'

'Of course. She'd been with me since I was quite small. But she died. People always die. It's not fair.'

Conn didn't know what to say. Kathleen had been clever about hiding her problems and must have been doing it all her life.

Why couldn't she read or write? Her governess must have tried hard to teach her. His heart sank as the implications of this sank in. She'd already said that she would find it difficult to manage on her own, so he couldn't see her allowing him to have their marriage annulled. And she was right. She really did need looking after. But why did it have to be him?

He'd dared to dream last night, dream of Maia, of marriage one day, children. Not big dreams but warm, cosy dreams. Now he could see only years of looking after Kathleen . . . hating her. But he couldn't just turn her loose in the world.

He wanted to weep. Men weren't supposed to weep, but he felt he had reason to at the thought of how bleak his life had become since that dreadful day when he'd been arrested.

Sighing, he urged his horse forward and led the way back to Galway House, handing his horse over to Sean and hurrying into the house, ignoring Kathleen.

When he stopped at the kitchen door to look back, his wife had disappeared into the stables.

Turning round, he saw Maia chatting to her sister as she prepared a tea tray for his mother. Her face was rosy and tranquil. She looked at him enquiringly, as if she cared how he was feeling.

The contrast between the two women was too great to be borne. He nodded and hurried across the room, taking refuge in his library, sitting with his head in his hands, sick to the soul.

10

Two days later was Sunday and as they got ready for church, it occurred to Conn that he could perhaps ask the advice of the clergyman who came every month to hold services in the barn next to the local shop. The one thing he'd decided after a restless night was to find a way to get this travesty of a marriage annulled. But he would look after Kathleen, see that she had somewhere to live.

He found her dressed in a huge crinoline skirt, the effect spoiled by the material being somewhat crumpled.

She greeted him with, 'That maid of yours wouldn't let Orla heat the flatiron to press my skirt. She said she was too busy getting ready for church and wanted the fire to burn down. And she couldn't clear the table to iron on, because places for lunch were set out there already. You're letting her take advantage of you, Conn. She's just being lazy. She should be looking after your guests, especially me, your wife.'

He took a deep breath. 'She's not lazy, Kathleen. She *is* too busy. Anyway, no one here wears crinolines. Don't you have something simpler you could wear?'

'For church? No, I don't. Your father always told me to dress up for church and so did my parents.' She smoothed down the material, seeming unaware of how incongruous her plain face and stocky body looked above such a wide skirt.

'It'll take up too much room on the benches. This isn't a proper church, as I told you. We hold our services in the barn.' He saw her face become flat and expressionless, a look he'd learned years ago meant she wasn't paying attention because she didn't want to hear what she was saying. Frustrated, he stared up at the sky, which was again full of heavy grey clouds. 'I suppose it's too late for you to change your clothes now. You'd better take an umbrella, though.'

'I don't have one. Besides, we'll be going in the carriage, so why should I need one? I can run from the carriage to the church door.'

'We use the cart and leave it in a field, so we have to walk across to the barn from there.'

'You go to church in a cart?'

'I don't have a carriage, just a gig and it'd not carry us all. There will be seven of us today, don't forget.'

She counted up on her fingers. 'Your mother, you, me, Ronan: that makes four.'

'Plus Xanthe, Maia and Sean.'

'Surely you don't let servants ride to church with you?'

'Of course I do. It's too far to walk.' He gave up trying to reason with her. 'Come on. We might as well get going.'

She hung back. 'My skirt will get dirty in a cart.'

'Sean cleans the cart out and puts cushions and blankets in the back for my mother.' He turned as Mrs Largan moved slowly across to join them. 'My dear, are you sure you feel well enough to come?'

She gave him one of her faint smiles. 'I think I should be there for Kathleen's first church service, don't you?' She turned to her daughter-in-law. 'That's pretty material, Kathleen. Is it the latest fashion to have the widest part of the crinoline near the hem? It's more a pyramid shape than a bell now.'

'Yes. Papa Largan liked me to dress well and he always bought me the latest fashions.'

Conn avoided his mother's eyes. He'd guess it had amused his father to have Kathleen look ridiculous and then force the local gentry to accept her anyway. His father had had a cruel streak.

Kathleen complained about the bumpiness of the road and the discomfort of riding in a cart for most of the journey, so no other conversation could flourish.

He saw his mother wince a few times as she was jolted, but unlike Kathleen she made no complaint. She never did.

They were among the last to arrive. He would have preferred to sit at one side, as he usually did, not wanting to upset the local worthies, but for once his mother drew him towards the front of the barn. So he sat with her and his wife on one of the benches local folk had made especially for these service, trying to ignore the dirty looks he was given by those nearby.

Livia Southerham arrived just before the service started, accompanied by Leo, who went to sit at the rear. Francis Southerham hadn't attended for some time. Conn's mother moved along the bench to make room, Kathleen did the same with an aggrieved sigh, and Livia joined them. She made a point of leaning across to shake Conn's hand. He could have told her it was a useless gesture, because no one would ever accept a convict socially even though they'd do business with him. It wasn't just here that he was ostracised; it was everywhere.

At least no one snubbed his mother. When she introduced her daughter-in-law, they were stiff but didn't refuse to speak to Kathleen, to his relief. The women were studying her clothes avidly and would no doubt ask her about the latest fashions afterwards.

As everyone settled down, his mother pulled out her prayer book and offered to share it with Kathleen, who simply shook her head.

Conn noticed that his wife spent most of the service looking round, paying little attention to the hymns or the brief sermon.

After the service, he hurried over to the clergyman. 'When you've finished speaking to people, I'd welcome your advice on a serious matter.'

The man inclined his head and Conn stepped back, knowing he had to let the other people take precedence. And anyway, he wanted to discuss the question of annulment privately.

His mother remained seated, waiting for him, and one or two of the ladies went to speak to her. Though they tried to include Kathleen in the conversations, she said very little.

'You wished to see me, Mr Largan?'

He turned with relief to the clergyman. 'Yes. Would you mind if we moved somewhere quieter? This is rather personal.'

The clergyman led the way to the little room just off the barn which had tools hanging on the wall and a sturdy workbench. He began to remove his surplice. 'How can I help you?'

'I wondered if you knew anything about having a marriage annulled.'

'I thought you were a Roman Catholic.'

'I'm not much of anything these days. And we all worship the same god, after all.'

'Whose marriage are you speaking of?'

'Mine. It's – um, never been consummated.'

'But your wife has just arrived here and is presumably living in your house!'

'She turned up uninvited. I could hardly refuse her shelter, could I? We're certainly not sharing a bed and never have done. I'm hoping to find her somewhere to stay in Perth.'

'I – don't know what to say. You really would be better handling this from England – or from Ireland perhaps, in your case.'

'I only had a conditional pardon after I arrived here, so I'd have to get special permission to go back and anyway, I don't really want to. I was hoping I could manage the annulment from here. I need to end this travesty of a marriage as quickly as possible.'

The clergyman sighed. 'I suggest you speak to your own Bishop, Mr Largan. If you go to Perth on horseback, it's only a day's travel and now that you people have your own cathedral, I'm sure you can find someone there to guide you.' He pulled out his pocket watch and glanced at it. 'Dear me. Is it that late already? You'll have to excuse me. I need to get on the road again. I have an evening service to deliver some distance from here.'

Conn realised there was no help to be gained from this man, thanked him and went out into the barn again. He waited at the rear until the women had finished speaking to his mother, Kathleen and Livia. One of the men was talking to Ronan, smiling and waving his hands about as he described something. Presumably they'd found out Ronan wasn't a convict.

If Conn had joined the group, they'd have taken their leave as quickly as possible, so he didn't. He hated to see how isolated his mother was here and tried to allow her time to chat to their neighbours whenever possible.

On the way home he bit his tongue as Kathleen poured scorn on the service and so-called church, but in the end she went on for so long he lost patience and snapped, 'Then why don't you go back to Ireland where they do have proper churches? You certainly weren't invited to come here.'

'I'm your *wife, even if you are a convict! I had no one else to turn to.*'

He'd heard those words too many times already. 'You're *not* my wife, not in any way that counts, and you never have been. Nor are you staying here for longer than necessary. You need to understand that clearly. I'll find you somewhere to live in Perth till we can get you back to Ireland.'

He heard some of his companions draw their breaths in sharply, but he didn't care who heard him.

'Your manners haven't improved,' Kathleen said.

'Neither have yours.'

Behind him in the cart his mother cleared her throat and he held back further sharp words. But it was difficult. Why could Kathleen not accept that her days at Shilmara had ended?

When they got back he went out to the stables and began saddling his horse, but before he'd finished Kathleen joined him.

'You shouldn't ride on Sundays,' she said.

'Go away and leave me alone.'

She didn't move and after a moment she said, as if he hadn't spoken so sharply, 'That's a fine horse. I'd like to take him out one day.'

'If you do, it'll be the last time I lend you any of my horses. This one is mine. He doesn't like being ridden by anyone else.'

She stretched out her hand and as if to give him the lie, Demon nuzzled her. It had always puzzled him why she got on so well with horses and so badly with people.

'I meant what I said. Demon is mine.'

She let out a huff of exasperation. 'Which horse can I take, then?'

'None of them today. I want to go riding alone.' He saw Sean hovering nearby and called, 'Don't saddle any of the other horses today. I need a peaceful hour or two.'

The old man winked and nodded.

Conn swung into the saddle and left without even looking at his wife.

The next morning he asked Ronan to come outside, where they could speak privately. 'Will you keep an eye on the farm for me if I go up to Perth?'

'Yes, of course. I presume the clergyman was no use yesterday.'

'No. He didn't want anything to do with me – I'm not only a Catholic but an ex-convict. These monthly services are supposed to be for all denominations, but he clearly doesn't see it that way. The last fellow we had was much kinder. This one told me to go to my own church, so I'll visit St Mary's Cathedral in Perth and see if the Bishop can help me end my marriage.'

'I hope he can. Kathleen's . . . difficult.'

'Very difficult. And Ronan . . . don't let her drive my mother mad, and don't let her pick on Maia and Xanthe, either. You're in charge of the farm and my mother's in charge of the house. Kathleen has no authority to do anything.'

'I'll do my best to keep her under control.' He smiled. 'I don't think that housekeeper of yours will be pushed into doing anything she doesn't think right.'

Conn smiled too. 'No. Xanthe is a very spirited woman. And a hard worker. She's put me in my place a time or two. But we feel extremely lucky to have her and her twin. And although Maia is gentler, she won't stand for any of Kathleen's nonsense either.'

As Conn was walking back to the house, his wife intercepted him. 'I heard you say you were going up to Perth. We need some more maids here, you know. I should come with you and select them. I can ride as well as you.'

'You're not coming. I'm going to see the Bishop about annulling our marriage.'

'I don't want to stop being your wife. I can't manage on my own.'

'I keep telling you, you've never been my wife in any way that matters.' He turned away, not wanting to start the arguments all over again.

But she shouted after him, not caring who heard her. 'They said it in church and your father said it too. I *am* your wife and you can't change that.'

As Conn was making preparations for his trip that evening, Bram Deagan came to find him. 'I wonder if I could ride up to Perth with you tomorrow, Mr Largan?'

Conn looked at him in surprise. 'Call me by my name, Bram. We've known each other a long time and I can't seem to face being called 'sir' these days.'

'Conn, then.'

'Have you thought more about my offer of employment?'

Bram hesitated. 'It's a grand offer, but I'm minded to try my luck at trading. I was talking to the captain of the ship that brought us here and we might go in together on a venture or two.'

'Do you have the money for that?'

'I have a little, thanks to Ronan, who gave me his mother's things instead of throwing them away. They might not seem much to you, sir, but I'm sure I can sell them and gain enough money to give me a start, at least.'

'I never realised you hankered after being a shopkeeper.'

'I don't know what I hanker after, and that's the truth, only that I never again want to feel as helpless as I did when Mrs Kathleen dismissed me.'

'Ronan told me she dismissed you for speaking to him about me.'

'Yes. The old master let her have her way and spoiled her till she thought the sun shone when he was there.' He shook his head sadly. 'Strange that all three of us wound up here in Australia, isn't it? Mrs Kathleen must have been desperate to come here, though.' He hesitated, then added, 'She tries to hide it but she gets upset about things. I've seen her when she came back from rides round Shilmara, her eyes red and puffy as if she'd been crying.'

'You're kinder to her than she is to you.'

'You should be kind to those born like her. It's not that she's slow-witted, but she is strange, for all she's a lady and her family trained her how to behave. Very strange.'

'Yes. They were clever and hid from me what she was like. I knew people of my class didn't marry for love, but for a solid financial or social gain, but I never realised . . . But my father must have done. He cared only for the money. Anyway, he's dead now and I'm going up to Perth because I'm seeking an annulment.'

'I hope you get it, but don't leave her on her own afterwards. She has no idea how to cope with the world outside Shilmara. She offended the other ladies on the ship and after Mrs Maguire died, she spent most of the journey on her own, just standing by the rails staring out at sea. I didn't want to feel sorry for her, but how could you not?'

Bram's kindness towards Kathleen made Conn feel guilty about his own longing to get rid of her, and also made the burden of providing for her seem even heavier. He still hadn't worked out how to find her a situation where she could cope. He changed the subject, tired of thinking of his wife and the problems she caused.

'Do you think there's money to be made from bringing things into the country to sell? Western Australia has a very small population.'

'Well, I'll have a good look round in Perth and I'll be better placed to tell you afterwards. But people here still need goods, after all. I'm not expecting to get rich, just to make a decent living. I might have to go on a voyage or two at first, to get the feel of what's available out there.' He waved one hand in a broad gesture.

'I might be tempted to invest a little money in such a venture myself. Would you be interested in having a partner?'

'I might, if you don't try to take over. I'd not want someone telling me what to do.'

'I might offer advice from time to time.'

'And I'd listen to it. But I'd have the final say.'

Conn looked at him, saw the determination in his face and nodded, holding out his hand. They shook, then he said, 'Fine. Come up to Perth with me and we'll maybe both look round once I've attended to my personal business.'

'I'm glad that fellow's gone,' Kathleen announced at breakfast, which she now took in the kitchen because she didn't like sitting alone in the dining room and couldn't persuade Mrs Largan to join her there.

'Who do you mean?' Xanthe asked, wondering if she meant Conn.

'That Deagan fellow. Ronan shouldn't have brought him here. I'd dismissed him, you know.'

'He seems a hard worker. He's been very helpful here.'

'That's not the point. I dismissed him for impudence. For talking about his betters.' Kathleen elevated her nose. 'The lower classes shouldn't do that.'

Xanthe suppressed a sigh of exasperation at this comment. She hadn't at first understood why Kathleen came here so often to chat to her, when she was so scornful about the lower classes. But gradually she began to realise that the poor creature was lonely and lost, still trying to make the same sort of life for herself as she had in Ireland.

'This bread is stale.'

'You can toast it. The toasting fork is there.'

'*Me?*'

'Why not? Do you have anything better to do?'

'You should be making fresh bread every day.' Kathleen sat frowning at the bread, then got up and took the toasting fork, but Xanthe had to show her how to use it.

'I don't have the time to make bread every day,' she said. 'Can't you see how much work there is to do and how few people to do it? You could help me if you liked. I can see time is hanging heavily on your hands.'

'I'm not a servant! Conn should hire more people.'

'There aren't any to hire. People bring maids out here but most of them get married within months. There are ten men for every woman, you see.' She'd said the same thing a couple of times before but it didn't seem to sink in.

Kathleen sat frowning. 'Why are there so many men?'

At least it was a new question. 'Because they bring only male convicts here. That's brought thousands more men here in the past few years but though some women have been brought out – people call them the "bride ships" – there are still far fewer of them.' She wasn't even sure whether her companion had understood this because Kathleen sighed and sat fiddling with her toast. She didn't seem to have much of an appetite.

'I think I'll go for a ride.'

'That'd be nice.'

'I'm a good rider.'

'Yes, everyone says so.'

Kathleen nodded. 'I like horses. I can ride anything.'

'Except Conn's horse. Sean says he won't go to anyone else.'

'Demon comes to me.'

'Well, don't ride him. It wouldn't do you any good to upset Conn, if you want him to help you.'

A bell rang just then and Xanthe wiped her hands on the kitchen towel. 'I have to answer that. It's Mrs Largan's bell.'

She left Kathleen still fiddling with her food and heard her muttering to herself about being a good rider.

11

It was a relief to get away from Galway House. It was usually his refuge from the world, but now Conn's spirits brightened as he rode up to Perth with Bram. There was nothing as pleasant as being out of doors on a sunny winter's day, without the searing heat of the summer sunshine.

'I wasn't guilty,' he said, needing to be sure his old friend understood that.

'I knew you weren't.'

Conn gave a small nod, which was all he could manage, and swallowed hard.

They got to Perth quite late in the day because they'd been careful to rest the horses regularly. After leaving their mounts at a livery stables Conn had used before, they sought lodgings at a house he knew. Today all the widow who owned it could offer them was a very small shared room with two narrow beds and little else.

'She treats you with respect,' Bram remarked.

'Her husband was a convict. He died on a road gang. She's worked hard to build up the lodging house. It's mostly emancipists and ticket-of-leave men who stay here.'

In the morning the two men had breakfast then parted company. Conn set off for the cathedral, intent on finding someone who could tell him how to get an annulment. He arrived at nine-thirty, surely a reasonable hour to find someone, but the early mass had finished a while since and the only person around was a woman sweeping the floor.

'Could you tell me where to find the priest?'

She stared at him incuriously. 'Having his breakfast, if he has any sense.'

'Where does he live?'

She gave him directions and he walked there slowly, not looking forward to this interview.

The priest was an older man, who listened to his story in silence. 'You don't feel – you've been given a sacred charge to look after this poor woman?'

'No, I don't.'

'You've admitted she can't look after herself.'

'I have. And I'll make sure she's cared for afterwards, though she does have an income of her own, which I've not touched and won't, not to mention a brother still living. But I want a family, children to carry on my name.' And not children who might be like their mother. 'Isn't that a reasonable thing to hope for?'

'Most people would say so. We'll have to make an appointment with the Bishop for you. I can't deal with this.'

'How quickly can we do that? I've a farm to run and an invalid mother to look after.'

'I'll send round to his excellency now. My housekeeper will give you a cup of tea while you wait.' He showed Ronan into a small cheerless room and left him there, with a few old newspapers to entertain him.

It was nearly two hours before a reply was brought that the Bishop would see Conn at two o'clock sharp the following afternoon.

He bit back a protest at this delay and thanked the priest for his help. Outside he stood for a moment, wondering what to do with himself for the rest of the day.

In the end, he walked down to the river and strolled along it in the sunshine, not worrying about tomorrow's meeting, not worrying about anything, just for a little while.

Bram spent the day exploring the city centre on foot, though it was a poor sort of city to his mind. He'd accompanied old Mr Largan to Dublin once when his master's manservant was ill and the memory of it had stuck in his mind ever since. Now that was a fine city, with some magnificent buildings. He'd slipped into Trinity College Library and stood marvelling at the sight of so many books, more than a man could read in ten lifetimes, all housed in a building as fine as any palace, he was sure.

To Bram, Perth was an incongruous mixture of architecture: tiny wooden houses, larger brick homes, shops with a floor above and attics, too – and a few imposing public edifices, especially two big churches and Government House with its turrets. There wasn't a proper town hall, though one man told Bram there was going to be one, but there was a fine Church of England Collegiate School, built in an old-fashioned style of red brick laid in patterns. Did the lads who attended such a school know how lucky they were to be offered a good education? Probably not.

And in the bright sunshine, with people bustling about, carts, horses and the occasional carriage passing by, and the river shining just down the slope, Bram realised that he liked this place, or perhaps he liked what it could become. Dublin had the River Liffey, Perth overlooked a wide expanse of water where the Swan River widened, with little boats dotted here and there on it. He hadn't grown up near the sea, but had learned to like and respect it on the voyage here – though only when it was calm. He'd had a few queasy patches when the sea was rough.

The people in Perth were as varied as the buildings. Some were well-fed and affluent, looking as if they owned the world, others were sturdy working folk moving quickly about their business and some – poor things – looked ragged and hungry. He hated to see that, still remembered his mother's tales of the famine years when the potato harvest had failed. Conn's father had made sure his own workforce didn't starve, but he'd not given them anything more than the basic food they needed, and Bram's mother spoke of gathering nettles to make soup. The needs of those not employed by old Mr Largan, even though they lived close by, had been totally ignored.

It was well known that Conn's mother had helped where she could in those terrible times and she was still blessed for that. But even she had been afraid of her husband and had only dared act secretly.

After getting his bearings, Bram looked closely at every shop he could find, studying what they had for sale, slipping inside some of them and listening to customers talking about what they wanted and, more important to him, what they couldn't find. Food supplies would never go amiss, he decided, if he set up a shop, especially the sorts of food you couldn't come by easily here. There were enough people with money to buy not only what they needed to eat but also the luxuries they fancied eating.

He saw ladies fingering dress materials and talking to one another in the accents of the rich, seeming to care nothing for who overheard them and raising their voices to address the shopmen who served them. Did they think the lower classes were all slightly deaf? Still, it was useful to hear their views of life in the Swan River Colony, since you could make more money from rich people than poor.

It was as he was leaving one shop that he saw a woman begging near the opposite corner. She could have been any age from thirty to sixty and she was skeletal and pale, despair showing clearly on her wasted face as one person after another walked past, ignoring her. Even as he decided to give her a coin, he saw her eyes roll up and she crumpled suddenly to the ground.

No one stopped to help her and he couldn't, just could not walk away and leave her. He moved quickly across the sandy street, avoiding a pile of horse dung and waiting for a small cart to pass.

She was still lying there on the edge of the road, hadn't stirred. He knelt beside her and lifted her head from the dirt, cradling it in one arm. To his relief she groaned and her eyes flickered open. She gasped as she saw his face above hers, then began to struggle.

He let go of her immediately, trying to reassure her. 'You fainted, miss. I came to help you.'

She leaned away from him, resting on one elbow, but made no attempt to get up and still looked dizzy.

'Are you hungry?'

She nodded.

'Let me help you up, then I'll buy you something to eat.'

She looked at him suspiciously. 'Why?'

'Because I've been hungry myself a time or two.'

'I won't let you use my body in payment.'

'Did I ask to?'

She sighed and closed her eyes. He thought she'd lost consciousness again, but when she began struggling to stand up, he risked helping her again. Once she was on her feet, she had to lean against him, but she weighed very little and he held her only lightly, so she'd know she could get away.

'Take it easy,' he said gently. 'How long since you ate?'

'A day or two. I've been ill. But I couldn't pay my rent and they threw me out, kept my things in payment.' Tears came into her eyes. 'I have nothing now but the clothes I'm wearing.'

From her accent, she was English, southern, he thought, slow speaking, not like those from London. He studied her. Her clothes were crumpled, as if she'd slept in them, but not ragged.

He couldn't save everyone in the world, he knew that, but every now and then he tried to help someone and this woman had touched something in him. 'I'll buy you some food first, then we'll go and get your things back.'

She studied his face as if trying to understand his motives. 'Why?'

'Because I'm an eejit and I do things like helping people for no payment.'

A smile dawned slowly on her face, then faded quickly. She clutched him as if she was dizzy again.

He spoke more gently again. 'I'm a newcomer here. Where can we find you something to eat and drink? Maybe a glass of milk first, or a piece of bread? You don't want to eat too much at first if you've not been eating properly.'

'There's a little shop down that side street.'

He helped her along, wishing he dare pick her up and carry her, which would have been far quicker. But he doubted she'd want that.

The shop was a mean little place and the milk looked dirty to him, but she took the enamel cup the shopkeeper offered and drank it thirstily.

He bought a piece of broken bread and tucked it in her hand. 'Better wait to eat this to make sure the milk stays down.'

She nodded and wrapped it in a piece of rag, stuffing it into a pocket in her skirt.

'How far to your lodgings?'

'A few streets away.'

'You're in no fit state to go walking around. Tell me where it is, how much you owe them and I'll bring your things to you.'

She gave him a suspicious look and pressed her lips together as if holding the information tightly back.

Annoyed, but trying to understand why she'd be so suspicious, he pulled out his battered pocket watch, a farewell present from his father. 'Hold on to that till I return, then we'll think what to do next.'

She stared at him open-mouthed as he pressed the watch into her hand and clasped her fingers round it. 'I'll look after it carefully. You'll still find me here when you get back, I promise.'

'I never doubted it for a second.' He listened to her instructions, then strode off briskly.

It took him longer than he'd expected to find her lodgings and force her sour-faced ex-landlady to give him her things in return for payment of the rent owing. It was only by threatening to go to the police and accuse her of theft that he got the carpet bag and two bundles back.

The amount owing had been so little that he'd easily had money enough and some to spare because he'd sold a couple of Mrs Maguire's possessions on the ship.

He wondered sometimes if the gentry knew how little made the difference between survival and starvation to poor families. He'd never forget that, he vowed, and he'd always try to help those in trouble. But he'd also try to help himself, now that he'd been given a chance to make something of his life.

When he returned to find the young woman, she was nowhere to be seen. He stood there, bitterly disappointed. He could usually trust his judgement of people.

Then she came out from behind the building and her face lit

up when she saw him standing there with the one bag and two pitiful bundles in one hand.

She blushed as she came towards him. 'I was just – attending to my needs.'

'Check first that everything is here,' he said.

She fumbled through her things and nodded, stroking a crumpled photograph of two elderly people.

'Your parents?'

'Yes. They're dead now. It's all I have of them. How did you get my bundles back?'

'I offered to pay the rent you owed.'

'They're worth more than that.'

'I guessed they must be when she refused, so I threatened to call in the police and accuse your landlady of theft.'

She gave a rusty laugh, which ended with a cough. 'She'd have hated that. I think – no, I'm sure she buys and sells stolen goods, just in a small way.'

'Then why were you staying in such a place?'

'A corner of her cellar was all I could afford.'

'What shall we do with you now?' he wondered, then saw her swaying again. 'Here, give me those bundles back and take my arm.'

'I'm sorry. I'm just – not feeling right yet.' She clutched him tightly.

'I'll take you back to my lodgings and see if they can find you a room.'

She looked down at herself, her lips quivering at the sight of her crumpled, dirty clothes. Her voice was so low he had to bend forward to hear what she said.

'Nowhere respectable will take me in looking like this.'

He grinned. 'They will when they hear my story. I think you're a cousin of mine from England and I turned up just in time to save you. What's your name, by the way?'

'Nancy.'

He waited but she didn't offer a surname so he didn't press the point. 'Nancy Deagan it is, and you're my uncle Niall's youngest daughter. Remember that now. You're Nancy Deagan.'

At the lodging house, he whispered, 'Leave this to me.' He found the landlady and asked her help for his cousin, whom he'd found in great distress.

She looked at him suspiciously and he said bluntly, 'I'm bringing you a decent young woman who needs help, Mrs Greeling, not a streetwalker. I don't want her in my bed – didn't I play with her as a child when we visited them in England? She's my cousin on my father's side, uncle Niall's daughter, and I promised her brother I'd look for her here. I need your help and surely you'll not be turning the poor girl away?'

Conn came back just then, listening to the conversation without betraying any surprise. 'You found her, then, Bram. Poor thing, she looks terrible.'

'You know her sir?' the woman asked, still suspicious.

'I've never met her before, but she's Bram's cousin and I knew he was going to look for her. I can offer her a job as a maid and I'd be grateful if you'd give her shelter till we leave. You know how hard it is to find maids here.'

'Very well, then. Since you vouch for her.'

'She might be grateful for a bath,' Conn added. 'I'll pay extra for that.'

'Very well, sir.'

Bram noticed how embarrassed Nancy looked at this statement, but there was no getting away from it: she was dirty enough to smell bad. 'Do you have clean clothes in your bundle, Nancy?'

'No. They're all dirty now.'

Conn slapped Bram on the back. 'Then we'd better go and buy your cousin some clothes from a second-hand dealer.'

Once they were out of earshot, he turned to Bram. 'You're still a sucker for a creature in distress, I see.'

Bram shrugged. 'She fainted right in front of me and no one tried to help her. I couldn't leave her lying in the street, now could I? I believe she's a decent young woman and if you really meant it about a job, I'm sure she'll accept.'

Conn shook his head, smiling ruefully at Bram. 'We're both of us too soft-hearted.'

'I don't think so.'

'If she proves suitable, this may give Xanthe the opportunity she needs.'

'Opportunity to do what?'

'She wants to leave and go travelling.'

'Can a maid in Australia afford to do that?'

'This maid can. She and her sisters were left some money by their uncle in England. He owned a big grocery shop.'

Bram's expression grew thoughtful. 'One day I'll have money to leave to my family. I'd never have managed that in Ireland, but from what people have said, I shall have a better chance here of making good. I'm going to open a shop.'

'Make some money for me, too, while you're at it. You always were a quick-witted fellow.'

Bram grinned. 'I'll do my best.'

Ronan walked into the kitchen to find Xanthe working on her own. 'I was hoping for a cup of tea.'

She stopped stirring whatever was in the big pan and gestured to the blackened kettle sitting simmering on the side of the hob. 'Push that over the heat. Would you mind making the tea yourself? I'm a bit behind today and I daren't stop stirring this at the moment.'

'Why are you behind?'

'Mrs Kathleen was here.'

'She seems to have attached herself to you.'

'I don't know why. She does nothing but complain and she won't help me at all.'

'She doesn't think it right.' He moved the kettle and fetched the big teapot. 'Her family filled her head with nonsense. You'll have a cup with me?'

'I think everyone would enjoy a cup. Where is Kathleen? Did Sean let her take a horse out?'

'He rode out with her, grumbling all the time. I think Conn told him to do that. She shouldn't go out on her own on these faint tracks. I'd not do it myself till I knew the countryside better.'

Following her instructions, Ronan brewed a pot of tea, then set out cups and saucers. 'Would there be something to eat with it?'

'Are you hungry already? You ate enough breakfast for me and my sister both!'

He grinned. 'I've been mending the front veranda. Some of those floorboards were loose. It's hungry work.'

'Are you a carpenter as well as a gentleman?'

'Sometimes. Like most lads, I enjoyed trying my hand at woodwork. I used to pester the estate carpenter to let me make things and he couldn't bear to see wood wasted, so he taught me properly.'

'Didn't your father mind?'

'My father didn't care what we did as long as we kept out of his way. My mother just cared that we were happy, when we were children at least. Later, what she cared about most was for us all to get married. I never gave her the grandchildren she wanted, nor did my older brother, Hubert, but Patrick did, at least.'

He looked so sad Xanthe laid her hand on his and he turned his over quickly to capture hers. 'You're a kind woman.'

'Am I? Sometimes, perhaps. It's Maia who's the really kind one. She'd do anything for anybody, my sister would.'

'What are you saying about me now?' Maia came into the room. 'Ah, you've just brewed a pot of tea. That's good. Mrs Largan didn't fancy her breakfast but she's a bit thirsty now.' She hesitated, then added, 'She's hardly eating a thing. I'm worried about her.'

'I've scones newly baked. And that jam that we had sent from Perth. It's not good jam, but it was all Conn could find, since most people make their own.'

'That'll be fine.'

Ronan pulled out a chair and sat down. 'I'm not moving till I've had a scone or two. You'd not see a man go hungry, surely, Xanthe?'

He spoke her name so easily and his smile was so warm that

Xanthe saw Maia staring at the two of them and couldn't help flushing as she realised her sister must have seen them holding hands. She'd have to tell her sister later not to read too much into that. She was just comforting a man who was feeling sad about losing his mother . . . that was all.

That morning Francis woke early, his breath catching in his chest in a way that frightened him. He looked at his wife, who was still asleep. He hated the way Livia had to do the menial work. Her beautiful hands were now red and rough. They'd asked around for a girl to help out in the house, but hadn't found one yet.

He slid from the bed and got dressed in the living room, then walked slowly outside. The sun hadn't fully risen yet and the world was bathed in a half-light that seemed to dim the colours. Birds were calling sleepily, one bird crooning nearby.

He walked down to the stables, feeling stronger by the minute, cheered by that. When he started to cough, he tried to hold it back, not wanting to wake anyone. But it wouldn't be held back and suddenly he was fighting for breath and the cough was trying to tear his chest apart.

The world went dim around him and he found himself lying on the ground, with no idea of how he got there. The coughing had eased now, but he needed to rest, was so tired, so very tired. He closed his eyes and let the first rays of the sun warm the clammy skin of his forehead.

Livia heard Francis coughing and sat up in bed as he went on and on. She'd never heard him sound so bad. It was heart-rending to hear him struggling for breath. She slipped out of bed and wrapped a shawl round herself before venturing outside.

She was in time to see him fall slowly to the ground and lie there. As she ran across, she saw him open his eyes, then close them. By the time she reached him, he was dead. There was blood everywhere, great clots of it, so bright in contrast to his pale face.

Leo had come out to join her and knelt beside Francis now, closing his eyes.

'I didn't think he'd die quite yet,' she said, feeling numb and disoriented.

'He died quickly, at least,' he said.

'Oh, Leo, what am I going to do without him?'

He shook his head. 'I can look after his horses.'

'But I can't look after a farm and I need to make money.'

'We'll ask Reece. He'll know what to do.'

She sat a moment or two longer, then bent to kiss her husband's forehead and stood up. 'Could you carry him to the veranda? I'll bring out a blanket for him to lie on. Then could you go and tell Reece what's happened, ask him to come and help me?'

Leo nodded but didn't move.

'You should have a drink of hot, sweet tea, Mrs Southerham. It'll help. I'll make it for you.'

Nothing would help, she thought wearily. She'd told Francis she'd open a school when he was gone, and it had comforted him, but she didn't feel capable of that.

When she'd covered Francis she found that Leo had made a pot of tea and sat down to drink a cup, just as he'd suggested. It gave her something to do, at least.

Who would she talk to in the evenings now? she thought suddenly. And how long would Francis's money last?

What was she going to do with her life? As a clergyman's daughter she could call herself a lady – but she couldn't afford to live as a lady. She was nearly forty, wasn't pretty, so had never attracted men's attention until Francis, dear Francis, so doubted she'd remarry. That was the easy way out for widows without children, to marry again. Only she wasn't practical at housework so what use would she be in this colony?

Then Reece appeared, followed by Leo, and the sad round of tasks began.

Leo washed the body for her. She shrank from that.

'Shall we bury him on this farm or on the hill next to Kevin?' Reece asked. 'It's a pretty spot up there for a grave.'

'Wherever you think best.' She didn't seem able to make a decision herself today.

'Come and spend the night with us.'

'I couldn't leave him alone here.'

'Leo will be here.'

'Weren't we lucky to find Leo? I don't know what I'd do without him.'

'He was lucky to find you. Pack what you need for the night. I'll ride over to tell Conn. Some of them will want to attend the burial, I'm sure.'

She did as he asked and nearly fell into Cassandra's arms when they got to Reece's farm, able at last to weep and accept comfort.

The next morning Conn decided to go out with Bram to inspect the Perth shops and work out what sort of goods it might be profitable to bring into the country. First they checked on Nancy, however.

She was a different person this morning, now that she was clean and wearing decent clothes. Her hair was straight, a soft brown in colour, shining clean now and tied back with a ribbon. Her eyes were grey – honest eyes, Bram thought. She looked first at him. 'I don't know how to thank you for this. Once I find work again . . .'

'What was your work?'

She flushed. 'I was working as a maid. Only my employer was – he . . .' Her voice trailed away and she flushed in embarrassment. 'When I wouldn't let him into my bed, he got his wife to dismiss me. I didn't have references or anywhere to stay, and though I tried to find work, ladies were suspicious of me – and I refused to work for a man on his own. I think my employer had told people I was a thief, because usually it's easy for maids to get other jobs. I fell ill and then . . . I had to sell some of my things.'

After studying her, Conn asked, 'Would you work for me and my mother?'

'Can I meet her first?'

'We live a full day's ride to the south in the country.'

As she hesitated, Bram said softly, 'You can trust Conn Largan with your life, and you'll like his mother, I promise you. I know it's hard to trust two strangers, but the landlady knows Mr Largan and his mother, so you can ask her about them, can't you?'

Her face cleared and she nodded. 'Yes. Thank you, sir. I'd like to work for you and I promise you won't regret hiring me.'

'Come and have breakfast, then,' Bram said.

She looked at him in shock. 'It wouldn't be proper for me to eat with you.'

'You're supposed to be my cousin, so I can't leave you to eat in the kitchen on your own, now can I?'

She ate very little and when they pressed her, said she couldn't fit any more food in, so Conn went to ask the landlady's advice about feeding up his new maid and she promised to keep an eye on the young woman while they were out.

'How will we get her back to Galway House?' Bram asked later as they left their lodgings to go exploring the city.

'She'll have to ride pillion.'

'I doubt she's strong enough for a day's riding, and it's asking a lot of the horses.'

Conn frowned. 'I think she'll have to try. It's the only way. We can take it in turns to have her ride behind us. I'm not being heartless, but I need to get back to my mother as quickly as possible. I don't like leaving her alone with Kathleen.'

The two men tramped the streets, listening to people and going in and out of shops. At one stage they found a small horse sale taking place on a bit of vacant land, so of course Conn had to stop and inspect the animals being offered. He frowned at most of them. 'Poor devils have been used hard,' he muttered to Bram.

But in one corner he found a couple of mares which he felt had promise. 'These look like they'll grow up to be strong workers.'

'They'll not be pretty looking.'

'That doesn't matter. I don't breed for show.'

Bram grinned. He might try to help people in distress, but Conn couldn't pass a good horse without stopping and if he said these mares had promise, then Bram was sure they were worth looking at. He'd have said they were only average himself, but he'd worked in the stables of landed gentry and their horses were for show and riding, so were a different type of animal. 'How will you be getting them back to the farm?'

Conn stood frowning for a minute or two, then slapped one hand against the palm of the other. 'I'll buy a small cart and tie these two behind it. The horse you're riding will pull it, and your *cousin* can ride in the cart. Afterwards, you can use the cart in your new business – we could make it my first investment.'

'Done. But we'll choose the cart carefully. I'll want it to be sturdy, though of course I can refurbish it myself.'

Conn nodded and looked at the sky. 'It doesn't look like rain, so if we have to camp rough overnight, so be it. We need a few more blankets at Galway House anyway so I'll buy some.

'After I've seen the Bishop we'll spend the rest of the day getting some extra provisions. Might as well take advantage of being here to choose them for ourselves rather than ordering them through our local shop. You get better quality that way.'

Just before two o'clock Conn presented himself at the Archbishop's Palace, a splendid building by Perth standards. He'd changed into his clean shirt and spruced himself up but felt apprehensive. He hated facing strangers as an ex-convict.

He was kept waiting for fifteen minutes, then shown in by the secretary, a man of middle years and quiet appearance.

After the formalities had been got through, the Bishop said, 'I believe you're an ex-convict, Mr Largan.'

'Yes. But I was innocent and I'm prepared to swear that on the Bible.'

The Bishop raised his eyebrows. 'The law doesn't think so.'

Conn shrugged. 'I can only tell the truth, your grace.'

'Well, whether you're innocent or not, you're still one of my flock and entitled to my help if you need it. My secretary says it's about an annulment. Kindly tell me the details.'

When Conn had finished the Bishop sat lost in thought for a few moments then sighed. 'It's a lengthy business, an annulment, unless you have useful connections in the church.'

'I don't. Not now, anyway.'

'And your wife? I gather she's not in agreement about this.'

'No. She's a strange woman, so rigid she can't cope with changes in her life. She knows she needs someone to look after her and now that all the others who might have helped her are dead or far away, she insists she's staying with me.'

'It would look better if she were not living with you.'

'I know. I intend to seek somewhere for her to live in Perth.'

'Let us know when she's settled and I'll see that someone calls on her and welcomes her to our flock.'

Conn walked out feeling better than he'd expected to. The Bishop hadn't been exactly encouraging, but he hadn't been discouraging either. Unfortunately, it was going to take a long time to get his annulment – if he got it. Nothing was certain. He couldn't ask Maia to wait for years for him. It wouldn't be fair.

He went back to the lodging house and found Bram waiting for him, sitting chatting to Nancy.

Bram waved to him. 'I've found us a small cart. The horses are safe in the livery stables, waiting for you and I've arranged for us to leave at first light.'

'Thank you. You always were efficient.' He smiled at Nancy. 'You're looking much better today.'

She nodded. 'I was healthy till I – couldn't earn my living and got soaked to the skin once too often.'

'That's good. Now, we'd better get to work, Bram. Since we've only a few hours of the day left to buy things for my mother and for Galway House, we'd better make a start. Tomorrow's going to be a long, hard day's travel.'

12

Maia happened to look out of the window as a cart and a man on horseback leading two young horses turned into the drive of Galway House. She'd recognise Conn anywhere. 'They're here!' she called.

She would normally have rushed to the door to greet them, but she met Kathleen in the corridor, so held back to let her go first.

'Get about your work!' Kathleen snapped. 'It's not for such as you to greet your master.'

'I need to tell him about Francis.'

'It's for me to do that. I'm his wife.'

Before anyone could stop her, she'd walked outside and said bluntly, 'Your friend Francis Southerham died yesterday. The funeral is tomorrow.'

Conn stared at her, thinking once again how oddly she behaved once she was away from the life she'd been trained in from birth. Then what she'd said sank in. Francis was dead!

Maia had come to the door. 'Leo rode over to tell us yesterday afternoon. We're all feeling sad and worried about Livia.'

Kathleen made an angry noise and shoved Maia backwards so forcefully that she stumbled and fell. 'I told you to get on with your work. You're a servant. You shouldn't join your betters like this.'

Conn pushed his wife aside and helped Maia get up. 'Are you all right?'

'Yes . . . sir.'

'Maia! Could you help me, please?' Mrs Largan had intervened several times to stop Kathleen picking on the maid. This time she was too late to prevent Conn betraying his feelings for Maia.

There was dead silence for a moment or two, then Kathleen said coldly, 'I will not live in the same house as your whore. She must leave.'

'She isn't my whore.'

'She is! I can tell how you feel for her. But you're married to me, and I'm *not* going to let you get rid of me.'

One hand pressed against her mouth, Maia ran to take refuge in her bedroom. After a quick glance at her mistress, Xanthe followed.

Mrs Largan went into the kitchen and sat down, pressing one hand against her chest, breathing shallowly and looking upset.

Conn came to join her, followed by his glowering wife. 'Are you all right, mother?'

'I shall be in a minute or two.'

Ignoring Kathleen completely, he beckoned to Nancy to join them. 'I've brought you a new maid, mother. This is Nancy. Bram found her in trouble in Perth. She'd lost her place after being ill, but she's getting better now and—'

'Can you find no one better than *her*?' Kathleen demanded. 'Anyone can see she's still ill and look at her clothes! They're all crumpled and worn. She's probably diseased if you found her on the street. Papa Largan said we should always choose country girls for maids and get them young.'

Conn rounded on her. '*Will you be quiet? Can you do nothing but cause trouble?*'

She picked up the nearest object, a cup, and hurled it and its contents at him, then ran outside, sobbing.

'I'll – um, wait in the hall.' Nancy made for the door and stood in the corridor.

Conn brushed the drops of tea from his shirt and rubbed his forehead which had started aching again. Then he took a deep breath and turned to his mother. 'I've got to find Kathleen somewhere else to live. This can't go on. Will you check if Maia is all right? I'd better not—'

'Her sister is with her. Give them a few minutes. Oh, Conn darling, you betray yourself every time you look at Maia. No wife would want to stay in the same house as the woman you love.'

'I can't help it.'

'Since you aren't free to marry her, it's not fair to Maia, either.'

'When was love ever fair?' Or life, he thought sadly.

'Nonetheless.' His mother squeezed his hand once. 'You should go to Francis's burial tomorrow, and take Maia and Xanthe with you. They'll want to say goodbye properly. The new girl – Nancy, did you say she was called? – can help me.'

'Kathleen's good at holding grudges. I doubt she'll let go of this one. I'm worried about Maia's safety.'

'I can't manage without her at the moment.' She looked at him, biting her lower lip, then confessed, 'I've been feeling very tired lately. I doubt I'll last much longer.'

He stared at her in dismay and dropped into the chair next to her, taking her hand. 'Are you feeling that bad?'

She shrugged. 'Yes. I get short of breath and very tired. And I've been in pain for such a long time. You shouldn't grieve for me, darling boy. I'm so glad I came to Australia. I've had some wonderful times with you here.'

Conn pulled her close, realising how much weight she'd lost. Her body felt frail and skeletal almost. Whey hadn't he noticed that before? He didn't want to believe what she was telling him, but she wasn't prone to exaggerating. *Please God, let her be spared for a while yet*, he prayed.

What would he do without her to keep him company, to lift his spirits and console him when people treated him like a criminal?

The kitchen door banged open and Kathleen came rushing out of the house, sobbing loudly. She headed for the stables, ignoring the three men.

'She always goes to the horses when she's upset,' Sean said. 'She's a poor lost soul, that one. I said at the time no good would come from forcing him to marry her. Wicked, it was, and not fair to her, either.'

Ronan started to unload the cart. After peering into the kitchen and seeing Conn and his mother in earnest discussion – on an unhappy topic, if his friend's expression was anything to go by – he left the boxes of goods on the back veranda until it was safe to interrupt and went to stand with Bram and Sean.

The three men studied the mares with an expert eye as they explored the small pen they'd been put into.

'He bought some new ones again,' Sean said with a smile. 'I thought he would. He usually does when he goes up to Perth, whether he plans to or not.'

'He says they show promise.' Bram moved closer to the fence.

Sean sucked on a gap in his teeth and went as far as to say, 'Could be he's right. I'll be keeping them here in the small enclosure till they've settled down. They're tired after the journey but they don't look too bad, considering.'

A few minutes later Conn came out to join them, looking sad, but didn't say what had upset him. 'What do you think of the new stock, then, Sean?'

'Could be all right once they've been fed and rested.' He hesitated then added, 'You look tired too. Did your errand go well?'

'As well as could be expected. It'll take time, years probably, given the distance.'

'Everything takes a long time here.' Sean's hand rested briefly on his master's shoulder then he went off with the horses.

'Who's the woman you brought back?' Ronan asked.

'A replacement for Xanthe. She fainted on the street and Bram went to her help. Doesn't he always?'

Conn and Ronan exchanged smiles. Bram shrugged.

'You can't leave Maia here on her own again, not with Kathleen on the rampage,' Ronan said. 'She's . . . a bit chancy when her temper's up, lashes out. She's always hitting poor Orla. You'll have to make better arrangements.'

'I know. But they're burying Francis tomorrow. Both Maia and Xanthe will want to attend that, for Livia's sake. They knew her back in Lancashire. I'll have to wait till afterwards to work something out for Kathleen.'

Xanthe and Maia returned to their mistress in the kitchen once Conn had left it, taking Nancy with them. She was looking so white and tired, Mrs Largan suggested Xanthe make up a bed for her, find her some food and let her lie down.

'I'm sorry, Mrs Largan,' Nancy said. 'I'll soon get better, then I'll earn my way, I promise.'

'It's a poor household that can't help someone in trouble. You're very welcome, my dear, and I hope you'll be happy with us.'

Xanthe took the new maid to a small room at the far end of their wing, guessing that if she let her sleep in Kathleen's wing, the latter would try to bully her. She explained the family situation in broad terms.

'And Bram? How does he fit in?'

'I'm not sure he does. He came with Ronan, but I don't think he wants to stay here.'

'He was talking about shops and trading.' Nancy stopped inside the door, setting her bundles on the floor. 'I can't believe I've got a room to myself.'

'It's not much bigger than a cupboard but we'll try to make you comfortable. Let me make up the bed then I'll bring you some food. The necessary is across the yard.' She showed Nancy where to go and hurried off for sheets and blankets. But there were no spare blankets left except for one ragged old one.

When she went to ask Conn if she could send a stable lad down to the local shop for some of the rough blankets they sold there, she could see no sign of him and asked Bram where he'd gone.

'He's gone to find Kathleen. Is it urgent?'

'We've no blankets for Nancy. I need to buy some more at the shop.'

'We bought some in Perth. They're in that bundle there.'

'Oh, good! How clever of him to remember.'

'We used some of them to overnight on the road, but it was

dry so they didn't get dirty. There are quite a few things to unpack. Shall I help you?'

'I'll do it afterwards. I need to get Nancy some food then make up a bed for her. She looks exhausted.'

When she went back to the tiny bedroom with some bread, cheese and a piece of cake, she found the new maid sitting on the edge of the straw mattress, looking greasy white with exhaustion. 'Here. Eat something before you sleep. You can leave the rest of the food under this cloth and if you wake in the night you can nibble a bit more.'

Tears filled Nancy's eyes. 'You're all so kind.'

'You won't find Mrs Kathleen kind. Just remember that although she's married to the master, she's not in charge here, so don't let her bully you. She doesn't even live here normally. You'll be working for Mrs Largan.'

She waited to see Nancy force a few mouthfuls down, then suggested, 'Shall I help you unpack your things and find a nightdress?'

Tears of shame filled Nancy's eyes. 'My clothes are all filthy except for these I'm wearing, which Mr Largan and Bram bought for me. I was living on the streets when I lost my job.'

'You poor thing! I'll lend you a nightdress, then, and bring some water to have a quick wash in. Though my nightdress will be too long for you. You only come up to my shoulder.'

'Thank you.'

When she'd left Nancy to sleep, Xanthe went back to the kitchen and found the men waiting for food. Kathleen was sitting on her own in the far corner, her eyes reddened, staring stonily out of the window. There was no sign of Mrs Largan and Maia. 'Perhaps Orla could help me get the food ready?'

'Orla is my maid, not a housemaid.'

When she looked up, Xanthe could see that Kathleen's face was flushed from weeping and that anger was still burning in her eyes. 'You don't need Orla at the moment.'

'She's *my* maid, my personal maid, not a housemaid.'

Conn opened his mouth and Xanthe spoke quickly to

forestall him. She didn't intend to let his wife spoil herself when the rest of them were working all the hours they were awake. 'Then you'll have your clothes looked after but must do without food.'

'What do you mean?'

'There are a lot of people to feed and I can't do it all. Unless we help one another here, we don't eat. You don't need your maid all the time, and if you had anything about you, you'd help us too.'

There was a pregnant silence then Conn said, 'Kathleen, she's right. There is far too much work for one person. Please let Orla help Xanthe whenever possible, so that we can all be fed.'

Kathleen folded her arms and said nothing. He took that to mean yes and went to bring Orla in from Kathleen's bedroom.

His damned wife sat scowling as the conversation resumed and made no attempt to join in. And with her there, the conversation didn't flow easily. They were all too aware of her glowering presence at the end of the table.

After the meal people scattered and Kathleen beckoned to Orla to follow her out.

When the maid came back, wanting some hot water for her mistress, Conn saw a red mark on her cheek.

'Did my wife hit you again?'

Orla looked at him pleadingly. 'It doesn't matter, sir, really it doesn't.'

'It does to me.' The vicious whippings and beatings he'd seen as a convict had sickened him to his soul and he'd vowed never to let that sort of thing happen in his own house or anywhere he could prevent it, for that matter. He strode down the corridor to his wife's bedroom and entered without knocking.

She jumped to her feet, snatching up the nearest object, a silver-backed hairbrush, as if to defend herself. 'What are you doing here? Get out at once!'

'You don't have to worry. I've no desire to touch you. I've come to tell you that if you hit Orla again, I'll take her away from you and let her work as a general maid, then you'll have to take care of your own clothes.'

'You can't do that!'

'As long as I'm your husband, the law says I can do anything I like.'

Tears filled her eyes. 'You're a terrible man. A criminal. I wish I'd never come here.'

'So do I. But you'll soon be moving out again. I intend to find you a house or lodgings in Perth.'

She looked at him in terror. 'No! I won't go and live on my own in a strange town. I won't!'

'You'll have to when our marriage ends. I've made a start on getting it annulled, but it'll probably take years to finalise it. In the meantime, remember . . . if you want to keep your maid, don't hit Orla again. And she's to help Xanthe and Nancy for a couple of hours every day.'

He noticed that Kathleen kept the hairbrush in her raised hand as long as he was in the room and once he was outside, he heard her run across and slam the door shut.

She was in no danger from him. The mere sight of her made him feel sick . . . and just as trapped as he'd felt in convict irons.

Conn decided to take Kathleen with him to the burial, to prevent her from causing trouble while he was absent. He explained that it would mean over an hour's ride each way and reminded her that it was a gentleman friend of the family who had died.

She brightened up at the thought of that and indeed, gave no trouble on the way there, riding beside him or one of the other gentlemen, chatting about the horses and the scenery around them.

That was how his father and her parents had trapped him. She was at her best on horseback.

They arrived at Lynch's Farm at about eleven o'clock and after introductions had been made, Leo helped them tend to the horses.

For once Kathleen was quiet, because she was used to funerals, knew how to behave at one, how to parrot condolences about 'a sad loss' and 'will be greatly missed' without meaning a word. When she was not going through the formalities, she watched

Maia, stiffening and glaring if the other woman went anywhere near Conn.

They walked up the hill, with Reece and Leo again carrying the coffin and lowering it gently into the grave.

Conn noticed that Kathleen spent the short time during the reading of prayers gazing at the view and watching some kangaroos which were sitting quietly nearby. But she came dutifully forward to toss a handful of earth into the grave when the others did.

Afterwards they enjoyed a simple stew with fresh bread, which Cassandra had prepared, then sat talking.

'Do you know what you're going to do now?' Conn asked Livia.

She shook her head. 'It happened so suddenly I wasn't really prepared. I told Francis I'd open a school, but I'm not eager to do that. And I couldn't anyway, unless I can sell the horses and the farm, because I have very little money left.'

'Do you want to go and live in Perth?'

'No. I'd rather stay here, near his grave, near the only friends I have in the colony.'

Conn was shocked to realise her predicament but as he thought about it, he got an idea. From then on he took little part in the conversation, sitting thinking furiously. After a while, he excused himself on the pretext of checking the horses.

Ronan joined him. 'Something wrong?'

'No. Well, not wrong, but I've been wondering if Livia would like a paying lodger, at least in the short term.'

'Kathleen?'

'Yes. Do you think she'd behave herself here?'

'If she was allowed to ride. And there's always Leo to keep an eye on things. He'd not let her hurt anyone physically.'

'Is it too soon to suggest it to Livia, do you think?'

'Do you have much choice? She sounds very worried about how she's going to manage.'

So when they rejoined the others, Conn asked Livia if he could speak to her and they walked over to a rough bench Reece had built to take advantage of the splendid view.

'I've a suggestion to put to you,' he said and explained about Kathleen.

'You mean – you'd pay me to have her staying here?'

'Yes. And Orla with her. I think you'd welcome a maid's help.'

'I'd be interested if I had room, but the house isn't big enough. There's only one bedroom, and let alone I don't want to share that, it'd not fit three of us. Francis bought this place for the view and the cleared meadows where he could graze horses, not because of the house. He wasn't very practical.'

'Hmm.' He looked at the tiny wooden house Reece and Cassandra lived in and noted how they'd added a new bedroom. 'Perhaps Ronan could help me build on another room for Kathleen and a lean-to of some sort for Orla. He's good with wood. And I'm sure my mother would let me bring some furniture across for Kathleen. How would you feel about it then? Please be honest with me. I don't want to force anything on you.'

Livia gave a shaky laugh. 'I don't need to think about it. I'd willingly have her. I don't want to move out but I'm desperately short of money. Francis wasn't very wise with it, you see.'

'Kathleen's not easy to deal with, but she loves horses and if you let her ride yours, she'll treat them well, I promise you.'

'Francis wasn't easy to deal with, nor was my father. I'm good at living with difficult people.'

He closed his eyes in relief. 'I'll tell her then.'

She pulled him back. 'No. Let me invite her to stay with me, as one lady to another. From what you tell me, that'd be more acceptable to her than being told what to do by you. And while I'm talking to her, you could ask Reece's help in building an extra room.'

Conn escorted her back to join the others in relief, unable to believe that this matter could be solved so simply. After a short time Livia asked Kathleen to come and check that the horses were all right.

Kathleen came back from their stroll and smirked at Conn. 'I've found somewhere to live myself, somewhere away from the sight of you and that Maia whore.'

She ignored Cassandra's gasp of outrage and went on, 'I can't wait to move out and live with someone of my own kind, a *lady*. Livia is going to let me ride Francis's horse. Poor thing, it needs exercise. And she likes riding too. She's going to read to me, as well. Papa Largan used to do that. I like hearing stories.'

Livia muttered to Conn, 'I said I'd let her ride it if Leo thought her a good enough rider. Does she always see things as she wants them to be?'

'Yes, I'm afraid so. But if she gives you too much trouble, you must tell me straight away and I'll find somewhere else for her to live.'

Livia shook her head. 'I'll manage. I must. It's the best solution to my problems, just for the present.' She flushed. 'How much are you willing to pay?'

He named a sum which made her sigh with relief.

'I want you to start building my new room tomorrow,' Kathleen said as they were getting ready to leave.

'We need to buy some wood first,' Conn said.

'I've got enough already sawn, I think,' Reece said.

'There, you see! You can start tomorrow. I want to come here as soon as possible. I'll feel *safer* here, living with another *lady*.' Kathleen went to mount her horse, with Leo's help, leaving them to discuss the practicalities.

'I'll pay you for the wood,' Conn said.

'All right. Find out how much it'd cost to buy some from a timber mill and knock a bit off the price, because mine isn't professionally milled. I think Kevin used to saw up wood to keep himself occupied. And at one time he thought his nephew would be coming out here and he'd need a bigger house, but that didn't happen.'

'Done.' Conn held out his hand and the two men shook to seal the bargain. 'And look, will you and Cassandra keep an eye on Livia and Kathleen? Let me know if things aren't going well.'

'Of course. I hadn't realised Livia was so short of money. Francis never discussed his finances.'

'She sounds to be desperate.'

'I wonder if she'd like to rent some of her land to me.'

'Thinking of expanding?'

'Now that Cassandra has some of her inheritance, we can try more things. We want to make cheeses. There's a rocky outcrop behind here with a sort of cave. I think we can deepen it and make somewhere cool to store the cheese as it ripens. Did you know you can make cheese from goat's milk? They'd be easier to rear here than cows, don't you think?'

'I miss cheese. Proper cheese, hard and well-ripened.'

'Exactly.'

'Bram and I are going into business together, opening a shop in Perth. By the time you have cheese ready to sell, that should be open and you could sell it there.'

'Sometimes things fall nicely into place,' Reece said with a satisfied smile.

On the way home Kathleen prattled about her coming move, insisting they had to start building the very next day.

'I'll have to find a carpenter first,' Conn said. 'And there aren't any near here that I know of.' He said that several times, but she wasn't listening.

'I don't mind helping you,' Ronan said. 'I'm sure we can put together something adequate, with Reece's help.'

'Are you sure?'

'Of course I am.'

'Then we'll go and camp out there, get the thing done as quickly as possible.'

'I'll help you too, if you like,' Bram said. 'I've not built a house before but I'm good with my hands. After that I must go up to Perth and wait for Dougal to return.'

Conn felt as if a burden had been lifted from his shoulders. He couldn't believe how well things were going. It was a long time since he'd felt even the slightest bit optimistic, but now there was quite a lot to be happy about.

He'd provided for Kathleen and would be getting her away from his mother and Maia. And one day, if he was patient, he might even be able to have what he wanted most, the woman he loved as his wife.

For two long weeks, Kathleen fussed about her coming move, making her maid's life a misery. Conn and Ronan were absent quite a lot of that time, building the room, so the other women had to cope with Kathleen and her moods as best they could.

Strangely it was Maia who could handle her best. She showed Kathleen how to make cakes and let her help as if she was a child, putting up with her occasional barbed remarks by ignoring them completely.

At Westview Conn felt guilty about how much he enjoyed being away from his wife. He worked hard, learning a lot about building the simple wooden houses they used in the colony, and admitted ruefully that he wasn't as good with wood as Ronan and Reece. He contented himself with fetching and carrying, helping where he could and following their orders. Every two or three days he rode back to Galway House to report progress and check that his mother and Maia were all right.

It was a great relief to everyone when the new room was finished. Kathleen and Orla got into the cart and he drove them across to Westview.

His wife didn't look back, but Conn saw Orla gaze over her shoulder a few times until they were out of sight. She looked wistful and unhappy, and had confessed to him the previous night that she'd rather have stayed at Galway House.

That wasn't possible, not if they were to be freed from the burden of Kathleen's presence and spiteful remarks. But he promised to raise her wages and keep the money safe for her, which cheered her up greatly.

'If I save enough, I can go home, can't I?' she said.

'If you give two years' service to my wife, I'll pay your fare home,' he offered impulsively. Her face lit up.

'Oh, sir! Oh, I'll do anything to go home, sir.'

13

A month later Xanthe decided it was time to look to her own future. She waited till she and her sister were in bed to speak. 'Nancy has worked out well, hasn't she?'

'Yes, she's a good worker and very efficient, too. We've caught up with a lot of the jobs round the place, things we had to leave before.'

'Yes, we have. So I think . . . I can leave now.'

There was silence and she heard Maia try to stifle a sob, but didn't let herself be softened by this. She'd known it'd be hard to move away from her sister, had discussed it with Cassandra, who would still be there if Maia needed help.

She'd miss Maia desperately, because they'd never been separated before, but she knew she had to strike out for a life of her own before it was too late. She was twenty-seven now, past looking for a husband but wanting a more interesting life than housework on a remote farm in Australia.

'I'd have come with you if Mrs Largan didn't need me.'

'She does need you, very much, because she's failing rapidly.'

'She's so brave about it. I admire her in many ways.'

'Afterwards, Conn will need you too. Sometimes I see him looking at his mother and there's such pain in his eyes. That poor man has had a lot to bear. And he's not heard a thing from the Bishop, has he?'

'He didn't expect to.'

'Has he talked to you, made any promises about what may happen if he gets his annulment?'

'No. He told me nothing is certain. He seems afraid even to hope.'

'You should find other employment . . . after Mrs Largan doesn't need you any more.'

'I don't know what I'll do – what he'll want – then.'

'You'll not give yourself to him out of marriage?'

There was another silence, then Maia said quietly, 'I can't promise you that. If he needs me . . .'

'Maia, no! You'd be the one to suffer if anything came of such a relationship. Think how it was in Outham when a girl was expecting a child out of wedlock.'

'It's different for me. I'd have enough money to look after myself – and a child. You're spending your inheritance on what you want. I shall do the same. Now, I'm tired and want to sleep. There's no use going over the same ground again and again. You've made your decision, you're determined to leave and nothing I say will change it.'

She turned her back to her sister and refused to say anything else.

It was a long time before Xanthe got to sleep, though. She was excited about her future but she was apprehensive and sad too.

The next day Xanthe went to find Conn, who was outside schooling one of the young horses. 'He's coming on nicely,' she said, having learned a lot about horses since she came to Galway House. 'When you've a moment, I'd like to speak to you.'

He looked at her as if he guessed what she was going to say. 'Now would be fine with me. Sean, will you take over, please?'

The old man came forward and Conn walked away. 'Shall we sit down?' He went to a bench that was set in an area of the garden he'd hoped his mother would enjoy when the bushes and cuttings grew bigger and waited till Xanthe had sat down.

'I think it's time for me to leave,' she began.

'You haven't changed your mind about staying in Australia? Maybe finding a more interesting job in Perth?'

'No. I find myself longing for soft rain and a greener country.'

'Shall you settle near Pandora?'

'I'm not sure.' She gave him a rueful smile. 'I'm not sure about anything except that I don't want to spend the rest of my life in the Swan River Colony.'

His voice grew sharper. 'And Maia?'

'Your mother needs her.'

He picked up a twig with a few dry gum leaves still attached and began shredding one absent-mindedly. 'My mother won't need her for much longer, I'm afraid.'

'I know. She's a very brave woman. I shall always think of her kindly.' Xanthe hesitated but couldn't leave without saying it. 'What about Maia . . . afterwards?'

'I don't know.'

'You'll . . . treat her with respect?'

'I love her. You know that I'd never willingly hurt her.'

'You should send her away once she's not needed here. Don't spoil her life.'

He looked at her with eyes filled with sorrow. 'That'll be a decision she and I will make later. I can't even think about it now, not with my mother failing.'

Xanthe let a few moments pass before she went on. 'At least your wife isn't here any longer.'

'Livia is working miracles at keeping her happy.'

'Your wife should have been brought up very simply, with horses to ride and the same tasks to do every day.'

'Yes. Fortunately, she's convinced herself that the present arrangement had nothing to do with me, but was arranged by herself and Livia. Though how long this will last, I don't know. Anyway, when do you wish to leave?'

'Quite soon, if that's all right with you. I read in the newspaper that the mail boat will be calling at Albany in a couple of weeks.'

'What if there's no cabin to be had?'

'Then I can go steerage. But I've already written to the shipping agent in Albany and asked for passage.'

'You seem to have thought of everything.'

'Yes. Ronan went to the highway for me and stopped the mail cart to book me a place on the next one going down to Albany and to give them my letter. I have to leave in two days' time.'

'So soon? Have you told Maia?'

'Not the details, no. I didn't want her weeping for my last two days.' She bent her head and said gruffly, 'I'm not doing this lightly, Conn. It'll hurt me too to be parted from her. But I'm hoping to see her again and we'll write. I just – can't settle in a place like this. It's a refuge for you, but a prison for me.'

Xanthe left early in the morning two days later. She got up very early and Maia got up with her, tears running down her cheeks the whole time they were making the final preparations.

Neither of them ate much. Neither of them said much. It had all been said during the long hours of a wakeful night.

'Are you sure you have to go?' Maia sobbed as the moment of parting came.

'We've been over and over this.'

'I can't believe I'll never see you again.'

Xanthe hugged her close, finding the strength somehow to speak calmly. 'That's not true. Of course we'll meet again, and we'll write often.'

'That's not the same. Let me come with you to wait for the mail cart.'

'No. It's best to get our farewells over in private.'

Conn came and put his arm round the sobbing Maia, while Ronan escorted a white-faced Xanthe out to the cart.

She was uncharacteristically quiet and he knew she was feeling desperately sad.

'Are you sure you're doing the right thing?' he asked gently.

'Is anyone ever sure of the future? I only know I can't live my life here.' She stared at her trunk and bag, then jumped down and began pacing to and fro by the road.

Ronan tried to think of something to say but only came up with, 'You're lucky to get a fine day to travel.'

'I'd not have cared if it rained. My only regret is leaving Maia behind. It's been very frustrating living in such an isolated place.'

'Conn seems to like it.'

'Conn is hiding away at Galway House.' She sighed. 'Who do you think made him seem guilty?'

'His father must have had a hand in that.'

She gaped at him. 'Surely not?'

'I've thought about it a lot. Conn was talking about getting an annulment. That'd have meant his father giving back the large dowry Kathleen's parents paid to get her married.'

'Are you sure?'

'I doubt we can ever be sure now because he's taken his secret to the grave. But why else would Susannah Largan have left her husband and come all this way to be with her son? Nothing else makes sense about the whole incident.'

'Does Conn suspect it?'

'Yes.'

'Poor man. He's been treated even more badly than I realised. But even so, I worry about leaving my sister with him.'

He shrugged. 'They'll make their choices. Don't we all?'

'How much longer are you staying in Australia?'

'Two or three months, I suppose. With my mother gone, I'm drifting a bit.' He grinned suddenly. 'I'll enjoy myself less with you gone.'

She didn't pretend to misunderstand. 'I've enjoyed your teasing. I always did wish we had a brother or two.'

'It's not brotherly I'm feeling towards you, Xanthe Blake.'

He caught her gaze and saw her eyes widen. 'Will you let me kiss you again? A farewell kiss.'

Mutely she raised her face towards him and he gathered her in his arms and kissed her till the world spun around. Then he realised she was pushing against his chest and he let her go.

'There's a vehicle approaching,' she said, reaching up to make sure her small, neat bonnet was straight.

The vehicle proved to be what people called the mail van, but was actually a spring cart, complete with driver and guard. It was drawn by sturdy horses and carried only two or three passengers per trip at a cost of four pounds.

The guard helped load Xanthe's luggage, then Ronan stood

back and watched the cart leave, not moving till it was out of sight.

He was going to miss her greatly. She interested him more than any other woman he'd ever met. She hadn't been raised to be a gentleman's wife and he knew she'd feel uncomfortable and be treated with condescension if he did the unthinkable and married her. It was only now as he stood alone by the muddy track listening to the last faint sounds of horses' hooves, cart wheels and harness rattling that he acknowledged to himself that he'd been tempted, very tempted to see if he could win her hand.

He laughed, but it wasn't a mirthful laugh, rather mockery at himself. He talked as if he only had to crook his finger and she'd fall into his arms. He couldn't even be sure of that. She was very firm about her desire to remain single. She wanted more than a life bearing and raising children.

Ironically, so did he.

'Ah, it's over now!' he muttered and turned to the patiently waiting horse, which was munching quietly in the nosebag of oats.

The big kitchen seemed very quiet that evening. Maia hardly said a word and every now and then swiped at her eyes with the corner of her apron. Nancy's cooking wasn't nearly as good as Xanthe's – or was it that Ronan had lost his appetite?

He stayed in the kitchen with Bram and the maids, instead of sitting with Conn and his mother that evening, explaining that he felt the two of them appreciated time alone together, now that time itself was running out for Susannah Largan.

Once he'd decided what to do with himself, Ronan would go back to Ireland. It was strange how difficult he was finding it to make plans, though. Perhaps it was the more relaxed lifestyle here, or he was still sad about his mother, or he was missing Xanthe. His thoughts and emotions had been in a tangle ever since he watched the big mail cart take her south towards Albany.

He hoped she'd be safe.

In the end he went to bed early, claiming he was tired. But he didn't find it easy to sleep, and the book Conn had lent him wasn't in the least bit interesting.

When rain began to beat heavily against the window panes, his first thought was that he hoped she was safe and dry somewhere.

Xanthe was safe indoors but she wasn't comfortable. She and the other passengers were lying on scratchy straw mattresses in a common lodging room at one of the staging posts. They'd been warned that they'd be expected to rise before dawn and be on the road by first light.

It seemed strange to be on her own, and it was more frightening than she'd expected. The man driving the cart kept looking at her in a way she detested. Thank goodness there was an older woman passenger, though she too had looked at Xanthe suspiciously until she'd asked the other woman if she minded her staying close by, explaining that the driver made her feel nervous.

It took several days to get to Albany, in spite of the changes of horses waiting for them at each stop.

Xanthe had dressed in dark, serviceable clothing and tried to make herself look as plain as possible, but even so, she found men staring at her as she walked to her lodgings in Albany after confirming with the shipping agent that a cabin was indeed available to her.

The town was in a splendid location on a huge bay dotted with islands. She had forgotten how bracing the sea air was and inhaled deeply as she stopped yet again to stare at the view.

'Are you waiting for someone?' a voice asked.

She swung round to see a strange gentleman, rather portly and going bald, smiling at her.

'No.' She turned round and walked away as quickly as she could.

Everywhere she went, it seemed, there was someone to stare at her, the gentlemen with admiration and that certain look that said quite clearly what they were thinking, the ladies in disapproval, though why they should look at her like that she didn't know.

In the end she went back to her lodgings and sat in her room, since the place was too small to have a parlour. She hadn't expected to be bored, would have liked to explore Albany.

She grew angry at herself for being so cowardly and after an hour of fidgeting in her room, she ventured out again, armed with information from the landlady about where she might be able to purchase some books and writing materials.

This time she glared fiercely at any man who looked like accosting her and walked at a very brisk speed indeed.

When she found the shop where she hoped to buy books, she found an elderly lady standing outside it, watching her.

'You're a very fast walker.'

Xanthe stopped, wondering if it was all right to speak to strange ladies, but then this one had a twinkling smile and looked so friendly, she relaxed a little. 'If I don't walk fast, strangers try to talk to me and I don't like that.'

'You're too pretty to be on your own.'

'I can't help how I look.'

'You're not a resident of the town, are you?'

'No. I'm waiting for the mail steamer.'

'Travelling to England?'

'Yes.'

'So am I.'

Another of those twinkling smiles had Xanthe smiling back involuntarily.

'Why don't we stroll around the town together? I've been here for two days and I'm very tired of my own company.' The old lady held out her hand. 'I'm Drusilla Pearson, *Miss*, but my friends call me Drue.'

'Xanthe Blake.'

'Now that's an unusual name.'

Within half an hour the two of them were fast friends, and they boarded the ship together the next day. She was delighted with the extra comfort afforded by travelling in a cabin, even though she had to share hers with a disapproving spinster who was travelling back to England to keep house for her brother after working as a governess in Australia.

Xanthe realised almost immediately how fortunate she had been to make Miss Pearson's acquaintance, because the other cabin class passengers at first looked down their noses at her because of the way she spoke and dressed.

There was dead silence at the table when someone asked about her family background and she told them the bald truth, scorning to pretend to be something she wasn't.

Drue broke the silence. 'I think you're a very unusual young woman and your father must have been a remarkable man to be studying Greek.'

'He was a remarkable man.' Tears came into Xanthe's eyes. 'I still miss him greatly. When we read books together, he brought the ideas they contained to life for me as no one else has ever done.'

She remained very much on guard with these people. They accepted her, after a fashion, because they were all travelling together and it'd have caused more embarrassment to try to snub her. Only with Drue could she fully relax and speak unguardedly, however.

It reminded her of how comfortable she'd felt with Ronan. She missed him, wished she could stop thinking of him. He was out of her reach in so many ways.

When they reached Galle, two weeks later, Xanthe was thrilled by the warm climate and the exotic people and food, and chose to stay for a while and catch the next suitable ship. This meant saying goodbye to Drue, but she knew by now that she was merely a novelty to Drue, who was very good-natured, but not the sort of woman you'd turn to in a crisis.

It still felt strange to be without Maia, and she turned sometimes to share a thought with her sister, then tears would come into her eyes as she remembered how far away Maia was now. At night she shed tears once or twice when the loneliness got her down. But when she asked herself if she'd done the right thing in leaving the Swan River Colony and in striking out on her own, she knew she had.

With all the loneliness and apprehension about her future, there was also excitement, the joy of learning new things from the people she was travelling with, and the pleasure of looking forward to new sights and experiences.

She continued to think of Ronan, how he smiled and teased. How he grew sad sometimes about his mother. How sharp his mind was, so that it was a pleasure to discuss something with him. And how good-looking he was. None of the men she'd met since leaving Australia was at all attractive.

She wasn't looking for a husband, but if she had been, Ronan would have been exactly the sort of man she'd have chosen. She might have chosen him, but he'd never have chosen to marry her. A gentleman born and bred looked for a woman of birth and fortune when he married.

And she wasn't stupid enough to give herself to him outside marriage.

She worried sometimes that her sister would do that with Conn, give herself to him. There was nothing she could do about it now, though, and anyway, that would always be Maia's own choice.

But at least Conn wouldn't hurt Maia willingly or abandon her if the worst happened.

14

Two weeks after Xanthe left Galway House, a neighbour called to bring Conn some letters which had been brought to the local shop, which was also the post office for the whole district.

One of the letters was for Ronan. The envelope was crumpled, as if it had had a hard journey, and it had a black border, the sign of mourning.

'Stop staring at it and give it to him,' his mother said.

'Someone's died, by the looks of it. And on top of his mother's death, too,' said Conn.

'It happened months ago and nothing you do now will change it.'

'He's out riding with Sean. I'll wait till he gets back. No need to hurry with sad news.' He looked at the letter beneath Ronan's and sucked in his breath in shock. 'Look, here's one from Kieran for you.' He passed it to her, knowing this was the first time his older brother had written, and hoping it wasn't carrying bad news.

She held the envelope in a hand that trembled slightly. 'I'm surprised to hear from him. Your father said when he wrote to me that no one in the family wanted to speak to me again if I didn't return.'

'Do you want me to read it for you?'

'No. I can face up to my own news.' She slit the envelope and pulled two pages out of it, reading them slowly, with the use of a magnifying glass.

Conn watched anxiously as he saw tears slide down her cheeks. He said nothing, waiting for her to tell him.

She bent her head for a moment when she came to the end of the letter, not looking at him as she spoke. 'It seems . . . to be a season for death. Your cousin Michael had an accident while out riding. He broke his back and lingered for a few days. It seems he confessed on his deathbed to having helped your father incriminate you. I brought Michael up like my own son and even though he betrayed you, I'd not have wished him dead. So young. So very young.'

Conn took her in his arms and held her as she wept against him, then she pulled away and said in a husky voice, 'There's more. Michael – he asked the priest to try to right the wrong and – and there was time to bring in a lawyer to take his statement. Kieran says it'll take a while but he has every hope of seeing you exonerated.'

Conn felt as if the ground was shaking beneath his feet and couldn't, for a moment, catch his breath, then he gulped and clapped one hand across his mouth to prevent himself from sobbing even more loudly than she had. Men weren't supposed to weep, and he hadn't all through his imprisonment and ordeal, but he couldn't hold back his emotions now, because the relief was so overwhelming. Sinking to the ground, he put his head in his mother's lap and let out a tide of pent-up anguish, ragged sobs shaking his whole body.

He felt her stroke his head gently as she had when he was a child but it was a while before he managed to stop weeping and even then he stayed where he was, taking comfort from that soft hand. As he started to get to his feet, she pushed his hair back from his damp forehead and kissed him there, another habit from childhood. She'd always said she was kissing something better, but no one could kiss away those horrifying years in prison and the stigma that they'd placed on his life.

'I'm so thankful I've been spared to hear this news, Conn darling,' she said as he got to his feet and sat down beside her on the sofa. 'I was so worried about who would comfort you and keep up your spirits once I wasn't here. Now, circumstances are going to change, even if it takes some time, and—'

'Don't talk about that! I can't bear to think of losing you.'

'Dear boy, I've been in severe pain for years and I'm weary of it, so very weary. Now, I'm getting a pain in my chest if I do something. It's . . . getting hard to cope with it all and I'm more than ready to die. But to have a child die before yourself, well, that seems utterly wrong. Whatever Michael had done to you, death is such a final thing – and he was like a son. He had no time to ask *your* forgiveness, but at least he spoke to a priest, repented and tried to make amends.'

'I don't think I could have forgiven him.'

'Was it so very bad? You've always refused to talk of that time.'

'Yes. Very bad.' He changed the subject. He'd promised himself never to talk of *that time* to her. 'I'm sorry that you have to grieve for him. I know for certain Michael loved you. We all do. You've been the best of mothers. But I don't want—'

She put one finger on his lips. 'Shh. You grow more used to the thought of death as you grow older. I'm quite reconciled to dying, especially now we've had this news.' She kept hold of Conn's hand. 'There's more news for you in the letter. Good news, this time. Here. Read it for yourself.'

He took the two sheets and they brought back so many memories, because Kieran was writing as he talked, not stiffly, as people do in a duty letter. He read slowly, savouring the sound of his brother's voice echoing behind the carelessly scrawled words. Then he came to the word 'Kathleen' and for a moment or two his mind refused to read on. He had to take several deep breaths before he could force himself to read the next part.

Have you had any news of Kathleen? I didn't know she was leaving until she'd gone. I tell you frankly, she's no loss to us. I never realised what she was like until after Father died and I had to cope with her. He found her amusing and encouraged her arrogance. I didn't.

Will you ask Conn if he still wants to seek an annulment? Is he still in a position to do so from non-consummation? If so, I'll set it in train here and he must do the same in Australia.

I know you said we should look after her, because she can't look after herself, but I couldn't face having her live at Shilmara. I did offer to buy her a house somewhere, and her brother is managing her money for her, though she complained at how little it was. She has no idea of how to manage money.

She flew into a rage when I refused to let her stay, and remained in a rage for days, smashing things until we had to set a watch on her. She was very attached to Shilmara, I grant you, considered it her home, but it can never be that again.

Then she packed up and left while I was away, not leaving any indication of where she was going. It wasn't till later that I found she'd gone off with Mrs Maguire to Australia, and taken poor Orla (do you remember her?) with her. No one has heard any more from either of them since.

It would be a relief to me and her brother to know Kathleen has arrived safely. I presume she went there to see Conn. Surely even she should realise she's the last person he would want to see? Or perhaps not. She'd grown very strange.

Life at Shilmara continues and you're about to become a grandmother again. This time we hope for a daughter . . .

Conn finished reading the letter and sighed. 'Good news for me on both counts, isn't it, though it's a sad way for it to happen? If someone's helping me with an annulment there, then I think I stand a much better chance of obtaining it, though it'll probably still take years.'

'It's wonderful news for you. It means that one day you can follow your heart. Maia's a wonderful young woman, so loving and kind.' She patted his hand again.

Once she'd have leaned sideways and given him a kiss, but now her movements were more limited and twisting was something she avoided. There was always a tightness to her smile, as if she was holding back pain. So he twisted round to kiss her instead. 'You're the best mother I've ever had, the very best.'

It was an old joke between them and it made her smile, as he'd hoped. She countered, as usual, by saying, 'And you're the best son I've got in all Australia.'

'Do you want me to write back for you? I know it hurts your hands to write.'

'We'll both write. I think I should write my own letter this time, don't you?'

He knew then that she thought it'd be the last she ever wrote to Kieran but he kept his pain at that thought to himself, as she always tried to hold back her physical pain.

'Well, that was good news in the midst of bad. Let's write straight away and send the letters up to Perth. I want to make sure Kieran is helping with the annulment and pushing it forward as quickly as possible. That's far more important than a pardon to me. Maybe your second cousin, the Bishop, will stir himself on my behalf.'

His father had forsaken his religion for the one followed by the English establishment, but his mother had remained true to the Catholic Church, even though that had caused considerable trouble with her husband.

His father had been quite happy for his younger sons to attend their mother's church, though he'd tried to make his heir change his religious allegiance. But like his mother, Kieran had refused and that was a good thing now if he was to help Conn.

At a sound outside, she looked up. 'I think that must be Ronan coming back from his ride. Better give him his letter before you settle into writing to your brother. You're lost to the world once you get a pen in your hand and you have a beautiful way with words. You should have been a poet, I think.'

As Ronan was coming back to the house from the stables, he saw Conn waiting for him on the rear veranda.

His friend handed him a letter, with, 'Bad news, I think.'

Ronan took it from him, freezing for a moment as he noticed the black border. 'It's Patrick's handwriting, so it's not him, at least. He'll not have had time to get my letter telling him of Mother's death, so who else have we lost in the family?' He frowned as he stuffed the letter in his pocket. 'I'd not have thought he'd have gone into deep mourning for a mere cousin or aunt, but perhaps his wife's family consider it necessary. Anyway, I'll read this in private, if you don't mind.'

In his bedroom he closed the door carefully then smoothed out the envelope, slitting it open with a feeling of dread. He read the letter, then sat down on the bed to read it again more slowly. He was so shocked by the news it contained that he couldn't move and sat staring into space for a long time, trying to come to terms with what this meant for him. Huge changes to his life, changes he didn't welcome, but couldn't refuse.

After a while, he got up and took off his riding clothes, washing carefully to get the smell of horses off himself before he put on his day clothes. His thoughts wandered like butterflies as he looked at himself in the mirror, anything rather than think about the news he'd just received. He was glad he hadn't had his new trousers made as tightly as fashion dictated. So uncomfortable. He put a handkerchief in his pocket and patted it, glad to have the new semi-circular pockets at the front, because they were more practical.

Trying not to think what it contained, he slipped the letter into the other pocket before joining his hostess and friend.

Conn was with his mother in the small sitting room where she spent her days during the winter. She looked so frail, Ronan worried that each day would be her last.

'May I join you?'

She gestured to a chair and asked quietly, 'Was it bad news?'

'I'm afraid so. And a dreadful shock, too. I can hardly believe it. It's from Patrick, my youngest brother. He normally lives in England but he was at Ardgullan House when he wrote. It seems . . . I can't believe it, but my brother Hubert has died suddenly – he was only thirty-four – and I've inherited the family estate.'

'Was there an accident?' Mrs Largan asked.

'No. He just dropped dead. For no reason that anyone could see.'

'This must be the season for deaths,' Conn said. 'We had similar news, only it's my cousin Michael who's died.' He shared the details, his voice breaking as he spoke of the possibility of his conviction being overturned.

Ronan went to clap him on the back and wish him a speedy

pardon or whatever it was they did when someone had been wrongfully accused. And a speedy annulment too.

After they'd settled down again, Mrs Largan rang for a tea tray and while they waited for Maia to bring it, she said, 'You'll go straight home, of course, Ronan.'

'Yes. I'll have to. Only it'll be nearly two months before there's another mail steamer. Perhaps I'll go and see what ships are leaving Fremantle.'

'There aren't a lot of ships that sail from there,' Conn said, 'and they're not usually steamers like the mail ships, so the journey takes longer.'

Ronan sighed. 'This really is an isolated place. Perhaps you'll move back to Ireland once your innocence is established, Conn?'

'I doubt it. I like it here. Look, I've been thinking. You could probably catch Bram's friend if you go straight up to Perth. He might be able to take you to Galle if you pay him well – he seems to have no fixed itinerary – and as Pandora told us, you can quickly get a ship to England from Galle. If I remember correctly, much of the Indian and Far Eastern trade uses that port for coaling or replenishing their food and water.'

'What a pity you didn't find out before Xanthe left!' Mrs Largan said. 'You could have gone together. I do worry about that girl travelling on her own. I don't care how sensible she is, a woman alone is vulnerable, especially one so young and beautiful.'

'Yes. It is a pity.' More than a pity, Ronan thought. It was as if fate was deliberately keeping them apart. He wondered if destiny would make their paths cross again, hoped it would.

If he had to go back, he was going to find her and see if his feelings for her were still as strong. And if they were, then to hell with convention. He might be the son and heir, but he was also a man in love.

But he didn't share those thoughts even with Conn. He simply set about packing and arranged to borrow the small horse and cart, with the oldest and most sensible stable lad to bring it back to Galway House again.

★　　★　　★

Bram had taken lodgings with Dougal's mother and sister in Fremantle, so Ronan found him quite easily. As the family of a ship's captain, even a small elderly ship like the *Bonny Mary*, they had a house large enough to contain spare bedrooms which they let out to selected lodgers, more for the company than from a need for money.

When he explained that he needed to get back to Ireland as quickly as possible, they offered him a room. It seemed that Dougal was due back any day now and if anyone could help, it would be him.

With relief, Ronan sent the lad and cart back to Conn with a note of thanks, explaining where he was and saying he'd write when he reached Ireland.

It was at times like this that the extreme isolation of the Swan River Colony was really brought home to you, Ronan thought. He spent most of the first day indoors, sheltering from a heavy downpour, alternating between reading a book – and a boring one, it was, too! – and chatting to Bram.

The following day was fine and he went out to stroll round Fremantle. He watched the convicts working on a bridge across the river, a huge wooden structure nearly a thousand feet long. He went on to look at the jail which dominated the town from the top of a limestone ridge, wondering if Conn had been incarcerated there when he arrived. He admired one newly built stone building of Gothic architecture, surprised when a passer-by told him it was the lunatic asylum. Did they have so many lunatics here?

In great contrast, some of the tiny wooden houses were as small as the poorest huts in Ireland, but it must be easier to live in such places in a warmer climate.

He tried to rein in his frustration at the delays and at least using up some of his energy by going for a long walk meant he slept better the second night.

It was three interminable days later that they heard the *Bonny Mary* had docked in Fremantle. Ronan was all for going straight down to the docks, but Dougal's sister said this wasn't the time to disturb him as he'd have the arrival formalities to go through and the cargo to unload.

It wasn't till late evening that Dougal arrived home, delighted to see Bram again and surprised to see Ronan. He was even more surprised to learn that Ronan was desperate to get back to Ireland and commiserated with him on his loss of a brother.

'But I can go nowhere till this cargo has been sold and another taken on. No!' He held up one hand. 'Not even if you pay me double. I will take you to Galle, and before the next mail steamer too, but not yet.'

Ronan could do nothing but continue to wait as patiently as possible.

Then, by a fortunate coincidence, another gentleman seeking a passage to Galle was directed to the *Bonny Mary* and a cargo consisting mainly of sandalwood was found, some of which could probably be sold in Galle while the rest would be taken on to Singapore.

In the end the ship managed to leave within the week, a very quick turn-round, Dougal said.

'I'd not have done this for anyone but a friend of yours,' he told Bram. 'I like to spend time with my family between voyages.' He puffed on his pipe, found it had gone out and needed refilling, so tapped out the dottle and began to fill it again.

'You know, Bram lad, now you've got the promise from your friend Conn of money to invest in your shop, you should come with me on a voyage or two and learn more about the sort of goods we can obtain. I'll probably be going on to the Straits Settlements after Galle. There's a very profitable British trading station on the island of Singapore these days and there's talk of it becoming a Crown Colony. We got the better of the Dutch when we gained a foothold there, I can tell you.'

Bram considered this suggestion. 'I don't really enjoy sailing, but I think you're right, Dougal lad. If we're to do well with our business association, I do need to see what goods we can find in the Orient. I'll ask Ronan if he minds sharing his cabin with me.'

The other gentleman who would be travelling with them was much older and of a studious disposition.

'He's so boring to talk to, I'm thinking this book he's writing will be a tedious read,' Bram said to Ronan after their first meal in their travelling companion's company the night before they set sail.

They left on a grey spring day and the weather continued cool and rainy for the first week of the voyage, keeping them in their cabins for long periods. Ronan was already bursting with unspent energy. Walking around a ship's deck wasn't nearly enough to tire him out, but to be confined to his cabin was driving him crazy. He would not, he decided, come to Australia again. The cost in boredom was too high.

He tried to use the time productively by planning what he would do once he got back to Ireland, but it still seemed unreal to him that he owned Ardgullan house and the estate, or that he was responsible for so many lives, not only those who worked for him, but those in his cottages in the village.

And one of his biggest responsibilities would be to provide an heir to carry on the family name. No escaping that.

But was he to marry for the estate, making a cool marriage to a woman of his own class, who would no doubt bore him to tears within the month? No. He wanted a woman who would argue with him, give as good as she got, and be worth talking to. You didn't just take a wife to bed, you lived with her day in, day out, and faced the world together – or you should do if things went well.

His brother Patrick had married a fortune and now lived with a woman who looked like a well-bred horse and had a whinnying laugh that made people wince. Perhaps Ronan had had too much freedom in his life or was more selfish, but he knew he couldn't do that. So, he decided, he'd wear the chains of the estate, but he'd not chain himself to a woman he didn't find attractive and interesting.

Inevitably his thoughts lingered at this stage on the woman he'd already met, the woman whose company he'd enjoyed and whom he still missed dreadfully.

The weather grew warmer. Ronan thought he was hiding his frustration well till Bram and Dougal began to tease him about it, likening him to a caged tiger.

The third week began with little wind and stifling heat. If they sat out on deck now, it was under a canvas awning, but in the heat of midday they retreated to their cabin and the sailors too did only essential jobs at that time, though many were dark-skinned and seemed to tolerate the sun better than Ronan, whose skin burned easily. Even the wind seemed to have come straight from a furnace and the sun shining off the water hurt the eyes.

Though it was hot in the cabin, it wasn't nearly as hot as outside on deck, and Dougal had a supply of books to share, as well as packs of cards to play silly games with, because Dougal frowned on gambling, saying he'd seen too many men lose their shirts that way.

One morning Ronan woke really early, found it impossible to get back to sleep in the stifling heat and went on deck to find Dougal there before him, studying the sky anxiously.

'Is something wrong?'

'I'm worried about a storm.'

'On a sunny day like this?'

Dougal nodded. 'Look at the barometer. Tropical storms can build up suddenly, or you can get hurricanes, though not usually at this season. If you're a praying man, you'd better pray we don't get one of those, or we're lost for sure.'

From then on Ronan too kept an eye on the sky. To his dismay he watched it growing darker and felt the quality of the air change, as it always did before a storm. The motion of the ship became more jerky as the waves grew higher and his stomach reacted badly to this.

All the tales he'd ever heard of shipwrecks and storms seemed to come back to him.

Bram was also affected by the rough seas and staggered across the heaving deck towards him from the rail, where he'd been vomiting over the side, looking distinctly greenish in colour. 'If I survive this voyage, I'm never going on a ship again. My stomach hasn't felt easy the whole time. Smaller ships are much worse than the larger ones in bad weather.'

'You'll have to travel back to Australia by ship.'

'Once I'm back there, then. That's it. No more sailing.'

Dougal came across to them, speaking curtly and with no sign of his usual smile. 'I'd be obliged if you two gentlemen would go back to your cabin and stay there until I tell you it's safe to come out. That way I won't have to worry about you falling overboard or getting in my crew's way.'

'What if I need to be sick?' Bram clutched his stomach again.

'Take a bucket with you. Now, hurry up. And *don't* come out for any reason whatsoever. I'll tell you when it's safe.'

Ronan stood at the door of the cabin for a few minutes and watched Dougal stride off to bang on their travelling companion's door and tell him the same thing. He kept shouting orders, stopping every now and then to study the horizon or the sky or the ship, always with a frown.

The next few hours would live in Ronan's memory as one of the worst times of his life. Both he and Bram were sick more than once and the cabin soon smelled foul, which didn't help.

The motion of the ship grew increasingly violent and they were tossed about however hard they tried to hold on to their bunks. Things he'd not thought to pack away were flung across the cabin, but he wasn't risking life and limb to put them away safely. Books, towels and clothing could be picked up later. The steward had made sure there were no pieces of crockery lying around to smash.

Just when Ronan felt things couldn't get any worse, there was a huge creaking sound and the ship seemed to stop in mid-air, then fall down into the abyss between waves with a sickening drop. He clung on to the edge of the top bunk, fending off a book that flew through the air.

Were they going to sink? He couldn't believe his life would end like this, desperately wanted to live. As the minutes passed slowly, he waited for water to come pouring under his cabin door, but it didn't, though it slapped against the sides of the ship loudly enough.

There was another of those wrenching movements and a loud cracking sound, followed by yells that sounded panicky.

'What the hell was that?' he asked Bram.

'I daren't think.'

However tightly he clung to his bunk, he couldn't hold on this time. When the ship heaved violently, he was thrown off it and yelled out involuntarily as he fell.

There was a burst of pain, after which the world went dark.

One morning Mrs Largan looked at Maia and said with a sigh, 'I don't think I'll get up today. I feel too tired.' She closed her eyes again.

This was so unlike her that Maia waited to see if her mistress woke again. When she didn't, Maia went to find Conn.

'I'm worried about your mother.'

'What's wrong?'

She explained and saw tears rise in his eyes. When she reached out to him, he took her hand and held it tightly.

'She thinks she hasn't much longer to live. I think she's right,' said Conn.

'Yes. She's been hiding from you for a while how tired she's felt. I've wanted to tell you, but she kept saying not yet. She didn't say anything this morning except that she didn't want to get up today.'

'I'll go and see her.'

Maia followed him along the corridor and they stood in the doorway of his mother's bedroom.

'There seems nothing of her,' he muttered. 'Has she grown thinner lately?'

'Yes. She hardly eats enough to keep a bird alive.'

'What should we do?'

Maia tugged him away and back to the library. 'I think you should let her go in peace. She's ready. She's been in great pain for as long as I've known her, and then on top of it she started fainting. I wondered if I should have told you, but she insisted it'd do no good. And I think she was right.'

'I can't think how I'll manage without her.'

'Nor I. She's taught me so much, not just information but how to face life, how to deal with people of all sorts. What a wonderful woman she is!'

There was silence and when she looked up, he was staring at her.

'You won't leave – afterwards? I know I've no right to ask it of you, but . . .' After a moment's hesitation, he told her about the possibility of both clearing his name and getting an annulment. 'And if I do get out of this farcical marriage, Maia, dearest Maia, you will marry me, won't you?'

'Yes, of course.'

'As simple as that?'

'We both know we love one another, so why pretend? It isn't the Lancashire way.'

With a low groan, he drew her into his arms and kissed her, holding her in his arms for a long time afterwards.

When he moved gently back she did too, smiling at him. She didn't care what other people said about her staying on here, didn't care about anything as long as she could be with Conn. He loved her and would need her support through the difficult days ahead.

And if everything did work out and they were able to marry, she'd be the happiest woman in the colony – in the whole wide world!

15

Xanthe was thrilled to see Point de Galle ahead of them. It seemed to her from a distance like one of the Greek islands her father had read about, a place of sun and sand, blue water and even bluer sky. On the rocky promontory at the south-west extremity of the island stood the fortified town, Galle, with hills rising behind it.

One of the young officers was delighted to tell her about Galle and for once she let him talk, though she didn't like the soulful way he looked at her. Making sheep's eyes was a very good way to describe it, and who was interested in spending time with a sheep?

The fort was quite large, apparently, overlooking the harbour and containing not only government buildings but an old church, a mosque and a hospital. He had to explain what a mosque was because she'd never even heard of such a place of worship.

She didn't accept the officer's offer to show her round because she didn't intend to give gossips any chance to blacken her name. It had been her salvation on the journey so far to have met Drue, who was like an unofficial chaperone, but her new friend was going on to Madras, so they would be parting company at Galle.

Xanthe had thought life would be so easy if you had money and didn't have to work for a living, but these people had so many rules and shibboleths she was finding it hugely difficult to fit in. She already knew they'd never make friends with her, because she didn't have enough money for them to overlook her origins, but she didn't want to be spurned outright, out of a sense of pride, if nothing else.

The purser told her where to look for lodgings, but advised consulting the P&O agent first about an onward passage. The agent apparently knew how to make arrangements to help passengers who didn't know Galle. She was relieved at that thought, had been wondering how she'd cope.

The agent said if she was in a hurry, she could leave immediately as a steerage passenger or else wait about ten days for a cabin on the next ship. She realised ruefully that she'd already grown accustomed to the extra comforts of taking a cabin. 'I'd rather wait, but is there any way I can hire a guide and a female companion to show me around the island?'

The agent smiled at her. 'Very sensible, Miss Blake. Best to observe the proprieties. People notice. I know a gentleman who sometimes acts as a guide. He's a native, but educated and a Christian. His eldest daughter sometimes accompanies him when there are ladies involved.'

She was delighted. 'Then I'll definitely wait for the cabin. Now, about lodgings?'

He studied her thoughtfully. 'The same gentleman also offers lodgings, which his wife manages. You'll be quite safe there, though some people prefer accommodation run by Europeans. I can arrange that too.'

'No need. The guide and his daughter sound ideal.'

So there she was, on a tropical island, staying with people who offered her new and exciting food to eat, showed her a different lifestyle and made her temporary stay extremely comfortable. Soft-footed servants forestalled her every need, washed her clothes and brought her refreshments.

She would have time to look around and try as many new things as she could.

Not till she was in bed did she admit to herself that it would have been even better – utterly perfect – if she'd had someone to share these new experiences with.

And of course that thought brought Ronan to mind again. It had been over three weeks now since she'd seen him. Was he well? Was he still at Conn's?

Was he thinking of her?

* * *

When Ronan regained consciousness, he found himself lying on a makeshift mattress on the floor. He tried to speak but it seemed too much effort and although the man kneeling beside him was asking him something, he couldn't make sense of the words, so he closed his eyes again.

Bram looked at Dougal. 'He's not really conscious.'

'No. He's lucky to be alive, with such a blow to the head. I shall have to leave you to look after him. We've a few repairs to make and we need to rig a temporary mast, but we've enough sail left to get us to Galle.'

'The quicker we get there the better. He needs to see a doctor. He's so pale. Does anyone on the ship have any medical knowledge?'

'I know how to deal with cuts and bruises, and I can get the ship's sailmaker to stitch up that cut to help it heal. He's done that a few times and he's quite good at it. I can set simple broken bones, but I'm no good at stitchery.' He laughed.

Bram didn't feel at all like laughing. 'What am I going to do about Ronan, then?'

Dougal stood up, his voice gentler than usual. 'There's nothing you can do except keep him as clean and peaceful as possible. You and he can stay here in my cabin till we arrive. Once yours is waterproof again, I'll use that. We'll be in Galle in two or three days because the storm pushed us along faster than usual. How did you enjoy your first taste of a storm at sea? Exhilarating to pit yourself against nature, isn't it?'

'Exhilarating!' Bram shuddered. 'How can you say that? I didn't enjoy it at all. In fact, it made me decide this will be my first and last voyage to the Orient with you.'

Dougal laughed again. 'Well, you'd better learn all you can, then. I'll leave you to your nursing. The sailmaker will be here shortly. Ask the steward if you need anything – or if you need me. Try to get Ronan to sip some water, if you can, or trickle it into his mouth. Someone once told me people can die of thirst while they're unconscious. When we get to Galle, we can find a doctor for your friend if he still needs help.'

He patted Bram on the back. 'People usually recover quite well on their own from head injuries, you know. There's nothing much doctors can do about them. They can't see inside someone's brain, after all.'

The sailmaker came and sewed up the cut, cleaning his needle in a flame first and chatting cheerfully as he worked. He made a very neat job of it, too.

When he wasn't pacing up and down, Bram sat on one of the chairs in this larger cabin. He kept an eye on Ronan, worried sick about his friend, and every now and then he trickled some water into his mouth, finding that if he did this a drop or two at a time, it seemed to go down easily enough.

When he was a child he'd seen one of the village lads die of a simple blow to the head, lying there unconscious until he simply stopped breathing. He'd seen others with cuts to the head that poured blood till you'd think they had major injuries, and yet they needed nothing except the cut washing and a little attention to it for a day or two, and they recovered fully.

Ronan's brother and mother had both died this year. Surely God wouldn't take him too?

What the hell am I going to tell people if you die? he thought as he looked at Ronan's pale, slack face with the livid scar surrounded by bruised flesh stitched together. *You don't even look like Ronan at the moment.*

Xanthe found her guide's daughter extremely good company. Anusha was about twenty, spoke perfect English and seemed to understand exactly what to explain to a stranger to help her understand this new world.

Anusha's father watched them indulgently and often absented himself from outings in Galle itself, though when they spent a day in the countryside to see a tea plantation or went outside the town to drink fresh coconut milk and eat fruits Xanthe had never even heard of before, he went with them.

'Better that he's with us for protection,' Anusha whispered to Xanthe.

In her letters, Pandora had said how much she'd hated the heat of Galle and Egypt, but Xanthe loved it. She wore as little as was respectable, thinking the other ladies foolish for keeping on their corsets. You could see at a glance from their rigid bearing that they were wearing them, and they looked flushed and uncomfortable. No wonder ladies fainted if they put corsets before common sense!

With just four days to go till she boarded her ship, Xanthe was strolling round the ramparts one day when she saw a schooner approaching.

'It's just a small trader,' Anusha said. 'That ship calls here sometimes. The captain's a big man with a beard.'

'Let's go and watch it dock.'

'If you wish.'

Xanthe hid a smile. If Anusha didn't want to do something, she always said 'If you wish'. Well, Xanthe did wish and since she was paying Anusha a daily rate for her companionship, she intended to do what *she* wanted.

They strolled to the harbour and watched the ship position itself at one of the moorings. A man came up on deck, looking worried as he talked urgently to the captain. Something about the man made Xanthe take a second look, then hurry towards the ship. It was Bram, surely it was?

The closer she got the more certain she became that it was him and without consciously thinking about it, she started running, calling out to him.

A couple of natives yelled something, so did a sailor on the ship. The captain and his companion turned towards her as she closed the distance between them.

'Xanthe!' Bram called. 'What are you doing here? We thought you'd be in Egypt by now.'

'I'm waiting for a passage on the next steamship. Are you on your way back to Ireland?'

'No.' He hesitated, then asked, 'I'll explain about myself later. Look, do you know of a doctor here? Ronan's on board but he's been hurt in a fall.'

She lost all desire to smile. 'He's hurt? Badly?'

'We're not sure. He got hit on the head and has been drifting in and out of consciousness for nearly three days. I don't know what to do for him, where to take him.'

'Wait!' She turned to Anusha, who had joined them at a more leisurely pace. 'A good friend of mine is on this ship and he's been injured. Is there a doctor who can see him? What should we do to help him?'

Anusha immediately lost her air of leisurely dignity. 'There's a good doctor in the next street to us and I'm sure my mother would take in your friend.'

'How do we get him there?'

Anusha studied Bram, then asked in an undertone, 'Will you be safe if I leave you with this man?'

'Yes, very safe. He's a friend of my family.'

'Then if you stay here, I'll make the arrangements.' She hesitated then added, 'Your friend can pay?'

'Oh, yes.' She thought it prudent to add, 'He's a gentleman, not rich but not short of money, either.' She didn't want anyone thinking they could charge ridiculous prices for anything.

'That's good. I won't be long.'

Anusha hurried off and Bram helped Xanthe board the ship, introducing her to the captain and explaining quickly what had been arranged. Then he turned to her. 'Do you want to see Ronan? We brought his bed up on deck. He's over there, under the awning.'

Swallowing hard, afraid of what she would find or that she would betray her feelings, Xanthe followed him across the deck.

It was worse than she'd expected. It was Ronan's face, but without the vivid, expressive life that was so typical of him. And his temple was badly bruised with a sewn line of flesh across it. He'd have a bad scar there when he recovered.

She looked again at his face and couldn't prevent the thought *if he recovered* from slipping into her mind. But she didn't let it stay there. She sat beside him and took hold of his hand, speaking as if he could understand her. 'It's Xanthe. I'm here with you now, Ronan, and I'm going to look after you until you're better. You've been hit on the head but you're in Galle and it's a delightful place. You're sure to recover quickly here.'

She kept hold of his hand, talking quietly about what she'd been doing while she waited for Anusha to return with help.

Watching them, Bram thought the love on her face far more beautiful than the mere arrangement of her features. One day, he wanted to be loved like that. Only, since he wasn't from a wealthy landowning family, surely he wouldn't face such diffi-culties about marrying the woman he loved? From things Ronan had let drop he was quite sure his friend loved this woman.

Both the Blake twins had been unlucky. One was in love with Conn, who wasn't free to marry, the other with Ronan, who might be free but would look for a woman of his own sort when he came to marry. The gentry always did.

He looked along the quay and saw two bearers approaching with a carrying frame, followed by the young woman who had been with Xanthe. He went across to her. 'Your friend's returned with some bearers.'

Xanthe looked up, seeming not to hear him for a moment, so hard had she been concentrating on the still figure beside her. Then she blinked and looked in the direction of his pointing finger. 'Oh. Good.' She bent over Ronan and said, 'We're going to carry you ashore now and get a doctor to help you.'

He opened his eyes, stared at her and whispered. 'Don't go. I know you're only a dream, but don't go.' Then he closed his eyes again.

That was a good sign, wasn't it? she thought.

The bearers came on board and under the directions of the two women lifted Ronan gently on to the frame.

'Someone is coming for his luggage,' the native woman said, in perfect English.

'I'll get it ready,' Bram replied. 'Tell me how to find Ronan later, after we've dealt with the cargo.'

'He'll be in our house, which is by the market. You can't mistake it, it has a blue awning over the front door.'

He watched them go, wondering if Ronan would recover –
surely he would? – then he turned back to Dougal, who was
directing the unloading of the cargo he wished to sell.

'This evening we'll go and see that Ronan is all right.'

Dougal nodded, his attention still mainly on the men unloading
the cargo and the crew member directing them.

Bram went to fetch a few things he'd got from Ronan's mother's
luggage, trinkets Dougal said would fetch more money in Galle.
He'd need every penny he could get if he was to succeed in his
new life in Australia.

Ronan gradually became aware that he felt far more comfortable
than he had for some time and sighed in relief that his bed was
no longer rising and falling beneath him. Even the pounding pain
in his head seemed to have abated.

Someone wiped his brow with a cool cloth and spoke to him
quietly. He knew that voice. Opening his eyes, he saw Xanthe
sitting beside him. 'Are you a dream?'

She smiled. 'What a question! Of course I'm not.'

'You've been in my dreams a lot.'

Her smile faded. 'Have I?'

'Yes. I missed you.' He closed his eyes but found no desire to
sleep so opened them again. 'Where am I?'

'Galle. You had an accident on board your ship. I gather you
hit your head during a storm and you've been unconscious for
days.'

'It hurts.' He tried to put his hand up to it, but it felt too much
of an effort.

'Could you drink some water for me? It's been boiled, so it's
quite safe to drink. The doctor said it was important to keep
giving you drinks, more important than food.'

'I'd love some. I'm very thirsty.'

'I can't give you too much at once.' She held him up and put
an engraved metal cup to his lips, allowing him to drink a little
then laying him down again.

He didn't want to lie down. He wanted to be held close to her soft breasts again. She smelled of something both spicy and flowery and she was wearing a brightly coloured garment like none he'd ever seen before. 'What are you wearing? Is that your nightgown?'

She laughed. 'No, of course not. It's an Indian garment that Anusha likes to wear round the house. It's called a sari. And I must say, it's very comfortable.'

'That vivid pink suits you.' He smiled at her, feeling too lazy to say much.

'Do you think you could drink a little more now?'

'Yes, please.'

After that his eyes began to feel heavy and he could only stay awake long enough to say, 'Don't leave me.'

'No, I promise I won't.' She wasn't at all sure he'd heard her because he was breathing softly and deeply. Was it her imagination or did he look a little better, with more colour in his cheeks?

The maid who'd been sitting in a corner, because Anusha's mother wouldn't let Xanthe tend Ronan on her own, came forward.

'I watch him for you now, Miss. Time for the evening meal.'

'Thank you. But come and fetch me if he asks for me. I'll be back after I've eaten.'

'No need. I see to him tonight.'

'I want to stay with him.' And no one was going to stop her doing so. But she tried to soften her words by adding, 'He knows me, you see.'

'Then mistress will say me sit with you.'

'I'll speak to her. I'm sure that's not necessary.'

But there was no budging her hostess on that point. The proprieties would be observed. Xanthe was young and unmarried. No scandal was going to touch her in this house.

The following morning Ronan woke to find Xanthe slumbering in a chair next to the bed, while a woman who looked like a maid sat quietly watchful in a corner. He had no idea where he was, just that it wasn't a ship, thank goodness. He didn't wake Xanthe but the maid came across to offer him a drink of water and that woke her. And he was so thirsty he couldn't bear to refuse.

'I'll see to him.' Xanthe took the metal cup from the maid. She lifted him and again he enjoyed the soft wonder of being held close by her as he drank.

Afterwards she looked down at him dubiously. 'Are you able to eat anything, do you think?'

'I'm not really hungry.'

'But you'll eat something to please me? Maybe a little fruit to start with?'

'Just to please you. Um – before that, is there a male servant who can help me see to my body's needs?'

'Of course.' She turned to the maid, who clearly understood English because she nodded and slipped out of the room briefly.

'You shouldn't give up your bed to sit by me,' Ronan said. 'Though I'm grateful, of course.' He raised one hand to his temple. 'My head's not aching as badly today. How long since the accident?'

'I don't know exactly. Several days, I think. You can ask Bram. He came yesterday evening but you were unconscious, so he said he'd come back this afternoon. He's had your luggage sent across from the ship. He'll be sailing soon, from what he said, going on to India then Singapore.'

'Good. And maybe this fellow who's coming to help me will be able to shave me.' He rubbed his chin and smiled ruefully. 'A fine way to appear before a lady.'

'I'm not a lady.'

'To me you're everything a woman should be.'

She looked at him warily. What did he mean by that?

'I missed you. Didn't you miss me at all?' he asked.

'Yes, I did.' She hadn't wanted to, though. Caring about him could lead nowhere. She prided herself on her common sense, so must keep reminding herself of that.

Just then two men came into the room and the maid tugged Xanthe's arm to take her outside. She wasn't allowed back in to see him for over an hour and when she did Ronan was sleepy.

'I'm sorry,' he said. 'I can't seem to get enough sleep.'

'Before you drift away, do you want me to see if there's another cabin free on the ship going to Suez? I'm leaving on it in two days. Otherwise you'll have to wait a week or two to leave – though perhaps that might be better.'

'No. It definitely wouldn't. Please see if you can get me on to that ship. My eldest brother has died and I've inherited the family estate. I have to get back to Ireland as quickly as possible.'

'I'll do my best.'

But she felt sad as she walked away. It was difficult enough to love a man of means, but the heir to an estate – why, Ronan was even further beyond her reach now than he had been before!

It was a good thing she was being sensible about this, not letting herself get carried away. These feelings would pass. Surely they would?

By dint of shuffling the passengers around and asking Xanthe to share a cabin with the daughter of an English family, the agent managed to find Ronan a berth on the outgoing ship.

He bade a rather emotional farewell to Bram, sorry to be losing his childhood friend. He clapped him on the shoulder and wished him well.

Bram looked at him very seriously. 'I want to thank you for giving me a chance to make something of my life.'

'Me? I've done very little.'

'You brought me here, you gave me your mother's things – which have given me some money to make a start with. That's not "very little", it's a lot.'

'Well, I shall hope to hear that you've grown rich then.'

Bram gave him a strange look. 'I'll do that or die trying.' Then, for all his threats never to go on board a ship again, he sailed away with his new friend, heading for other exotic-sounding ports to investigate trading possibilities.

And Ronan was left to continue his journey with Xanthe.

★   ★   ★

Within five minutes of making the acquaintance of her new cabin mate, Xanthe realised why she and her family had agreed so quickly to the changes: Ronan was now a very eligible gentleman and Marianne was on her way back to England to find a husband. Marianne was as fair as she was dark, and very pretty, dressed in exquisite clothes that Xanthe envied.

As was soon evident, the young woman considered Xanthe long past the age of snaring a husband, even before she found out that her cabin mate had once been a mill girl.

Ronan, still recovering, spent most of his time sitting on deck. But he soon found himself besieged by Marianne's parents, who were determined to take charge of his convalescence, since it was inconceivable that a single woman like Xanthe should spend time with him on her own.

In the end Xanthe gave up trying to sit with or chat to him on her own, because if she did, Marianne and her mother were sure to join them.

One night, however, it was so hot that Xanthe couldn't bear the stuffy cabin for a minute longer and in spite of Marianne's shocked protests, she got dressed again in one of the saris Anusha had helped her choose at the market and went up on deck. She jumped in shock as Ronan's voice came out of the shadows.

'How did you escape them?'

'I waited till Marianne was in bed, then got dressed again and came out.'

'What's the betting she'll get dressed too, fetch her mother and come searching for you, all in the interests of propriety?'

'At least I'll have a few minutes on my own first.'

'I don't suppose . . . no, it wouldn't be fair to you.'

'What?'

'I don't suppose you'd like to come and sit in a little refuge I've found? I'm sure they won't find us there. It's outside our area of the deck, a place the crew usually use, but they're asleep by this time, the steward says. He's the one who showed it to me the other night when I said I just wanted some peace and quiet without people pestering me.'

'Let's go there quickly.'

He took her hand and led her through the moonlight into a shadowy part of the deck, where a narrow gap let them into a small area with a couple of benches along the sides. 'Shh! I heard something.'

They stood very still and sure enough, Mrs Garston's strident tones carried through the night. 'Where can she be?'

'I can't think, Mama! She said she was just going up on deck for a few moments.'

'She'll be meeting a man, I'm sure she will. A female who's worked in a mill won't have moral scruples like our sort of people do. Their sensibilities are blunted by the free life they lead. I'd never have let you share a cabin with her if I'd known her background.'

'She seems decent enough, Mama. She doesn't flirt with anyone and spends most of her time reading. I'm sure she's read everything in the ship's library. It's a wonder she's not cross-eyed.'

'Addling her brain. I'd not allow you to do that. Gentlemen don't want wives who're cleverer than they are.'

The voices faded away and Xanthe let out her breath in relief.

'I'm sorry you heard such remarks about yourself,' Ronan said.

'It doesn't matter. I'm quite aware of how they feel about me.'

'Are you aware of how I feel about you? I—'

'Ronan, please don't!'

'Don't what?'

'Say anything personal. It doesn't matter what you feel about me. We're so far apart there can be no – permanent friendship between us.'

'It's not friendship I want. Xanthe, won't you—'

But she'd gone, fleeing from him with an inarticulate murmur of distress. And before he could catch her up, she was safe inside her cabin again. He went back on the deck, knowing he could at least safeguard her reputation.

When he met Marianne and her mother strolling along, he affected pleasure at seeing them and agreed to take a turn round the deck with them.

'You haven't seen Xanthe, have you?' Marianne asked.

'Should I have?'

'She came out for a walk.'

'I'm on my own, as you can see. And since I've enjoyed a little fresh air now, I think I'll go back to my cabin and try to sleep. Perhaps I'll have more luck this time.'

For the rest of the two-week journey to Suez, Xanthe took good care to keep away from him. He knew it was sensible of her. And he knew it'd be wrong of him to pursue her now that he was the heir to Ardgullan.

But he didn't want to be sensible. He wanted . . . oh, he wanted her. Just Xanthe, with her lively comments on life and her beautiful expressive face.

16

Mrs Largan didn't leave her bed again. She faded away as quietly as she'd lived, trying not to be a trouble, smiling when her son sat with her, thanking Maia for looking after her so carefully.

Conn was sitting with his mother when she died, holding her hand. When he heard a sigh, then felt the hand in his go slack, he looked at her face and knew what had happened. Still, he felt her throat for a pulse, not wanting to accept that she'd died. When he couldn't find one he sat staring at her, feeling utterly lost. He couldn't imagine life without her.

'Oh, no!'

Maia's soft voice made him turn and say, 'Yes, she's gone.' He raised his mother's hand to his lips then laid it across her chest, kissing her cheek as well before standing up.

Maia came to kiss his mother's other cheek, tears streaming down her face. Shaking her head slowly and sadly, she fumbled for a handkerchief, couldn't find one and mopped her eyes with her apron instead.

He tried to think what to do and couldn't.

She waited, her head on one side, as if waiting for him to speak. When he didn't, she said quietly, 'Shall I lay her out for you? I'd like to perform that last service for her.'

'Would you?'

'Yes, of course.'

'Do you need help lifting her, Maia?

'No. I'm sure Nancy will help me.'

'We'll need a coffin.' He couldn't even think how to get one, felt so numb and stupid.

'Mr Carling makes coffins. You could ride across and ask his help.'

His words were bitter. 'Would he make one for a person like me?'

'Of course he would.'

While he was gone, Maia tended to Mrs Largan, with Nancy in attendance.

'Poor lady, she was only skin and bone,' Nancy said. 'She must have been pretty when she was young.'

And a little later, 'How will the master manage without her? He was devoted to her. It was lovely to see them together.'

'He'll manage well enough once he's over the shock. We all do when we lose someone, don't we? Life goes on, whether we want it to or not.'

Nancy's face twisted in distress and she nodded.

There was no way of getting a clergyman to officiate at the burial, but Conn made an area of the garden into a burial ground and said he'd plant it with his mother's favourite flowers.

Cassandra and Reece came across from Lynch's Farm for the informal ceremony, bringing Livia with them.

To everyone's consternation, Kathleen insisted on coming too, wearing black, talking too loudly, mouthing trite condolences Conn didn't want from her and spoiling the burial itself by asking in a loud voice, 'Why are those servants here?'

'Because I asked them to attend,' he replied in a tight voice.

'You shouldn't have done that. It's not seemly. Tell them to go back to the house and get on with their work.'

'The servants loved her too. She'd want all the people who loved her to be present as she's laid to rest.'

When Kathleen opened her mouth to protest, he snapped, 'Be quiet or go away!'

He looked so fierce even she closed her mouth, though she glared at the servants throughout the informal ceremony.

Afterwards, one by one, they came to shake his hand and offer their condolences. Kathleen tried to stand next to him, but Reece grasped her forearm and pulled her back, shaking her when she protested and telling her in a savage undertone to be quiet.

The furious look Conn gave her made her blink and for once she understood that she'd really upset him.

Cassandra went into the kitchen to help Maia, seizing the opportunity to ask, 'Do you want to come back and live with us now? You know you'll always be welcome. We can easily build on another bedroom.'

Maia linked her arm in her sister's for a moment or two and leaned her head against her sister's shoulder. 'Thank you. If I need somewhere to go, be sure I'll come to you. But for the moment, Conn needs me.'

'It's not right for you to stay here, love.'

'Isn't it? I think it is.'

'Maia, he's not for you.'

'I know that. But he needs me desperately. If that's all I can do for him, be here in his time of distress, then I'll do it gladly.'

Maia was glad when the visitors left, especially glad to be free of Kathleen's scowls and pointed remarks. She watched Conn say farewell to them, then go and shut himself in the library, his main place of refuge from the world.

After helping Nancy clear up, she went into her bedroom and allowed herself to weep for the mistress she'd loved – and also for herself. She had so much love for Conn and didn't dare show it openly but he'd said he wanted to marry her one day, if he could, so surely she could dream a little. She longed for a home and family, children to love and raise. His home, his children.

She knew her sister had similar feelings for Ronan. What a pair she and Xanthe were, ignoring the decent young men who'd tried to court them for years, and falling in love with two gentlemen.

Her father had told her tales of Eros, the Greek god of love, son of Aphrodite. If there was such a being, he had a lot to answer for!

After Mrs Largan's funeral, Livia noticed a change in Kathleen. She'd never been exactly docile, because she was too used to getting her own way, but had settled down reasonably well, spending most of her days with the horses and sitting with Livia in the evenings.

Now she seemed to be having moments where her mind went blank, at least it did if her facial expression was anything to judge by. And she was talking to herself, breaking off and looking guilty if anyone came near her.

What was happening to her?

She was so different from Leo, who was also slow-thinking. He was innately kind and seemed to sense what would hurt someone. Even Kathleen responded well to him, because he knew so much about horses and was allowing her to help school Francis's horses and to keep an eye on a pregnant mare.

Once or twice Kathleen fell into black moods and tried to quarrel with him but he simply stared at her then turned away to do some job or other. She would come stumping into the house to complain about him to her hostess, but Livia insisted he was in charge of the animals and knew exactly what he was doing.

In the evenings, Livia usually read to her guest, something which seemed to calm her down quite well. But now, instead of listening intently, Kathleen let her attention wander, jerking back to gaze at Livia as if she was listening, but not asking questions as she had before, just – staring.

Kathleen had nightmares too, thrashing around in her bed and waking everyone with screams and cries.

Livia began to understand that this life couldn't go on and to think about her own future again. She didn't want to spend her life tied to this strange young woman, but taking charge of Kathleen had given her time to adjust to her loss and think about her future, not to mention money to buy food without dipping into her meagre savings.

She knew for certain now that she didn't want to return to England, where she had no one to turn to. But what did she want to do with herself? She started scanning the newspapers when she could get them to see if there were advertisements for governesses. Surely she could manage to teach girls?

In the meantime she was saving all the money Reece and Cassandra were paying her to use her fields for two cows they'd purchased, which made her feel safer. And she was learning from Orla of all people how to be frugal. Kathleen no longer seemed interested in having a maid look after her and Orla had turned happily to helping Livia.

Now that there was no Francis to make foolish purchases and insist they were necessary, Livia found she could live more cheaply than she'd expected.

After working out where her money went, she wrote to the bookseller in Perth to say that her husband had died and she could no longer afford to purchase books from him. She sighed wistfully as she looked at the letter, but it had to be sent.

But she also sent a message to the local shop that she wanted to receive her own copy of *The Perth Gazette*. It came out on Fridays but arrived later in the country. She'd have to send Leo to pick up her copy. Surely she'd find some form of employment in it? There were lots of advertisements.

When she went outside and looked at the sky, she sighed again at the sight of rain clouds building up to the west, because Kathleen was much harder to control when it was stormy. It was as if something unpleasant in her that was normally under control was stirred by the dark forces of the storm.

Livia hadn't expected that and grew a little nervous, so asked Leo to help keep an eye on Kathleen in stormy weather.

He nodded. 'The horses get edgy too. She's more like them than like you, isn't she? She's not a real lady. Something inside her head doesn't work properly.'

Out of the mouths of babes and sucklings, she thought. Now where did that saying come from? She spent a pleasant hour searching the Bible and found it in Psalms.

By that time Kathleen had come in, gone to wash and flung herself down in a chair.

'Why don't you do some embroidery?'

'I hate embroidery.'

'Ladies often keep themselves occupied with fancywork.'

'I *don't want to!* Read to me.'

In the end, for the sake of peace, Livia did this. But she lay awake and worried that night. Kathleen seemed to be behaving more and more strangely, and she couldn't understand why her guest had changed.

By the time the ship got to Suez, Ronan was feeling much better, though he still grew tired more quickly than usual. He listened to the other passengers making plans to visit ancient monuments or go and inspect the diggings for the canal. He was worried that Xanthe would join them and delay him. He needed to get home as quickly as possible, but he intended to make sure she got home first.

He bribed the steward to find out what Xanthe was intending.

'Miss Blake is intending to go and inspect the Suez Canal diggings, sir,' the steward told him. 'Thank you. Most generous.' He pocketed the tip.

Ronan paced the deck, worrying about that, and wondered whether he could feign a relapse that required her attention. Then destiny intervened again, or chance, he didn't care what it was called. One of the other passengers, a gentleman to whom Ronan had taken an instant dislike, attached himself to the group intending to go and see the sights.

He'd been making a nuisance of himself to Xanthe intermittently, but had stopped when his overtures got him nowhere. However, one evening Ronan found him trying to force himself upon her in a quiet part of the deck. He took the fellow by the scruff of the neck and threw him away by force, so furious he had trouble controlling himself.

'Are you all right?' he asked Xanthe after the fellow had slunk off.

'Yes. Thank you so much for helping me. I can't understand why he thought— Why will men not leave me alone?'

'Have you looked at yourself in the mirror lately?'

She flushed and bit her lip, obviously embarrassed by this. 'I don't dwell on my appearance. Ronan . . . isn't there some way I can stop them?'

'No way has ever been found of stopping men lusting after a beautiful woman.'

'*You* don't annoy me with unwanted attentions. Nor do most other gentlemen. It's just a few, like him.'

'I think my mother brought me up with better manners. And besides . . . you and I are good friends, are we not? I'd hate to spoil our friendship.'

Their eyes met and for a moment neither said a word, then she nodded. 'Yes, I too value our friendship.'

'If you go on an expedition with that group, there will be no one to protect you. I doubt the Garstons will make the effort.'

'Could you not come too?'

'Not this time. I really do have to get home.'

'Of course. I knew that really. I shouldn't have asked.' She crossed her arms across her breasts in a protective gesture. 'In that case, I don't think it'd be wise to go.'

'I'm afraid not.'

'It's not fair. Men have such a better time in life.'

'It's not at all fair, I agree! Look, I know you want to travel, but please, Xanthe, take care where you go and with whom.' At any other time he'd have delayed his own journey to escort her, but he didn't want to do that. Not this time. Who knew what state everything would be in back at Ardgullan?

She looked so downhearted he ached to take her in his arms. But he didn't. She was right that their worlds were too far apart. But apart from his duty to his family and the estate, he knew that other people would look down on her if he married her and make her life a misery. Or else they'd treat her as an oddity, just as some of the gentlefolk on the ship did.

'Being sensible isn't as much fun, is it?' he said with a sigh.

'No. But I *will* get to Greece one day. Whatever else happens, I intend to do that for my father. I shall investigate Mr Cook's tours once I'm settled in England again. I've read that they take tours to Switzerland now. Surely going with a group would be a safe way to travel? There has to be a way.'

★   ★   ★

A few days after Mrs Largan's death, Maia sat at the kitchen table, toying with her food and watching Conn eat his evening meal. He seemed lost in thought and hardly said a word. Afterwards he wandered out towards his library without offering his usual thanks for the meal.

He'd eaten very lightly, claiming he wasn't hungry, saying he'd eaten plenty at midday. But he hadn't. She'd prepared his tray herself and taken it into the library and she'd seen the tray when Nancy brought it back to the kitchen, with the food rearranged, but not much of it eaten.

In her usual cheerful way Nancy had suggested offering the leftovers on the various plates to the three stable lads, who came in daily from their nearby homes, one of them staying each night in case help was needed. They had no qualms about clearing every scrap of food and she was smiling as she brought it back. 'I've gone hungry too often to see good food going to waste.'

When Maia went to bed that night she couldn't sleep. She lay worrying about Conn, who hadn't even gone out riding today, claiming he had accounts to attend to. But she'd walked along the veranda a few times to check on him and had seen him staring into space each time, not even aware of her presence outside the window.

She was just dozing off when she heard a door open and foot-steps move along the veranda. The sounds had come from Conn's bedroom. She could hear leaves rustling underfoot, which meant he'd gone out into the garden.

Getting up she hurried across to the glazed door that led out from her bedroom to the veranda and was just in time to see him disappearing along the garden path. She could guess where he was going: to his mother's garden, the one he'd had cleared for her but which had never been finished because Mrs Largan had preferred to sit on the veranda. He'd gone to stand there a few times since her death.

Maia hesitated. It was none of her business if he chose to go walking at night. But whose business was it, then? Who was there now to care how Conn was feeling and jolly him out of his sad moods as his mother had? Ronan had gone back to Ireland, leaving no one but her. Such a lonely man, her Conn.

Well, she was here still, had refused to leave and go to live with Cassandra, because she knew he needed her. Flinging her shawl round her shoulders, she left her hair flowing freely down her back. Mrs Largan had worn little night bonnets and so had Mrs Kathleen, but Maia didn't like being trussed up to go to bed. Even her nightgowns were simple affairs that she'd learned to make herself, hanging loose from a shoulder yoke, sleeveless in summer.

The night was chilly, with not even a memory of the heat of summer, but luckily it wasn't raining and the three-quarter moon gave enough light for her to follow Conn along the path.

She stopped at the edge of the cleared space with its rough bench. He was standing there, hands thrust deep into his dressing-gown pockets, bare feet thrust into the felt slippers his mother had instructed Maia in making. She wasn't a skilled needlewoman but was competent nowadays, thanks to her former mistress.

He didn't even notice her, heaving a sigh and gulping as he pulled out a handkerchief and scrubbed at his eyes.

'Oh, Conn!' She'd spoken before she realised it.

He swung round. 'Maia! What are you doing here? Is something wrong?'

'No, nothing's wrong. I heard you get up and followed you. I was worried about you.' She moved forward, sure he needed a loving touch.

He took a step backwards. 'Go back to bed, Maia. It's not right for you to be out here alone with me. It's not right for you even to stay at Galway House now.'

'You need someone to look after you and your house with Xanthe gone – and someone to talk to, as well.'

His voice grew harsh. 'Don't you understand that I'm trying to do the right thing by you? I want you, Maia, and have done for a long time. But I'm not free yet. It'd be wrong to take advantage of you. Love isn't enough; you deserve marriage. If I can one day, if you're still free, I will – but not now.'

'Even if you get your marriage annulled, you can't marry a woman from my background. I've always known that. Oh Conn, I love you so much. Surely we don't need to pretend any longer?'

'It'd ruin you if we . . . if I . . . and I won't do that. Not only am I a married man, but I'm a convict and can't be sure of getting my conviction overturned. You came free to this colony and can hold your head up in any society. I should give you the chance to find someone else.'

'What does that matter to me?'

'It ought to matter. You should leave Galway House. In fact, I'll take you to your sister's tomorrow. It's for your own good, Maia.'

'I won't go. It'd tear me apart to leave you. You say you love me, Conn. Has that changed?'

'Of course it hasn't.' He took another step backwards as she moved towards him. 'I love you too much to ruin you, Maia. If I manage to free myself from Kathleen, and if you're still free then – and it'll take years – I'll ask you to marry me and to hell with what other people think. But I'm not free now.' He moved again, bumped into a tree and could go no further.

Smiling she moved close to him and put her arms round his neck. 'I'm being shameless, I know, but if you love me, that's all that matters to me. We've waited long enough to show our love.' As he tried to pull away, she tightened her hold.

He stared down at her and slowly, so slowly she thought she would die from waiting, he bent his head and kissed her, a long loving kiss, not a devouring one, but a kiss that seemed to say everything he felt.

Conn drew back and brushed a strand of hair from her forehead. 'Are you sure, my darling?'

'Very sure.'

He'd tried to resist her, but he was only human and couldn't summon up the strength to keep pushing her away, especially not with her looking at him with that loving expression. 'Then become my love, darling Maia, and to hell with the world.'

With a laugh that was almost a sob she took his hand and let him lead her into the house, into his bedroom and into his loving embrace.

She began to unbutton her bodice.

'Let me, my love.'

The darkness no longer seemed hostile and heavy, but warm and enfolding. Her body felt so right in his arms. But before he made love to her, he held her at arm's length and asked one final time, 'Are you still sure?'

'How many times do I have to tell you?'

'Every day for the rest of my life. And Maia, darling . . . I may not be able to marry you now, but when I can, when this annulment comes through, I shall do so joyfully.'

'But I'm—'

'Shh! You're my love, the woman I want to spend the rest of my life with.'

'Then stop talking and make me yours.'

As they lay together afterwards, he thought he hadn't been so happy for a good many years and knew that his mother would have understood. He vowed that he'd love and protect Maia while ever there was breath in his body.

On that thought he frowned. That wasn't enough. He must make sure she was protected financially in case something went wrong and he was no longer there. She and any children they might have. He was still lawyer enough to draw up a will and would do that the very next day, get it signed . . .

She murmured and nestled closer in her sleep and he laid his head beside hers, smiling in the darkness. Tomorrow he'd think carefully. Tonight was for loving.

17

Ronan and Xanthe called a truce and went sightseeing together in Alexandria as they waited for the ship to leave. They had two days to spare and he wasn't going to leave her to the mercies of some chance-met travelling companions or a local guide who might be a murderer for all he knew

They didn't even discuss it, they simply let themselves enjoy everything the guide showed them, the ancient buildings, the people in the streets who looked so different from people in England or Australia, the markets which surely sold everything on earth.

'Many English and French people come now,' the guide said proudly. 'Since the Cairo railway opened ten years ago is easier to travel. I speak both these languages. *Très bien, monsieur.*'

A little later he said, 'You don't complain about too hot.'

'I love the warmth,' Xanthe said.

His eyes slid over her uncorseted body, not offensively but as if assessing her. 'You dress wisely.'

That evening some of their fellow passengers complained bitterly about the heat. What else had they expected in this part of the world? Ronan wondered.

When they got back to the hotel on the second evening, Xanthe looked at him sadly. 'So it ends.'

'What do you mean?'

'We'll be back to the confines of a ship with people watching every look we exchange.'

'Does that matter?'

'Yes. I'm not a loose woman and I'm not going to act like one. It's been . . . delightful . . . but now I have to pack my bag ready to board the ship early tomorrow.'

When she didn't join the others for the evening meal, he knew she had gone back to avoiding him. He understood why, respected her for it – but he missed her. It felt as if half of him was missing, the half that laughed and teased and was just – there. Making him complete.

Three days out from Alexandria Xanthe sat on deck, ostensibly part of a group of ladies but not listening to them. It had happened again. A man had grabbed her on deck at dusk the previous night, fumbling with her breasts in a way that disgusted her. For a moment shock had held her dumb, then she'd started kicking and scratching, screaming for help at the top of her voice.

He'd run away before anyone got to her, but it had caused talk and she felt dirtied by the encounter, still shuddered when she remembered what he'd done. He'd had a checked cloth tied round his head, like some of the Arabs she'd seen in Alexandria, so she'd not known who he was.

After that incident she hadn't dared walk about the deck on her own unless there were other people nearby, and certainly not at dusk, however much she longed for a breath of fresh air.

The stewardess assured her that a careful watch would be kept in future and she'd be quite safe. Safe this time, Xanthe thought. Safe while I'm on the ship. But what about next time? What if this happened again in some far-away place where there was no one to rescue her? Some would say the man had done nothing, but he had! He'd left her feeling nervous.

Her plans were beginning to seem utterly naïve and unrealistic. How could she travel on her own when some men treated her that way? She wasn't rich enough to hire bodyguards and a female companion, even if she'd known of suitable people. She was even beginning to worry about how safe Mr Cook's tours would be for a woman on her own. They had seemed the answer to her desire to travel. But how could she be sure?

She was furious about all this, but she wasn't going to let it stop her doing *something*. At the very least she could travel around her own country and could afford to hire a sturdy lass from her home town of Outham to go with her. But it wouldn't be the same. She wanted to do so much more, see so much more.

One day she might go back to Australia to see her sisters, then visit the eastern side of the continent, Sydney and Melbourne. When she was older. When men had stopped looking at her like that.

Perhaps she wasn't the stuff of which lady travellers were made, after all?

'A penny for them.'

She jerked in shock and realised that Ronan had sat down next to her. He didn't say anything, just stared at her, almost as if she'd done something wrong. So she put her chin up and stared right back. The other ladies were talking in an animated fashion and she doubted anyone would hear them if they kept their voices low, but she wasn't going to speak first.

'I heard about your trouble yesterday evening.'

'The whole ship's heard of my trouble. If you intend to say I told you so, I'll remind you that I fought him off even before help arrived.'

'Yes. I'm glad about that.' He went back to staring.

'What do you want?' she asked in the end.

'I don't know. But I'm not here to say I told you so, just to see for myself that you're all right, not too upset by the incident.'

'Of course I'm upset. And mostly because you were right. I'm trying to work out how to travel without facing such *incidents* again.'

'There is no way. You're too beautiful.'

'Then I'll find a way to make myself ugly.' She glanced at the other ladies, but they were laughing about something. 'Shh. Keep your voice down.'

'It'd be impossible to make yourself ugly, because part of your beauty comes from inside. Oh hell, Xanthe, I can't bear to see you at risk.'

'It's none of your business.'

'I think it is. I've fallen in love with you. Surely you realise that?'

She loved him too but she wasn't going to say that, so shrugged. 'It doesn't matter. You'll get over it. You have to. I do understand your situation, Ronan. You have your duty to your family and I'm not going to become your or anyone else's mistress.'

'I wouldn't ask that of you.'

'Then we should both agree to stay away from one another, shouldn't we?'

'Not exactly. What I'm going to ask is that you wait until I've had time to visit my estate and think about my future in the light of what I find there. Don't . . . go travelling abroad, not yet. Please?'

'Sit and wait for you,' she mocked. 'In case you beckon to me. Then what do I do, come running like a tame puppy dog?'

'You know that I can't just rush into marriage. Dammit, Xanthe, you said you understood that.'

She sighed and the fire went out of her. 'I do, really. Dad read us enough Greek tragedies for us to understand how people like you feel about family duty. You don't just have a house to think of, but your land and your dependants.'

'Yes. The trouble is, I still don't feel that I own Ardgullan. All my life I've known it would belong to Hubert, that one day his sons would inherit. But although he became the landowner, he didn't marry and he didn't have sons, so that duty has now passed to me. And I wasn't prepared for it. I'm still not sure I even want it.'

'You do have another brother. Perhaps he could take it on.'

'Patrick's so English, he'd sell Ardgullan, I'm sure. He enjoys living in England, says he'd never live in Ireland again and is bringing up his children to be very English. And that's a good thing, I suppose, because his wife is very scornful of the Irish and she'd make a dreadful châtelaine for Ardgullan. How she lowered herself to marry him, I don't know – except that he's a handsome devil and women have always flocked to him.'

'You're quite good-looking yourself,' she said coolly. 'You must have had similar success with women.'

'A few. Not that many. But not one of them made me want

to spend the rest of my life with her. I'd think how suitable a young lady was, like choosing a horse, really, birth and breeding so important. My mother would be urging me to ask her hand in marriage and I'd think seriously about doing that, because I would like to have children one day. Then I'd realise I couldn't bear to spend my whole life tied to her, listening to her prattling on about nothing. It was too high a price to pay.'

'Well, one day you'll have to choose one woman and put up with her.'

Her mocking tone might have fooled others, but he could hear the pain behind it.

She looked at him, trying to smile and failing, so being Xanthe she got to her feet and with a curt, 'I'm tired', hurried off towards the cabins.

And he let her go. Because he was so confused about what would be fair to her that he didn't know what to think.

After that, however, she avoided him completely, finding excuses to get up and leave if he took a seat next to her, so that he learned to sit opposite her at meals, to sit nearby if he wanted to join the same group of people, and never ever to stand beside her at the rails, because she'd immediately walk away.

She was wrong, though. She didn't understand why he was still hesitating. He didn't think he could live happily with anyone else but her, even out of duty. But he didn't want to subject Xanthe to a lifetime of snubs and social snobbery. That was what worried him most, the thought of seeing her glorious spirit broken.

He kept trying to tell her that, to explain, but she wouldn't listen. Perhaps she didn't understand how cruel his class could be to those they considered their inferiors. But he did. And they could be even more cruel to those who had fallen from grace, like Conn.

The visit to Gibraltar was quite short and though Ronan tried to get Xanthe to go ashore with him, he found she'd already arranged to visit the place with some other passengers. He walked round on his own, scowling up at the huge rock, glaring at anyone who tried to invite him to buy something, and returning to the ship before the others.

He was sitting on deck when she came back. Their eyes met and she looked away first. She hadn't been looking happy lately. It was as if some fire within her was half-quenched.

On a grey, chilly day in early November the ship eased its way into Southampton and the steerage passengers crowded against the rails, talking excitedly. The cabin passengers were much more sedate in their behaviour, though even they expressed pleasure at having the long voyage over.

Xanthe stood by the rail, staring at the harbour and beyond it the town, trying to take in the fact that she was back in England, something which at one stage in her life she'd never expected to happen. She didn't know whether to feel pleased or sad about arriving, because after today she'd not be seeing Ronan again. It'd take the strain away not to have him nearby, but the thought of not seeing him again was more painful than anything she'd ever experienced in her life before.

She expected him to join her, to say farewell at least, but he didn't. She felt hurt by that, more deeply hurt than she should have allowed herself to be. After all, she was the one who had kept him at a distance, he was only doing what she'd told him to do, leaving her alone . . . Wasn't he?

Or had he just seen her as pleasant company on the voyage? No, she knew that wasn't so. She knew he did love her – but in his own way, which wasn't enough to bridge the yawning chasm between them.

But why hadn't he at least come to say goodbye to her?

As Xanthe boarded the train for London, the carriage door opened and a man got in: Ronan.

'I thought this was a ladies only carriage,' she said coolly.

'You can make a fuss and have me thrown out, but the train isn't full and it's leaving shortly, so unless you complain, no one else will.' He waited, one eyebrow cocked.

She wasn't going to complain. She was delighted to see him, though she didn't intend to tell him that.

As the train set off, he leaned back with a sigh. 'I'm glad I don't have to travel in another compartment this time.'

'I thought you'd be going to Ireland, not Manchester.'

'I wanted to see you safely home first.'

She tried to think of something clever to say to that and could come up with nothing, so kept her mouth closed.

'This is the first time I've really had a chance to talk to you alone since Alexandria. And now that the train has left, we're trapped in this compartment until the next stop and you can't get rid of me.'

It was out before she could stop herself. 'I don't want to get rid of you.'

'Ah, Xanthe!' He reached out as if to gather her into his arms, but she fended him off.

'Don't do that! You'll only make it harder.'

He leaned back again. 'Then at least let me explain why I'm hesitating – about us.'

'What is there to explain? You're landed gentry and I'm a mill lass. I'm not stupid. It's quite obvious you can't marry me.'

'I'd marry you tomorrow if I thought I could do so without ruining your life.' His voice was savage. 'Surely you have some idea by now of how snobbish the gentry are after seeing how they treat Conn? And they're just as bad when someone makes what they consider an unsuitable match. I can't bear the thought of you being made miserable, of you having no real friends *for the rest of your life*. And not just you, but any children we might have. They'd suffer too. *That* is why I'm holding back.'

'Oh.'

'Our paths crossed and from then on I was lost. I didn't fall in love with you because you're beautiful but because you're Xanthe, lively, intelligent and so very dear to me.'

'Oh.'

'Is that all you can say? You're not usually lost for words.'

She felt her face soften into a smile. 'I don't know what to say.

I don't think you do, either. Are you really coming all the way
to Outham?'

'To Manchester. I can get a train to Liverpool and cross to
Ireland from there.'

'And afterwards?'

'I must talk to people, take over my inheritance, feel my way.
Xanthe, will you promise me not to go to Europe yet? Will you
promise to wait till you hear from me before you go travelling?'

She felt angry suddenly. 'In case you decide you can squeeze
me into your life? I just . . . sit and wait like a child, to be told
what to do? No, I shan't promise anything of the sort.'

'That's not what I meant.'

'Oh?'

'Well, I didn't mean it in that sense.'

They were still arguing as they drew into the next station and
suddenly she could bear it no longer. She opened the window
and called out, 'Porter, can you please ask this gentleman to move
to another carriage? He boarded the train in a hurry and didn't
realise this was a ladies only carriage.'

'You have a damnable temper, Xanthe Blake,' he said in an
undertone.

'And you're a – a patronising humbug, Ronan Maguire.
When you do decide what you want, not to mention what I'm
allowed to have, let me know, and then I'll tell you whether I
agree. Or not.'

She sat staring stonily ahead as the porter got into the carriage
to fetch Ronan's luggage and after both men had left her alone
there, she cried on and off all the way to Manchester, angry at
herself for caring and at him for taking so long to decide what
to do, for not . . . She pushed that thought away each time.

Ronan was there on the station in Manchester, his eyes
searching the crowd for her.

She walked past him, nose in the air, and found one of the
frequent local trains waiting to depart. As she got into it, she
glanced quickly back and saw him watching her. He raised
one hand.

And heaven help her, she waved back, couldn't stop herself.

Soon she'd be home again. She'd see Pandora and Zachary, have other things to occupy her mind than a stubborn Irishman. It'd take time, but she'd get over him – or at least learn to live without him.

When she got out of the train in Outham, she stopped in shock because it no longer felt like home. Everything seemed grey and dirty, and it was raining hard, even the puddles taking on a grey sheen.

She walked to Blake's Emporium from the station, followed by a lad with her trunks and luggage on a cart. If she looked bedraggled and wet when she arrived, it might hide the fact that she'd been crying.

Ronan watched Xanthe's train leave, wondering if she would wait for him before setting off on her travels and whether he'd been right to ask her to wait, then he set off on the long, weary journey home.

He arrived late the following day, feeling exhausted and underneath everything else, utterly miserable. He'd taken a train as far as he could, then hired a carriage to take him and his luggage from Enniskillen to his home.

As he was driven through the village which had the same name as his family home, he stared out of the carriage window in shock. Had the houses always been so tumbledown? Had the people always looked so gaunt and wretched? Why had Hubert not done something about that? The Maguires owned most of the houses here, after all. Surely there had been enough money to repair leaking roofs and broken window panes.

Well, Ronan owned the village now, and was responsible for the houses and their inhabitants' welfare. Shame on him if he did nothing about this misery!

Passing the Dower House brought memories tumbling back: his mother strolling round the garden, laughing at him, picking flowers to brighten up her rooms, being driven out in the old carriage that Hubert kept for her use to visit a friend.

Would she still be alive if he hadn't gone to Australia, or had the doctor been right and the problem would have flared up anyway? He'd never know, but he'd always feel guilty.

The big house looked sad and unloved, with rain weeping down the walls and windows, forming puddles in the drive – not softly falling rain today, but driving rain that rattled against the carriage like shotgun pellets.

He got out and hurried into the house, holding tightly to his hat. The door was opened for him before he reached it and the housekeeper stood there, as she had for so many years. For the first time he felt a sense of homecoming.

'Welcome back, sir. We're glad to have you back.'

He took off his hat and shook the rain from it. 'Thank you for your welcome. How are you, Mary? You're looking well.'

'I am well, sir. You know I never ail.'

'Is my brother here?'

'No, sir. Mr Patrick comes every few weeks to make sure everything is all right, but he doesn't stay. He leaves it to Mr Devlin to run the place.'

'Well, he's been the land agent here for a long time.'

'Mr Devlin's not well, sir. He's doing his best, but he's getting old. We all are.' She patted his arm with the easy familiarity of one who'd known him as a child. 'I'm glad you're back now, so I am.'

Her Irish accent was stronger today, which usually meant she was emotional.

He slipped off his overcoat and let her take it from him. 'I'll just – walk round the house, get used to being back. Perhaps you could make me a cup of tea and a bite of something to eat? Give me a call when it's ready.'

'Yes, sir. I'll have your luggage brought in and put in the master's bedroom.'

He hesitated to take the room his father and then Hubert had occupied, then shrugged. It was just a room. If he didn't like it, he could move to another easily enough. There were plenty of them, that was for sure.

He walked through the drawing room, which felt damp and neglected, the rugs worn and the curtains faded. That led into the dining room, where the big oval table was as shiny as ever, but the carpet had worn patches in it.

He crossed the hall, hesitated then went into the small room that had been his mother's private parlour before his father died, used only by family. Some of the wallpaper was hanging loose above the window and the rug was frayed at one corner. The books on the shelves were Hubert's books. His brother had been a great reader. The small easy chair he remembered so clearly had gone and been replaced by a much bigger one, upholstered in scuffed brown leather. It looked out of place. This had always been a woman's room.

'Shall I bring the tea tray in here, sir?'

He turned to see Eilis standing there. 'I didn't know you worked here now.'

'When we heard about your mother dying, God bless her, Mr Hubert closed up the Dower House and said I should come here as a maid, though to tell the truth, there wasn't much work for me. He didn't have many visitors.'

Ronan had played with Eilis as a child, known her when she worked for his mother. He had so many links to the people here. 'Did you ever suspect that my brother was ill?'

She hesitated. 'He grew very quiet, sir, the last few months, didn't want to do anything much but read.'

'He always did read a lot.'

'Yes, sir. But this was different. He hardly moved from this room after your mother left, even had his meals brought in here. And he left everything he could for Mr Devlin to decide about. He died in that chair, sir. We found him there one morning.'

Ronan stared round again. 'Well, I think we'll clear out my brother's things now, so that I can use this room. It's a pleasant place to sit of an evening. Can you see to that for me?'

'Of course, sir.'

'If there's anything you're doubtful about moving, put it to one side and ask me before you finish.'

'Yes, sir. Would you like to have your tea now before it gets cold?'

'I'll take it into the library.' He wasn't using the room till that chair was removed. He drank two cups of tea sitting in solitary state behind the desk that had been his father's, wishing he could have it out of an Australian tin mug that held as much as the fancy teapot.

Even this room didn't please him. He'd been brought in here for punishment as a lad. His father had used a strap for serious offences, kept it in the bottom drawer. It felt strange to be sitting on the other side of this desk. When he opened the drawer, he found the strap still there and threw it on the fire in a sudden fit of anger that anyone would hit little boys with it.

After that, he felt hungry suddenly and ate the cakes, drinking all the tea in the small teapot.

He wondered what to do next and couldn't seem to make up his mind. Loneliness sat heavily on his shoulders.

What was Xanthe doing now? Was she any happier than him?

When Dot opened the door, she gaped at the visitor. 'It's Miss Xanthe, isn't it? Come in, come in! Eeh, you're all wet.'

Behind Xanthe the lad who'd brought the luggage cleared his throat. 'I'll need help with that big trunk, miss.'

'I'll fetch a shop lad to help and tell Mr Zachary you're here.' Dot darted off down the short corridor that led from the hall of the living quarters into the shop and returned with her master. A sturdy lad followed him, nodded to Xanthe and went outside to help with the luggage.

Zachary beamed at his sister-in-law. 'Why didn't you send us a telegram to let us know you were coming, Xanthe?'

'I'd forgotten about such luxuries after staying in Australia. They don't have telegrams there, or trains either.'

'No. I remember. Very primitive. But beautiful too. Well, it's wonderful to see you. You know you're always welcome.'

She looked up the stairs. 'Is Pandora all right? Or is she out? I'd expected her to come rushing down.'

'She'll be feeding little Hebe, I expect.'

'She's had the baby? It's a girl? And you called her by a Greek name?'

'Yes. We thought your father would like that.'

'Oh, he would, he would!'

The two lads came down the stairs again and she fumbled in her pocket for her purse, taking out some coins. When they'd gone, she said, 'I can't wait to see my new niece and my sister.'

Pandora was indeed feeding little Hebe. Zachary stood in the doorway of the bedroom, smiling fondly as his wife shrieked in surprise, startling the rosy-cheeked infant into letting go for a moment and wailing in protest.

As Hebe settled back to the important business of life and her sister held out one hand, Xanthe went across to kiss her.

'What a beautiful baby!'

'She is, isn't she. Looks like our side of the family, I think.'

'Thank goodness,' Zachary said. 'My side isn't noted for its good looks.'

'Sit on the bed, Xanthe, and don't you dare leave till I've finished this!' Pandora ordered. 'Go away, Zachary. I shall cheer up now I've got my sister to talk to.'

When he'd gone, Xanthe looked at her in surprise. 'Why do you need cheering up?'

Pandora pulled a face. 'Because feeding a baby is very boring and not the most comfortable thing in the world. I know it has to be done and I love her dearly, but honestly, Xanthe, it's driving me mad. I must be a bad mother. Other women seem to get all the happiness they need from being wives and mothers, but I need to feed my mind as well.'

'Are you sorry you got married?'

'Never. Zachary is a wonderful man. It's just – Father brought us up to use our brains and no one wants a woman to do that, especially a married woman. A married woman's life can be very tedious! I'm warning you: don't get married unless you love a man quite desperately.'

Xanthe bit her lip, blinking as tears came into her eyes.

Pandora's eyes narrowed. 'Something's wrong. And you've been crying. I don't think Zachary noticed because you're so bedraggled, but I know you better.'

So it all came tumbling out, what had happened, how she had fallen in love with Ronan, how it could lead nowhere. Once little Hebe had been laid in her cot and left to the young nursemaid whose main responsibility she was, they moved to the parlour and continued to exchange news.

'I can see how you'd find Ronan attractive,' Pandora said. 'And he seemed a nice man, as well. I never thought, though, that you'd fall in love so foolishly. You've always been so practical.'

'No one can be practical about love.'

Pandora smiled. 'No. You're right. And you say Maia is in love with Conn? That's terrible. Do you think she'll really let him love her – out of wedlock?'

Xanthe nodded. 'One day it's bound to happen. Every time they're together you can see how much they love one another. And his wife is a dreadful woman, really strange and slow-witted, but vicious with it.'

'Well, there's nothing we can do about it. Maia can be stubborn for all her gentleness. Are you quite sure Ronan loves you?'

'Yes. But he can't marry someone like me.'

'I don't see why not. He won't marry someone else if he loves you, surely? It wouldn't be fair.'

'That's the way things are for the gentry. They don't marry for love, but for breeding and property. He said he was thinking of me, how hard it would be for me not to be accepted, to be criticised . . . What do I know about such things? He may be right. Anyway, I can hardly force him to marry me, can I? Oh, let's not talk about it any more. We'll just see how things go.'

Zachary joined them for tea, then went back into the shop, which didn't close until nine o'clock at night.

In spite of her sadness, Xanthe was enjoying Pandora's company. Her sister looked a different person from the unhappy woman who'd left Australia because she was ill from homesickness. Even though she complained about the tedium of caring for a child and overseeing the house, she looked to be in excellent health, her cheeks rosy and her eyes sparkling with life. And for all her complaints about motherhood, she clearly adored little Hebe.

As Xanthe lay in bed, her last thoughts as she drifted towards sleep were of Ronan. Had he arrived home yet? Was he thinking of her?

Would she ever see him again?

18

The following morning Ronan found his land agent in the small room off the stable block which they called by the grand title of the estate office. John Devlin came hobbling towards him with a stick, breathing laboriously.

'Are you all right?'

'I can't seem to shake this chestiness, sir. Sorry about that. Please take a seat. How can I help you?'

'I wanted to talk to you about the estate, the cottages in the village, repairs, everything really. The place is looking – well, very run down.' He waited.

John sighed. 'I'm sorry about that, Mr Ronan,' he said. 'I mean, Mr Maguire. I tried to get things done, really I did, but Mr Hubert would never spend money if he could help it, even on important repairs. I've done what I could, managed to stop the cottages falling down, but that was all.'

'I'm not blaming you. I know my father was a bad landlord and it seems Hubert followed suit. But I mean to do better. I think there's too much work for a man of your age, so would you mind if I took on a deputy land agent? He and I could both come to you for help, but you could take things more easily. Then, once you're ready to retire – and you don't need to do that till you want – I'll continue paying you your wages and—'

'I couldn't take money I'd not earned, sir. It wouldn't be right. Though I would be grateful if you could pay me the wages owing.'

'*You haven't been paid?*'

'No, sir. Quite a few people haven't.'

'What did Hubert do with the money?' He bit off further words out of loyalty to his brother. 'You've given your life to this estate,

John Devlin, so I'll pay you as soon as I can, and make sure you're comfortable when you retire.'

The older man gave a weary sigh. 'I doubt I'll make old bones, sir, so I'll not be a burden on you for long. It's my wife I'm worried about, after I'm gone.'

'I'll see that she's all right, too. But don't talk about dying. Talk about getting better. I can't do without you. No one knows the estate like you do. I'm bound to need your advice about all sorts of things. I'm very ignorant because I never took an interest.' He saw John's face brighten and was pleased by that. 'Now, do you have any idea who could act as your deputy?'

'Well . . . yes, I do. Brian Cahill, Peter's youngest. He's a sensible fellow. Not fancy spoken or anything, but he knows the estate and he's been helping me out a bit.'

'I'll send for him at once, then. Or perhaps you'd like to speak to him at first?' He smiled at John and said coaxingly, 'See if you don't get well again now I'm back. I'm going to insist on it.'

His land agent laughed. 'You could always cajole people into doing what you wanted, even as a lad.'

Could he? Ronan wondered as he walked away. He wasn't sure about that. Xanthe had a mind of her own, and the local ladies here had their own ways and standards too. He knew they wouldn't approve of his marriage plans. Could he cajole them into accepting her?

There was going to be a lot to sort out during the next few days, what with inspections, discussions and long talks to both John and Brian, but first he had to see the lawyer about his inheritance, find out how much money there was and where it was kept. He needed to make a start on repairs before the worst of the winter weather.

The day after her arrival in Outham Xanthe woke to almost-clear skies and a freshly washed world that made her itch to go outside. It wasn't warm, not at this time of year, and full winter would soon be upon them, but it was bright and clear. After an early breakfast with her sister and brother-in-law she went for a long walk round the town, meeting people she'd known in the old days.

At a more acceptable hour, she went to call on the Minister's wife. Phoebe Rainey had helped her and her sisters in many ways in the old days, and was the first on her list for visiting.

Xanthe enjoyed a pleasant hour with her old friend and found herself elevated now to calling the Minister's wife Phoebe. She shared all the news from Australia and only when it came to her own plans was she more reticent.

As the hours passed, she kept wondering what Ronan was doing today. Had he found his inheritance in good condition? Did he still care about her? Were matchmaking mothers already descending on him?

To Xanthe's surprise and then amusement, she found herself the target of matchmaking. After the first Sunday service she was hemmed in by people wanting to talk to her. The sisters or mothers of young men she had grown up with or met at chapel, her former neighbours, so many people were waiting to speak to her. She was invited to visit them, they spoke casually of 'our Henry' or 'our Robert' and she didn't dare say she already had a 'fellow' – because she didn't know for certain that she did have Ronan.

Pandora was also amused by this but she saw it as a test. 'Go and visit them,' she whispered. 'Meet their brothers and sons. See if you're attracted to any of them, or whether your feelings for Ronan hold strong.'

'I won't be attracted and my feelings won't change.'

'How do you know?'

'How did you know you loved Zachary? From what you told me, it didn't take you long.'

'That's different. We were thrown together on the journey so we got to know one another more quickly than usual.'

'And you think Ronan and I weren't thrown together on the journey?'

'You didn't – do anything wrong!'

'If you mean what I think, no, I didn't give myself to him.' She almost wished she had, then he'd feel compelled to marry her straight away instead of delaying and worrying about how happy she'd be in his milieu. She pushed those thoughts away again. 'Anyway, I shall be bored to tears if I go and take tea with everyone who's invited me.'

'Do it for me, then. I don't really like the thought of you marrying so far above you. It won't work out, I know it won't. I want you to be as happy as I am with Zachary.'

Why was everyone so certain that Ronan wasn't the right man for her? Xanthe wondered. Surely when two people loved one another, they could overcome their differences. It wasn't as if he lacked money to support her or she was badly educated, and didn't know how to use a knife and fork. Thanks to Mrs Largan her table manners were impeccable and her former mistress's reminiscences had given her a fair idea of how to conduct herself in society.

She found things to fill her days, but whatever she did, she missed Ronan dreadfully! He was in her thoughts so often, she'd not have been surprised to see him walking beside her.

When he went into the family lawyer's office in Enniskillen, Ronan was greeted by an unsmiling Mr Hatton, who exchanged brief greetings with his client, gestured to a seat and pulled a pile of papers towards him with a sigh.

'I've had copies made of all the main documents and accounts, which I'll give you before you leave, but if I may sum up the situation?'

At Ronan's nod, he continued, 'I'm sorry to tell you that your father didn't leave the estate in a sound position financially. As you know, he enjoyed a lavish lifestyle and . . . well, he gambled at times, not hugely, but enough to make serious inroads into the family's reserves of money. In short, he acted as if he was a very wealthy man to whom money didn't matter, but although he was comfortably circumstanced when he inherited, he was by no means wealthy – and grew poorer over the years.

'Your brother found matters in confusion when he inherited

because I had not been consulted by your father about certain business arrangements. Hubert was determined to rebuild the family fortunes, but he too made several unwise investments, one in a bank which failed, and another more recently in a ship which was lost at sea. He – um – remained overly optimistic about recouping the family fortunes and took risks that I did advise against, believe me.'

His shudder as he revealed this convinced Ronan more than words could ever have done.

Squaring his shoulders, the lawyer took a deep breath and added, 'What's more, I'm sorry to say this but if you too are inclined to gamble, I shall have to ask you to find another lawyer because I don't wish to be involved in your losing the family estate.' He folded his arms across his narrow chest and waited, his expression grave.

Ronan was lost for words and for a few seconds could only stare at him and try to take in what he'd been told. After a few moments, he managed to say, 'I'm not a gambler, Mr Hatton, and I'm not reckless with money. My own inheritance is not only intact but has, I believe, grown over the years. I can give you the name of the lawyer who handled my great-aunt's estate if you wish to check that. I'd be grateful if you'd remain our family lawyer, and believe me, I shall be grateful for your advice and I promise to heed it most carefully.'

After studying him for a moment or two Mr Hatton inclined his head. 'Then perhaps we may save the estate – in time, given stringently careful management.'

'Are things that bad?'

'I'm afraid so. There are creditors, some of them local tradesmen, who have been waiting only for your arrival to present their accounts and demand payment – usually long-overdue. And some of the servants' wages haven't been paid for a while.'

'I had no idea it was so bad! How long has this been going on?'

'For several years.'

'Why did Hubert not say something?'

'He believed he could retrieve the situation.'

'The creditors must be paid first, of course, before I start any renovations.'

'If you wish.'

When they'd gone through the figures and agreed on the next steps to be taken, Ronan prepared to take his leave. Mr Hatton held up one hand to stop him and cleared his throat before saying, 'There is one way to re-establish your fortunes quickly and that is to marry an heiress.'

Ronan could feel his face go rigid. 'I don't think I can bring myself to do that, Mr Hatton. I am – er, in love with a young lady and we've spoken of marriage.'

'Ah. May I ask if she brings any money to the match?'

'A little, a thousand or two, I believe, and not all of it is immediately available.'

The lawyer looked at him scornfully. 'That wouldn't be nearly enough. You should give the matter of a suitable wife your serious consideration. Your first duty is to your family estate. As it happens, I am acquainted with a certain gentleman who has risen in the world and is anxious to establish his daughter among the gentry. I could introduce you and—'

Ronan shook his head. 'No. I'm deeply in love and I just – couldn't do that.' He might not be able to marry Xanthe now – for how could he ask her to live in poverty while he struggled to build up the estate again? – but she had spoiled him for other women.

'But you are not yet engaged to her?'

'No. We agreed to wait until after I'd seen how things stood at Ardgullan.'

Mr Hatton shuffled the papers together. 'You should, in all fairness to her, hold back until we see exactly how matters stand.'

When he got home, Ronan thought long and hard, then came to the conclusion that he must write to Xanthe, explaining the situation and offering to release her from any promises – if she considered they'd made promises to one another. He wasn't even sure of that. Judging by the lawyer's long face and head shaking, it might be years before he was even in a position to take a wife.

He could walk away from this unwanted inheritance and live perfectly comfortably on his own money, marry even, but his conscience wouldn't let him do that. He was the landowner. People's lives depended on him running Ardgullan efficiently. And if he had to plough his inheritance into it to save the estate, then he must do so.

But duty was a cold bedfellow.

A few days later Zachary came upstairs just after the shop opened, carrying a letter. He held it out to Xanthe. 'This came for you in the post. I think it must be from Ronan. Who else could be writing to you from Ireland?'

She took the letter from him, nodding and smiling as she recognised the handwriting. 'If you don't mind, I'll open it in my room.'

When she'd gone, Zachary and Pandora exchanged glances. 'I hope it's good news,' she said softly. 'She tries not to show it, but she's fretting for him.'

In her bedroom Xanthe stared at the envelope, wondering if Ronan was going to be noble again and worry about making her happy? If so, she'd have to do something about it. It wasn't in her nature just to wait around for someone else to decide what was good for her or what was bad.

Taking a deep breath and hoping for the best, she opened the envelope carefully, spreading the single sheet of paper out on her dressing table.

My dearest Xanthe

I've come home to find things in a very bad way, the money gone, the estate run down, debts piled up. I'm not even sure whether I'll be able to keep Ardgullan once I've paid everything off.

Therefore, with the deepest regret, I feel I can't hold you to any promises. A man can't marry if he hasn't got a home to offer to his wife and family. You must consider yourself free to meet and marry someone else.

My regret runs very deep but my duty is clear.
With all my love
Ronan

She read the letter again, hearing his voice saying the words, sensing the anguish behind them. Then she sat down by the window, wondering what she was going to do.

One thing was certain. She wasn't going to let him be noble about this and ruin both their lives. There was no other man for her, she was quite certain of that, and she knew he loved her. She needed to find out more details about his situation, work out if she'd be a help or a hindrance to him.

There was no getting away from it: she needed to see him, talk to him, get to know Ardgullan!

Once he'd sent the letter to Xanthe, Ronan spent a sleepless night before sending a message to Mr Hatton that given his circumstances he'd ended his connection with the young lady from Australia and for the sake of his family estate, would be interested in meeting suitable young women – though he didn't wish to raise any false hopes and could promise nothing at this stage.

He received a letter back by return post, suggesting he come to Enniskillen and discuss Miss Georgina Johnson, daughter of a very rich, self-made man, who was a very amiable young lady.

Ronan wrote back quickly, before he could change his mind, to say he'd come the following day. Then he spent a sleepless night dreaming of Xanthe.

Was it fair to any young lady, he wondered, to marry when his heart was given to another?

When he arrived, he found to his surprise that Mr Hatton had already arranged a meeting.

'You said "discuss". Why are you trying to rush me into this?'

The lawyer looked a little uncomfortable. 'Mr Johnson can be very – persuasive and he's eager for his daughter to marry into the landed gentry. She's been – difficult to persuade and has refused other offers.'

'Then why should she consider me?'

'I think her father is pressing her hard. And I must stress that she's only considering you at the moment. So it would do no harm for you both to meet.'

Although it was a chilly day, after he'd left the lawyer's rooms, Ronan went for a walk along the lough, ending up, as he always did, at the castle with its twin towers. Long ago the junior branch of his family had ruled from that castle. He smiled. He was from an even more junior branch of the Maguires, but still, the castle had been the inspiration for his boyish imagination. He'd dreamed of being a knight there, rescuing fair maidens and wielding a gleaming sword.

A troop of soldiers marched by from the Royal Inniskilling Fusiliers, on their way to the barracks. This was one of two regiments who took their name from the town and the sight of them brought him suddenly back to reality. He was no knight in shining armour, just a man struggling to save his family estate.

That afternoon he went to tea at the Johnsons'. He took an instant dislike to Mr Johnson, but was pleasantly surprised by his daughter. Georgina wasn't beautiful but had a fresh, honest face.

Mr Johnson pulled out his pocket watch a few times and declared that he must return to his office. His sister-in-law, Miss Lawson, who was acting as chaperone to her niece, escorted him to the door, which left Ronan alone with Georgina for a few minutes.

'You don't really want to marry me, do you?' she asked abruptly.

He was surprised by this question, but tried to answer it honestly. 'I can't afford to marry for love, but you can be sure that I'd respect you and treat you kindly.'

'Which is more than my father does,' she said bitterly. 'I will – consider this seriously.'

He thought she looked deeply unhappy but before he could ask her to tell him why she was so reluctant to marry, her chaperone returned.

After a few more minutes Ronan took his leave.

He'd expected to dislike Georgina Johnson, but he didn't.

It wasn't the same as loving someone, though. Could he really bring himself to marry her?

Maia had never been so happy in her life. Nancy seemed to accept her new status. Maia was not only sleeping with Conn but spending the evenings with him in the small sitting room.

Sean and the other servants also treated Maia with as much respect as they always had.

And there was Conn, always Conn, smiling at her, dropping a kiss on her cheek as he passed, chatting to her in the evenings, loving her in bed.

Then she went to church that first Sunday. They'd planned to do this in the same way as they always had. She'd take her place with the other servants while Conn sat with the gentry. They were a little late but people were still chatting outside, something they did both before and after the service.

When Maia greeted a neighbour, the mother of one of the stable boys, the woman turned away without responding and one by one, other women did the same. She stood there feeling her cheeks burning at the thoroughness of the snub. Except for Livia and her sister, who had driven across to attend the service, all the women in the congregation had made it plain that they did not intend to associate with her any longer.

They knew!

She walked inside the barn with her sister, feeling wobbly and afraid.

'What's happened?' Cassandra asked as they sat down. 'Why are people treating you like a pariah?'

Face burning, Maia bent over her hymnbook. 'I'll tell you afterwards. Have you time to come and visit us for an hour or two?'

'I'd rather not. Livia and Kathleen drove here with us and Livia doesn't think it'd be good for Kathleen to go to Galway House.'

'No. No, I suppose not. I hadn't noticed that Kathleen was here.'

'She's outside talking to someone she considers "suitable". I think she judges people only by their appearance and the way they speak.'

After the service Conn, who was looking angry, was held up at the front of the barn, so Maia and her sister walked outside and went to stand away from the others. Reece, after a glance at his wife, picked up little Sofia and went to chat to a man he knew.

'Tell me what's wrong?' Cassandra asked again. 'There must be some reason why people are treating you like this.'

Maia took a deep breath. 'It's because – I've become Conn's mistress and – and people seem to have found out. I think the stable boy must have noticed and told his family. You should have seen how his mother looked at me!'

'Oh, no! Maia, I can't believe you'd do that. What would Father say?'

'He'd be upset, but I love Conn so much. I'd do it all over again.'

He came up to join them just then, his cheekbones burning red with anger. He put one arm protectively round Maia's shoulders and looked at Cassandra. 'I'm sorry this has happened. But I promise you that no woman will ever be loved more than your sister. And once I'm free, I'll marry her as soon as I can, willingly and happily, and to hell with class differences.'

Reece had followed Conn, also looking annoyed. 'I hope you live to make good that promise, Largan. In the meantime, she's the one who will suffer most, not you.'

There was a scream of outrage from across the yard and Conn whirled round, to see Kathleen storming towards them, fury making her face even uglier. He moved to stand between Maia and her.

When she'd tried and failed to push him aside, Kathleen screeched at the top of her voice, 'Whore! She's nothing but a whore!' and everyone stared at them.

'Stop it this minute!' he said.

'You protect *her*. But I'm your wife. I won't have it. I won't!'

Kathleen suddenly went mad, trying again to fight her way past Conn to attack Maia, so that it took the combined efforts of Reece, Conn and two other men to drag her back.

When Kathleen eventually gave up struggling she yelled at him as he dragged her towards Reece's cart, 'She's all you deserve. A whore is good enough for a convict!'

Livia ventured forward and laid one hand on her arm, murmuring something. Kathleen quivered, looking as if she was going to erupt in anger again. Then suddenly the fight went out of her, her mouth trembled and she began to sob, as noisily as a child.

'Come and sit in the cart. We'll drive you home soon,' Livia said gently.

'It's wrong!' Kathleen said, repeating it again and again. 'It's wrong, isn't it? Wrong. She should be whipped. She's a whore.'

Reece went back to his wife while Conn kept an eye on Kathleen. 'We brought them here so we'll have to go. We don't want her to start screeching again.'

'No. I suppose not.' Cassandra hugged her sister, tears in her eyes. 'Will you be all right, Maia?'

She straightened her shoulders. 'Of course I will. Conn will look after me.' She gave Cassandra another hug. 'I shan't come to the monthly service again so we'll have to find another way of meeting. I'll be all right, truly I will. I'm quite safe with Conn.'

She waited alone, head held high, until he came back to her. The way he looked at her said he understood exactly how she was feeling, so when he offered his arm, she took it without a word and allowed him to escort her to the wagon, where Sean was waiting.

But on the way home Maia wept silently, unable to stop the tears falling.

Sean was sitting in the back of the cart, scowling in the direction of the church. He exchanged glances with his master and said suddenly, 'I think I'll stretch my legs a bit.' He got off the cart and as they left him behind, Conn put one arm round Maia and left the horse to find its own way home. 'My darling, I'm sorry. So very sorry.'

'It wasn't your fault.'

'I can't bear to see you weep like this. What can I do?'

She looked at him blankly. 'Do? Why, nothing. We can't change what we've done, and I don't want to. But . . . I don't think I'll go to church again. I'm not strong enough to outface ostracism each month.'

'How did they find out?'

'Does it matter?'

'Of course it does. Someone working for me must have told people, and that sort of disloyalty I can do without.'

But he had no need to dismiss anyone. One of the stable lads sent a message that his parents didn't want him working there any more and he was sorry to let Mr Largan down. For a while the other stable lads stared at Maia as if she'd changed overnight, but after Sean had spoken to them sharply a few times, they stopped doing it.

Maia didn't let herself weep again, because it wouldn't do any good and would only hurt Conn, who was feeling guilty.

He held her close that night, not making love, but she could feel his love surrounding her.

'What have I done to you, my darling? I should be taken out and hanged for being so selfish.'

'They'd have to hang me too, then, Conn, because I came to you willingly. And in spite of – everything – I don't regret it.'

'No. Heaven help me, neither do I. You're all the world to me, my darling.'

When they reached Westview, Kathleen jumped down from the cart and vanished into the stables. Without saying anything, Leo went after her.

'Sometimes only he can calm her down,' Livia said.

'She seemed different today,' Reece said with a frown. 'More uncontrolled and so very angry. It's not as if she and Conn are even living together. They're trying to get an annulment.'

Livia couldn't hold back a sigh. 'She sets a lot of store on doing things the right way. The correct way to behave must have been dinned into her as a child and young woman. But she does seem to be getting stranger, almost by the day, and I'm finding it harder to keep her peaceful. I couldn't manage at all without Leo.'

'If you need help, don't hesitate to come for me,' Reece said, still not signalling to the horse to move on.

'I'll be all right, I'm sure.'

'Perhaps Conn should find some other solution for her.'

'What other solution is there? And what other solution to my present problems could *I* find? Francis left me nearly penniless. I won't dip into my meagre capital because it's all I have behind me. The money Conn gives me is what keeps me going in my daily needs.'

'You know we'd never see you go hungry. And later, when we get the rest of Cassandra's money, we'd like to buy your land.'

'I know. But I need more than food. I need to find a more pleasant way of life and I can't decide what to do. Perhaps I will open a school, after all. Or buy a house in Perth and offer lodgings to people. I don't intend to stay here for ever. But I'm not ready to change things yet.'

As Reece drove the cart back down the slope and turned into their own drive, he shook his head sadly.

'You're worried about Kathleen, aren't you?' Cassandra asked, cuddling little Sofia.

'Yes. She's getting quite strange at times. You must have noticed.'

'I have.'

'Leo told me the other day that her head isn't right inside and he doesn't know how to mend it. I think that sums up the situation. But Livia really needs the money Conn pays her. I don't like to think of a lady like her struggling on her own.'

'There's nothing else we can do to help? Perhaps invite Kathleen to tea?'

'I'm not exposing you and Sofia to Kathleen. Don't ever leave our daughter alone with her.'

'Of course not.' She looked down with a fond smile at the sleeping infant. 'Wasn't she good at the service today?'

'Very good. She's a happy child.'

Reece continued to worry about the situation but didn't talk about it any more, even to his wife, because he didn't want Cassandra worrying about her sister. He felt he had to keep an eye on Kathleen, though, and he wished Maia and Conn hadn't decided to act on their love yet. But it was too late to worry about that now.

The following evening he sat reading the newspaper someone had passed on to him at church. It was a few weeks old and contained an article about the new Lunatic Asylum in Fremantle. He read it carefully and studied the engraving of the building, which seemed to be a fine example of the gothic style.

'Have you seen this?' He showed it to Cassandra. 'I couldn't help thinking when I saw it that if Kathleen's behaviour continues to deteriorate, that's where she'll wind up.'

She stared at him in shock. 'Surely not?'

'Where else could she be kept? She's a strong woman physically. It took four of us to subdue her today and she left her mark on each of us.' He touched the scratch on his cheek. 'I'd not like to face her on my own – and I don't like to think of Livia alone with her.'

'She has Leo and Orla.'

'Yes, thank goodness. But he's only one man and Orla's not a big woman. I doubt even the three of them together could hold Kathleen down if she went as mad as she did today.'

'Conn's father has a lot to answer for, making him marry a woman like her.'

'I agree. But some people will do anything for money, even sacrifice their children's lives.' He gave her a kiss on the cheek. 'Now, let's talk of more cheerful things. Tomorrow I'm going to start work on digging out that cheese cellar. We have to have somewhere to keep the cheese cool in the summer heat. When the cellar is ready I'm going to offer to buy milk from people around here, so that I don't have to keep too many cows myself.

Lots of people have too much milk, but need to keep a cow for their own family's needs. That money of yours is going to be put to very good use, I promise you.'

'I think you're only intending to make cheese because you love eating it so much,' she teased.

He smiled. 'I do love it. But I also see a way of making money. Not the only way, but one of them. I'm thinking of selling timber too, but for that we'd need a sawpit and someone to help me saw the trees into planks.'

'You can't do everything at once, Reece.'

'I know. But I enjoy planning things. And do you realise we've still not explored all of our property? It's amazing to think how many acres Kevin owned. I didn't realise till we saw the deeds. I want to get to know every slope, every tree, every rock.'

'Even you haven't got that good a memory. It's not like English land, though, is it? Some of the soil is very poor, even I can see that.'

'In which case we should look at what grows naturally and see if there's anything we can profit from.'

'Stop dreaming and come to bed, Reece Gregory. I'm tired, even if you're not.'

He folded up the newspaper carefully, because it would be passed to another family once he'd finished with it. Livia had her own newspaper now and didn't offer to share her copies with anyone. She clearly had some purpose in keeping them.

But as he lay in bed, he thought again about the new Lunatic Asylum and Kathleen. Surely it wouldn't come to that? Poor Conn had had far too much to bear in recent years.

19

In late January Xanthe got up and looked out at the snow falling. She'd not be able to go out for a proper walk until it melted, let alone travel.

Christmas had passed without a word from Ronan, though she'd written to wish him a happy festive season. He hadn't written back to her, though.

Well, she'd made a decision last night. She'd given him enough time to sort out his life. She wasn't going to wait any longer. She was going to do something about it.

Pandora looked at her the next morning and said, 'You're growing thinner and you look unhappy.'

'Does it show? I try to put on a cheerful face when I'm with people.'

'To me, it shows clearly – and Zachary commented on it the other day. Why, even his sister Hallie asked me if you're unwell.'

'She's a lovely girl.'

'Yes. She's nearly as bad as you, wants to see a bit of the world before she settles down and her mother complains that she's too fussy about the young men who come courting her.'

Her sister's words gave Xanthe an idea. She didn't act on it straight away. She'd learned the hard way not to do that, especially when her ideas didn't suit what people thought right for a young woman. But she thought things over carefully for the next few days.

When she'd made up her mind, she said thoughtfully, 'I think I need a change of scene. I could go into Manchester one day, perhaps. Do you think Hallie would come with me? I'd ask you, but I know you'd not leave Hebe for a whole day.'

Pandora pulled a face. 'No, I couldn't do that.' She looked down at her little daughter and smiled fondly.

'She's a very good baby, isn't she? I love it when she smiles.'

'Yes, thank goodness. How our mother managed with four of us, I don't know, especially when two of her children were twins.'

'We live in luxury, compared to her.'

Pandora nodded, then a shadow passed across her face. 'It hasn't always been easy for us, though, has it? At least Cassandra and I are happily married. I do worry about you and Maia.'

Xanthe changed the subject. She didn't want any more lectures about accepting invitations, going out walking with young men, or the futility of loving a landed gentleman. She knew all the arguments, but she knew Ronan, too, or at least she thought she did.

And she'd given him enough time! She was going to see Hallie and ask if she would help.

But there was another reason for going. She had a strong feeling that he was unhappy and needed her. She had feelings sometimes about her twin, knew whether Maia was happy or unhappy. But she'd never had this special feeling for anyone else.

Which just went to show that he was the right man for her.

Maia was sick for the second morning running and when she looked up, Conn had come back into the bedroom and was staring at her.

'You're expecting a child!'

She nodded. 'Yes.'

He came to enfold her in his arms. 'That's wonderful. There's no other woman I'd want to mother my children. But I wish—'

'That it hadn't happened yet. I do too. Still . . .' she beamed at him. 'I've always wanted children, always.'

'I'm going to make a money settlement on you straight away, so that whatever happens, you'll have enough money to support yourself and the child.'

'I have some money of my own.'

'Then you'll have more. And I don't want you doing any more heavy work from now on.'

She pulled a mocking face at him. 'No, sir.'

His expression grew sad. 'I'm sorry my first child will be born out of wedlock. Nothing we do will hurry the Church in the question of annulment, but I did reply to my brother's letter and write to the Bishop in Perth as well, to make sure the matter is under consideration. There hasn't been time for Kieran to get back to me but I did get a letter from Perth, saying it was under way – whatever that means.'

He held her at arm's length again to say softly, 'A child. Our child. How we shall love it!'

Although it was a bitterly cold day, Xanthe and Zachary's sister went for a walk, because it was the only way they could be sure of privacy. Hallie lived with her widowed mother in the house where she and Zachary had grown up. She no longer needed to worry about finding a job, because he made sure they had everything they needed, but neither he nor their mother seemed to understand that she wanted more than to spend her days doing housework, shopping, sewing and reading.

After Xanthe had explained the situation to her friend, she let it sink in while they walked round.

'What do you intend to do about it?' Hallie asked.

'I want to go to Ireland and confront Ronan, only . . . I've already found out that a young woman travelling on her own can be considered fair game by a certain type of man. So I wondered if you'd like to come with me? I'd pay for everything, of course.'

'Oh, I'd love to! I've never been anywhere.' Then Hallie's smile faded and she stopped walking. 'But I don't think Zachary will allow it.'

'Leave Zachary to me. What about your mother?'

'I think she might let me go. She knows I long to see more of the world. And she could invite her cousin Martha to stay with her. Martha rents one room and is always short of money, so to have her food found for a week or two will help her.' Her face became very determined. 'In any case, I shall make it clear to them both that I'm going with or without their blessing.'

'How do you think I should broach the matter to your brother?'

After a moment or two's thought, Hallie said slowly, 'I think it'd help if you asked Zachary to help you plan the trip without telling him you've asked me to come. Let him persuade you to take someone with you.'

Xanthe gave her a hug. 'I knew you'd be the right person to ask.'

That evening over tea, Xanthe said, 'I've waited long enough. I'm going to Ireland to see Ronan. If he won't set a date for us to marry, I'll do it for him.'

Pandora's gasp echoed round the room.

Zachary stared at her in dismay. 'But you can't just go and demand that he marry you! You said he had no money.'

'I know he loves me and wants to marry me. That's enough for me. And what *he* considers enough money to support a wife and what I would consider enough are two very different things. I don't need keeping in style. He's being too stupidly noble for words and I've given him long enough to come to his senses. Anyway, I have the strongest feeling that he *needs* me, that if I don't go to see him now, he'll never marry me, so I'm going if I have to walk barefoot all the way.'

'I think she's right,' Pandora said.

Zachary turned to her, dismay on his face. 'You're *encouraging* her to go travelling on her own?'

'She's already come from Australia on her own.'

'She had Ronan with her.'

'Not when she started off. She went as far as Galle on her own. She should be allowed to follow her heart. You and I did, after all.'

'Well, I won't have her travelling on her own. And in winter, too. No, no, it's not to be thought of.'

Pandora winked at Xanthe then said to her husband, 'Rubbish! Besides, the solution to that is easy. She can take someone with her. How about Hallie? Your sister's dying to see something of the world. I know you promised to take her to Blackpool in the summer, but that's a long time to wait.'

'Two young women, both of them pretty, travelling alone. Definitely not!'

'You're getting stuffy as you get older, my love.'

He gaped at this unexpected dig.

Pandora looked at him sadly. 'You are, you know. But as you're not Xanthe's guardian and she's over the age of twenty-one, you can't stop her. All you can do is make sure she travels safely.'

Interested, Xanthe let them argue. In the end, he said, 'Well, if Hallie agrees to go, I'm making sure the whole journey is carefully planned. Every single detail. I'm not leaving that to anyone else.'

'No one could do it more carefully than you,' Pandora said. 'Who will you ask to help you?'

He thought for a moment, then said, 'Mr Featherworth told me he always has a railway guide in case he has to travel suddenly. I'll go and borrow his.'

It was a full hour before he came back waving a book in a bright yellow wrapper at them. 'Here you are! *Bradshaw's Monthly Railway Guide.* I called in at Mother's on the way back and persuaded her to let Hallie come with you – though she too thinks you're foolish for rushing off like that. But Hallie's as reckless as you are and thinks it's going to be an adventure. *I* think you'll both be very uncomfortable, travelling in the depths of winter, and will soon regret your hasty decision.'

When he'd gone back down to the shop to supervise the staff during the final hour of opening, Pandora cocked one eyebrow at her sister. 'Well, you've got what you wanted, haven't you?'

Xanthe went across to hug her. 'Yes, yes, yes! And you're the best of sisters for helping me like that!'

Pandora hugged her back. 'I don't want to lose you, but I know what it's like to love someone who's being stupidly noble. Zachary was exactly the same about marrying me, because I was part-owner of the shop. I had to put my foot down and make him see sense before he'd agree to marry. So I do understand.'

Xanthe heaved a sigh of relief. 'That's settled then. I'm sorry we'll be travelling in the middle of winter, though. It'd be far more interesting in the summer, I'm sure. Maybe you could all come and visit me there, after I'm married.'

'You're that sure Ronan will still want to marry you?'

'Yes, but all sorts of things can happen and I don't want to leave anything to chance.' She sighed and her eyes grew dreamy. 'I can't wait to see him again.'

Only when she was in bed did she allow herself to remember his letter saying she was free to marry someone else. As if she would!

And she'd not let him marry anyone else, either.

Ronan sat in the library at Ardgullan, feeling depressed. He'd managed to save the estate, but at what cost? He'd used up all his own inheritance to pay off the most pressing debts and was living as frugally as a monk.

If any more debts came in, he didn't know how he'd pay them. Mr Hatton thought they were all accounted for, but even he did not go so far as to guarantee that.

The last time he'd been to see the lawyer, Mr Hatton had again raised the question of him marrying Miss Johnson.

'I've spoken to her father and he thinks it a fair match, is prepared to lend you money to modernise the house.'

'What does she think?'

Mr Hatton looked surprised. 'I don't know. I deal with her father.'

'Well, I'm still considering it and so is she.'

And it was still the last thing he wanted, but if it was a choice between that and losing Ardgullan . . . no, what was he thinking about? He couldn't, wouldn't! Look what had happened to Conn in an arranged marriage?

No, Ronan would rather sell up and seek employment – except that he didn't know how he'd earn a living. Unlike Conn he hadn't trained for any profession, had lived what now seemed an idle and self-indulgent life until now.

The future looked very bleak.

And his dreams were still filled with Xanthe, smiling, teasing, challenging. How could he ever marry another woman?

A few days later Mr Hatton sent his clerk with a letter saying another debt had surfaced and it seemed as if it was genuine, so would have to be paid.

Ronan read and reread his letter, despair filling him. Mr Hatton was pressing him to reconsider the suggestion of marrying Miss Johnson. It was now the only way to keep the family estate.

After a wakeful night, his heart heavy with grief, Ronan wrote to his lawyer to say he was willing to consider it.

Then he went out for a long ride in the rain, where no one could interrupt him, or want him to do something, or above all, see how upset he was at the mere thought of marrying someone other than Xanthe.

Did duty demand that you give up everything you truly wanted for the sake of the family name and estate?

He still wasn't sure he could do it. But he was caught in a cleft stick and had no idea what he would do if he lost the family estate *and* his money, because no one was going to pay much for a run-down place like Ardgullan House.

If he had no money at all, there was no way he could marry Xanthe, so it wasn't a choice between her and Georgina Johnson, but between losing everything or marrying money.

20

Livia was woken by a sound she couldn't identify. Then she realised it was coming from Kathleen's bedroom. Her guest was talking away, but who was she talking to?

A figure appeared in her doorway: Orla.

'Are you awake, Mrs Southerham?'

'Yes.'

'I think she's gone mad. I daren't go near her. I've never seen anything as shameful in all my life.'

Getting up, Livia went barefoot into the living area and saw that Kathleen's bedroom door was half open and the room was a blaze of candlelight. Had all the candles in the house been lit? What on earth for?

She went closer and saw Kathleen sitting naked on the bed, gesticulating wildly and talking earnestly to someone – only of course there was no one else there. Livia glanced sideways at Orla, who looked terrified, and suddenly she was afraid, too, because Kathleen was a strong woman.

She tiptoed away, followed by the maid. 'You stay here and keep an eye on her.'

'I'll watch from outside but I daren't go near her. Not for the life of me, I daren't.'

The door squeaked as Livia opened it but the voice inside didn't falter. She stood on the tiny veranda for a moment or two, getting used to the dimness outside compared to the brightness in the guest bedroom. The moon was less than half full, but it gave her enough light to pick her way down to the lean-to by the stables, where Leo slept.

She rapped on the door, glancing over her shoulder to make

sure Kathleen hadn't followed her and that Orla was all right. She had to knock a second time before it opened and Leo stood staring at her, clad in his nightshirt.

'Mrs Southerham? Is something wrong?'

'Yes. Kathleen's behaving very strangely and I'm a bit afraid of her.'

He stared at her, his brow furrowed as if taking this in slowly, then said, 'Reece told me to help you if you were worried. What do we need to do?'

She explained, embarrassed at the thought of him seeing Kathleen naked, but even less willing to go back into the house on her own and try to persuade her guest to put on some clothes. She'd tried her hardest to settle Kathleen down, but it wasn't working and she would now have to ask Conn to find somewhere else for his wife to stay – somewhere she could be cared for and protected against herself.

'I'll get dressed and come back to the house with you,' Leo said.

'I think we'd better take some ropes. We may have to tie her up.'

He vanished inside and came back a few minutes later, fully dressed, though with his buttons wrongly fastened, and carrying two short lengths of rope.

Still Livia hesitated to go back to the house. 'She's very strong. Can you manage her on your own, Leo? Or should we go and fetch Reece first?'

'I think I can manage her long enough for you and Orla to slip the ropes over her feet or hands. I've made a sliding loop on each piece, like I do for horses. You just need to pull it tight.'

They went back up the slope to the brightly lit house. Orla was standing outside, a shawl over her nightdress. They could hear Kathleen singing now and when they went inside, Livia was upset to see that the younger woman was still naked.

Kathleen turned round to stare at them as they went into her bedroom. 'I was waiting for you, Leo. If Conn can have a lover, I can have one too.' She smiled at him, a smile meant to be enticing, but which looked wrong on her heavy features, like a grotesque cartoon creature in *Punch* magazine.

'Put your clothes on now, Kathleen,' Livia said. She could feel herself blushing at the sight of her guest's nakedness and she could see that Leo was embarrassed too.

Behind them Orla muttered something and crossed herself but Kathleen ignored Livia and continued to smile at Leo.

'It's time to get dressed now,' Livia repeated.

'You don't get dressed to entertain a lover.' Kathleen stared down at herself and stroked her fingers along her thigh. 'I'm sure Conn and his whore don't get dressed when they're together. You'd better take your clothes off, Leo. You're the only man round here so you'll have to do for a lover till I can get up to Perth. There are lots of fine gentlemen there.'

As she rose and moved towards him, he took her by surprise and flipped her down on the floor, lying sideways across her.

Livia tried to get the rope round Kathleen's ankles, but she kicked out, knocking Livia flying, then tried to roll over and get rid of Leo. But he was very strong and by working together, Livia and Orla got the loop of rope over one kicking foot.

While Kathleen was shrieking at them and kicking out with her free foot, Leo managed to twist one of her arms behind her back. She yelled out in pain and forgot to kick for a moment, during which time Livia got the loop over her other foot and tightened it. Orla immediately grabbed the other rope to deal with her hands.

It was several minutes before they managed to get Kathleen tied and helpless, by which time all three of them had been kicked and bumped about. When they stood back, she jerked around on the floor like a landed fish.

'Shall I cover her, ma'am?' Orla asked.

'Yes. We'll use a sheet from her bed.' Livia pulled one off and they tried to cover her, but she tossed it off.

Livia suddenly remembered the laudanum Francis had taken occasionally towards the end and went to find it. Leo watched her put some into a glass and nodded to Orla. He held Kathleen's head motionless while Orla pried her mouth open and tipped the liquid in.

Kathleen choked and cursed, biting Orla before she could take her hand away, and using the sort of words no lady was supposed even to know.

'We need to wait a while,' Livia said quietly, though she could have shouted for all the attention Kathleen was paying to them.

Gradually the laudanum worked and she began to subside, her struggles to free herself grew less violent. In the end she fell asleep.

'She'll sleep for a while now,' Livia said.

'The Lord be praised.' Orla crossed herself and flung the sheet over Kathleen's plump white body.

Livia sat down on the edge of the bed, feeling suddenly exhausted. 'Could you please go and fetch Reece, Leo? We'll have to take Kathleen back to Conn and the sooner the better, before she harms herself or one of us.'

When he'd gone she turned to Orla. 'Do sit down. You must be exhausted too. She's been very difficult to manage lately.'

Orla nodded and sank down on the end of the bed. 'She's gone quite mad now, hasn't she, ma'am?'

'Yes.'

'Then I don't have to work for her any more, do I?' She bent her head and began to weep, her shoulders shaking. 'I'm free.'

'You could have worked for someone else before now, if you'd wanted to,' Livia said, a bit puzzled as to why a maid would stay with an unpleasant mistress in a country so short of maids that a dozen people would have come offering Orla a job if they'd known she was available.

'I didn't dare. If she'd written to the new master, they'd have turned my family out of their house. She made sure I knew that.'

'Oh, Orla, it wasn't true. I'm sure it wasn't. It might have been with the old master, but he's dead and I'm sure Conn's brother would never turn them out. Conn speaks well of him, says he's kind. You'll easily find another job. I'd employ you myself, but I don't have the money to pay you at the moment. You can stay

on here for as long as you like and I'll give you a good refer-
ence. At least you'll have a roof over your head and you won't
go hungry.'

'What will happen to Mrs Kathleen?'

'I fear they'll have to lock her away. What else can you do with
someone like that?' After a moment or two she stood up. 'We
should get dressed while we can.'

About an hour after it got light, Conn heard the sound of a cart
approaching. He went outside and saw Reece driving his ugly
but capable mare round to the back of the house, with Leo sitting
in the cart behind him. He went out to see what had brought
them across so early in the morning and his heart sank when he
saw his wife lying bound in the tray of the cart, glaring at them.

As soon as she saw him she began cursing and screaming
abuse, thrashing around till she'd tossed off the blankets and
revealed her nakedness.

Reece let Leo go to the horses' heads and jumped down from
the cart. 'I'm sorry, but Kathleen's gone completely mad. She
took off all her clothes and tried to get Leo into bed with her.
Livia couldn't get her to see sense. It took the three of them to
hold her down and tie her up. We tried to get her dressed, but
she struggled so we gave up. She'd already scratched and bitten
people, so in the end we just covered her up.'

He waited till Conn had taken this in, then added, 'Livia
sends her apologies. She can do no more to help you. And Orla
is terrified to go near Kathleen, so she's staying at Westview
with Livia.'

Conn looked down in horror at his wife, whose madness showed
in her eyes, as well as her behaviour. 'What am I going to do
with her now? We don't have enough people to keep her under
control, and no one here is nearly as strong as Leo.'

'Even Leo couldn't look after her on his own. We had to give
her laudanum and it's worn off now. We don't have much left,
I'm afraid but I brought the bottle for you.'

Conn forced himself to go up to the cart, wincing as Kathleen cursed and spat in his direction. 'What the hell am I going to do with her?' he repeated in a whisper.

'There's only one thing you can do,' Reece said quietly. 'Take her to the new Lunatic Asylum in Perth.'

'Lock her away?'

'Can you think of any other solution?'

Conn shook his head.

'You'll need to set off as soon as you can. Already she's soiled herself and we daren't untie her.'

An hour later, Conn set off, taking Leo with him to help keep Kathleen under control. They had a little more laudanum but were saving it for when they got to areas with more people, hoping to keep her subdued.

Nancy watched them go, keeping an eye on her mistress, who had tears in her eyes. She'd never wish this to happen to her worst enemy and the wild rage in Mrs Kathleen's eyes had shocked and upset her, as it had everyone.

'Has she always been strange, that one?' she asked Maia.

'She's never been – normal. Mrs Largan said once that Kathleen's aunt was just the same, always strange and went quite mad as she grew older. Only I can't help thinking . . . what if something I did caused this?'

'You weren't even there.'

'But she knew about me and Conn, and I could see how that upset her, even though she didn't love him. She was like a lost child, didn't know where she belonged.'

'It's still not your fault.' Nancy went across the room and because Maia was looking pale and upset, forgot her place and gave her mistress a quick hug. 'No one knows what makes people go mad, but it's nothing you did, I'm sure. Come and sit down. I'll make you something to eat.'

'I'm not hungry.'

'You're eating for two now, remember. You should eat something, for the baby's sake. I'll boil you an egg, shall I? Just one, softly boiled, with some of yesterday's crusty bread.'

Maia tried to eat but after forcing down less than half the egg, she pushed her plate away. 'I can't.'

'Well, you've got something down you, at least. You look exhausted. Why don't you go and have a rest? I can manage here. It'll be easy enough with the master away.'

When Maia had gone, Nancy finished off the food. Since the terrible days of being achingly hungry, she couldn't bear to see even a crumb go to waste.

Sitting back, she licked a smear of dried egg yolk from the back of one finger and looked round the kitchen. She loved it here at Galway House. She was learning more all the time about how to run a big house properly and every night she prayed they'd not bring in someone else to take over as housekeeper.

No one else would love this house more than she did. No one, not even her master. It was her refuge and salvation, she knew that. And if she never had to leave it again as long as she lived, she'd die happy.

Xanthe continued to feel anxious about Ronan as she and Hallie made their preparations to travel to Ireland. She didn't know why she felt they had to hurry, but she did, and very strongly.

She didn't want to upset Zachary, who only had her best interests at heart, but his interference and fussing slowed down their preparations by a couple of days at least.

In the end, however, her brother-in-law could think of nothing else to check or arrange, so he escorted her and Hallie to the station very early one morning and saw them on the first train. As it began to pull slowly away from the station, he stood waving goodbye till he was lost in a cloud of steam blowing back from the engine.

Xanthe leaned her head against the seat with a sigh of relief. 'I don't want to upset you, but your brother's a fusspot.'

'Zachary needs to look after people,' Hallie said apologetically. 'He's always been very protective about his family.'

'I know. I shouldn't complain really. Anyway, we're on our way now.'

They changed trains in Manchester, going to Liverpool, from where they took the packet to Dublin.

'See,' Xanthe said. 'We're coping perfectly well without a man to do all this for us.'

One of the stewards described the sea as 'lively' but neither of them suffered any seasickness. Hallie was fascinated by her first sight of the sea and could not be persuaded to go below deck for long as she wanted to look out over the water.

In Dublin they rested, tired by their journey, but though Hallie pleaded to spend an extra day or two looking round the city, Xanthe refused, insisting on pressing on.

They could only go as far as Enniskillen by train and had to spend a night there before their hired carriage came to carry them to the small village near to which Ardgullan House was situated. That day the weather, which had been cold but fine, turned rainy and they made slow progress on the muddy roads.

Xanthe continued to worry about Ronan. What was he doing? Why did she feel so strongly that he was in trouble?

As they came to a small lake, which they'd already learned was called a lough here, the coachman slowed down to shout to them, 'The village is on the other side, but the big house standing on that small promontory is the place you want. You can see the standing stones at the top of the slope. That's how it got the name Ardgullan House, from the stones being high up on the promontory.'

The village was on the far side of the house, so Xanthe had a clear view of it. As she watched, another carriage came from a different direction and turned into the gates, looking like a toy in the distance. Who was visiting Ronan? She hoped they'd conduct their business quickly because she wanted to see him, feel his arms round her and make him see sense about marrying her.

When they came to the gates, they found them open and no signs of anyone coming out of the gatekeeper's cottage to ask their business. To the right, about a hundred yards down the drive was a pretty house and she guessed this would be where his mother had lived. It looked closed up now, all the curtains drawn and the garden bare and wintry.

At long last they drew to a halt in front of the big house, a neat square of grey stone, with a portico over the front door.

The coachman's lad jumped down and went up to knock on the front door.

Xanthe didn't intend to sit waiting in the carriage, so opened the door herself and jumped down, hurrying up the steps just as the door was opened by a pleasant-faced woman.

'I'm here to see Mr Maguire,' she said before the coachman's lad could speak.

The woman looked at her in puzzlement, then beyond her to where Hallie was still sitting in the carriage. 'Is he expecting you?'

'No. But I know him from Australia and he knows my family.'

'He's busy at the moment, I'm afraid, talking to his lawyer and the Johnsons.'

'Can you just tell him I'm here? I'm sure he'll want to see me.'

After a hesitation, the woman said, 'I daren't interrupt. I think they're arranging his marriage. She's a rich young lady and the estate's in a bad way. So if you could come back another day, miss, it'd be much better? It really is a bad time to visit him.'

21

The journey to Fremantle seemed to take for ever. In the back of the cart Kathleen continued to shriek and yell until her voice was hoarse. Conn's throat ached just from listening to her.

'She's in a very bad way,' Leo said. 'If she was a horse, we'd have to put her down.'

'You can't put people down like you do animals.'

'I know, but I don't think they'll be able to cure her. She'll have to go into that lunatic asylum to be looked after.' After a pause, he added in a gruff voice, 'My stepfather used to threaten to send me to the lunatic asylum and that made my mother cry.'

'Why would he do that? You're not mad.'

'No, but I'm slow-thinking and that annoys some people. I know it annoyed him. And he didn't like to see his stepson working with the horses like a servant.' He sighed. 'I hope my mother is happy. I think about her a lot.'

'Would you like me to write her a letter for you?'

Leo sat frowning, then shook his head. 'He'd hide it and she wouldn't know I'd written.'

'Does she have a friend you could write to? He'd not be able to stop her getting the letter then.'

It took a few minutes for this idea to sink in, then Leo nodded several times, looking excited. 'Yes, yes! We could send a letter to Mrs Farsham in the village. The vicar's wife. Yes, she'll tell my mother. I heard her say once that she doesn't like my step-father.' He beamed at Conn. 'Will you do that for me, write the letter?'

'Of course I will.'

'Thank you.' Leo brushed a tear from his cheek.

'Your mother may even write back to you, then Livia or I could read it to you whenever you wanted.'

Leo's voice got even gruffer. 'I'd like that. I'd keep her letter very safe.'

They drove on in silence for another mile or two, then he said, as if carrying on his former conversation, 'I thought Mrs Kathleen might get better if she worked with the horses, because she loves them, but she kept getting worse. Later I got scared she'd hurt them when she flew into a rage so I wouldn't let her go near them without me. She got very angry about that and said I had to obey her because she was a lady. But she didn't act like a lady. And I won't let anyone hurt another living creature, whoever they are.'

When they began to pass through more settled areas, Conn worried that his wife might start screaming again and people think they were ill-treating her, but fortunately she stayed asleep. Perhaps the slow rocking of the cart and the sound of the harness jingling had lulled her. Whatever it was, he felt relieved not to have to listen to that dreadful screaming and cursing.

'I was right. We shan't be able to reach Fremantle in one day,' he said as they stopped to rest and water the horses. 'It's a good thing we brought blankets and supplies. In another hour or two we'll start looking for somewhere to camp overnight.'

There were sounds from the cart and then Kathleen began to heave about, tossing off the blankets. When she couldn't get free, she began screaming again, shrieking that they should set her free and calling out for help. They went to check on her only to find she'd soiled herself. Conn shuddered.

'I'll clean her,' Leo said. 'I don't mind. I do it for the horses.'

'You'd better leave her lower clothes off if she's going to do this. We'll put them on again before we get to Fremantle.'

When Leo touched her Kathleen stopped screaming and instead tried to persuade him to make love to her. It was horrifying, grotesque, making Conn feel sick with disgust.

Then another cart came up to them and as Leo covered her

with a blanket, she started screaming for help again. The man driving it reined in to gape at them in shock. The woman beside him clasped his arm, looking afraid, and the man sitting in the back took up his rifle, holding it in a threatening way.

'What's happening?' the driver asked. 'Why is that woman screaming?'

It was hard to say the words out loud, but Conn knew he had to get used to it. 'She's gone mad. She's my wife. We're taking her to the new lunatic asylum in Fremantle because we can't control her.'

'I'm not mad,' Kathleen called. 'And I'm not his wife. They've kidnapped me. Help me! Please help me!'

'She doesn't sound mad,' the man with the rifle said.

'She's very cunning.'

Kathleen managed to kick off the blanket covering her and the woman on the other cart gave a little scream and averted her eyes.

Just as Conn was desperately trying to think how to convince them he was telling the truth, Kathleen suddenly changed her tone and began offering herself to the newcomers in a voice hoarse from screaming.

Leo picked up the blanket and tied it round her with a rope this time.

'I'm sorry,' the driver said. 'She is cunning, isn't she? She nearly had us fooled. It must be hard for you.'

'It is. Very hard.' Conn unclenched his fists only with an effort. 'I'm sorry you've been troubled.'

'We'll let people know you're coming,' the driver said. 'It may make it easier for you if she starts claiming you've kidnapped her.'

'Thank you.'

When they'd gone Conn covered his face with his hands for a moment or two, trying to pull himself together.

What he'd do if they refused to take her at the asylum, he couldn't even begin to imagine.

★　　★　　★

Livia hadn't realised how much she relied on Leo to do the hard work about the place, not to mention simply being there, cheerful and willing, until she had to cope without him.

'He's a nice fellow, Leo, isn't he?' Orla said, echoing her thoughts. 'Always smiling and works hard without needing telling. I miss him.'

'Yes. It's going to be difficult to look after the horses without him.'

'I don't know much about caring for horses.'

'I do.'

'Then I'll take over inside the house, if you like? I can cook and wash and clean for you now Mrs Kathleen's not here to stop me.'

'That'd be a big help.'

Orla's eyes gleamed and she added, 'Now that she's gone, we can put her things in the big tent and I can give that bedroom a good bottoming. She wasn't very clean in herself.'

'You may as well sleep there now.'

Tears came into Orla's eyes. 'You'd let me sleep in a room of my own?'

'Yes, of course. You have to sleep somewhere. It can't be pleasant sleeping out in the tent, even though the nights aren't cold at this time of year.'

'Summer's very hot here, isn't it?' Orla said. 'I've never seen such sunshine. I like it though.'

'I'll go down to the stables, then.' But Livia found the work harder than she'd expected. She fed the horses and mucked out the stables as best she could, wishing there were someone to talk to. Occasionally she stopped because she imagined she could hear Francis's voice calling to her and that upset her.

Later in the afternoon she heard the crunching of leaves and the occasional cracking of a twig being stepped on and stopped work again. It took her a few moments to realise that the footsteps were real. Suddenly nervous, she peeped out of the stable to see who it was. To her relief it was Reece striding briskly along the bush path that joined the two properties. She called out to him and he turned towards the stables.

'Livia! Are you all right? I thought you'd like to know that we got Kathleen to Galway House safely. Conn and Leo are taking her up to Fremantle.' He took the shovel out of her hand. 'Let me finish this for you. It's not suitable work for a lady. Why don't you hire the Bronsons' middle lad for a few days to do this sort of job till Leo gets back?'

She hesitated, then nodded and handed over the shovel to Reece. Short as she was of money, today's struggles had convinced her yet again that she wasn't cut out to be a farmer's wife – not that she needed convincing.

As she walked slowly up the slope, she thought ruefully that she'd come here to follow her husband's dream, not her own. Her dreams had been of a home and family, but she'd never got with child – well, Francis had never been very ardent. And he'd been a child himself, in some ways, a wilful, playful man who had brought happiness into what had been a very dull life for her, but had given her no stability.

After a few years of marriage, knowing Francis might not have more than a year or two to live, she'd agreed to follow yet another of his dreams and come to Australia. But like all the others, this one had remained a mirage and never come true.

Ah, but he'd made such beautiful dreams! And she'd loved him dearly, for all his faults.

After his death, however, reality had set in and she knew she had to do something different with her life. But what? She felt so drained and weary after nursing him for so long, she couldn't seem to reach any decisions about her future, let alone make definite plans. All she wanted was to rest and live quietly for a while.

She'd thought having Kathleen to stay would give her a breathing space and money to live on, but her lodger had only brought more anxiety and trouble.

She realised she'd stopped walking but didn't move yet, continuing to look at the small wooden house. At least there was one good outcome from Kathleen's visit. Reece and the other men had built her a second bedroom on the side of the little wooden house. The new planks of its exterior were still fresh and warmly coloured, unlike the silver-grey of the old, unpainted wood. Perhaps when she tried to sell the farm, that extra room would make it more attractive to families.

She'd have to sell it, of course she would, but she was terrified of going out into the world on her own. She hadn't advertised the farm for sale yet in the newspaper, because she knew Reece and Cassandra wanted to buy it.

'Are you all right, Mrs Southerham?'

Orla's voice brought her out of her reverie. 'What? Oh, yes, I'm fine. Just thinking about something. Let's make a cup of tea, shall we? I'm sure we could both do with a sit-down.'

As her words sank in, Xanthe stared in horror at the maid who'd opened the door of Ardgullan House. Ronan was arranging to marry someone else? He couldn't be! Had she come too late?

For a moment she almost turned and ran back to the carriage, then something inside her stiffened her spine. If he was thinking of marriage to someone else, he must be desperate. But she wasn't going to let him sacrifice himself – or her – just for a house, even a huge one like this.

Without consciously planning what to do, she pushed past the maid and stood in the hall. 'Where is he?'

'Please, miss! I daren't—'

But the woman's eyes had gone instinctively towards a heavy carved door to the right. Xanthe moved in that direction, feeling she was on the right track when she heard a gasp from behind her.

She opened the door quietly and found herself facing a group of people who had solemn expressions, and were all so still they looked to be carved from stone.

Ronan was standing in front of the hearth where a fire was sputtering miserably. His face had a shuttered look and his whole demeanour was grim and joyless, so unlike his usual self. Whatever he was doing, she'd guessed right: he wasn't happy about it. Xanthe knew him too well to mistake his mood. Her spirits lifted just a little. There was hope. She was sure there was hope.

The young woman sitting on a sofa also looked stiff and unhappy, her red hair tightly pinned back but tendrils escaping as if they had a will of her own. She was dressed in a huge crinoline, which meant she had to sit on the edge of the sofa so that it could spread out in front of her. Her hands were clenched tightly in her lap and she was staring at the floor in front of her skirt, not at Ronan. That puzzled Xanthe. Surely if he was the man she was to marry, she should be looking at him, smiling even? And why weren't the two of them alone? Why were the other people there? It seemed a strange way to arrange a marriage to her.

The older woman sitting on the sofa beside the young one was sour-faced and watchful, as if ready to pounce on any mistake in behaviour or speech.

Two older men were sitting opposite them on another sofa, one richly dressed, presumably the father, the other dressed in more sombre garments. A lawyer? Was this a marriage or a business arrangement?

In the time it had taken her to assess the situation, Ronan had turned towards the door, saying, 'Ah, here's the tea now. Shall we—' He broke off to stare at Xanthe, his expression changing to one of incredulity. For a moment he hesitated, then he took a step towards her, mouthing her name, his love showing on his face.

She didn't wait for him to have second thoughts, but ran across the room and threw herself into his arms. Before he could speak, she said, 'I won't let you do it, Ronan! You'll be miserable for the rest of your life, just like Conn.'

He pulled her close with an inarticulate murmur, cradling her closely, ignoring the muttering of the other occupants of the room. 'Xanthe! I can't believe it's you.' He dropped a light kiss on her cheek, saying with a shaky laugh, 'I think the sun has just come out.'

Pushing her to arm's length, he smoothed her hair back from her forehead. 'How did you happen to come here at just this moment?'

'I knew you needed me. I didn't know why, but I just knew it, so I came as quickly as I could.'

'Maguire!' It was an angry roar that echoed round the room.

Ronan jerked as if he'd forgotten they weren't alone and let go of her. They both turned towards the voice.

The richly clad older gentleman had stood up and was glaring at them. 'What the hell do you think you're doing, Maguire?'

'Coming to my senses.' He turned back to Xanthe. 'Don't go. I must sort this out before we do anything.'

She patted his cheek with one hand and went across to stand by the window, joy filling her heart. He did love her. That was all that mattered. Somehow they'd work everything else out.

Ronan went across first to the younger woman. 'Miss Johnson, I owe you my deepest apologies, but it would be unfair to marry you when I love someone else.'

She looked up at him and said simply, 'I love someone else too. But Papa wanted me to marry into the gentry so he wouldn't let me marry Paul.'

'Don't marry for money. It won't make you happy.'

She smiled, suddenly looking pretty. 'You're right.'

'Georgina, hold your tongue!' the older woman snapped.

'I've held it for too long, let you both bully me and make me unhappy.' She stood up, moving away from the sofa and shaking her skirt a little so that her crinoline spread out evenly around her. Then she looked at Ronan again. 'I think if things were different I'd have liked you, Ronan Maguire.' She turned to Xanthe. 'I wish you happy, whoever you are. I can see how much he loves you.'

'I wish you happy too.'

Georgina shook her head and her smile faded. 'Father won't let me marry Paul. He's threatened to ruin him if I do. But from now on I shan't let him force me into marriage with someone else. On that at least I can stand firm.'

'Georgina, I said, hold your tongue!'

She turned to her father. 'I've enough of your stubbornness in me, Father, now that I've seen a young woman with the courage to come to the man she loves. It's Paul or no one for me.'

'We'll see about that.' Her father turned to Ronan. 'You'll lose this house. I'll make sure of that.'

'But I won't lose the woman I love. That's much more important.' He walked across to put one arm protectively round Xanthe's shoulders.

She smiled at him. 'Maybe we can manage to keep the house. You'd be surprised at how economically I can live.'

The lawyer came forward. 'You're making a serious mistake, Maguire.'

'No, I'm not. I've seen what can happen in a forced marriage. I don't know why I ever let you push me so far.' His voice grew gentler. 'Bear with me, Hatton. I intend to have a very good try at keeping my family estate. But whatever happens, I'll keep the woman I love.'

'Come, Georgina,' the older woman said.

The father followed them, tossing over his shoulder again, 'I'll make sure you regret this, Maguire.'

'Then you'll make yourself and your daughter look like spiteful fools,' Xanthe snapped. She didn't intend to let him have all his own way, the bully!

He stopped to gape at her. 'Young woman, mind your own business.'

'Ronan is my business. Your conscience is yours.'

He looked at her as if he couldn't believe how pertly she was answering him back, then grunted and turned away.

In silence Ronan walked with his visitors to the door, waited to see them drive away, then came back into the house.

Hallie, who had been sitting on a hard wooden chair in the hall, shamelessly eavesdropping, stood up. As he noticed her for the first time, she said, 'I'm Hallie Carr, Zachary's sister. I came here with Xanthe.'

He took her hand, clasping it in his for a moment and smiling at her. 'I'm so glad you did. We need a chaperone if we're not to upset the local gossips beyond remedy. How is your brother?'

'He's well, thank you.'

Ronan looked at the maid, who was standing at the back of

the hall, with an anxious expression. 'Mary, could you please get bedrooms ready for Miss Carr and Miss Blake? No, better that they share one, I think. Miss Carr, if you'll kindly give me a few moments alone with Xanthe . . . ?'

The maid had relaxed into a smile now. 'There's a good fire in the kitchen if you don't mind waiting there, miss. It's a raw day outside and none of the other rooms are heated yet.'

Inside the drawing room Ronan closed the door and walked across to the fire, taking Xanthe in his arms and kissing her until she sagged breathlessly against him.

'You're not angry at me, then?' she asked with a smile.

'You know very well I'm not. I'm deeply grateful to you for making me realise what was important. Very grateful. I was so caught up in the debts and problems, I wasn't thinking straight. I meant what I said to Mr Johnson: if I lose this house, then so be it. I can live without it. But I'm quite sure I can't live without you.'

Somehow they found themselves sitting on the sofa so recently vacated by Miss Johnson, holding hands as they exchanged news in incoherent snatches.

'Shall you really lose this house?' Xanthe asked.

'I may. But I'll try very hard not to.'

'You can have all my money. I know it's not a lot, but—'

'We'll go over the figures together and see what we can do to save Ardgullan, though I'm not good at accounts, I'm afraid. Those rows of figures seem to tell me something different every time I look at them.' He gazed round with a sigh. 'It's a damp old place and I'm not even sure it's worth it, but I would like to save it. Maguires have lived here for generations.' He hesitated, then asked quietly, 'Are you sure . . . of everything?'

She rolled her eyes and gave him a mock slap. 'How can you ask that when I've shamelessly thrown myself at you?'

'Darling, I had to ask one final time. Now, we need to get hold of a special licence. I don't intend to wait a minute longer than I must to marry you. You don't want a big fuss of a wedding, do you?'

'No. I just want to be legally married. Besides, we can't afford a big fancy wedding. We have to economise in every way possible, and believe me, after living through the Cotton Famine, I'm very good at managing on very little. I'll have your servants so frugal your bills will halve, I promise you. And we'll go over your accounts together, see where we can cut back.'

'Are you – good at accounts?'

'Not as good as Pandora. But I'm a quick learner.'

'Don't ask me to teach you, then, because I'm hopeless with figures.' He pulled her suddenly to him and hugged her close. 'But I think with you at my side I can cope with anything.'

'Good. Now, show me round this house of yours. Where's poor Hallie? You haven't left her sitting in the hall, have you? And what about the carriage we hired? I have to pay off the men.' Taking his hand, she pulled him out of the room, almost running in her eagerness to share her happy news with her friend.

And for the first time in weeks, Ronan laughed aloud for sheer joy.

The following day they visited Mr Hatton in his rooms and when he heard what they intended to do, he looked at them in consternation. 'You wish to get married *immediately?*'

Ronan nodded, half-turning to smile at Xanthe.

'And I shall be taking over the accounts for Ardgullan from now on.' She smiled happily at the lawyer, who looked even more shocked at this statement. 'But I wish to hire a clerk for a few days to help me learn how to do that properly. Do you know anyone who could come for a few days?'

'But ladies don't do accounts.'

'I'm not a lady, as you must have realised from the way I speak. And when things are in such a dire state, I intend to do everything I can to help. What's more, my friend Hallie is going to stay for a while and help out too. She's better at the housekeeping side of things than I am. She actually likes that sort of thing. But first Ronan and I must get married. Even with Hallie to chaperone me, it's not right for me to stay in his house.'

Ronan grinned, enjoying the way she'd taken the wind from

Mr Hatton's sails with her plain speaking. His lawyer was a good man but he clearly wasn't used to a woman taking charge and he kept opening his mouth as if to speak, then closing it again. He decided it was time to interrupt. 'The most important thing is: how quickly can we marry?'

'Within two days if you're prepared to pay extra for a special licence.'

He ignored the lawyer's pained expression. 'Then that's what we'll do. It's the one thing I won't economise on.'

The journey to Fremantle was a nightmare, with Kathleen creating a disturbance whenever they stopped. He grew tired of explaining what was wrong, furious at her rapid changes from almost-sanity to that mindless screaming.

When they stayed overnight he let her walk about, but kept her arms tied behind her. As he helped her back into the cart she began kicking out at him and another battle took place before he and Leo could get her tied up again. He couldn't leave her hands tied behind her back or she'd not be able to lie down, so after a struggle, he tied them in front of her.

When they came into areas with more houses, Kathleen seemed to sense that there were people around, in spite of the sides of the cart hiding much of what they passed. She grew even more agitated, shrieking and yelling for help. Desperate to stop that, Conn tipped the last of the laudanum down her throat.

He felt more numb than anything by now, as well as literally bruised where she'd kicked him. He was aching to be rid of her.

When they got there, he reined in the horse and looked at the Lunatic Asylum. It was an impressive new building but he wondered if those incarcerated inside cared what it looked like – or perhaps this outer appearance was for the benefit of the population, to make people feel good about how they treated the poor creatures who were insane. After all, there were laws about what should be done. It wasn't like the uncivilised old days of bedlams where mad people were treated like sideshows.

When they were admitted, he explained about Kathleen, who

was still in the cart under Leo's care. The female attendant who'd opened the door went out with him to inspect her, wrinkling her nose at her foul state.

'We've kept cleaning her,' Conn said, 'but we've been on the road for two days and have had no facilities for a thorough wash. She – um, tries to act inappropriately with men we meet on the road, or she screams and screams.'

'Hmm.' The woman studied him as carefully as Kathleen, then said in a reluctant tone, 'I suppose you'd better see the doctor. But I doubt he'll admit her. There are only fifty places and you seem to have enough money to care for her privately.'

Conn looked at her in horror. 'I can't care for her as well as look after my farm, and I can't find help out in the country. It'd need three strong people to care for her. She can get very violent.'

When they attempted to get Kathleen out of the cart, she roused and began to curse them. Her voice might be slurred, because of the laudanum, but her vocabulary was vicious and crude.

Conn apologised, feeling further humiliated by this behaviour.

The woman shrugged. 'We're used to it. I'd better fetch help. She's a strong woman.'

Conn left Leo in charge of the cart and followed the attendant inside.

When two strong men came outside, Kathleen began screaming and kicking again and they had a struggle to get her into the asylum.

The attendant indicated that Conn should follow them and he watched grimly as his wife was manhandled into a cell then chained to a bed by a waist chain. She didn't stop shrieking the whole time.

'Ah, here's the doctor,' the female attendant said. 'This is the husband, doctor, but I think you'd better examine the patient before we talk. She's a lively one.'

The doctor nodded to Conn and asked him to wait outside, then went in to examine Kathleen.

From the corridor Conn could hear her suddenly change to a normal way of speaking and he felt panicked at the thought that she might fool them. Surely they wouldn't be taken in by her?

When the doctor came out, he regarded Conn thoughtfully, then turned to the female attendant. 'How was she behaving when she was brought in?'

'Screaming and shouting, kicking. In a bad way.'

'Cunning, then, because she acted as if she was normal with me.'

There was an even louder scream from inside the cell and the doctor went to stare inside. This time Kathleen began shrieking and cursing him, tugging at the waist chain.

'Strange how the eyes change when they're mad,' he said absent-mindedly. 'Now, come to my office, Mr Largan and we'll discuss the situation.'

Once they were both seated, he said, 'We need to consider whether there is any physical cause for your wife's problem, which will determine whether we can relieve the condition or not. Does she throw fits? No? Has she had any injuries to the head? A high fever, perhaps?'

Conn shook his head to all these, hesitated, then said, 'She's always been – strange, as far as I can work out. They beat her regularly as a child to make her learn to behave, I gather. I believe my father colluded with her parents to keep me ignorant of how strange she really was when we married. She brought a very large dowry, you see, which my father took for the family estate.'

'And you agreed to this?'

'Yes. He could be very – persuasive – and his anger was upsetting my mother, who was an invalid. After I was convicted—'

'You're a convict?' The doctor's expression suddenly changed and he looked at his companion as if he had grown horns.

Conn spoke hastily. 'I was a lawyer and was wrongly accused. Since then the guilty person has confessed, so my family in Ireland is seeking to overturn my conviction. But this all takes time.'

'And your wife? How did she take your transportation? Is that what shocked her into madness?'

'I never saw her again after I was arrested until she came here. She stayed with my father. But he died and then a few months ago, she suddenly turned up here. At first she seemed no different, but gradually her behaviour deteriorated. I tried paying for her to stay quietly on an isolated farm with a lady of our acquaintance, but she rapidly grew too difficult to control, so in the end I've been forced to bring her here. My wife is a very strong woman and I can't control her. I don't know what to do. I'm at my wits' end.'

The doctor tapped his fingers on the table, looking thoughtful.

The seconds ticked slowly past, then he looked at Conn and said, 'You say you've not consummated your marriage, but I have to tell you, Mr Largan, that your wife is not a virgin. Not only that, but she has contracted syphilis, which might be exacerbating her condition.'

The words seemed to echo in Conn's brain, as he tried to take in this shocking information. '*No!* No, that's not possible. She refused to let me consummate the marriage, used to fight like a wildcat if I went near her. I'm seeking an annulment on those grounds.'

'I'm sorry, Mr Largan, but there can be no mistake, and the syphilis will gradually lead to what we call general paralysis of the insane. This is incurable.'

Conn gulped and tried to control his emotions but couldn't and fumbled for his handkerchief. 'Forgive me. Such a shock.'

'I'm sorry to be the bearer of bad news, Mr Largan. Given the situation, we shall, of course, admit her.'

'Thank you.'

The doctor looked at him. 'You're sure you never touched her?'

'Yes. Quite sure.'

'You should thank your Maker on your knees for that. If you had, you might have been afflicted with the same scourge as her.'

Conn answered a few more questions, handed over the clothing they'd brought with them for Kathleen and then walked back out to the cart.

Leo looked at him. 'She's not coming back, is she?'

'No. No, she's not.'

'You'll be better without her.'

'Yes.' He tried to pull himself together. 'Shall we seek lodgings for the night or shall we get some food and start on our way home?'

'I don't like it here. People stare at me.'

'Then we'll set off back. But first we need to clean the cart.'

'I did that while you were inside.'

Conn clapped Leo on the shoulder. 'I don't know how I'd have managed without you. You're a good lad.'

Leo beamed at him. 'And you'll write to my mother for me?'

'Yes. I'm happy to do that for you. It'll take months to get a reply, though.'

Conn was glad to leave the town behind, but he couldn't leave his main worry behind, a far worse worry than the one he'd arrived with. How the hell had Kathleen contracted syphilis? Who had taken advantage of her while she'd been living with his father? He couldn't imagine who would even want her. But it meant she wasn't a virgin, which he had assumed she must be. How was he going to prove he'd not touched her now? *How was he going to get an annulment?* He'd not be able to marry Maia now. He'd ruined her. A fine way of showing his love, that was!

22

Ronan took his bride and her friend home to Ardgullan House after the brief wedding, which took place in a draughty church with Hallie and a cousin of Bram, who was working as coachman and general groom, acting as witnesses. The latter drove them home and Ronan watched Xanthe chat cheerfully to her friend in the carriage. She didn't seem in the least upset at having such a simple wedding and it occurred to him that the people among whom she'd grown up would probably have married in a similar way.

When they got home, he saw a carriage in his drive and Kieran Largan standing outside the front door. The latter turned and at the sight of Ronan smiled and waved, waiting for him to draw up.

Ronan helped the two ladies down and offered them both an arm. 'Kieran! I'm delighted to see you. Let me introduce my wife Xanthe and her friend, Miss Carr. Ladies, this is Conn's brother.'

The visitor blinked at them in shock. 'You're married?'

'Yes. We got married today, actually.'

'Then let me be the first to congratulate you. You're not from round here, Mrs Maguire?'

When his wife didn't seem to recognise her new name, Ronan replied for her. 'Xanthe's from Lancashire, but we met in Australia at your brother's house.'

'Look I'll come over again in a day or two. Don't let me interrupt your festivities.'

'There are no festivities, except in our hearts.'

'We couldn't afford a fancy wedding,' Xanthe said with her usual directness. 'Why don't you come in for a few moments,

Mr Largan? You obviously want to speak to Ronan. Would it be about your brother?'

'Er – yes. Did you know my brother Conn well in Australia?'

'I used to work for him as his housekeeper and my sister Maia is still – um, working for him.'

Looking startled at her frankness, Kieran turned to Ronan, head on one side, to see what he wanted.

'My wife knows everything that's happened to your brother. Come and have a drink of wine to celebrate our marriage, then you can tell me what you came for. If there's anything I can do to help you – or Conn – you know I will. Have you heard from him?'

'I have, actually. He wrote a week or two after you left and the letter arrived yesterday. He sends his regards to you, hopes you've not found things in too bad a state.'

'I must write and tell him we're married. I doubt he'll be surprised.'

Kieran looked at Xanthe, seeming a little embarrassed as he added, 'Conn also asked me to look after your sister if anything happened to him. He says he intends to marry her as soon as his annulment comes through. I'm sorry if this news upsets you, Mrs Maguire.'

'I prefer to know.' Xanthe sighed. 'And actually, it's not a surprise. Everyone could see how much they loved one another.'

'You can be sure that I will look after her if it's ever needed. Conn knows that he can rely on me this time. I let our father persuade me to do nothing last time, to my shame.'

Ronan put his arm round Xanthe. 'Maia would always find a home with us, as well.'

They sat down and he changed the subject. 'I'll go and find a bottle of wine. The cellars are in a dreadful state but my brother bought in some wine, so we won't go short of that, at least.' He came back a few minutes later rubbing his hands together to warm them. 'Mary's cleaning the bottle and bringing in some glasses. Brr. Those cellars are cold.'

After Kieran had proposed a toast to the newly-weds and

Ronan had responded on behalf of himself and his wife, Xanthe took Hallie away and left the gentlemen to chat. 'It seems so far away now, Australia,' she said wistfully as she led the way into a small sitting room across the hall.

'Do you wish you were back there?'

'No. I think life will be more interesting here in Ireland with Ronan. I never wanted to stay in Australia. But I hate being so far away from Maia when she's in such a difficult position. Still, Cassandra is nearby. I'd not have left my twin there on her own otherwise.'

She looked round the room thoughtfully and changed the subject. She didn't want to dwell on her sister and Conn. 'What do you think? This would make a nice room to sit in, except when we have guests, and it'll cost a lot less to heat.'

Hallie followed her lead. 'It's a lovely room and it seems quite big enough to me. I'm amazed at how big the rooms are here and how many of them there are. It'd take a lot of people to keep it all immaculate, wouldn't it?'

'Far too many. I'm thinking of closing down half the house, or more even. We shan't be using it, after all.'

Kieran watched the door close behind his neighbour's new wife and raised his glass. 'You're a lucky man. She's beautiful.'

Ronan smiled. 'That's the least of it. I've not married her for her beauty but for her courageous spirit and her intelligence. She's a very special woman.' He looked down at his wineglass, then said quietly, 'We knew before we left that your brother was deeply in love with her twin sister. Maia's gentler, but still intelligent and beautiful.'

'He's very eager to get this annulment through, but the Church won't be hurried on these things.'

'It never was a marriage with Kathleen.'

'I was horrified when I found out that Father had persuaded him to marry her. He did it while Julia and I were on a long visit to her grandparents in England. She was very fond of them and knew they were both unwell. They left her a good legacy afterwards. If my father had still been alive, he'd have been trying to get his hands on it.'

'I'm glad you're in a comfortable position.'

'I would have been even without Julia's legacy. That's partly why I came here. I hear you're hard pressed.'

Ronan nodded.

'How bad are things?'

'I may keep Ardgullan House or I may not. I've offended Reginald Johnson and he's threatened to make sure I lose the whole property.'

'If a few thousand pounds will make the difference, I'll be happy to lend it to you. My father worshipped money. I don't think Conn ever realised how he'd been cheated and I didn't know until I inherited that my father had taken most of Kathleen's dowry.'

Ronan looked at him in shock. 'How could he do that?'

'He arranged it secretly with her family. They must have been bribing him to get rid of their daughter.'

'It's kind of you to offer to lend me the money but I couldn't take it from you because I'd have no way of paying it back.'

'I could wait. You've been a good friend to Conn and I feel my family owes you a great deal. I feel guilty about inheriting all the money. It seems as if Conn has paid for everything, and paid very dearly too, not only losing his freedom, but his profession and his whole way of life.'

'I felt desperately sorry for him when he was sentenced,' Ronan admitted.

'I always knew he was innocent,' Kieran said. 'No wonder my mother ran away from Shilmara after Conn was transported. She must have known my father was involved. He was talking about going after her right until he died, planning it too, for all I know. He hated anyone to get the better of him.' After another pause, Kieran asked quietly, 'How is Conn coping with his new life? Tell me the truth, now.'

'He's become very quiet and withdrawn. I think he only seeks a peaceful life now, and Maia can give him that. She's a very restful woman. Will Michael's statement get Conn's conviction quashed?'

'My lawyer thinks so. But it'll take time. Probably as long as the annulment. I'll send Conn out some more money and explain why. I'll feel better if I make sure he can wait for both verdicts in comfort.' He drained his glass. 'Well, I won't keep you on your wedding day. Could you please ring to let them know I'll need my carriage?'

'Yes, of course. Oh look, Feargus is out there.' Ronan went to the window and hauled it up, letting in a whirl of damp air. 'Hoy, Feargus! Mr Largan needs his carriage.'

The man walking past raised one hand in acknowledgement.

Ronan turned to see Kieran grinning. 'There's no use standing on one's dignity with staff who've worked for nothing for years and we don't have a dozen maids to run round after us. Besides, Feargus taught me to ride. He's more like an uncle than a head groom.'

The two men shook hands at the front door ten minutes later.

'Don't forget!' Kieran called as he got into his carriage. 'Bring your wife round to meet mine. I think she and Julia will get on well.'

After dinner, Hallie excused herself and Ronan took Xanthe into the library. He pulled a leather box out of a drawer and held it out to her. 'These were my mother's. I can't offer you much, but at least some of the family jewels are still left for my bride gift to you.'

She opened the box, surprised at how many brooches, necklaces and bracelets it contained. When she looked at him, she was frowning. 'Why haven't you sold these when you're so short of money?'

'Some of them have been in the family for over a hundred years. And they aren't particularly valuable. These brooches, for instance, have small stones, even if they're pretty.'

'That's not the point. They'd be worth quite a lot of money and you need every penny.'

'Hubert would have sold them already if he could have got his hands on them, but my mother kept them safe from him by hiding them and taking some of her favourites to Australia. I found them among her things after she died and as I knew where her hiding place was, I found the others after I got back.

'I felt then and I still feel now that I should only use them as the very last resort. If Mr Johnson is intending to ruin me, you should keep these safe because we may have to use them to pay our fares back to Australia and start up a new life there.'

'You think he really can ruin you, take your house away?'

Ronan's expression became grim. 'I'm sure he'll try. He's got plenty of money, not to mention a reputation for ruthlessness, so I'll be on my guard. And I certainly behaved badly towards his daughter, so in that sense he has a right to be angry with me.'

'I feel sorry for her. She seems very unhappy.'

'Yes. But at the moment I'm more concerned about your happiness.'

She picked up a diamond bracelet, letting it dangle from her fingers. 'I don't need jewels like these to make me happy. If we sold them, wouldn't it give us enough to pay off the debts?'

'I don't know, but I'm not inclined to risk everything I have. More debts keep coming to light, you see. Let's just wait and see.'

'Very well. I hope you have a good hiding place, because I'd worry about leaving them around.'

'I'll show you the family hidey-hole when we go up to bed.' He sighed. 'I wish I were better at figures, Xanthe. Or at business generally. I've led a very idle life, I'm afraid, and I'm an outdoor sort of fellow. I love riding and walking, going on exploring trips, not sitting in front of a ledger. But I will do my best – my very best – for you and for Ardgullan.'

'I know you will. But I'm going to deal with the accounts from now on. I'm not just helping out for the moment, I'm taking over.'

He looked at her in shock. 'You are?'

'Yes. I'm not stupid and I've always been quick at arithmetic. It can't be that hard to keep track of sums of money and to work out what there is left to spend on renovations each year.'

'Is there nothing you won't try?'

She beamed at him. 'No. Well, I don't want to try anything physically dangerous, so you won't get me hunting, but I started to learn to ride in Australia and I'd like to continue. I've already discussed the present situation with Hallie and she's offered to take charge of the house for the first week or two and do an inventory. That'll leave you free to take over the farm and see what improvements you can make there, and work out what you can sell to give you more money. Don't you have trees you can sell for timber or horses you can sell . . . or something?'

'I doubt the trees here are particularly valuable. This isn't rich land. And as for selling the horses, what would people say about that?'

'They'd say we were being sensible, cutting our coat to suit our cloth. There has to be a way to find some money, just enough to keep us going.'

He planted a quick kiss on her cheek. 'Does nothing ever get you down?'

'Losing you would.'

'I feel the same way.' His breathing grew deeper as he pulled her closer. 'Ah, darling, let's stop talking about money and make our marriage real.'

He watched her nod and put the jewels carefully back into the box, then he picked it up and led his bride up the stairs. He felt happier than he had since his arrival in Ireland and it was all due to her. She made him feel anything was possible, even saving his family home. She was indomitable. That was the word for her. And he'd do his very best to be worthy of her.

Inside the bedroom she wouldn't allow him to touch her till the jewels were safely locked away in the secret cupboard, then she moved into his arms and their troubles faded. They kissed and moved to the bed, not hurrying, because from now on they had all the time in the world to be together and love one another.

Conn arrived back at Galway House from Fremantle feeling weary in body and spirit. Leo hadn't pestered him to chat on the journey back, not even when they were sleeping under the stars, a time when confidences were frequently exchanged. Whatever else he was slow at, Leo seemed to understand people's feelings and needs, to sense that his companion on this journey wanted to be quiet.

The sight of Galway House made the guilt come rushing back again. Conn got down from the cart, anxious to find his beloved, leaving it to Leo and Sean to unharness the horses and give them a well-deserved rest.

He saw Maia waiting for him on the little veranda at the rear of the kitchen, her smile glowing with love and he forgot about guilt, forgot about everything except her.

Behind him, Leo and Sean watched the reunion and the old man wiped a tear from his eye.

'He deserves some love, that lad does. Always was too soft for his own good, and that father of his was a hard man, hard on his children and a harsh master to his servants, too. All *he* cared about was money. I'd not have stayed at Shilmara but for the mistress.' He clapped Leo on the shoulder. 'Well, we can't stand here all day. Come on, lad. You and I will see to the horses then we'll have a nice cup of tea in the stables. Those two won't want disturbing for a good while.'

It wasn't until they were sitting together after their evening meal, with Nancy dismissed for the evening, that Maia asked, 'Aren't you going to tell me what's wrong, Conn darling?'

He sighed and took her hand in both his, holding it as if it was the most precious thing on earth. 'I had some bad news at the asylum. The doctor examined Kathleen and – he said she wasn't a virgin. Worse, she has – it's dreadful, I hate even to say the word – syphilis. Who she lay with I can't think.'

Maia was more concerned about the deep sadness on his face

than about her own situation. 'That won't make much difference to me, will it?'

'It'll make a big difference. The annulment plea is based on a claim that I never consummated our marriage. But if she lay with someone, I can't prove that it wasn't me, so I doubt we'll get the annulment now. She'll die of this dreadful disease, but that may not be for years yet.'

'Will your word that you've never touched her not count for anything?'

'I shouldn't think so. I wonder if I ought to withdraw my plea before we face further humiliation.'

She didn't speak at first, thinking this through carefully. 'Darling, the only thing that would destroy me would be to lose you. The rest I can face.'

His voice was savage. 'Well, I'm not sure I can face a lifetime of this. You don't *deserve* the way people will treat you from now on. I shouldn't have taken advantage of you. And our children don't deserve to be born with the label 'bastard' on them, either. It's a poor legacy for a father to give them.'

'How did you take advantage of me?'

'You know how. By taking you into my bed.'

She chuckled, a soft, contented sound. 'I came willingly and would do it all over again if I had to. Darling Conn, I'm not some doll to be picked up and put down at will. I have a mind of my own and I use it.'

'But look how badly you were treated at the monthly church service! I saw how that upset you.'

'I wasn't prepared for it. And I've been thinking about my situation. One of the fears for women in my position is to be left without money. I have money of my own and you've set up a trust for me and any children I may have, so I feel perfectly safe in that way. Stop worrying, Conn. What matters is that I'm far happier with you than I would be without you.'

He put his arm round her shoulders and she nestled against him. 'It all seems very simple, Conn darling. You're my man, whether married or not, my dearest friend and the father of my child. I've never been so happy in my whole life as I am living here quietly with you. I have no need to go out into the world and face other people's scorn.'

'The world might come here, though.'

'We'll worry about that when it happens.' She wouldn't tell Xanthe about how she'd been treated, though. It would only make her sister worry. She'd write about her happiness and the coming child. Letters were a poor substitute for seeing people you loved.

The major sadness in her life was not being a fallen woman, but being so far away from her sister. She missed talking to Xanthe, sharing her thoughts and feelings, missed it dreadfully.

How was Xanthe getting on? Had she started travelling or had she and Ronan come together? She did hope so. They suited one another so well.

It was infuriating to have to wait months for news. But at least she could sense that Xanthe was all right. She always knew when something was wrong with her twin.

The day after their wedding, Ronan went across to the land agent's office to go through some more details of his inheritance and Xanthe summoned the cook and Mary. She kept Hallie with her as they waited for the two servants.

The cook was the first to arrive, a thin woman with iron-grey hair and an immaculate pinafore. Today she had a worried look on her face and as soon as she was invited to sit down, she burst into speech. 'I'm sorry if the food isn't fancy enough for you, Mrs Maguire, but indeed we've not got half the things we need for me to do better.'

'That's not why I summoned you, Mrs Sullivan. I'm very pleased with the food you've been preparing. I enjoy your cooking and so does my husband. It's not that. Let's wait for Mary so I don't have to say everything twice.'

Mary arrived, breathless from hurrying. 'Sorry, ma'am, but I was going through the linen when I got your message and the girl couldn't find me. Why she didn't look in the storerooms the first time, I don't know.' She took the seat indicated, glancing quickly at Mrs Sullivan, then looking at her mistress and clasping her hands so tightly in her lap that the knuckles were white.

Xanthe couldn't think of a delicate way to explain, so said bluntly, 'You'll know that my husband inherited a lot of debt because of his father and brother?'

They both nodded, looking at her even more apprehensively.

'Let's speak frankly, then, about what this means for us. We're going to have to be very careful with the housekeeping if we're to help Mr Maguire to keep his home.'

Mary put up her hand as if to cross herself, then jerked it back glancing nervously at her mistress.

Xanthe was used to this habit of making the sign of the cross by now so said quietly, 'I see no harm in you crossing yourself, Mary, if it comforts you. Why did you stop?'

'Mr Hubert didn't like us doing it. He didn't like us going to mass, either. I was always frightened he'd dismiss me for being a Catholic.'

'Well, Ronan and I don't mind whether you attend Catholic services or not, if that's what you want to do. But that's not what I need to talk about today. Look . . . I want to ask your help in cutting right down on expenses in this house.'

That surprised them and was it relief she saw on their faces too? Of course it was! They'd have been afraid of losing their jobs with a new mistress in the house. 'I don't mean anyone has to go hungry, but surely there's food that's cheaper, ways of economising? I'm not a fine lady, so I don't need to be pampered or have more food on the table than anyone can eat and Ronan, as you must be aware, will eat anything put before him.'

Mrs Sullivan let out a huge sigh of relief and admitted, 'I was worried you were going to close the house down, ma'am.'

'I hope not. Can you help us live more cheaply?'

'I can do that, ma'am, and willingly. And you're right. The master won't even notice. I remember him as a lad, such a cheerful little soul, he was.'

'That's wonderful.' Xanthe turned to Mary. 'I'm asking the

same thing of you. I don't want to dismiss anyone, but can we run the house more economically? I thought we might close down those rooms not in use. I'd need you to tell me which ones would be best.' She saw relief writ large on another face.

'Indeed, ma'am, now I know what's needed I'll see to that personally. And yes, we can get out the dust covers and close several of the rooms. Some of them are never used.'

'Mr Maguire and I will use the small room next to the library for our sitting room and we'll eat our meals in there too, to save on heating and cleaning. We'll keep the drawing room for when we have visitors, but we'll only light a fire in there if visitors actually turn up.'

'Leave it to me, ma'am.'

'That's wonderful. Now, Miss Carr is going to help you in any way she can and will be making an inventory of what's in this house. You could perhaps help her to turn out the store cupboards and check everything that's usable. She and I learned to be economical in a hard school when the mills in our town closed down for lack of cotton and many of the people were hungering. I'm going to learn how to do the accounts. Ronan tells me he's no good at figures, so I can't be worse than him at it. Mr Hatton is sending a clerk to help me for a few days, till I get the hang of it. We'll need to find him a bedroom.'

When the two senior servants had gone, she turned to Hallie. 'Do you think I handled that all right?'

'You did it well. They were very polite and attentive.'

'That's because everyone loves Ronan. They say nothing at all about his brother Hubert, but their expressions speak for them. He wasn't liked.'

Xanthe twirled round and beamed at her friend. 'I know things are in a terrible state, but it's wonderful to have some purpose in life again.'

The young clerk from Mr Hatton's rooms arrived two days later. Mr Flewett was very nervous of them and seemed surprised that he was expected to eat with them. Within a day he'd lost his fear of Xanthe and was enthusiastically guiding her through the mysteries of keeping the accounts for a large country residence.

'You're doing well, Mrs Maguire,' he said the second evening. 'You have a real head for figures.'

'Thank goodness for that!' Ronan raised his teacup in a mock toast to her.

When they were alone that night he teased her about Mr Flewett being half in love with her. She just grinned at him. 'Poor man. He's very downtrodden. I don't like the way Mr Hatton treats his clerks.'

'For goodness' sake, don't start trying to reform old Hatton. He's a plain, old-fashioned man and will never change.'

After four days of tuition Xanthe felt confident enough to send Mr Flewett on his way and commandeer for her office another of the little rooms that seemed tucked into corners everywhere in this rambling house.

23

Two weeks later, Mr Hatton arrived at Ardgullan House in a hired carriage, looking harried. Xanthe sent Mary to fetch Ronan in from the stables, whispering that the lawyer looked anxious and the master was to hurry. She took the visitor through to the library, lighting a taper from her sitting-room fire to get the big fire going in there.

Ronan wasted no time changing his clothes, but came straight into the house. As soon as he saw his lawyer's sombre expression he asked, 'What now?'

'Another debt has turned up, and it's for twenty thousand pounds.'

'What? How is that possible?' Ronan demanded. 'Who is owed that much money?'

'Mr Johnson.'

'I don't believe it. He'd have said something about it before now if he'd been owed such a huge sum. What's it for?'

'He says it was a loan for Hubert to make one of his investments. He has the estate down as security.'

Ronan was silent, trying to think this through. 'My brother was involved in risky investments, yes, but surely he'd not have borrowed to finance them? And especially not from Johnson.'

'He said that since you were about to marry his daughter he decided not to call in the debt but now that you weren't going to marry her, he wanted to be paid, and quickly. He presented your brother's IOU to me yesterday.'

'I find this hard to believe.'

Mr Hatton hesitated then said slowly, 'So do I. If it wasn't for Hubert's signature, which I'd recognise anywhere, I'd think it was a – well, some sort of sham.'

'Why do you say that?'

'Because your brother wasn't on particularly close terms with Johnson. He told me more than once that he neither liked nor trusted him.'

There was silence as the implications of this sank in, then Ronan asked bluntly, 'Do you think the IOU is a forgery, then?'

'I'm puzzled, I must admit. Only – it looks like Hubert's signature. No mistaking that squiggle at the end of his name.'

More silence until Xanthe felt like shouting at them to put it into words. When they didn't, she said it for them. 'This is a trick, then. Mr Johnson told us before he left that he'd have the house off you, Ronan, and this is his way of doing it.'

Mr Hatton stared unhappily down at his hands.

'Well?' she urged. 'There must be some way of proving that this is a fraud, surely? I don't think that horrible man would ever have forgiven a debt that big, whoever you were. He looked too . . . too . . .'

'Predatory,' Ronan finished for her. 'But how the hell do we prove that this is a trick if he's made so good a copy of my brother's signature that even Mr Hatton wonders if it's genuine?'

No one answered until the lawyer said, 'What do you want me to do about it? I think we'll have no alternative but to pay – and to do that you'll have to sell the estate. There is no way you can raise such a big loan by mortgaging Ardgullan, not in your present circumstances. And even if you do sell, I don't think the estate will bring in that much money so it and everything on it will be forfeit to Johnson.'

Ronan spoke slowly, still trying to think his way through this. 'Do nothing yet. Ignore it for the time being and if Johnson presses for payment, say you've let me know and are awaiting my response. I'm not going to rush into anything.'

'That'll only hold him for a few days.'

'Every day will help. Now, if you have no more nasty surprises for us, can we offer you some refreshments before you go?'

Mr Hatton glanced towards the windows. 'Thank you, but no. It looks as if a storm is brewing.'

'Could be. Thank you for coming to see me yourself today. I'll see you to the door.'

When the lawyer had left, Ronan came back to sit with Xanthe. 'I don't know what to do. I can hardly throttle Johnson, can I, which is what I'd *like* to do? And if he goes to court for the money he says he's owed, I have no way of proving him a liar.'

'My father always said the main thing in a crisis is not to rush into anything.'

'Well, as I can't think of anything to do, rushing certainly doesn't come into it.' After a while, Ronan went outside again, but the energy had gone from him. Watching him, Xanthe saw how heavy his tread was, how his shoulders sagged.

She went back to sit by the fire, hands clasped round her knees, feet toasting on the fender, and thought long and hard about the situation. There must be something they could do. Surely that horrible man couldn't just steal their home?

She continued to mull the problem over during the rest of the afternoon, but no hint of a solution came to her.

The whole house was sunk in gloom. The servants knew only that another debt had cropped up. Hallie knew the truth about what they suspected, but since she was unable to help in any way, she continued to go through the house, sorting out cupboards of things which hadn't been touched for decades.

It wasn't until the middle of the night that Xanthe woke abruptly with the thought of Georgina Johnson. Ronan had said she seemed a decent young woman, unlike her father, and indeed, Xanthe had thought she had a pleasant face, the sort that reflected a pleasant nature. Would *she* know what her father was up to? Would she help them? Or was she so under her father's thumb that she would continue to live with him and give up the man she loved?

Wasn't it worth a try to seek her help? She'd been honest about her feelings after Xanthe's arrival, glaring at her father as she spoke. If that was the start of a rebellion against a bullying parent, perhaps she could be persuaded to help.

Why did she not marry her young man? If her father threat-ened to put him out of business, the two of them could make a new life elsewhere. Or was Georgina afraid of what her father might do? How ruthless was Mr Johnson? Theft was clearly not beyond him. Was murder? Even Ronan admitted the man was feared in the district.

Xanthe knew the Johnsons lived in a huge new house just off the main road to Enniskillen. She decided to try to see Georgina and ask for her help, because it was the only thing she could think of to do for Ronan.

But how to get in touch with her? She couldn't just knock on the door and pay a morning call, she was sure, and anyway, she didn't want to alert Mr Johnson to what she was doing.

No, she had to find some way to see Georgina in secret. And in the meantime she'd continue to rack her brain about other things she might do. Getting Georgina's help was a forlorn hope.

Only . . . something in Xanthe said it was the right thing to do.

The next day Xanthe confided in Mary, who had been born in the area and might be able to help her without Ronan finding out. 'How can I get a message to Georgina Johnson without her father knowing? It's very important indeed.'

Mary pursed her lips, then said, 'I might be able to help. My second cousin's daughter is a maid in their house. But I'd need your promise that if Brenda lost her job because of helping us, you'd give her a place here.'

'Of course we would. But it doesn't seem right to put the girl at such risk.'

Mary gave one of her wry half-smiles. 'Brenda's not happy there. She's frightened of Mr Johnson and is already looking for another place.'

'How can we get a message to her?'

'I can go to market in Enniskillen and call at the back door of the house on my way back. They know me there. I've dropped by to see her a few times now.'

Xanthe forgot herself and gave the housekeeper a hug.

Mary stiffened in surprise, then smiled and patted Xanthe's arm. 'You write your letter, ma'am. I'll go and see Brenda tomorrow.'

The following day Xanthe couldn't settle to anything. It seemed a long time before Mary came home, driving the shabby little pony trap the servants used to go shopping. It was quite a long drive into Enniskillen so they didn't go every week.

Ronan was standing in the enclosure next to the stables, trying out one of the young horses he had been thinking of selling till this latest blow struck them, so Xanthe didn't give in to her first instinct to rush out and ask how the mission had gone, but waited impatiently for her housekeeper in the kitchen. She didn't want to raise his hopes because he was very downhearted about it all.

Mary came in, shaking the raindrops off her cloak. 'Brenda took your note up to Miss Georgina and brought a message back from her. She'll meet you tomorrow at her old nurse's cottage at about ten o'clock in the morning. I'm to take you there. The village isn't too far away.'

'Do you think she's willing to help us?'

'I don't know. Brenda said her mistress had to rush off, because her father came home early and she had to go down and pour his tea.'

'Can't he pour his own?' Xanthe muttered, but she'd already learned that ladies did the tea-pouring in the elevated world she now inhabited. There were a lot of silly little customs like that to learn. Thank goodness for Mrs Largan's patient instruction when she'd been learning to be a housekeeper! It was certainly paying off now.

The following morning Xanthe set out with her housekeeper, ostensibly to take food to a family Mary knew who needed help. They had a basket of leftover bits and pieces to show to Ronan if he asked where they were going, but it turned out that he'd already gone out himself, so it wasn't needed.

'There are plenty who'll take the food, though, and say thank you for it,' Mary said. 'It's mostly things left over from your meals. Mrs Sullivan only gives away the leftovers she can't use, things like the fat you've cut off your meat and left on your plate. She's not wasting your money, well only a little. There are one or two old folk in the village who rely on us to support them, you see, ones whose children have moved away. We didn't think you'd mind. They'd starve without our help and they eat very little.'

'Are they as poor as that?'

'Some of them. None of the village folk have much to spare these days, you see, so can't help them as much as they'd like.'

Xanthe made a mental note to go on helping people like these, remembering her own hungry days – well, she would help them if she was still here. Strange how quickly she'd settled in here, begun to feel at home, didn't want to leave. This was partly because of the friendliness of the servants and the local people she'd met.

Miss Johnson's old nurse lived in a small cottage in the village to which she'd retired when she became too frail to work. There was a carriage standing outside with a coachman and groom sitting on it, keeping a watchful eye on the cottage. Mary murmured that this was the place, but didn't point and drove straight past. 'Good thing I have friends in the village,' she said as they slowed down further along the only street.

'You seem to have friends everywhere.'

'Wasn't I born round here?'

They left the horse and trap with Mary's friend then as she took Xanthe along a narrow, overhung path at the rear of the row of cottages it began to rain. She turned through a neat little garden to tap on a back door.

When Georgina answered it, Mary said gruffly to Xanthe, 'I'll wait for you out here, ma'am.'

'You'll get wet if you do,' Georgina said. 'That rain's setting in. Come and sit in the kitchen.'

That, thought Xanthe, showed that Georgina had a kind heart, which boded well for her mission. She hung back when the other would have led the way into the tiny front parlour of the cottage. 'Won't those men see us from your carriage if we go in there?'

'The windows are covered with muslin because Nurse doesn't like people looking in as they pass. As long as we keep our voices down, the coachman won't know you're here. Oh, and Nurse is deaf, so she won't hear what we're saying but I've explained to her who you are.'

Xanthe nodded politely to the old woman then explained the situation to Georgina. 'We think your father has forged the promissory note.'

Georgina hesitated, biting her lip, then nodded. 'He did. A man came to the house late one night, someone Father's used before for forging documents, so I crept downstairs to see if I could find out what was going on. I heard them mention Hubert Maguire and they laughed because his signature was so easy to copy.'

Xanthe sucked in her breath, amazed to have been told this so quickly.

Georgina gave a bitter laugh. 'It sometimes makes it easier to live with my father if I know what he's doing and what I should avoid talking about. He's not an easy man, even with his own family. Since he had a hard life, he doesn't see why anyone else should have a soft one.'

'Will you help us, then?'

'Yes. I know he's my father, but he's not a good man and I hate him. In return I want your help in escaping so that Paul and I can get married, not just getting away from my home but getting out of Ireland. I'm twenty-two now so I don't need my father's permission to marry, but he'll come after us if I just run away without a good plan. He'd have me stopped on the road and probably arrange for Paul to be killed.'

'Is your father that bad?'

'Yes. Since my mother died, he's hardly let me out of his sight. You saw my watchdogs sitting outside.' She gestured to the window. 'You've also met my aunt who lives with us. She doesn't come with me to visit my nurse because the two of them hate one another.'

'How exactly are you going to help us?'

'All I can think of is to sign a statement saying I overheard my father talking to the man who forged your brother-in-law's signature. I can also give you the forger's name. And – I'll also say I heard my father threaten to make Ronan sorry, which I did, several times. You'll have to ask that lawyer of yours if that's enough. It's all I can do for you. You can send a message to my maid again when you're ready.'

'You'd better have your things packed, then, ready to leave.'

'There's no way I'd dare do that, because someone would notice and tell him. I'm hoping you'll give me some clothes. You're a bit taller than me, but I can easily take up the hems. I'll just have to snatch what I can when I leave, my jewels especially.' She closed her eyes and added in a low voice, 'I can't wait to leave him. Every servant in the house is terrified of upsetting him and even my aunt is nervous when he's around. It's a miserable way to live.'

'I have to ask – are you sure your courage won't fail you at the last minute?' This point had been worrying Xanthe.

'Oh, yes. I'm very sure.'

Her expression was so grimly determined, Xanthe believed her.

'It's partly because of you, you know. I can't forget how you came after the man you loved. I envied you that day. Ronan's face lit up when he saw you.' She sighed.

'How will you live after you marry Paul?'

'He has some money saved. We'll go to England and sell my jewels. They really are mine because my aunt and mother left them to me. Father thinks he has most of them locked away, but I know where he hides the box and how to open it. He doesn't trust banks and anyway, he likes me to wear them when we go out, to show off his wealth.'

'Why go to England?'

'Paul has relatives there who'll help him. He'll lose a lot by going there, because he'll have to abandon the family business to his cousin. But he says it'll be worth it. He can always open another workshop – he's a very skilled clockmaker. We've been wanting to marry for three years, but my father refused even to consider it. I've had to wait till I turned twenty-one – and until I found the courage.'

'If your father is as bad as you say, you might even find it safer to go to America or Australia. It'd be far harder for him to find you there.'

Georgina looked at her thoughtfully. 'You're right, I suppose. But it's such a long way, isn't it?'

'People there are just the same as they are here.'

Was the signed statement going to be enough? Xanthe wondered as she and Mary drove home, stopping at cottages here and there to distribute small amounts of food. The light rain soon had them soaked to the skin, in spite of the umbrella she held over them. It seemed to rain a lot in Ireland. Anyone coming from Lancashire was used to rain but to her surprise it seemed to rain more here, if the recent weeks were anything to judge by.

It was a huge contrast to Western Australia where it hardly rained at all for the warmer half of the year.

She couldn't wait to ask what her husband thought of her plan. Surely he would help?

Ronan stared at her in shock after hearing what she'd done. 'I can't believe you got in touch with Georgina Johnson. Is there nothing you're afraid of?'

'Losing you.'

He had to give her a kiss for that and said against her hair, 'Georgina's right about you inspiring other people. You give me courage too, my darling, and not just courage but a desire to settle down and become a steady provider – and father of a family too, one day. I was an idle fellow till I met you.'

He looked down, saw her frown and added, 'I know you've never wanted children, but I hope you'll give me one or two. There are ways to limit the size of families these days, you know. They're not infallible methods, but they're good enough that you can be sure I'll not burden you with one child after another.'

She smiled at him mistily and raised one hand to caress his cheek. 'Thank you. That did worry me a little, though not enough to stop me marrying you. I'd like to have a child or two with *you*. Maia said I'd change if I loved someone enough, and I have done. But there were women in the streets where I grew up who hated their husbands, because they were forced to have one child after another till they were worn out and sometimes died.'

'I'd never do that to you.' He caught hold of the hand that had caressed his cheek and carried it to his lips, smiling to see her draw her breath in sharply as he placed a lingering kiss in her palm. She was so responsive, so loving.

'Hadn't we better go and see Mr Hatton about this?' she asked when she got her breath back.

'Yes, I suppose so. The sooner the better, really. It's the only chance that I can see to keep Ardgullan.'

They went into Enniskillen that afternoon, the drive seeming much shorter when Ronan drove them in a smart new four-wheeled dog cart that had been one of his brother's last purchases.

'This is quicker than the carriage Hallie and I hired,' Xanthe commented.

'That heavy old thing! It can hardly rumble along at a walking pace. Only visitors are foolish enough to hire it. Even our carriage at Ardgullan is more modern than that one. But this dog cart is a very useful vehicle and luckily we have a pair of horses to draw it. They're sturdy animals, these two. I'd not sell them except as a final resort, but I've taken your advice and looked at our other horses and there are a few I can sell.

'Hubert would never sell any, but some don't serve any real purpose and they all cost money to feed. Maybe, if we do manage to keep Ardgullan, I'll take a leaf out of Conn's book and breed horses.'

She was glad to hear Ronan making plans. She'd worried that he might not be able to settle down to the steady hard work that would be needed to bring the estate back to prosperity. 'That sounds like an excellent idea. I'll help you in any way I can.'

He chuckled. 'What? Are you an expert on horse breeding now, as well as everything else?'

She tilted her chin and stuck out her tongue at him. 'Well, I do know a little about it. I lived at Conn's house for a few years and there wasn't much to see except what went on in the yard at the back, so I often watched what he and Sean were doing. I'm a quick learner.'

'You are, indeed.' His smile faded and he said wonderingly, 'Ah, you're the light of my life, Xanthe girl. You'll be the making of me.'

She felt a glow of happiness at his words in spite of all the worries they were facing.

When they explained to the lawyer what she'd arranged, Mr Hatton gloomily admitted that if they had such a statement from Mr Johnson's own daughter it'd put the debt in doubt, at least. 'He might even withdraw his claim to avoid a scandal. But then he could bring out that promissory note again at a later date. And I should warn you, he's a dangerous man to cross. He never forgets it when he thinks someone has done him a wrong and there have been whispers of convenient deaths. I feel guilty now about bringing the two of you together.'

Ronan definitely wished Mr Hatton hadn't done that, but you couldn't change the past. 'We'll face whatever happens when we have to,' Ronan said. 'Now, what do we do? I don't intend to let him steal my home without a fight.'

'You'd better get Miss Johnson to come in here and make the statement in front of witnesses of my choosing.'

'After which we'd better help her get out of the country immediately,' Xanthe said. 'It needs careful planning.'

Mr Hatton gave her one of his disapproving glances but said nothing. She wished Ronan had a more cheerful and modern-thinking lawyer. This man seemed to resent her even opening her mouth.

As she walked out she smiled at Mr Flewett. The young clerk

was standing at a high desk, writing industriously, but he stopped work to wink at her behind his employer's back.

Three days later, Georgina slipped out of her father's house just before dawn, carrying two bundles. Ronan and his wife picked her up at the gate, again using the dog cart. Xanthe had packed a bag of clothes and other necessities for Georgina.

They brought Hallie with them, partly because it was time for her to return to her mother and partly because Mr Johnson and his minions would not be looking for two ladies travelling together.

By the time they reached Enniskillen, Mr Hatton was in his rooms, having got up earlier than usual by arrangement, something he'd been very grumpy about.

Looking as gloomy as ever, he showed them all into his office. 'Mr Rawdon is already here. He's been waiting for half an hour. It's a good thing Mr Flewett came early to let him in. I have trouble thinking straight if I have to get up this early. It's an uncivilised hour.'

Paul Rawdon was dressed as a manservant and grinned at Georgina, tugging on his forelock.

She let out a cry of joy and rushed across to hug him, which had the lawyer looking even more disapproving.

'If we could sit down and see to the important business first?' Mr Hatton waited for them to take the chairs set out in front of his big desk. 'Now, I've had two copies of the statement prepared and young Flewett is waiting outside to witness it.'

'Wouldn't it be better to have someone not employed by you as the second witness?' Paul Rawdon suggested. 'It would look less like collusion between you and your client. I've got two friends waiting for me outside. I brought them along for protection, just in case. Let me bring them in and we'll have one of them witness the document.' He looked directly at Ronan. 'I don't trust Mr Johnson in the slightest.'

'Neither do I.'

After the statement had been signed, Mr Hatton started to put the two pieces of paper away. Xanthe waited for Ronan to speak and when he didn't, she said, 'I think we ought to take one of those statements.'

Mr Hatton glared at her. 'Are you insinuating that I won't keep them safely?'

'No, of course not. But it's so important, I'll – I mean, *we* will both feel safer to have one in our keeping.'

Bristling, he rolled one up and tied a red cord round it, shoving it across his desk so hard it nearly fell off. 'Here, then. Take it. But make sure you don't lose it.'

As Ronan slipped it into his inside pocket, flattening it a little to do so, Paul's friend took out his pocket watch. 'We need to get you three to the station if you're to catch the first train.'

'I think we should start playing our roles from the minute we leave here,' Paul said. 'From now on, I'm your man-servant, and you two are sisters. Georgina, you did well to darken your hair. They'll be looking for a woman with bright red hair not brown.'

She grimaced, touching it gently with one hand. 'It's shoe polish! I could find nothing else.'

Xanthe listened in approval. Rawdon seemed very sensible to her, as did Georgina. She hoped the two of them would get away from Mr Johnson. And surely, travelling with Hallie would help disguise them?

On the way there Paul gave Ronan an address in England which would find them. 'I'm not running any further than that. My relatives there will help me set up another business. I'll make sure we keep an eye out for trouble once we're away from Johnson's influence, believe me.'

As the Maguires stood waving goodbye Xanthe said regret-fully, 'I'm going to miss Hallie. And I'm sorry Georgina has to move away from the district. I think she and I could have become good friends.'

'What about Kieran's wife? She took the trouble to pay a call on us. Can you not make friends with her?'

'She was so polite and formal I wasn't sure. Only time will tell. They probably all think you've made a poor match.'

'*I* don't think I have. Though I do wonder sometimes if I've caught me a tiger by the tail.'

'Did you really want a meek wife?'

He grinned. 'No. That'd be boring. I didn't want any wife till I met you. I wonder what Mr Johnson will say when he hears from Hatton? More to the point, I wonder what he'll do.'

'I hope he flies into a fury and dies of an apoplexy!' She added hesitantly, 'Once all the fuss has settled down, could we not find ourselves another lawyer? Mr Hatton is an old fuddy-duddy. He's not only set in his ways but he disapproves of me.'

'Let's make sure of Ardgullan first and then see what we need. His family have been lawyers to my family for years so I'd not like to dismiss him.'

24

Mr Hatton wrote to tell them he'd informed Mr Johnson that they repudiated the debt claim and had sent him a copy of his daughter's statement. Nothing more was heard, but Xanthe felt twitchy, as if a storm was brewing. They were all sure Mr Johnson wouldn't take this meekly.

A week after Georgina's flight to England they received a letter from her saying she and Paul had been kindly received by his relatives and had got married by special licence.

'Why are you looking so worried?' Ronan asked. 'We've spiked Johnson's guns. He'll be more concerned to look for his daughter now than pursue us.'

'I hope you're right.'

'Oh ye of little faith!'

But though she said nothing more to Ronan, she still felt worried. Something bad was going to happen, she was sure. She had these presentiments sometimes and they were never wrong. A man like Johnson wouldn't stop at the first major setback.

But how far would he go to get his own back?

Maia contented herself with her home and her beloved Conn, letting him drive her across every week or two to visit her sister, who had also stopped attending the Sunday services at the barn because she was so angry about how people had treated her sister.

'I'm worried about Xanthe,' Maia announced on one of these visits. 'You know how I get a feeling sometimes when she's in trouble – well, I've got it now.'

Cassandra looked at her in dismay. 'Are you sure?'

'Yes.'

'I hope it's nothing too bad. That's the worst thing about living here. We won't hear from her for months.'

Maia was cradling her swelling stomach with one hand, her eyes gazing sightlessly into the distance. 'I always know she's still alive. That's a great comfort to me. But I'll feel it if the trouble continues. I just can't help it.'

The following day a letter arrived from Perth for Conn, a summons to attend a preliminary hearing about his application for an annulment.

'I shall have to go,' he said, reading it through again. 'Will you be all right here?'

'Of course I will. I've Nancy and Sean to look after me.'

'Don't go to the shop on your own.'

'I've no need of anything. I only go with you now. I'm a coward, I know, but the way people speak to me . . . hurts. No, I'll stay snugly at home and Sean will go to the shop for me if necessary, though it won't be. I don't let our stocks run down.'

'I hope I won't be delayed, but don't worry if I'm not back as quickly as I'd like. It may take a day or two.'

'No, I won't. Will you be riding or taking the cart?'

'I think I'll ride, unless you want me to buy a lot of things in Perth.'

'Not this time. It's more important that you see about the annulment.'

In Perth Conn found himself speaking to a priest who acted as secretary to the Bishop.

'You realise it'll be a mortal sin to lie about this,' the priest said.

'I'm not lying.'

'You're a ticket of leave man, so your morals are clearly not of the highest. His Excellency is very worried about that.'

'I've already stated that I was falsely accused and you can tell the Bishop that I heard recently from my brother in Ireland. The man who arranged the false evidence against me confessed on his deathbed to a priest and signed a written statement to that effect. So although it'll take time I expect to have my conviction quashed.'

His companion nodded and for a moment looked at him with almost sympathy. 'It must have been hard, knowing you were innocent.'

'Yes.' He never talked of his days in prison or the journey out here.

'His Excellency will be pleased to hear that news and it will make your plea more credible, I'm sure.'

Conn bit back a sharp comment, wishing the man would just hurry up.

'Now, to your marriage. You say it was never consummated.'

'Never.'

'And yet your wife came out to join you in Australia.'

'She had nowhere else to go after my father died. My brother wouldn't have her living with him, nor would her brother.'

'Where is she now? Has she been living with you? That won't look good.'

'I could hardly throw her out. She stayed in my house at first, but my mother was there and Kathleen slept with her maid in another wing until I found her somewhere else to stay.'

'And that was where?'

Conn sighed. 'She was staying an hour's drive away with a lady of my acquaintance, but unfortunately my wife grew stranger and stranger and in the end she went completely mad. She's now been admitted to the Fremantle Lunatic Asylum.'

But this made the priest look very sour and disapproving. 'If that's the case, one can't help worrying that you might be claiming this non-consummation to get rid of a wife who was going mad.'

'I'm not. Kathleen wasn't mad when we married, but she'd never let me touch her, fought like a tiger the one time I tried, just after we were married. I wanted children, you see. I still do.'

'Which is the true purpose of marriage. Well, in that case we must have your wife examined by a doctor.'

'The doctor at the asylum has already examined her.'

'So he can vouch for her virginity?'

Conn closed his eyes, but didn't see any point in lying about something which could be checked up easily. 'On the contrary. She's not a virgin – and that's *not* my doing – and she has contracted syphilis.'

An intake of breath was his only answer, so he waited, not knowing what to say or do next.

The priest was looking at him with eyes narrowed. 'I shall have to speak to the doctor myself. Can you stay in Perth for a few more days?'

'Yes. I'll do anything to get out of this sham of a marriage.'

But Conn didn't feel hopeful as he went in search of lodgings. He had no idea what was going to happen next, after what he'd told them, and his experiences over the past few years hadn't left him feeling optimistic.

There was only one thing he was certain of: he wasn't going to visit Kathleen, had had nightmares about her since he left her at the asylum, hoped he need never set eyes on her again.

The following week Mr Hatton's young clerk turned up at Ardgullan House, getting down from a cart which had stopped by the gates and then driven on.

Xanthe was looking out of her window enjoying the peaceful February morning, mercifully without rain for once, so she saw him arrive. As he hurried through the gates, carrying a shabby carpet bag, even at this distance she could see that he looked terrified.

She ran into the hall and as she flung the front door open, Ronan came from the side of the house and joined her under the portico.

When Mr Flewett saw them, he ran the rest of the way. 'You haven't heard?'

'Heard what?'

'Mr Hatton's rooms burned down early this morning and he's dead. When I was going to work – I go in early to light all the fires – I saw that the entrance was black and smouldering, but the neighbours had put out the fire by then. I noticed two men watching the house, and recognised them as

Johnson's men because they'd come to see Mr Hatton with him and waited for their master in the outer office with me. So I hid in an alley until they left.' He paused for breath, looking extremely distressed.

'Come and sit down,' Ronan said gently. He led the way inside and saw Mary standing at the back of the hall. 'Could you fetch us a tea tray, please?'

'Have you eaten?' Xanthe asked.

Mr Flewett shook his head.

'Then bring some bread and ham as well, Mary.'

In the sitting room, their visitor collapsed into a chair, looking white and shocked.

'I came here because I fear for my life,' he said in a low voice. 'Please don't send me away.'

Xanthe exchanged a quick glance with her husband, but let him do the prompting.

'Why do *you* fear for your life?'

'Because I heard Mr Hatton had been found on the stairs – dead. The fire had started downstairs, you see. People thought he'd fallen and been overcome by the smoke some time around dawn. But I know he sleeps very soundly, because I've had to wake him up once or twice and it wasn't easy. I doubt he'd have been woken up, even by smoke.'

'Does he live above his rooms, then?' Xanthe asked.

'Yes, on the floor above and we store old documents in the attics. I go in every day about seven o'clock to light the fires, then his housekeeper comes in half an hour later. We have instructions never to wake him till nine o'clock.'

'Perhaps this time he smelled smoke and went to investigate,' Ronan said gently.

'Well . . . that's the other thing. I can't see any *reason* for a fire to start. Mr Hatton told me once that when he was younger, he lived in a house that burned down, and he was terrified of the place catching fire. That's why he didn't risk servants living with him and acting carelessly. He personally put out the fire every night. He didn't even leave smouldering embers, but poured water over them. And he had gas lighting upstairs and down, so he didn't use candles. There was no need.'

As this information sank in, Xanthe looked at her husband apprehensively. Could Mr Johnson really have murdered their lawyer?

'Can I stay here, please?' Mr Flewett pleaded. 'Just until I can think where to go? I don't want Mr Johnson to find me.'

'Won't your family miss you?'

'I don't have any family. My parents are dead and I've no brothers and sisters. Mr Hatton was a distant relative but he sent me away to school till I was old enough to work for him. I always lodged with his housekeeper. He wasn't a gregarious man. But he did look after me when I could have been sent to an orphanage and now that he's dead, I don't know what I'm going to do without him.'

The poor young man was so distraught Xanthe patted his hand and said soothingly, 'Well, you're safe here for the moment and we'll certainly not turn you out.'

Ronan looked at her. 'Johnson must have been trying to destroy the evidence, the paper Georgina signed.'

'Or punishing Mr Hatton for doing it, or perhaps he acted for both reasons. Poor man, he didn't deserve that.' She felt a hollow apprehension in the pit of her stomach. 'What are we going to do? Will Johnson come after us next?'

Ronan was silent for a few minutes, then said, 'I'm going to talk to the people in the village. They'll keep watch with me in case this place is attacked. I'd be grateful if for once *you* would keep out of danger. This is a time for a display of strength. Can you even fire a gun?'

She shook her head. 'No, but I could learn.'

'I'll teach you myself once the present trouble is over. For now, I need to alert our people to the danger.'

She knew this was no time to assert her independence. 'I'll stay indoors, I promise you.'

There was a knock on the door and Mary brought in a tea-tray, with a plate of ham sandwiches.

'I'll get started. You tell the maids.' Ronan left the room.

Mary watched him go in surprise and turned to her mistress for an explanation.

There followed what seemed to Xanthe a most amazing time. She found one of the maids nearby wherever she went in the house, unless she was with the young clerk, and for once the doors and windows were all locked.

After a hearty meal, Mr Flewett seemed to have recovered from his panic and when Ronan came in for his dinner asked what he could do to help.

'Nothing for the moment. It's dark now, but I have people keeping watch in the grounds. Can you fire a gun?'

Mr Flewett shook his head. 'I've never even touched one.'

'Then I'll give you a knife later, just in case you're attacked. You'd be best staying with my wife. Even if you don't use the knife, I'll feel better to know you're carrying some sort of weapon.'

'I'll have one too, please,' Xanthe said. She locked eyes with her husband until he rolled his eyes and said, 'Oh, very well. If you must. But I don't want you getting close enough to use it.'

That evening it seemed as if the clock hands were moving more slowly than usual. Conversation languished and Xanthe found herself listening for footsteps, or breaking glass or some sign that their enemies were close.

'It's more like Australia than England here in the countryside,' she said at one stage. 'People have to take care of themselves there because there are no police nearby.'

'We have to take care of ourselves here in Ardgullan, too,' Ronan said. 'Each village is a little world of its own. I'm fortunate the local people don't blame me for my brother's behaviour. He let them languish, didn't care whether they starved or not, didn't do repairs on their houses, was only interested in his investments.'

'One of the investments has paid off, at least,' Mr Flewett volunteered.

They turned as one to stare at him.

'What do you mean?'

'I forgot to tell you, I was so upset about Mr Hatton, but we got the news late yesterday. Your brother had invested in a ship's cargo and it was thought that the vessel had sunk, but it hadn't. It limped into a small port in India and had to wait for repairs, then it went on to sell its cargo at a profit, so it was away far longer than usual. You've got quite a lot of money coming to you from it.'

'Ah!' Ronan gave a grim smile. 'That's another reason why Johnson acted quickly, I should think. He knew that if I had money, I'd keep my home whatever he did, and no doubt he wanted to make sure we couldn't use his daughter's statement to have him arrested for fraud.'

As he opened his mouth to continue speaking, Xanthe heard something and stiffened. 'Shh! Listen!'

'I can't hear anything,' Ronan said.

'I can.' Mr Flewett looked at his hostess. 'Voices in the distance. Faint.' He looked at Ronan apologetically. 'I've always had very good hearing.'

'I'd better go out and investigate,' Ronan said.

Xanthe grabbed his arm. 'Don't! You've got men out there. Let them keep watch.'

He lifted her hand gently away, giving her his crooked smile, the one he reserved for her only. 'I can't ask them to do something I'm not prepared to do myself.'

'Should I come with you?' Mr Flewett asked.

Ronan's smile became a grin. 'No. Stay with my wife. You're not used to the countryside and would soon give yourself away – which I'm hoping our intruders will do as well – if that's who it is.' He turned back to Xanthe. 'I'm going out through our sitting-room window. Wait in the kitchen with the curtains drawn and the outer door locked. I'll come back into the house that way. Don't open the back door unless you hear my voice.'

She couldn't bear the thought of him going out into danger, but she knew she'd never stop him so she did as he'd asked and took Mr Flewett to the kitchen. 'The knives are kept in this drawer.' She selected one for herself that felt right in her hand

and then, almost as an afterthought, put a smaller one into her side pocket. 'Now we wait.'

'That's hard to do,' he said. 'I'm sorry if I've brought trouble on you by seeking refuge here.'

'It would have come of its own accord, I'm sure. Shh. Let's keep quiet and listen.'

They heard faint sounds from time to time, but nothing to tell them exactly what was happening. She felt helpless – and angry.

Conn spent most of the day pacing up and down in his lodgings in Perth, or standing by the gate, watching people pass in the street. He'd hate to live in a town, where so many of the smells were unpleasant and where there were too many people to know who the passers-by were. He'd felt like that in Dublin, too.

He was summoned to see the priest later in the afternoon and went hurrying off to the Bishop's Palace, which might be a 'palace' by Perth standards, but seemed small to him. He was coming to hate this place, he decided as he walked through the door.

He was kept waiting for a quarter of an hour by the large, ticking clock, and though he tried to contain his impatience, by the time he was at last shown into a small room to see the priest, his nerves were so tautly strung he had trouble speaking calmly.

'I've been to see the doctor at Fremantle,' the priest said. 'I believe in investigating these matters very carefully. You married for better for worse, so we must be sure it was in no way a marriage before we let you loosen the ties.'

'And?'

'He says she's had the disease for some time and if you'd had congress with her at any time since your marriage, you'd also have contracted it. You are therefore to present yourself at the Lunatic Asylum tomorrow so that he can examine you.'

'And if I don't have the disease? Which I'm sure I don't, by the way?'

'Then we can proceed with the annulment claim.'

'How long does that take?'

'From here? Probably two years. Does that matter?'

Conn closed his eyes in anguish. 'Yes. The woman I want to marry is carrying my child.'

'You've sinned.'

'It didn't feel like a sin. I love her dearly and want to marry her.'

'There is no way to avoid the child being born out of wedlock.' He bent his head, rustling through the papers on the desk. 'I'll send a clerk with you to take the doctor's deposition about your state of health. Afterwards you should go home. If you're not diseased there is nothing else you can do but wait for things to take their course.'

Three hours later Conn was on his way home, feeling disgusted by the examination, but not at all surprised to have been told that he definitely didn't have the disease.

But waiting was sometimes very hard and he was longing to regularise his position with Maia.

When he reached his home the following day, he stopped for a moment to breathe a prayer of thankfulness. Here, the world felt a warmer, kinder place to live. Sean grinned as he took the horse and dared to ask how things had gone, Nancy smiled cheerfully at him as he went into the kitchen and forestalled his question.

'She's lying down, sir. No, she's fine. I just persuaded her to take a little rest, for the baby's sake.'

He walked through a house that was sparkling with cleanliness to the bedroom where Maia was dozing on the bed. She woke as he went in.

'You're back.' Her smile was a glory of love.

He took off his horsy outer garments and lay down on the bed beside her with a happy sigh, reaching out to take her hand. 'Just to come home to you makes me feel good.'

After he'd told her what had happened, they stayed where they were for a while, with Maia nestled in the curve of his left arm and the quiet peace of the countryside outside broken only by bird calls and farm sounds.

'Whatever happens, I love you,' he said drowsily.

There was no answer. Her breathing was deep and even, and when he looked, her brow was smooth, her long eyelashes casting shadows on her cheeks.

His love for her was so deep he didn't know how to put all he felt into words. Whatever had happened to him had been worth it because it had brought him to a woman he'd never have met otherwise and who was the perfect wife for him.

Some of the bitterness fell away as that thought sank in and he smiled as he too fell asleep.

25

After he left the house to search for the intruders, Ronan crouched in the shadows, wishing it were summer and there was foliage to hide behind. He had to wait a moment or two for his eyes to grow accustomed to the darkness.

When shapes began to take on clearer form and meaning, he moved cautiously forward. Seeing the outline of a figure standing in the shrubbery about a hundred yards away from the house, he slowed down, moving cautiously from shadow to shadow, trying to ensure the stranger didn't see him.

When he was as close as he dared go, he pressed himself against the trunk of a tree he'd climbed many a time as a lad to watch what the man did.

The other stood for a time then moved towards the house, passing Ronan's tree without seeing him. He made more noise than he needed to, which puzzled Ronan. One of the younger villagers he'd asked to keep watch round the house moved out of the shadows opposite Ronan to follow the intruder.

Good! That part of his plan was working as he'd hoped.

Just as Ronan was about to follow them, he heard something else and stayed where he was. Another stranger came out of the shadows, cudgel in hand, cap pulled down to his eyes, again taking little trouble to be quiet. How many of them were there? And why were they making so much noise?

To his puzzlement the first intruder stopped some thirty yards from the house, leaning against a tree, watching, not seeming in a hurry to move on. What was he watching for? Why was he just staying there?

★   ★   ★

Xanthe heard a noise upstairs. It sounded to be coming from the servants' quarters. She didn't recognise the sound and that worried her. The servants were in the cellar, at Ronan's request, so who could be up there?

When she looked across at Mr Flewett she could see that he'd heard the noise too. She put one finger to her lips and he nodded.

She thought she heard a whisper of sound on the servants' stairs, as if someone was coming down them very quietly. Looking across at Mr Flewett, she pointed and again he nodded. It would be better, she decided, to wait and let the person come to them.

The light in the oil lamp was turned low and she wished now that she'd turned it right out. If this person could move through the house so easily in the darkness, with little light from the crescent moon getting through the drawn curtains, then he'd find the kitchen relatively bright.

An idea came to her and she gestured to Mr Flewett to move behind the door and went to sit by the table, the knife in her lap, her hands clasped on the surface in front of her. She hoped the clerk would be able to take the intruder by surprise and that between them they could knock him senseless.

If not, she'd be in trouble.

The door moved slightly but no one came in.

She rubbed her forehead and feigned a yawn, listening intently but trying not to show it.

It took her by surprise when something whizzed across the room and hit her forehead, sending sharp pain through her so that she didn't know what she was doing for a moment.

By the time she'd recovered from the shock, the intruder had her by the throat.

'Not a word or I'll throttle you!' he growled.

She kept perfectly still, praying that Mr Flewett was unharmed and would come to her aid.

'We're going outside, you an' me. You'll keep very silent if you enjoy breathing. Nod if you understand that.'

She nodded and as he yanked her to her feet she saw the knife she'd been holding lying on the floor. He kicked it out of the way

with a contemptuous laugh and let go of her throat for a moment
as he pulled her towards the outside door.

There was a sudden clatter and Mr Flewett hurtled across the
room, clumsily giving warning of his attack before he reached
his target.

With an angry roar, the intruder flung her to one side and
turned to smash one fist into Mr Flewett's face, making him yell
in pain and shock. But although he was much smaller, the clerk
put up a good struggle, giving Xanthe enough time to act.

She picked up the teapot and darted forward to crash it down
on the intruder's head. Surprise and hot tea made him yell out.

Thrusting her hand into her pocket, she took out the other
knife to defend herself with, praying it'd be enough.

When crashes and yells suddenly rang out from the kitchen, the
intruders started to run forward. Ronan took the second one by
surprise, wrenching his cudgel from his hand.

By that time Paddy from the village was there to finish the job
and thump him into oblivion. 'I've got him, sir.'

Ronan nodded and ran towards the kitchen, desperate to find
out what was happening to his wife. But he had to pause to help
subdue the other intruder, who had used a knife to injure one
of his opponents. Ronan moved on only when another villager
came to join in the fray.

The kitchen door was locked, as he'd ordered. Ronan kicked
out at the door, so terrified that someone was hurting his wife
that he found the strength to crash the door open. He was just
in time to see the intruder lying in a pile of broken crockery and
a puddle of something dark and wet. Then his wife stabbed a
knife into the intruder's shoulder and the man roared with pain.

As Ronan ran across the room, his wife picked up the heavy
bread board and smashed it down on the man's head with a
loud thwack.

Hearing someone approach, she turned swiftly round, panting
as she held the board up to protect herself. Then she let her arms
drop as she saw her husband.

Mr Flewett had seized one of the kitchen cloths and picked up the knife that had fallen on the floor. He hacked at the cloth and used the long pieces of linen to tie the intruder's hands behind his back, ignoring the blood pumping out of the stab wound on the man's shoulder.

Sounds outside took Ronan away from his wife to stare out of the door, ready to defend them if necessary. But after a moment he turned with a grin and beckoned to her. Paddy and three other men had the two intruders trussed up and were marching them at knife point across the yard.

'What shall we do with them, sir?'

'Keep tight hold of them. I want to speak to this fellow.' He went back inside and jerked the bound man to an upright position. 'What were you doing in my house?'

The man pressed his lips together.

Grim-faced now, Ronan hit him on the wound, causing him to scream in pain. 'I'll kill you rather than let you go without finding out what exactly you're doing here,' he threatened, meaning every word. 'When my wife's in danger I'd do anything to protect her, and that includes killing you.' He raised his fist again as if to deliver another blow and the man squealed for mercy.

This was a side of her husband Xanthe hadn't expected to see. She watched in amazement as he questioned the man sharply, ignoring the way he sobbed with pain as he answered the questions.

'Your wounds will be tended to after you've answered my questions. Now, tell me who sent you.'

He hesitated, then as Ronan bunched his fist again, said hastily, 'Mr Johnson.'

'Why did you come inside the house?'

'He wanted her taken away and killed.' The man gestured to Xanthe. 'Said he'd make you pay in the way that would hurt you most, because you'd never know what had happened to her.'

Ronan closed his eyes for a moment, thanking all the fates that Xanthe hadn't been captured. Then he opened his eyes and something about the way he looked must have frightened his captive, who flinched. 'I'll be taking you to the local magistrate and if you don't answer his questions promptly, I'll make the way I just hit you seem like a love tap.'

'Shall I bind a cloth round him to stop the bleeding before we set off?' Xanthe asked.

'No. Let him bleed.'

'I'll get my cloak, then.'

'You're not going anywhere.'

'I'm coming with you. It was me he tried to kidnap. You weren't here, so I'll need to answer questions too.'

'I want you safe.'

'I'll be safe now.'

But as they were all going out of the back door a shot rang out and Xanthe dropped to the ground.

Ronan covered her body with his and the men outside went running into the woods again.

Maia woke in the night with a scream. Conn jerked upright in the bed. 'What's wrong? Is it the baby?'

She began sobbing.

'What *is* it?'

'It's Xanthe. She's been hurt. I can tell.' Maia began rubbing her shoulder. 'Here. Ah, it hurts, it hurts.'

He took her in his arms and tried to comfort her, but she wouldn't be comforted. All her thoughts were for her twin and she was hardly aware of him.

Two hours later the local doctor stepped back from the bed at Ardgullan. 'She ought to be all right, Mr Maguire. She was lucky. The bullet went straight through the fleshy part of her arm. I've bound the wound and you're to leave it bound up for several days. I'll come back to check on her every day.'

As Mary showed out the doctor, Xanthe groaned and Ronan went to her side. 'You're going to be all right, my darling.'

'Not if you leave this bandage on so tightly.'

'The doctor says we're not to touch it.'

'He's old and so are his ways. I want Mary back here with a
bowl of soapy water and a clean bandage. I don't want the wound
wrapping so tightly. It's made it feel worse. I've read about new
ways of treating gunshot wounds, developed in the Crimea, and
I'm not having it done this way. It needs to be kept clean, not
left to fester.'

'Is there anything you've not read about?'

Even through her pain she managed a near smile. 'What else
did I have to do with myself in Australia?'

He couldn't persuade her to leave the bandage alone, at least
for tonight, and Mary, standing on the other side of the bed, took
her mistress's side.

'He's good at setting broken bones, that one, or for getting
bullets out, but for nothing else. Did you see how dirty his hands
were?'

Xanthe looked at him pleadingly. 'Please don't leave it dirty.'

'You're supposed to be resting quietly, not complaining about
the doctor's methods,' Ronan told her.

'When have I ever kept quiet?'

There was a commotion below and a voice boomed out.
'Where's Maguire?'

'I sent Paddy for the magistrate,' Ronan said. 'That's him
now. He has a loud voice because he's half deaf. I'll have to
go down and speak to him. Stay there. You are not to get out
of that bed.'

She didn't protest but turned to Mary. 'I want it cleaning.'

The housekeeper nodded and slipped downstairs. The housemaid appeared a minute later looking frightened.

'Please, ma'am, I have to sit with you.'

Xanthe nodded and closed her eyes till she heard footsteps
and looked up to see Mary and the kitchen maid come in
with a ewer of hot water and the materials to wash and cleanse
the wound.

Though it hurt badly, Xanthe urged them to continue their
work.

By the time Ronan came back two hours later, she was sleeping, if rather fitfully, and her shoulder sported a new bandage made from a torn-up clean sheet.

Mary was sitting by the bed.

'How is she?'

'Clean.'

'I'll sit with her now.'

'We'll both sit with her this night, what's left of it anyway. I'm better at bandaging than you are.'

After a pause, she said with a sniff, 'I suppose Mr Johnson will find a way to wriggle out of this. He always does.'

'Not this time. Our magistrate says the evidence is overwhelming and there's no way he'll escape prison, if not a hangman's rope. He'll be under arrest by now.'

She crossed herself. 'Thank the Lord for that.'

But he was most thankful of all that his wife had survived. What would he have done without her? He reached out to brush a strand of hair off her forehead, just for the sheer pleasure of touching her.

He was a very lucky man. Fate had given him far more than he'd deserved. He'd make sure he spent the rest of his life more usefully, making Xanthe happy and, he hoped, their children, and caring for his estate and the people on it.

In Australia, Maia sighed with relief. 'The pain's eased a little now.'

'Do you always feel her pain?'

'Sometimes. If it's bad. Not small things. I can sense when she's unhappy, too.' She gave him a wan smile. 'She's happy at the moment. I wonder what happened to hurt her.'

'An accident?'

'We'll not know exactly what for three months or more. But she's alive, that's what matters.' With a sigh Maia lay back on the pillows and fell asleep, even though it was broad daylight.

Conn watched her for a while then he too fell asleep.

The following day a messenger arrived at Galway House from Perth. 'Mr Largan? The priest sent me to speak to you.'

'Come in. You must be hungry and thirsty, travelling in this heat.'

'I'll give you the message first. He said it was urgent.' The stranger held out an envelope which had C. Largan scrawled across it.

Conn took it from him, strangely reluctant to open it, then muttered in annoyance at himself and moved aside to read his message in privacy. 'Dear God!'

Maia came across to join him. 'What is it? Not bad news?'

'I'll tell you in a minute. Let me take this fellow into the kitchen and tell Nancy to give him refreshments.'

When he came back Conn took her into the library.

'Tell me,' she urged.

He handed her the two pieces of paper the envelope had contained.

The first one was from the priest and said simply,

Have stopped annulment procedures in view of this news. I leave any final rites to you. Clearly she cannot be buried in consecrated ground.

The second letter was longer and was from the doctor.

I regret to inform you that Mrs Kathleen Largan took her own life yesterday by cutting her throat. I don't know how she was able to obtain the knife but she did a thorough job of it and was dead when we found her.

I trust you'll inform Mr Largan of this. I consider it a merciful release because she was very unhappy even in her madness, crying and wailing for hours on end. The one she cried out for when she wept was 'Papa Largan' and from what I could make out, it was he who had used her as a wife, shocking as that seems, not Mr Conn Largan. He must have been diseased.

I'll arrange for a burial in a place we have for people like her.
Yours, etc

Maia sat staring at the letters, then looked at Conn with tear-filled eyes. 'How sad!' He tried to speak, but he was so sickened and disgusted by what his father had done that he couldn't say a word.

Maia put her arm round him. 'Your father must have been a—'

'Don't speak of him. Don't ever say his name again. I hope he rots in hell.' He swallowed hard. 'I always wondered what had driven my mother to flee after she'd endured so many years with a difficult husband, and now—' his voice broke, but he forced himself to finish, 'I'm fairly sure from things she said that always puzzled me . . . She knew, Maia. She knew about Kathleen. And never said a word.'

They sat together for a long time, then Maia moved her arm away. 'Shall you change the burial arrangements, Conn?'

'No. I'll leave the poor creature in peace now. She was more sinned against than sinning.'

He went to stand by the window. 'I didn't want her to die.'

'I know, my darling.'

After a few moments he came back and laid a hand on her belly. 'Has it occurred to you that we can now marry and this little one will not bear the stigma of being a bastard?'

She smiled. 'Only just in time.'

'We'll go to the church service on Sunday and ask to be married. And to hell with anyone who looks scornfully at you!'

She blushed rosily. 'Oh dear, I'm going to look such a mess.'

'To me you always look beautiful.'

'And you always say the nicest things. Do they train lawyers to do that?'

'No. But love gives wings to my words.' He folded her in his arms and they stood for a long time, not speaking, not even moving, just quietly happy to be together.

But he found it difficult to sleep that night. He was glad he could marry Maia, of course he was, but it upset him that this was at the cost of Kathleen's death and what his father had done would haunt him for years, he was sure. His father must have known he was diseased and hadn't cared that he'd passed on that vileness to Kathleen.

There had been so many deaths in the past year. He hoped they would have a time of peace from now on. They'd surely earned it.

He put his arms round Maia and even though she was asleep, she snuggled up to him and the mere fact of her presence comforted him, always would.

He must not dwell on the past. He must look forward to a future filled with love and children and happiness. How could a man not be happy who had a Maia to love?

Epilogue

Eighteen months later: late 1868

In Australia the party started in the late morning on a day agreed by letters passed between the sisters. Cassandra and Reece drove up to Galway House, accompanied by Leo, Livia, Orla and the girl who was now helping Cassandra round the house and with the two children.

As everyone got out of the cart, Sofia stood guard over her new little sister. 'Be careful with Demi,' she kept telling people. 'She's very little.'

Maia smiled at Cassandra. 'I didn't think you'd use the full name for such a little child.'

'I wanted to but Sofia couldn't say Demetria easily and it somehow got shortened.'

'Dad wouldn't have minded. He'd love the way we've all chosen Greek names for our children.'

Maia turned to smile at her little son. Karsten was tottering along the veranda on his chubby little legs, clutching a toy dog she'd made which he took everywhere with him.

It was a sunny late spring day, perfect for sitting outside in the middle of the day, and they gathered on the back veranda, which had been enlarged specially for such family events.

Not until they were all seated did Maia stand up. 'I have something to announce.'

They looked up.

'Not another baby!' teased Livia.

'No. Not this time. It's Conn, his conviction has been quashed and he's a free man now.'

There was silence then everyone cheered and clapped.

Conn came to slip his arm round his wife's waist. 'It won't make much difference to the way Maia and I live. We're both quiet homebodies. But it will make a big difference to our children one day.' He looked at Maia. 'There's only one thing we regret – that all four sisters couldn't be together today.'

'Perhaps when the Suez Canal is opened – they think it'll be next year – it'll get easier to travel to Australia,' Reece said. 'Ronan and Xanthe have already said they intend to come back here for a visit.'

Cassandra shook her head, looking sad. 'Pandora won't be able to. She gets terribly seasick, and anyway I doubt you'll get Zachary to leave his beloved shop for several months. So maybe one day we all ought to go back there for a reunion.'

'Perhaps we will. Who knows what the future will hold?' Maia said softly, giving her little son a luminous smile and a quick kiss.

Conn made a beckoning gesture towards the kitchen window and Nancy came out of the house with a tray. As they all took a wineglass, he whispered to her, 'Get some for yourself and Sean, so you can both join in the toast.' He waited till she'd done this, then raised his glass. 'To the Blake sisters. Thank goodness they came into my life!'

'And mine,' Reece echoed as people clinked glasses and drank a heartfelt toast. He saw that his wife's eyes were overbright and knew she was thinking of her two sisters on the other side of the world. Some things you could do nothing about.

In Ireland, on a sunny late autumn day Ronan called out, 'They're here!'

Xanthe came running to join him at the door as the carriage drew up. Zachary got out of it as soon as it stopped and Pandora nearly fell out after him in her eagerness to see her sister. The two ran across the lawn and hugged each other, not weeping – the Blake sisters were not the sort to weep for no reason – but smiling and hugging, blinking hard, then holding each other at arm's length to smile again.

'It's been a long time,' Xanthe said. 'We've visited you twice and this is the first time you've come to see us.'

'You know Zachary doesn't like to leave the shop.'

The two men were shaking hands. 'Thank goodness we're here!' Zachary said. 'Pandora's been twitching with impatience ever since we left Enniskillen. And she's not a good traveller.'

'How did she cope with the sea crossing?'

'She felt nauseous but that was all.'

Hallie, standing at the edge of all this joy with her mother, was soon drawn into the family circle, while the nursemaid looking after Master Hector Carr and his sister Hebe stood watching wide-eyed.

Then they were swept into the house, where Pandora's new baby was cooed over and Hebe was kissed and told how big she was growing, everyone agreeing that she was going to be tall like her mother and aunt.

Though Xanthe's son had been brought down to meet his cousins, he stayed obstinately asleep the whole time.

'He does nothing but sleep, that one,' said Xanthe. 'I should have found out the Greek word for sleepy and called him that, instead of Andreas. Maia writes that her Karsten is just the same. She wishes one of us had had twins, but I find one baby at a time quite enough trouble.'

After a while the nursemaids took the little ones up to the nursery and the rest of the party retired to the drawing room to bring one another up to date and share the latest letters from Cassandra and Maia.

'They'll be just finishing their party now, going to bed,' Xanthe said wistfully. 'I wish . . .' She didn't finish her sentence and pinned a determined smile to her face to hide her emotions. One day she'd go to see her twin. She'd make sure of that.

She had settled down here at Ardgullan House, but she and Ronan still had plans to travel. After all, holidays were being organised to all sorts of places for groups of people by Mr Cook. Travelling for pleasure was getting easier all the time.

Ronan had already brought up some wine from the cellar and he poured glasses for them all, then called for their attention. 'I propose a toast. To the Blake sisters, who have brought us all together! May we one day manage a reunion of the whole family.'

CONTACT ANNA

Anna Jacobs is always delighted to hear from
readers and can be contacted:

BY MAIL

PO Box 628
Mandurah
Western Australia 6210

If you'd like a reply, please enclose a
self-addressed, business size envelope, stamped (from
inside Australia) or an international reply coupon
(from outside Australia).

VIA THE INTERNET

Anna has her own web domain, with details
of her books, latest news and excerpts to read.
Come and visit her site at
http://www.annajacobs.com

Anna can be contacted by email at
anna@annajacobs.com

If you'd like to receive an email newsletter about
Anna and her books every month or two, you are
cordially invited to join her announcements list.
Just email her and ask to be added to the list, or
follow the link from her web page,
or send a blank email to
AnnaJacobs-subscribe@yahoogroups.com